Shannow edged to the right to a break in the undergrowth and stepped out onto the walkway some fifteen yards from the Hellborn group. There were five in all, and each held a weapon pointed at his three companions. The Hellborn leader was still speaking. "Tonight we shall be in hell, with servants and women and fine food and drink. Your souls will carry us there."

"Why wait for tonight?" asked Shannow.

The Hellborn swung to face him, and Shannow's guns thundered. The Hellborn leader was hurled back, his face blown away; another man spun back, his shoulder shattered. Shannow stepped to his right and continued to fire. Only one answering shot came his way; it passed a few feet to his left, smashing into the stone head of a statue demon and shearing away a horn.

The last echoes faded away. Amaziga was kneeling beside Gareth. "Jesus wept, Shannow!" whispered the young man. "You really are death on wheels . . ."

By David Gemmell
Published by Ballantine Books:

LION OF MACEDON
DARK PRINCE

KNIGHTS OF DARK RENOWN

MORNINGSTAR

The Drenai Saga
  LEGEND
  THE KING BEYOND THE GATE
  QUEST FOR LOST HEROES
  WAYLANDER

The Stones of Power Cycle
  GHOST KING
  LAST SWORD OF POWER
  WOLF IN SHADOW
  THE LAST GUARDIAN
  BLOODSTONE

Bloodstone

A Jon Shannow Adventure

David Gemmell

A Del Rey® Book
BALLANTINE BOOKS • NEW YORK

A Del Rey® Book
Published by Ballantine Books
Copyright © 1994 by David Gemmell

All rights reserved under International and Pan-American Copyright Conventions. Published in the United States by Ballantine Books, a division of Random House, Inc., New York. Originally published in Great Britain in 1994 by Legend Books, Random House UK Ltd.

http://www.randomhouse.com

Library of Congress Catalog Card Number: 97-91992

ISBN 0-345-40797-0

Manufactured in the United States of America

First American Edition: December 1997

10 9 8 7 6 5 4 3 2 1

Bloodstone is dedicated with love to Tim and Dorothy Lenton for the gift of friendship and for shining a light on the narrow way at a time when all I could see was darkness.

Acknowledgments

My thanks to my editors John Jarrold at Random and Stella Graham in Hastings and to my copy editor Jean Maund and test reader Val Gemmell. I am also grateful for the help so freely offered by fellow writers Alan Fisher and Peter Ling. And to the many fans who have written during the years demanding more tales of Jon Shannow—my thanks!

Bloodstone

Prologue

*I*HAVE SEEN *the fall of worlds and the death of nations. From a place in the clouds I watched the colossal tidal wave sweep toward the coastline, swallowing the cities, drowning the multitudes.*

The day was calm at first, but I knew what was to be. The city by the sea was awakening, its roads choked with vehicles, its sidewalks full, the veins of its subways clotted with humanity.

The last day was painful, for we had a congregation I had grown to love, peopled with godly folk, warmhearted and generous. It is hard to look down upon a sea of such faces and know that within a day they will be standing before their maker.

So I felt a great sadness as I walked across to the silver and blue craft that would carry us high toward the future. The sun was setting in glory as we waited for takeoff. I buckled the seat belt and took out my Bible. There was no solace to be found.

Saul was sitting beside me, gazing from the window. "A beautiful evening, Deacon," he said.

Indeed it was. But the winds of change were already stirring.

We rose smoothly into the air, the pilot informing us that the weather was changing for the worse but that we would reach the Bahamas before the storm. I knew this would not be so.

Higher and higher we flew, and it was Saul who first saw the portent.

"How strange," he said, tapping my arm. "The sun appears to be rising again."

"This is the last day, Saul," I told him.

Glancing down, I saw that he had unfastened his seat belt. I told him to buckle it. He had just done so when the first of those terrible winds struck the plane, almost flipping it. Cups, books, trays, bags all flew into the air, and there were screams of terror from our fellow passengers.

Saul's eyes were squeezed shut in prayer, but I was calm. I leaned to my right and stared from the window. The great wave had lifted and was hurtling toward the coast.

I thought of the people of the city. There were those who were even now merely observing what they saw to be a miracle, the setting sun rising again. They would smile, perhaps, or clap their hands in wonder. Then their eyes would be drawn to the horizon. At first they would assume that a low thundercloud was darkening the sky. But soon would come the terrible realization that the sea had risen to meet the sky and was bearing down on them in a seething wall of death.

I turned my eyes away. The plane shuddered, then rose and fell, twisting and helpless against the awesome power of the winds. All the passengers believed that death would soon follow. Except me. I knew.

I took one last glance from the window. The city looked so small now, its mighty towers seemingly no longer than a child's finger. Lights shone at the windows of the towers; cars still thronged the freeways.

And then they were gone.

Saul opened his eyes, and his terror was very great. "What is happening, Deacon?"

"The end of the world, Saul."

"Are we to die?"

"No. Not yet. Soon you will see what the Lord has planned for us."

Like a straw in a hurricane the plane hurtled through the sky.

And then the colors came, vivid reds and purples washing over the fuselage, masking the windows. As if we had been swallowed by a rainbow. Then they were gone. Four seconds, perhaps. Yet in those four seconds I alone knew that several hundred years had passed.

"It has begun, Saul," I said.

◇ *1* ◇

THE PAIN WAS too great to ignore, and nausea threatened to swamp him as he rode, but the Preacher clung to the saddle and steered the stallion up toward the Gap. The full moon was high in the clear sky, the distant mountain peaks sharp and glistening white against the skyline. The sleeve of the rider's black coat was still smoldering, and a gust of wind brought a tongue of flame. Fresh pain seared him, and he beat at the cloth with a smoke-blackened hand.

Where are they now? he thought, pale eyes scanning the moonlit mountains and the lower passes. His mouth was dry, and he reined in the stallion. A canteen hung from the pommel, and the Preacher hefted it, unscrewing the brass cap. Lifting it to his lips, he found that it was filled not with water but with a fiery spirit. He spit it out and hurled the canteen away.

Cowards! They needed the dark inspiration of alcohol to aid them on their road to murder. His anger flared, momentarily masking the pain. Far down the mountain, emerging from the timberline, he saw a group of riders. His eyes narrowed. Five men. In the clear air of the mountains he heard the distant sound of laughter.

The rider groaned and swayed in the saddle, the pounding in his temple increasing. He touched the wound on the right side of his head. The blood was congealing, but there was a groove in the skull where the bullet had struck, and the flesh around it was hot and swollen.

He felt consciousness slipping from him but fought back, using the power of his rage.

Tugging the reins, he guided the stallion up through the Gap, then angled it to the right, down the long wooded slope toward the road. The slope was treacherous, and the stallion slipped twice, dropping to its haunches. But the rider kept the animal's head up, and it righted itself, coming at last to level ground and the hard-packed earth of the trade road.

The Preacher halted his mount, then looped the reins around the pommel and drew his pistols. Both were long-barreled, the cylinders engraved with swirls of silver. He shivered and saw that his hands were trembling. How long had it been since those weapons of death had last been in use? Fifteen years? Twenty? *I swore never to use them again. Never to take another life,*

And you were a fool!

Love your enemy. Do good to him that hates you.

And see your loved ones slain.

If he strikes you upon the right cheek, offer him the left.

And see your loved ones burn.

He saw again the roaring flames, heard the screams of the terrified and the dying . . . Nasha running for the blazing door as the roof timbers cracked and fell on her, Dova kneeling beside the body of her husband, Nolis, her fur ablaze, pulling open the burning door, only to be shot to ribbons by the jeering, drunken men outside . . .

The riders came into sight and saw the lone figure waiting for them. It was clear that they recognized him, but there was no fear in them. This he found strange, but then he realized they could not see the pistols, which were hidden by the high pommel of the saddle. Nor could they know the hidden secret of the man who faced them. The riders urged their horses forward, and he waited silently as they approached. All trembling was gone now, and he felt a great calm descend on him.

"Well, well," said one of the riders, a huge man wearing a double-shouldered canvas coat. "The Devil looks after his own, eh? You made a bad mistake following us, Preacher. It would have been easier for you to die back there." The man produced a double-edged knife. "Now I'm going to skin you alive!"

For a moment he did not reply; then he looked the man in the eyes. *"Were they ashamed when they had committed the abomination?"* he quoted. *"No, they were not ashamed, and could not blush."* The pistol in his right hand came up, the movement smooth, unhurried. For a fraction of a second the huge raider froze, then he scrabbled for his own pistol. It was too late. He did not hear the thunderous roar, for the large-caliber bullet smashed into his skull ahead of the sound and catapulted him from the saddle. The explosion terrified the horses, and all was suddenly chaos. The Preacher's stallion reared, but he readjusted his position and fired twice, the first bullet ripping through the throat of a lean, bearded man, and the second punching into the back of a rider who had swung his horse in a vain bid to escape the sudden battle. A fourth man took a bullet in the chest and fell screaming to the ground, where he began to crawl toward the low undergrowth at the side of the road. The last raider, managing to control his panicked mount, drew a long pistol and fired; the bullet came close, tugging at the collar of the Preacher's coat. Twisting in the saddle, he fired his left-hand pistol twice, and his assailant's face disappeared as the bullets hammered into his head. Riderless horses galloped away into the night, and he surveyed the bodies. Four men were dead; the fifth, wounded in the chest, was still trying to crawl away and was leaving a trail of blood behind him. Nudging the stallion forward, the rider came alongside the crawling man. *"I will surely consume them, saith the Lord."* The crawling man rolled over.

"Jesus Christ, don't kill me! I didn't want to do it. I didn't kill any of them, I swear it!"

"By their works shall ye judge them," said the rider.

The pistol leveled. The man on the ground threw up his hands, crossing them over his face. The bullet tore through his fingers and into his brain.

"It is over," said the Preacher. Dropping the pistols into the scabbards at his hips, he turned the stallion and headed for home. Weariness and pain overtook him, and he slumped forward over the horse's neck.

The stallion, with no guidance from the man, halted. The

rider had pointed him toward the south, but that was not the home the stallion knew. For a while it stood motionless, then it started to walk, heading east and out into the plains.

It plodded on for more than an hour, then caught the scent of wolves. Shapes moved to the right. The stallion whinnied and reared. The weight fell from its back . . . and then it galloped away.

Jeremiah knelt by the sleeping man, examining the wound in the temple. He did not believe the skull was cracked, but there was no way to be sure. The bleeding had stopped, but massive bruising extended up into the hairline and down across the cheekbone almost all the way to the jaw. Jeremiah gazed down at the man's face. It was lean and angular, the eyes deep-set. The mouth was thin-lipped yet not, Jeremiah considered, cruel.

There was much to learn about a man by studying his face, Jeremiah knew, as if the experiences of life were mirrored there in code. Perhaps, he thought, every act of weakness or spite, bravery or kindness, made a tiny mark, added a line here and there that could be read like script. Maybe this was God's way of allowing the holy to perceive wickedness in the handsome. It was a good thought. The sick man's face was strong, but there was little kindness there, Jeremiah decided, though equally there was no evil. Gently he bathed the head wound, then drew back the blanket. The burns on the man's arm and shoulder were healing well, though several blisters were still seeping pus.

Jeremiah turned his attention to the man's weapons: revolvers made by the Hellborn, single-action pistols. Hefting the first, he drew back the hammer into the half-cocked position, then flipped the release, exposing the cylinder. Two shells had been fired. Jeremiah removed an empty cartridge case and examined it. The weapon was not new. In the years before the Second Satan Wars the Hellborn had produced double-action versions of the revolver with slightly shorter barrels and squat rectangular automatic pistols and rifles that were far more accurate than these pieces. Such weapons had not saved them from annihilation. Jeremiah had seen the destruction of Babylon. The Deacon had ordered it razed, stone by stone, until nothing remained save a flat, barren plain. The old man shivered at the memory.

The injured man groaned and opened his eyes. Jeremiah felt the coldness of fear as he gazed into them. The eyes were the misty gray-blue of a winter sky, piercing and sharp, as if they could read his soul. "How are you feeling?" he asked, as his heart hammered. The man blinked and tried to sit. "Lie still, my friend. You have been badly wounded."

"How did I get here?" The voice was low, the words softly spoken.

"My people found you on the plains. You fell from your horse. But before that you were in a fire and were shot."

The man took a deep breath and closed his eyes. "I don't remember," he said at last.

"It happens," said Jeremiah. "The trauma from the pain of your wounds. Who are you?"

"I don't remem . . ." the man hesitated. "Shannow. I am Jon Shannow."

"An infamous name, my friend. Rest now and I will come back this evening with some food for you."

The injured man opened his eyes and reached out, taking Jeremiah's arm. "Who are you, friend?"

"I am Jeremiah. A Wanderer."

The wounded man sank back to the bed. *"Go and cry in the ears of Jerusalem, Jeremiah,"* he whispered, then fell once more into a deep sleep.

Jeremiah climbed from the back of the wagon, pushing closed the wooden door. Isis had prepared a fire, and he could see her gathering herbs by the riverside, her short, blond hair shining like new gold in the sunlight. He scratched at his white beard and wished he were twenty years younger. The other ten wagons had been drawn up in a half circle around the river-bank, and three other cookfires had been lit. He saw Meredith kneeling by the first, slicing carrots into the pot that hung above it.

Jeremiah strolled across the grass and hunkered down

opposite the lean young academic. "A life under the sun and stars agrees with you, Doctor," he said amiably.

Meredith gave a shy smile and pushed back a lock of sandy hair that had fallen into his eyes. "Indeed it does, Meneer Jeremiah. I feel myself growing stronger with each passing day. If more people from the city could see this land, there would be less savagery, I am sure."

Jeremiah said nothing and transferred his gaze to the fire. In his experience savagery always dwelled in the shadows of man, and where man walked evil was never far behind. But Meredith was a gentle soul, and it did a young man no harm to nurse gentle dreams.

"How is the wounded man?" Meredith asked.

"Recovering, I think, though he claims to remember nothing of the fight that caused his injuries. He says his name is Jon Shannow."

Anger shone briefly in Meredith's eyes. "A curse on that name!" he said.

Jeremiah shrugged. "It is only a name."

Isis knelt by the riverbank and stared down at the long, sleek fish just below the glittering surface of the water. It was a beautiful fish, she thought, reaching out with her mind. Instantly her thoughts blurred, then merged with the fish. She felt the coolness of the water along her flanks and was filled with a haunting restlessness, a need to move, to push against the currents, to swim for home.

Withdrawing, she lay back . . . and felt the approach of Jeremiah. Smiling, she sat up and turned toward the old man. "How is he?" she asked as Jeremiah eased himself down beside her.

"Getting stronger. I'd like you to sit with him." The old man is troubled, but trying to hide it, she thought. Resisting the urge to flow into his mind, she waited for him to speak again. "He is a fighter, perhaps even a brigand. I just don't know. It was our duty to help him, but the question is: Will he prove a danger to us as he grows stronger? Is he a killer? Is he wanted by the Crusaders? Could we find ourselves in trouble for harboring him? Will you help me?"

"Oh, Jeremiah," said Isis softly. "Of course I will help you. Did you doubt it?"

He reddened. "I know you don't like to use your talent on people. I'm sorry I had to ask."

"You're a sweet man," she said, rising. Dizziness swept over her, and she stumbled. Jeremiah caught her, and she felt swamped by his concern. Slowly strength returned to her, but the pain had started in her chest and stomach. Jeremiah lifted her into his arms and walked back toward the wagons, where Dr. Meredith ran to them. Jeremiah sat her down in the wide rocking chair by the fire, while Meredith took her pulse. "I'm all right now," she said. "Truly."

Meredith's slender hand rested on her brow, and it took all her concentration to blot out the intensity of his feelings for her. "I'm all right!"

"And the pain?" he asked.

"Fading," she lied. "I just got up too quickly. It is nothing."

"Get some salt," Meredith told Jeremiah. When he returned, Meredith poured it into her outstretched palm. "Eat it," he commanded.

"It makes me feel sick," she protested, but he remained silent, and she licked the salt from her hand. Jeremiah passed her a mug of water, and she rinsed her mouth.

"You should rest now," said Meredith.

"I will, soon," she promised. Slowly she stood. Her legs took her weight, and she thanked both men. Anxious to be away from their caring glances, she moved to Jeremiah's wagon and climbed inside, where the wounded man was still sleeping.

Isis pulled up a chair and sat down. Her illness was worsening, and she sensed the imminence of death.

Pushing such thoughts from her mind, she reached out, her small hand resting on the fingers of the sleeping man. Closing her eyes, she allowed herself to fall into his memories, floating down and down through the layers of manhood and adolescence, absorbing nothing until she reached childhood.

Two boys, brothers. One shy and sensitive, the other bois-

terous and rough. Caring parents, farmers. Then the brigands came. Bloodshed and murder, the boys escaping. Torment and tragedy affecting them both in different ways, the one becoming a brigand, the other . . .

Isis jerked back to reality, all thoughts of her illness forgotten as she stared down at the sleeping man. I am staring into the face of a legend, she thought. Once more she merged with the man.

The Jerusalem Man, haunted by the past, tormented by thoughts of the future, riding through the wild lands, seeking . . . a city? Yes, but much more. Seeking an answer, seeking a reason for being. And during his search stopping to fight brigands, tame towns, kill the ungodly. Riding endlessly through the lands, welcome only when his guns were needed, urged to move on when the killing was done.

Isis pulled back once more, dismayed and depressed—not just by the memories of constant death and battle but also by the anguish of the man himself. The shy, sensitive child had become the man of violence, feared and shunned, each killing adding another layer of ice upon his soul. Again she merged.

She/he was being attacked, men running from the shadows. Gunfire. A sound behind her/him. Cocking the pistol, Isis/ Shannon spun and fired in one motion. A child flung back, his chest torn open. Oh, God! Oh, God! Oh, God!

Isis clawed her way free of the memory but did not fully withdraw. Instead she floated upward, allowing time to pass, halting only when the Jerusalem Man rode up to the farm of Donna Taybard. This was different. Here was love.

The wagons were moving, and Isis/Shannon rode out from them, scouting the land, heart full of joy and the promise of a better tomorrow. No more savagery and death. Dreams of farming and quiet companionship. Then came the Hellborn!

Isis withdrew and stood. "You poor, dear man," she whispered, brushing her hand over the sleeping man's brow. "I'll come back tomorrow."

Outside the wagon Dr. Meredith approached her. "What did you find out?" he asked.

"He is no danger to us," she answered.

* * *

The young man was tall and slender, with a shock of unruly black hair cut short above the ears but growing long over the nape of his neck. He was riding an old, swaybacked mare up and over the Gap and stared with the pleasure of youth at the distant horizons, where the mountains reared up to challenge the sky.

Nestor Garrity was seventeen, and this was an adventure. The Lord alone knew how rare adventures were in Pilgrim's Valley. His hand curled around the pistol butt at his hip, and he allowed the fantasies to sweep through his mind. He was no longer a clerk at the timber company. No, he was a Crusader hunting the legendary Laton Duke and his band of brigands. It did not matter that Duke was feared as the most deadly pistoleer this side of the Plague Lands, for the hunter was Nestor Garrity, lethal and fast, the bane of warmakers everywhere, adored by women, respected and admired by men.

Adored by women . . .

Nestor paused in his fantasy, wondering what it would be like to be adored by women. He had walked out once with Ezra Feard's daughter, Mary, taken her to the summer dance. She had led him outside into the moonlight and flirted with him.

Should have kissed her, he thought. Should have done some damn thing! He blushed at the memory. The dance had turned into a nightmare when she had walked off with Samuel Klares. They had kissed. Nestor had seen them down by the creek. Now she was married to him and had just delivered her first child.

The old mare almost stumbled on the scree slope. Jerked from his thoughts, Nestor steered her down the incline.

The fantasies loomed back into his mind. He was no longer Nestor Garrity, the fearless Crusader, but Jon Shannow, the famed Jerusalem Man, seeking the fabled city and with no time for women, much as they adored him. Nestor narrowed his eyes and lifted his hat from where it hung at his back. Settling it into place, he turned up the collar of his coat and sat straighter in the saddle.

Jon Shannow would never slouch. He pictured two brigands riding from behind the boulders. In his mind's eye he
could see the fear on their faces. They went for their guns.
Nestor's hand snapped down. The pistol sight caught on the
tip of his holster, twisting the weapon from his hands. It fell to
the scree. Carefully Nestor dismounted and retrieved the
weapon.

The mare, pleased to be relieved of the boy's weight,
walked on. "Hey, wait!" called Nestor, scrambling toward her.
But she ambled on, and the dejected youngster followed her
all the way to the bottom, where she stopped to crop the dry
grass. Then Nestor remounted.

One day I'll be a Crusader, he thought. I'll serve the
Deacon and the Lord. He rode on.

Where was the Preacher? It should not take this long to find
him. The tracks were easy to follow to the Gap. But where
was he going? Why did he ride out in the first place? Nestor
liked the Preacher. He was a quiet man and throughout Nestor's
youth he had treated him with kindness and understanding.
Especially when Nestor's parents had been killed that summer
ten years earlier, drowned in a flash flood. Nestor shivered at
the memory. Seven years old—and an orphan. Frey McAdam
had come to him then, the Preacher with her. He had sat at the
bedside and taken Nestor's hand.

"Why did they die?" the bewildered child had asked. "Why
did they leave me?"

"I guess it was their time, only they didn't know it."

"I want to be dead, too," the seven-year-old had wailed.

The Preacher had sat with him then, quietly talking about
the boy's parents, of their goodness and their lives. Just for a
while the anguish and the numbing sense of loneliness had left
Nestor, and he had fallen asleep.

The previous night the Preacher had escaped from the
church despite the flames and the bullets. And he had run
away to hide. Nestor would find him, tell him that everything
was all right now and it was safe to come home.

Then he saw the bodies, the flies buzzing around the terrible
wounds. Nestor forced himself to dismount and approach

them. Sweat broke out on his face, and the desert breeze felt cold on his skin. He could not look directly at them, so he studied the ground for tracks.

One horse had headed back toward Pilgrim's Valley, then had turned and walked out into the wild lands. Nestor risked a swift, stomach-churning glance at the dead men. He knew none of them. More important, none of them was the Preacher.

Remounting, he set off after the lone horseman.

People were moving on the main street of Pilgrim's Valley as Nestor Garrity rode in, leading the black stallion. It was almost noon, and the children were leaving the two school buildings and heading out into the fields to eat the lunches their mothers had packed for them. The stores and the town's three restaurants were open, and the sun was shining down from a clear sky.

But a half mile to the north smoke still spiraled lazily into the blue. Nestor could see Beth McAdam standing amid the blackened timbers as the undertakers moved around the debris, gathering the charred bodies of the Wolvers. Nestor did not relish facing Beth with the news. She had been the headmistress of the lower school when Nestor was a boy, and no one had ever enjoyed the thought of being sent to her study. He grinned, remembering the day he had fought with Charlie Wills. They had been dragged apart and then taken to Mrs. McAdam; she had stood in front of her desk, tapping her fingers with the three-foot bamboo cane.

"How many should you receive, Nestor?" she had asked him.

"I didn't start the fight," the boy had replied.

"That is no answer to my question."

Nestor had thought about it for a moment. "Four," he had said.

"Why four?"

"Fighting in the yard is four strokes," he had told her. "That's the rule."

"But did you not also take a swing at Mr. Carstairs when he dragged you off the hapless Charlie?"

"That was a mistake," Nestor had said.

"Such mistakes are costly, boy. It shall be six for you and four for Charlie. Does that sound fair?"

"Nothing is fair when you're thirteen," Nestor had said, but he had accepted the six strokes, three on each hand, and had made no sound.

He rode slowly toward the charred remains of the little church, the stallion meekly following his bay mare. Beth McAdam was standing with her hands on her ample hips, staring out toward the wall. Her blond hair was braided at the back, but part of the braid had come loose and was fluttering in the wind at her cheek. She turned at the sound of the approaching horse and gazed up at Nestor, her face expressionless. He dismounted and removed his hat.

"I found the raiders," he said. "They was all dead."

"I expected that," she said. "Where is the Preacher?"

"No sign of him. His horse headed east, and I caught up with it; there was blood on the saddle. I backtracked and found signs of wolves and bears, but I couldn't find him."

"He is not dead, Nestor," she said. "I would know. I would feel it here," she told him, hitting her chest with a clenched fist.

"How did he manage to kill five men? They were all armed. All killers. I mean, I never saw the Preacher ever carry a gun."

"Five men, you say?" she replied, ignoring the question. "There were more than twenty surrounding the church, according to those who saw the massacre. But then, I expect there were some from our own . . . loving . . . community."

Nestor had no wish to become involved in the dispute. Wolvers in a church was hardly decent, anyhow, and it was no surprise to the youngster that tempers had flared. Even so, if the Crusaders had not been called out to a brigand raid on Shem Jackson's farm, there would have been no violence.

"Anything more you want me to do, Mrs. McAdam?"

She shook her head. "It was plain murder," she said. "Nothing short."

"You can't murder Wolvers," Nestor said, without thinking. "I mean, they ain't human, are they? They're animals."

Anger shone in Beth's eyes, but she merely sniffed and

turned aside. "Thank you, Nestor, for your help. But I expect you have chores to do, and I'll not keep you from them."

Relieved, he turned away and remounted. "What do you want me to do with this stallion?" he called.

"Give it to the Crusaders. It wasn't ours, and I don't want it."

Nestor rode away to the stone-built barracks at the south end of town, dismounting and hitching both horses to the rail outside. The door was open, and Captain Leon Evans was sitting at a roughly built desk.

"Good morning, sir," said Nestor.

Evans looked up and grinned. He was a tall, broad-shouldered man with an easy smile. "Still looking to sign up, boy?"

"Yes, sir."

"Been reading your Bible?"

"I have, sir. Every day."

"I'll put you in for the test on the first of next month. If you pass, I'll make you a cadet."

"I'll pass, sir. I promise."

"You're a good lad, Nestor. I see you found the stallion. Any sign of the Preacher?"

"No, sir. But he killed five of the raiders."

The smile faded from Captain Evans's face. "Did he, by God?" He shook his head. "As they say, you can't judge a man by the coat he wears. Did you recognize any of the dead men?"

"Not a one, sir. But three of them had their faces shot away. Looks like he just rode down the hill and blasted 'em to hell and gone. Five men!"

"Six," said the captain. "I was checking the church this morning; there was a corpse there. It looks like when the fire was at its worst, the Preacher managed to smash his way out at the rear. There was a man waiting. The Preacher must have surprised him, there was a fight, and the Preacher managed to get the man's gun. Then he killed him and took his horse. Jack Shale says he saw the Preacher riding from town, said his coat and hair were ablaze."

Nestor shivered. "Who'd have thought it?" he said. "All his

sermons were about God's love and forgiveness. Then he guns down six raiders. Who'd have thought it?"

"I would, boy," came a voice from the doorway, and Nestor turned to see the old prophet making his slow way inside. Leaning on two sticks, his long white beard hanging to his chest, Daniel Cade inched his way to a seat by the wall. He was breathing heavily as he sank to the chair.

Captain Evans stood and filled a mug with water, passing it to the prophet. Cade thanked the man.

Nestor faded back to the far wall, but his eyes remained fixed to the ancient legend sipping the water. Daniel Cade, the former brigand turned prophet, who had fought off the Hell-born in the Great War. Everyone knew that God spoke to the old man, and Nestor's parents had been two of the many people saved when Cade's brigands had taken on the might of the Hellborn army.

"Who burned the church?" asked Cade, the voice still strong and firm, oddly in contrast to the arthritic and frail body.

"They were raiders from outside Pilgrim's Valley," the captain told him.

"Not all of them," said Cade. "There were townsfolk among the crowd. Shem Jackson was seen. Now, that disturbs me, for isn't that why the Crusaders were not here to protect the church? Weren't you called to Jackson's farm?"

"Aye, we were," said the captain. "Brigands stole some of his stock, and he rode in to alert us."

"And then stayed on to watch the murders. Curious."

"I do not condone the burning of the church, sir," said the captain. "But it must be remembered that the Preacher was told—repeatedly—that Wolvers were not welcome in Pilgrim's Valley. They are not creatures of God, not made in his image, nor true creations. They are *things* of the Devil. They have no place in a church or in any habitat of decent folk. The Preacher ignored all warnings. It was inevitable that some . . . tragedy . . . would befall. I can only hope that the Preacher is still alive. It would be sad . . . if a good man—though misguided—were to die."

"Oh, I reckon he's alive," said Cade. "So you'll be taking no action against the townspeople who helped the raiders?"

"I don't believe anyone *helped* them. They merely observed them."

Cade nodded. "Does it not strike you as strange that men from outside Pilgrim's Valley should choose to ride in to lance our boil?"

"The work of God is often mysterious," said Evans, "as you yourself well know, sir. But tell me, why were you not surprised that the Preacher should tackle—and destroy—six armed men? He shares your name, and it is said he is your nephew or was once one of your men in the Hellborn War. If the latter is true, he must have been very young indeed."

Cade did not smile, but Nestor saw the humor in his eyes. "He is older than he looks, Captain, and no, he was never one of my men. Nor is he my nephew—despite his name." With a grunt the prophet pushed himself to his feet. Captain Evans took his arm, and Nestor ran forward to gather his sticks.

"I'm all right. Don't fuss about me!"

Slowly and with great dignity the old man left the room and climbed to the driving seat of a small wagon. Evans and Nestor watched as Cade flicked the reins.

"A great man," said Evans. "A legend. He knew the Jerusalem Man. Rode with him, some say."

"I heard he *was* the Jerusalem Man," said Nestor.

Evans shook his head. "I heard that, too. But it is not true. My father knew a man who fought alongside Cade. He was a brigand, a killer. But God shone the great light upon him."

The Deacon stood on the wide balcony, his silver-white beard rippling in the morning breeze. From that high vantage point he gazed affectionately out over the high walls and down on the busy streets of Unity. Overhead a biplane lumbered across the blue sky, heading east toward the mining settlements, carrying letters and possibly the new Barta notes that were slowly replacing the large silver coins used to pay the miners.

The city was prospering. Crime was low, and women could walk without risk, even at night, along the well-lit thoroughfares.

"I've done the best I could," whispered the old man.

"What's that, Deacon?" asked a slender, round-shouldered man with wispy white hair.

"Talking to myself, Geoffrey. Not a good sign." Turning from the balcony, he reentered the study. "Where were we?"

The thin man lifted a sheet of paper and peered at it. "There is a petition here asking for mercy for Cameron Sikes. You may recall he's the man who found his wife in bed with a neighbor. He shot them both to death. He is due to hang tomorrow."

The old man shook his head. "I feel for him, Geoffrey, but you cannot make exceptions. Those who murder must die. What else?"

"The Apostle Saul would like to see you before setting off for Pilgrim's Valley."

"Am I free this afternoon?"

Geoffrey consulted a black leather-bound diary. "Four-thirty to five is clear. Shall I arrange it?"

"Yes. I still don't know why he asked for that assignment. Perhaps he is tired of the city. Or perhaps the city is tired of him. What else?"

For half an hour the two men worked through the details of the day, until finally the Deacon called a halt and strolled through to the vast library beyond the study. There were armed guards at the doors, and the Deacon remembered with sadness the young man who had hidden there two years before. The shot had sounded like thunder within the domed building, striking the Deacon just above the right hip and spinning him to the floor. The assailant had screamed and charged across the huge room, firing as he ran. Bullets had ricocheted from the stone floor. The Deacon had rolled over and drawn the small, two-shot pistol from his pocket. As the young man had come closer, the old man had fired, the bullet striking the assassin just above the bridge of the nose. The youngster had stood for a moment, his own pistol dropping to the floor. Then he had fallen to his knees and toppled onto his face.

The Deacon sighed at the memory. The boy's father had

been hanged the day before, after shooting a man following an argument over a card game.

Now the library and the municipal buildings were patrolled by armed guards.

The Deacon sat at a long oak table and stared at the banks of shelves while he waited for the woman. Sixty-eight thousand books, or fragments of books, cross-indexed, the last remnants of the history of mankind, contained in novels, textbooks, philosophical tomes, instruction manuals, diaries, and volumes of poetry. And what have we come to? he thought. A ruined world, bastardized by science and haunted by magic. His thoughts were dark and somber, his mind weary. No one is right all the time, he told himself; you can only follow your heart. A guard ushered the woman in. Despite her great age, she still walked with a straight back, her face showing more than a trace of the beauty she had possessed as a younger woman.

"Welcome, Frey Masters," said the Deacon, rising. "God's blessing to you and to your family."

Her hair was silver, the lights from the ornate arched and stained-glass windows creating soft highlights of gold and red. Her eyes were blue and startlingly clear. She smiled thinly and accepted his hand, then sat opposite him.

"God's greeting to you also, Deacon," she said. "And I trust He will allow you to learn compassion before much longer."

"Let us hope so," said the Deacon. "Now, what is the news?"

"The dreams remain the same, only they are more powerful," she said. "Betsy saw a man with crimson skin and black veins. His eyes were red. Thousands of corpses lay around him, and he was bathing in the blood of children. Samantha also dreamed of a demon from another world. She was hysterical upon wakening and claimed that the Devil was about to be loosed upon us. What does it mean, Deacon? Are the visions symbolic?"

"No," he said sadly. "The Beast exists."

The woman sighed. "I, too, have been dreaming more of late. I saw a great wolf, walking upright. Its hands held hollow talons, and I watched as it sank them into a man, saw the blood drawn out of him. The Beast and the wolf are linked, aren't they?" He nodded but did not answer. "And you know far more than you are telling me."

"Has anyone else dreamed of wolves?" he asked, ignoring the comment.

"Alice has seen visions of them, Deacon," said Frey Masters. "She says she saw a crimson light bathing a camp of Wolvers. The little creatures began to writhe and scream; then they changed, becoming beasts like those in my dream."

"I need to know *when*," said the Deacon. "And *where*." From his pocket he took a small golden stone, which he twirled against his fingertips.

"You should use the power on yourself," said the woman sternly. "You know that your heart is failing."

"I've lived too long, anyway. No, I'll save its power for the Beast. This is the last of them, you know. My little hoard. Soon the world will have to forget magic and concentrate once more on science and discovery." His expression changed. "If it survives."

"It'll survive, Deacon," she said. "God must be stronger than any demon."

"If He wants it to survive. We humans have hardly made the earth a garden, now, have we?"

She shook her head and gave a weary smile. "Yet there are still good people, even though we know that the path of evil offers many rewards. Don't give in to despair, Deacon. If the Beast comes, there will be those who will battle against it. Another Jerusalem Man, perhaps. Or a Daniel Cade."

"Come the moment, come the man," said the Deacon with a dry chuckle.

Frey Masters rose. "I'll go back to my dreamers. What would you have me tell them?"

"Get them to memorize landscapes, seasons. When it comes, I need to be there to fight it. And I will need help." Standing, he held out his hand, and she shook it briefly. "You have said nothing of your own dreams, Frey."

"My powers have faded over the years. But yes, I have seen the Beast. I fear you will not be strong enough to withstand it."

He shrugged. "I have fought many battles in my life. I'm still here."

"But you're old now. *We* are old. Strength fails, Deacon. All things pass away . . . even legends."

He sighed. "You have done a wonderful job here," he said. "All these fragments of a lost civilization. I would like to think that after I am dead men and women will come here and learn from the best of what the old ones left us."

"Don't change the subject," she admonished him.

"You want me to spare the man who killed his wife and her lover?"

"Of course—and you are still changing the subject."

"Why should I spare him?"

"Because I ask it, Deacon," she said simply.

"I see. No moral arguments, no scriptural examples, no appeal to my better nature?"

She shook her head, and he smiled. "Very well, he will live."

"You're a strange man. Deacon. And you are still avoiding the point. Once you could have stood against the Beast. Not any longer."

He grinned and winked at her. "I may just surprise you yet," he said.

"I'll grant you that. You are a surprising man."

Shannow dreamed of the sea, the groaning of the ship's timbers almost human, the waves like moving mountains, beating against the hull. He awoke and saw the lantern above his bed gently swaying on its hook. For a moment the dream and the reality seemed to blend. Then he realized he was in the cabin of a prairie wagon, and he remembered the man . . . Jeremiah? . . . ancient and white-bearded, with but a single long tooth in his upper mouth. Shannow took a deep, slow breath, and the pounding pain in his temples eased slightly. With a groan he sat up. His left forearm and shoulder were bandaged, and he could feel the tightness of the burned skin beneath.

A fire? He searched his memory but could find nothing. It doesn't matter, he told himself; the memory will come back. What is important is that I know who I am.

Jon Shannow. The Jerusalem Man.

And yet . . . Even as the thought struck him, he felt uneasy, as if the name were . . . what? Wrong? No. His guns were hanging from the headboard of the bed. Reaching out, he drew a pistol. It felt both familiar and strange in his hand. Flicking the release, he broke open the pistol. Two shells had been fired.

Instantly, momentarily, he saw a man fall back from his horse, his throat erupting in a crimson spray. Then the memory vanished.

A fight with brigands? Yes, that must have been it, he thought. There was a small hand mirror on a shelf to his right. He took it down and examined the wound in his temple. The bruising was yellow, fading fast, and the groove in his skull was covered by a thick scab. His hair had been trimmed close to his head, but he could still see where the fire had scorched the scalp.

Fire.

Another flash of memory! Planks ablaze and Shannow hurling his body at the timbers time and again until they gave. A man beyond with pistol raised. The shot hitting his head like a hammer. Then that vision also faded.

He had been in a church. Why? Listening to a sermon, perhaps.

Easing himself from the bed, he saw that his clothes were folded neatly on a chair by a small window, the burned coat having been cleaned and patched with black cloth. As he dressed, he looked around the cabin of the wagon. The bed was narrow but well made of polished pine, and there were two pine chairs and a small table by the window. The walls were painted green, there were elaborate carvings around the window in the shape of vine leaves, and a strange motif had been carved above the door: two overlapping triangles making a star. A bookshelf sat on two brackets above the bed. Buckling his gun scabbards to his hips, Shannow scanned the books. There was a Bible, of course, and several fictions, but at the end was a tall, thin volume with dry, yellowed pages. Shannow pulled it clear and carried it to the window. The sun was setting, and he could just make out the title in faded gold leaf. *The Chronicle of Western Costume* by John Peacock. With great care he turned the pages. Greek, Roman, Byzantine, Tudor, Stuart, Cromwellian . . . Every page showed men and women dressed in different clothing, and each page carried dates. It was fascinating. Until the coming of the planes many men had believed that only three hundred years had passed since the death of Christ. But the men and women traveling in those great ships of the sky had changed all that, consigning the previous theories to the dust of history. Shannow paused. How do I know that? He replaced the book, then moved to the rear of the cabin, opening the door and climbing unsteadily down the three steps to the ground.

A young woman with short blond hair was walking toward him, carrying a dish of stew. "You should still be in bed," she admonished him. In truth he felt weak and breathless and sat back on the wagon steps, accepting the stew.

"Thank you, lady." She was extraordinarily pretty, her eyes blue-green, her skin pale tan.

"Is your memory returning, Mr. Shannow?"

"No," he said, then began to eat.

"It will in time," she assured him. The outside of the wagon was painted in shades of green and red, and from where he sat Shannow could see ten other wagons similarly decorated.

"Where are you all going?" he asked.

"Where we like," said the girl. "My name is Isis." She held out her hand, and Shannow took it. Her handshake was firm and strong.

"You are a good cook, Isis. The stew is very fine."

Ignoring the compliment, she sat down beside him. "Doctor Meredith thinks you may have a cracked skull. Do you remember nothing at all?"

"Nothing I wish to talk about," he said. "Tell me about you."

"There is little to tell," she told him. "We are what you see, Wanderers. We follow the sun and the wind. In summer we dance, in winter we freeze. It is a good way to be."

"It has a certain charm," said Shannow. "Yet is there no destination?"

She looked at him in silence for a moment, her large blue eyes holding his gaze. "Life is a journey with only one destination, Mr. Shannow. Or do you see it otherwise?"

"It doesn't pay to argue with Isis," said Jeremiah, moving into sight.

Shannow looked up into the old man's grizzled face. "I think that is true," he said, rising from the step. He felt unsteady and weak and reached out to grasp the edge of the wagon. Taking a deep breath, Shannow moved into the open. Jeremiah stepped alongside, taking his arm.

"You are a tough man, Mr. Shannow, but your wounds were severe."

"Wounds heal, Jeremiah." Shannow gazed at the mountains. The nearest were speckled with stands of timber, but farther away, stretching into an infinite distance, were other peaks, blue and indistinct. "It is a beautiful land." The sun was slowly sinking behind the western peaks, bathing them in golden light. Off to the right Shannow focused on a rearing butte, the sandstone seeming to glow from within.

"It is called Temple Mount," said Jeremiah. "Some say it is a holy place where the old gods live. For myself I believe it to be a resting place for eagles, nothing more."

"I have not heard the name," Shannow told him.

"The loss of memory must cause you some anguish," said Jeremiah.

"Not tonight," Shannow answered. "I feel at peace. The memories you speak of hold only death and pain. They will come back all too soon; I know this. But for now I can look at the sunset with great joy."

The two men walked toward the riverbank. "I thank you for

saving my life, Jeremiah. You are a good man. How long have you lived like this?"

"About twelve years. I was a tailor, but I longed for the freedom of the big sky. Then came the Unifier Wars, and city life became even more grotesque. So I made a wagon and journeyed out into the wilderness."

There were ducks and geese on the river, and Shannow saw the tracks of a fox. "How long have you nursed me?"

"Twelve days. For a while the others thought you were going to die. I told them you wouldn't; you have too many scars. You've been shot three times in your life: once over the hip, once in the upper chest, and once in the back. There are also two knife wounds, one in the leg and a second in the shoulder. As I said, you are a tough man. You won't die easy."

Shannow smiled. "That is a comforting thought. And I remember the hip wound." He had been riding close to the lands of the Wall and had seen a group of raiders dragging two women into the open. He had ridden in and killed the raiders, but one of them had managed a shot that had clipped Shannow's hipbone and ripped through his lower back. He would have died but for the help of the man-beast Shir-ran, who had found him in the blizzard.

"You are miles away, Mr. Shannow. What are you thinking?"

"I was thinking of a lion, Jeremiah."

They strolled back up the riverbank and toward the campfires in the circle of wagons. Shannow was weary and asked Jeremiah to lend him some blankets so that he could sleep under the stars.

"I'll not hear of it, man. You'll stay in that bed for another day or two, then we'll see."

Too tired to argue, Shannow pulled himself up into the wagon. Jeremiah followed him.

Fully clothed, Shannow stretched out on the narrow bed. The old man gathered some books and made to leave, but Shannow called out to him. "Why did you say I had an infamous name?"

Jeremiah turned. "The same name as the Jerusalem Man.

He rode these parts some twenty years ago. Surely you have heard of him?"

Shannow closed his eyes.

Twenty years?

He heard the cabin door click shut and lay for a while staring through the tiny window at the distant stars.

"How are you feeling, and do not lie to me!" said Dr. Meredith. Isis smiled but said nothing. If only, she thought, Meredith could be as assertive in his life as he was with his patients. Reaching up, she stroked his face. The young man blushed. "I am still waiting for an answer," he said, his voice softening.

"It is a beautiful night," observed Isis, "and I feel at peace."

"That is no answer," he scolded.

"It will have to suffice," she said. "I do not want to concentrate on my . . . debility. We both know where my journey will end. And there is nothing we can do to prevent it."

Meredith sighed, his head dropping forward, a sandy lock of hair falling across his brow.

Isis pushed it back. "You are a gentle man," she told him.

"A powerless man," he said sadly. "I know the name of your condition, as I know the names of the drugs that could overcome it. Hydrocortisone and fludrocortisone. I even know the amounts to be taken. What I do not know is how these steroids were constructed or from what."

"It doesn't matter," she assured him. "The sky is beautiful, and I am alive. Let's talk about something else. I want to ask you about our . . . guest."

Meredith's face darkened. "What about him? He is no farmer, that is for sure."

"I know that," she said. "But why has his memory failed?"

Meredith shrugged. "The blow to the head is the most likely cause, but there are many reasons for amnesia, Isis. To tell you more I would need to know the exact cause of the injury and the events leading up to it."

She nodded and considered telling him all she had learned. "First," she said, "tell me about the Jerusalem Man."

He laughed, the sound harsh, his face hardening. "I thank

God that I never met him. He was a butchering savage who achieved some measure of fame vastly greater than he deserved. And this only because we are ruled by another merciless savage who reveres violence. Jon Shannow was a killer. Putting aside the ludicrous quasi-religious texts that are now being published, he was a wandering man who was drawn to violence as a fly is drawn to ox droppings. He built nothing, wrote nothing, sired nothing. He was like a wind blowing across a desert."

"He fought the Hellborn," said Isis, "and destroyed the power of the Guardians."

"Exactly," said Meredith sharply. "He *fought* and *destroyed*. And now he is seen as some kind of savior, a dark angel sent by God. I wonder sometimes if we will ever be free of men like Shannow."

"You perceive him as evil, then?"

Meredith stood and added several sticks to the dying fire, then returned to his seat opposite Isis. "That is a difficult question to answer. From all I know of the man he was not a murderer; he never killed for gain. He fought and slew men he believed to be ungodly or wicked. But the point I would make, Isis, is that *he* decided who was wicked and *he* dispensed what he regarded as justice. In any civilized society such behavior should be deemed abhorrent. It sets a precedent, you see, for other men to follow his line of argument and kill any who disagree. Once we revere a man like Shannow, we merely open the door to any other killer who wishes to follow his example. Men like the Deacon, for instance. When the Hellborn rose against us, he destroyed not only their army but their cities. He visited upon them a terrible destruction. And why? Because *he* decided they were an evil people. Thousands of ordinary Hellborn farmers and artisans were put to death. It was genocide, an entire race destroyed. That is the legacy of men like Jon Shannow. So tell me, what has this to do with our guest, as you call him?"

"I don't know," she lied. "He claims to be Shannow, so I wondered if it would have a bearing on his . . . What did you call it?"

"Amnesia."

"Yes, his amnesia. You asked about the event that led to his being wounded." Isis hesitated, preparing her story. "He watched his friends being murdered, horribly murdered, some shot down, others burned alive. His ... home ... was set ablaze. He escaped and took up weapons he had put aside many years before. He was once a warrior but had decided this was wrong. But in his pain he tracked the killers and fought them, killing them all. Does that help?"

Meredith sat back and let out a long breath. "Poor man," he said. "I fear I have misjudged him. I saw the guns and assumed him to be a brigand or a hired man. Yes, indeed it helps, Isis. The mind can be very delicate. I trust your talent, and taking everything you have told me as true, it means our guest went to war against not only a vile enemy but his own convictions. His mind has reeled from the enormity of anguish and loss and closed itself against the memories. It is called protective amnesia."

"Would it be wise for me to explain it to him?" she asked.

"Under no circumstances," he told her. "That is what is meant by protective. To tell him now could cause a complete disintegration. Let it come back slowly, in its own time. What is fascinating, however, is his choice of new identity. Why Jon Shannow? What was his occupation?"

"He was a preacher," she said.

"That probably explains it," said Meredith. "A man of peace forced to become something he loathed. What better identity to choose than a man who purported to be religious but was actually a battle-hardened killer? Look after him, Isis. He will need that special care only you can supply."

"Everyone is wrong and you're right; is that what you're saying, Mother?" The young man's face was flushed with anger as he rose from the dinner table and strode to the window, pushing it open and staring out over the tilled fields.

Beth McAdam took a deep breath, struggling for calm. "I am right, Samuel. And I don't care what *everyone* says. What is being done is no less than evil."

Samuel McAdam rounded on her. "Evil, is it? Evil to do the work of God? You have a strange idea of what constitutes evil. How can you argue against the word of the Lord?"

Now it was Beth who became angry, her pale blue eyes narrowing. "You call murder the work of God? The Wolvers have never harmed anyone. And they didn't ask to be the way they are. God alone knows what caused them to be, but they have souls, Samuel. They are gentle, and they are kind."

"They are an abomination," shouted Samuel. "And as the Book says, *'Neither shalt thou bring an abomination into thine house, lest thou be a cursed thing like it.'* "

"There is only one abomination in this house, Samuel. And I bore it. Get out! Go back to your murdering friends. And tell them from me that if they ride onto my lands for one of their Wolver hunts, I'll meet them with death and fire."

The young man's jaw dropped. "Have you taken leave of your senses? These are our neighbors you're talking of killing."

Beth walked to the far wall and lifted down the long-barreled Hellborn rifle. Then she looked at her son, seeing not the tall, wide-shouldered man he had become but the small boy who once had feared the dark and wept when thunder sounded. She sighed. He was a handsome man now, his fair hair close-cropped, his chin strong. But like the child he once had been he was still easily led, a natural follower.

"You tell them, Samuel, exactly what I said. And if there are any who doubt my word, you put them right. The first man to hunt down my friends dies."

"You've been seduced by the Devil," he said, then swung away and strode through the door.

As Beth heard his horse galloping away into the night, a small form moved from the kitchen and stood behind her. Beth turned and forced a smile. Reaching out, she stroked the soft fur of the creature's shoulder.

"I am sorry you heard that, Pakia." Beth sighed. "He has always been malleable, like clay in the hands of the potter. I blame myself for that. I was too hard on him, never let him win. Now he is like a reed that bends with every breeze."

The little Wolver tilted her head to one side. Her face was almost human yet fur-covered and elongated, her eyes wide and oval, the color of mixed gold, tawny with red flecks. "When will the Preacher come back?" she asked, her long tongue slurring the words.

"I don't know, Pakia. Maybe never. He tried so hard to be a Christian, suffering all the taunts and the jeers." Beth moved to the table and sat down. Now it was the slender Pakia who laid her long fingers on the woman's shoulder. Beth reached up and covered the soft, warm hand. "I loved him, you know, when he was a real man. But I swear to God, you can't love a saint." She shook her head. "Wherever he is, he must be hurting. Twenty years of his life gone to dust and ashes."

"It was not a waste," said Pakia, "and it is not dust and ashes. He gave us pride and showed us the reality of God's love. That is no small gift, Beth."

"Maybe so," Beth said, without conviction. "Now you must tell your people to head deep into the mountains. I fear there will be terrible violence before the month is out. There's talk of more hunts."

"God will protect us," said Pakia.

"Trust in God but keep your gun loaded," Beth said softly.

"We do not have guns," said Pakia.

"It's a quote, little one. It just means that . . . sometimes God requires us to look after ourselves."

"Why do they hate us? Did not the Deacon say we were all God's children?"

It was a simple question, and Beth had no answer to it. Laying the gun on the table, she sat down and stared at the Wolver. No more than five feet tall, she was humanoid in shape, but her back was bent, her hands long and triple-jointed, ending in dark talons. Silver-gray fur covered her frame.

"I can't tell you why, Pakia, and I don't know why the Deacon changed his mind. The Unifiers now say you are abominations. I think they just mean different. But in my experience men don't need too much of an excuse for hate. It just comes natural to them. You'd better go now. And don't come back for a time. I'll come into the mountains with some supplies in a little while, when things have cooled down a mite."

"I wish the Preacher was here," said Pakia.

"Amen to that. But I'd sooner have the man he once was."

Nestor counted the last of the notes and slipped them into a paper packet, which he sealed and added to the pile. One hundred forty-six lumbermen and seven haulers were to be paid that day, and the Barta notes had arrived only late the previous night from Unity. Nestor glanced up at the armed guards outside the open doorway. "I've finished," he called.

Closing the account ledger, Nestor stood and straightened his back. The first of the guards, a round-shouldered former lumberjack named Leamis, stepped inside and leaned his rifle against the shack wall. Nestor placed the payment packets in a canvas sack and handed it to Leamis.

"A long night for you, yongen," said the guard.

Nestor nodded. His eyes felt gritty, and he yearned for sleep. "The money was due yesterday morning," he said wearily. "We thought there'd been a raid."

"They went the long way, up through the Gap," Leamis told him. "Thought they were being followed."

"Were they?"

Leamis shrugged. "Who knows? But Laton Duke is said to be in these parts, and that don't leave anyone feeling safe. Still, at least the money got here."

Nestor moved to the doorway and pulled on his heavy top-coat. Outside the mountain air was chilly, and the wind was picking up. There were three wagons beyond the shack, carrying trace chains to haul the timber. The drivers were standing in a group chatting, waiting for their pay. Turning to Leamis, Nestor said his farewells and strolled to the paddock, where the company horses were held. Taking a bridle from the tack box, he warmed the bridle bar under his coat; pushing a chilled bridle into a horse's warm mouth was a sure way to rile the beast. Choosing a buckskin gelding, he bridled and saddled him and set off down the mountain, passing several more wagons carrying loggers and lumbermen to their day's labor.

The sun was bright as Nestor turned off the mountain path and headed down toward Pilgrim's Valley. Far to the north he could see the squat, ugly factory building where meat was canned for shipment to the growing cities, and a little to the east, beyond the peaks, smoke had already started to swirl up from the ironworks, a dark spiral, like a distant cyclone, staining the sky.

He rode on, past the broken sign with its fading letters, welcoming travelers to "Pi . gr . . s Val . . y, pop. 827." More than three thousand people now dwelled in the valley, and the demand for lumber for new homes meant stripping the mountainsides bare.

A low rumbling sound caused him to rein in the buckskin, and he glanced up to see the twin-winged flying machine moving ponderously through the air. It was canvas-colored, with a heavy engine at the front and fixed wheels on the wings and tail. Nestor hated it, loathed the noise and the intrusion on his thoughts. As the machine came closer, the buckskin grew skittish. Nestor swiftly dismounted and took firm hold of the reins, stroking the gelding's head and blowing gently into its nostrils. The gelding began to tremble, but then the machine was past them, the sound disappearing over the valley.

Nestor remounted and headed for home.

As he rode into town, Nestor tried not to look at the charred area where the little church had stood, but his eyes were drawn to it. The bodies had all been removed, and workmen were busy clearing away the last of the blackened timbers. Nestor rode on, leaving his mount with the company ostler at the livery stable and walking the last few hundred yards to his rooms above Josiah Broome's general store.

The rooms were small, a square lounge leading through to a tiny, windowless bedroom. Nestor peeled off his clothes and sat by the lounge window, too tired to sleep. Idly he picked up the book he had been studying. The cover was of cheap board, the title stamped in red: *The New Elijah* by Erskine Wright. The Crusader tests would be hard, he knew, and there was so little time to read. Rubbing his eyes, he leaned back, opened the book at the marked page, and read about the travels of the great saint.

He fell asleep in the chair and awoke some three hours later. Yawning, he stood and rubbed his eyes. He heard sounds of shouting from the street below and moved to the window. A number of riders had drawn up, and one of them was being helped from the saddle, blood seeping from a wound in his upper chest.

Dressing swiftly, Nestor ran down to the street in time to see Captain Leon Evans striding up to the group. The Crusader captain looked heroic in his gray shield-fronted shirt and wide-brimmed black hat. He wore two guns belted high at his waist, the gun butts reversed.

"The bitch shot him!" shouted Shem Jackson, his face ugly with rage. "What you going to do about it?"

Evans knelt by the wounded man. "Get him to Doctor Shivers. And be damn quick about it; otherwise he'll bleed to death." Several men lifted the groaning man and bore him along the sidewalk, past Broome's store. Everyone began to speak at once, but Leon Evans raised his hands for silence. "Just one," he said, pointing to Jackson. Nestor did not like the man, who was known for his surly manner when sober and his violent streak when drunk.

Jackson hawked and spit. "We spotted some Wolvers on the edge of my property," he said, rubbing a grimy hand across his thin lips. "And me and the boys here rode out after 'em. We come near the McAdam place, when she ups and shoots. Jack went down, then Miller's horse was shot out from under him. What you going to do about it?"

"You were on her property?" asked Evans.

"What's that got to do with anything?" argued Jackson. "You can't just go around shooting folks."

"I'll talk to her," promised Evans, "but from now on you boys stay clear of Beth McAdam. You got that?"

"We want more than talk," said Jackson. "She's got to be dealt with. That's the law."

Evans smiled, but there was no humor in his expression.

"Don't tell me the law, Shem," he said quietly. "I know the law. Beth McAdam gave fair warning that armed men were not to hunt on her property. She also let it be known that she would shoot any man who trespassed on her land in order to hunt Wolvers. You shouldn't have gone there. Now, as I said, I'll speak to her."

"Yeah, you speak to her," hissed Jackson. "But I tell you this: Woman or no woman, no one shoots at me and gets away with it."

Evans ignored him. "Get on back to your homes," he said, and the men moved away, but Nestor could see they were heading for the Mother of Pearl drinking house. He stepped forward. The captain saw him, and his dark eyes narrowed.

"I hope you weren't with those men," said Evans.

"No, sir. I was sleeping up in my room. I just heard the commotion. I didn't think Mrs. McAdam would shoot anybody."

"She's one tough lady, Nestor. She was one of the first into Pilgrim's Valley; she fought the lizard-men, and since then there have been two brigand raids out on the farm. Five were killed in a gun battle there some ten years back."

Nestor chuckled. "She was certainly tough in school. I remember that."

"So do I," said Evans. "How's the studying going?"

"Every time I try to read, I fall asleep," admitted Nestor.

"It must be done, Nestor. A man cannot follow God's path unless he studies God's word."

"I get confused, sir. The Bible is so full of killing and revenging—hard to know what's right."

"That's why the Lord sends prophets like Daniel Cade and Jon Shannow. You must study their words. Then the ways that are hidden will become known to you. And don't concern yourself about the violence, Nestor. All life is violence. There is the violence of disease, the violence of hunger and poverty. Even birth is violent. A man must understand these things. Nothing good ever comes easy."

Nestor was still confused, but he did not want to look foolish before his hero. "Yes, sir," he said.

Evans smiled and patted the young man's shoulder. "The

Deacon is sending one of his apostles to Pilgrim's Valley at the end of the month. Come and listen."

"I will, sir. What will you do about Mrs. McAdam?"

"She's under a lot of strain, what with the Preacher gone and the burning. I think I'll just stop by and talk with her."

"Samuel says he thinks the Devil has gotten into her," said Nestor. "He told me she threw him out of the house and called him an abomination."

"He's a weak man. Often happens to youngsters who have strong parents. But I hope he isn't right. Time will tell."

"Is it true that Laton Duke and his men are nearby?" asked Nestor.

"His gang was shot to pieces down near Pernum, so I doubt it," said the Crusader. "They tried to rob a Barta coach heading for the mines."

"Is he dead, then?"

Evans laughed. "Don't sound disappointed, boy. He's a brigand."

Nestor reddened. "Oh, I'm not disappointed, sir," he lied. "It's just that he's ... you know ... famous. And kind of romantic."

Evans shook his head. "I never found anything romantic about a thief. He's a man who hasn't the heart or the strength for work and steals from other, better men. Set your sights on heroes a little bigger than Laton Duke, Nestor."

"Yes, sir," promised the youngster.

◊ 2 ◊

It is often asked, How can the rights of the individual be balanced evenly with the needs of a society? Consider the farmer, my brothers. When he plants the seeds for his harvest of grain, he knows that the crows will descend and eat of them. Too many birds and there will be no harvest. So the farmer will reach for his gun. This does not mean that he hates the crows or that the crows are evil.

The Wisdom of the Deacon
Chapter IV

BETH SWUNG THE ax. It was an ungainly stroke, but the power of her swing hammered the nine-pound blade into the wood, splitting it cleanly. Wood lice crawled from the bark, and she brushed them away before lifting the severed chunks of firewood and adding them to the winter store.

Sweat ran freely on her face. Wiping it away with her sleeve, she rested the ax against the wood-store wall, then hefted her long rifle and walked to the well. Looking back at the ax and the tree round she used as a base, Beth pictured the Preacher standing there and the fluid poetry of his movements. She sighed.

The Preacher . . .

Even she had come to regard Shannow as the man of God in Pilgrim's Valley, almost forgetting the man's lethal past. But then he had changed. By God he had changed! The lion to the lamb. And it shamed Beth that she had found the change not to her liking.

Her back was aching, and she longed for a rest. "Never leave a job half done," she chided herself aloud. Lifting the copper ladle from the bucket, she drank the cool water, then returned to the ax. The sound of a horse moving across the dry-baked ground made her curse. She had left the rifle by the well! Dropping the ax, she turned and walked swiftly back across the open ground, not even looking at the horseman. After reaching the rifle, she leaned down.

"You won't need that, Beth, darlin'," said a familiar voice.

Clem Steiner lifted his leg over the saddle pommel and jumped to the ground. A wide grin showed on Beth's face, and she stepped forward with arms outstretched. "You're looking good, Clem," she said, drawing him into a hug. Taking hold of his broad shoulders, she gently pushed him back from her and stared into his craggy features.

The eyes were a sparkling blue, and the grin made him look boyish despite the gray at his temples and the weather-beaten lines around his eyes and mouth. His coat of black cloth seemed to have picked up little dust from his ride, and he wore a brocaded waistcoat of shining red above a polished black gun belt.

Beth hugged him again. "You're a welcome sight for old eyes," she said, feeling an unaccustomed swelling in her throat.

"Old? By God, Beth, you're still the best-looking woman I ever saw!"

"Still the flatterer," she grunted, trying to disguise the pleasure she felt.

"Would anyone dare lie to you, Beth?" His smile faded. "I came as soon as I heard. Is there any news?"

She shook her head. "See to your horse, Clem. I'll prepare some food for you." Gathering her rifle, Beth walked to the house, noticing for the first time in days how untidy it was, how the dust had been allowed to settle on the timbered floor. Suddenly angry, she forgot the food and fetched the mop and bucket from the kitchen. "It's a mess," she said as Clem entered.

He grinned at her. "It looks lived in," he agreed, removing his gun belt and pulling up a chair at the table.

Beth chuckled and laid aside the mop. "A man shouldn't surprise a woman this way, especially after all these years. Time has been good to you, Clem. You filled out some. Suits you."

"I've lived the good life," he told her, but he looked away as he spoke, glancing at the window set in the gray stone of the wall. Clem smiled. "Strong-built place, Beth. I saw the rifle slits at the upper windows and the reinforced shutters on the ground floor. Like a goddamn fortress. Only the old houses now have rifle ports. Guess people think the world's getting safer."

"Only the fools, Clem." She told him about the raid on the church and the bloody aftermath when the Preacher had strapped on his guns. Clem listened in silence. When she had finished, he stood and walked to the kitchen, pouring himself a mug of water. Here there was a heavy door with a strong bar beside it. The window was narrow, the shutters reinforced by iron strips.

"It's been hard in Pernum," he said. "Most of us thought that with the war over we'd get back to farming and ordinary life. Didn't work out that way. I guess it was stupid to think it would after all the killing in the north. And the war that wiped out the Hellborn. You had the Oathmen here yet?" She shook her head. Crossing the room, he stood outlined in the open doorway. "It's not good, Beth. You have to swear your faith in front of three witnesses. And if you don't . . . well, at best you lose your land."

"I take it you swore the Oath?"

Returning to the table, he sat opposite her. "Never been asked. But I guess I would. It's only words. So tell me, any sign of him since the killings?"

She shook her head. "He's not dead, Clem. I know that."

"And he's wearing guns again."

Beth nodded. "Killed six of the raiders, then vanished."

"It will be a hell of a shock to the righteous if they find out who he is. You know there's a statue to him in Pernum? Not a good likeness, especially with the brass halo around his head."

"Don't joke about it, Clem. He tried to ignore it, and I think he was wrong. He never said or did one-tenth of the things they claim. And as for being the new John the Baptist . . . well, it seems like blasphemy to me. You were there, Clem, when the Sword of God descended. You saw the machines from the sky. You *know* the truth."

"You're wrong, Beth. I don't know anything. If the Deacon claims he comes direct from God, who am I to argue? Certainly seems that God's been with him, though. Won the Unifier War, didn't he? And when Batik died and the Hellborn invaded again, he saw them wiped out. Scores of thousands dead. And the Crusaders have mostly cleaned out the brigands and the Carns. Took me six days to ride here, Beth, and I didn't need the gun. They got schools, hospitals, and no one starves. Ain't all bad."

"There's lots here that would agree with you, Clem."

"But you don't?"

"I've no argument with schools and the like," she said, rising from the table and returning with bread, cheese, and a section of smoked ham. "But this talk of pagans and disbelievers needing killing and the butchery of the Wolvers—it's wrong, Clem. Plain wrong."

"What can I do?"

"Find him, Clem. Bring him home."

"You don't want much, do you? That's a big country, Beth. There's deserts and mountains that go on forever."

"Will you do it?"

"Can I eat first?"

Jeremiah enjoyed the wounded man's company, but there was much about Shannow that concerned him, and he confided his worries to Dr. Meredith. "He is a very self-contained man, but I think he remembers far less than he admits. There seems to be a great gulf in his memory."

"I have been trying to recall everything I read about protective amnesia," Meredith told him. "The trauma he suffered was so great that his conscious mind reels from it, blanking out vast areas. Give him time."

Jeremiah smiled. "Time is what we have, my friend."

Meredith nodded and leaned back in his chair, staring up at the darkening sky. A gentle wind was drifting down across the mountains, and from there he could smell the cottonwood trees by the river and the grass from the hillsides.

"What are you thinking?" asked Jeremiah.

"It is beautiful here. It makes the evil of the cities seem far away and somehow inconsequential."

Jeremiah sighed. "Evil is never inconsequential, Doctor."

"You know what I mean," chided Meredith. Jeremiah nodded, and the two men sat for a while in companionable silence. The day's journey had been a good one, with the wagons moving over the plains and halting in the shadows of a jagged mountain range. A little to the north was a slender waterfall, and the Wanderers had camped beside the river that ran from it. The women and children were roaming a stand of trees on the mountainside, gathering dead wood for the evening fires, while most of the men had ridden off in search of meat. Shannow was resting in Jeremiah's wagon.

Isis came into sight, bearing a bundle of dry sticks, which she let fall at Jeremiah's feet. "It wouldn't do you any harm to work a little," she said. Both men noticed her tired eyes and the faintest touch of purple on the cheeks below them.

"Age has its privileges," he told her, forcing a smile.

"Laziness more like," she told him. She swung to face the sandy-haired young doctor. "And what is your excuse?"

Meredith reddened and rose swiftly. "I am sorry. I . . . wasn't thinking. What do you want me to do?"

"You could help Clara with the gathering. You could have cleaned and prepared the rabbits. You could be out hunting with the other men. Dear God, Meredith, you are a useless article." Spinning on her heel, she stalked away, back toward the wood.

"She is working too hard," said Jeremiah.

"She's a fighter, Jeremiah," Meredith answered sadly. "But

she's right. I spend too much time lost in thoughts, dreaming, if you like."

"Some men are dreamers," said Jeremiah. "It's no bad thing. Go and help Clara. She's a little too heavily pregnant to be carrying firewood."

"Yes . . . yes, you're right," Meredith agreed.

Alone now, Jeremiah made a circle of stones and carefully laid a fire. He did not hear Shannow approach and glanced up only when he heard the creak of wood as the man sat in Meredith's chair. "You're looking stronger," said the old man. "How do you feel?"

"I am healing," said Shannow.

"And your memory?"

"Is there a town near here?"

"Why do you ask?"

"As we were traveling today, I saw smoke in the distance."

"I saw it, too," said Jeremiah, "but with luck we'll be far away by tomorrow night."

"With luck?"

"Wanderers are not viewed with great friendliness in these troubled times."

"Why?"

"That's a hard question, Mr. Shannow. Perhaps the man who is tied to a particular piece of land envies us our freedom. Perhaps we are viewed as a threat to the solidity of their existence. In short, I don't know why. You might just as well ask why men like to kill one another or find hatred so easy and love so difficult."

"It is probably territorial," said Shannow. "When men put down roots, they look around them and assume that everything they can see is now theirs: the deer, the trees, the mountains. You come along and kill the deer, and they see it as theft."

"That, too," agreed Jeremiah. "But you do not share that view, Mr. Shannow?"

"I never put down roots."

"You are a curious man, sir. You are knowledgeable, courteous, and yet you have the look of the warrior. I can see it in you. I think you are a . . . deadly man, Mr. Shannow."

Shannow nodded slowly, and his deep blue eyes held Jeremiah's gaze. "You have nothing to fear from me, old man. I am not a warmaker. I do not steal, and I do not lie."

"Did you fight in the war, Mr. Shannow?"

"I do not believe that I did."

"Most men of your age fought in the Unifying War."

"Tell me of it."

Before the old man could begin, Isis came running into view. "Riders!" she said. "And they're armed."

Jeremiah rose and walked between the wagons. Isis moved alongside him, and several of the other women and children gathered around. Dr. Meredith, his arms full of firewood, stood nervously beside a pregnant woman and her two young daughters. Jeremiah shaded his eyes against the setting sun and counted the horsemen. There were fifteen, and all carried rifles. In the lead was a slender young man with shoulder-length white hair. The riders cantered up to the wagons and then drew rein. The white-haired man leaned forward onto the pommel of his saddle.

"Who are you?" he asked, his voice edged with contempt.

"I am Jeremiah, sir. These are my people."

The man looked at the painted wagons and said something in a low voice to the rider on his right. "Are you people of the Book?" asked White-hair, switching his gaze back to Jeremiah.

"Of course," the old man answered.

"You have Oath papers?" The man's voice was soft, almost sibilant.

"We have never been asked to give oaths, sir. We are Wanderers and are rarely in towns long enough to be questioned about our faith."

"I am questioning it," the man said. "And I do not like your tone, Mover. I am Aaron Crane, the Oath Taker for the settlement of Purity. Do you know why I was given this office?" Jeremiah shook his head. "Because I have the gift of discernment. I can smell a pagan at fifty paces. And there is no place in God's land for such people. They are a stain upon the earth, a cancer upon the flesh of the planet, and an abomination in the eyes of God. Recite for me now Psalm 22."

Jeremiah took a deep breath. "I am not a scholar, sir. My Bible is in my wagon—I shall fetch it."

"You are a pagan," screamed Crane, "and your wagon shall burn!" Swinging in his saddle, he gestured to the riders. "Make torches from their campfires. Burn the wagons." The men dismounted and started forward, Crane leading them.

Jeremiah stepped into their path. "Please, sir, do not do . . ." A rider grabbed the old man, hurling him aside. Jeremiah fell heavily but struggled to his feet as Isis ran at the man who had struck him, lashing out with her fist. The rider parried the blow easily and pushed her away.

And Jeremiah watched in helpless despair as the men converged on the fire.

Aaron Crane was exultant as he strode toward the fire. This was the work he had been born for, making the land holy and fit for the people of the Book. These Movers were trash of the worst kind, with no understanding of the demands of the Lord. The men were lazy and shiftless, the women no better than common whores. He glanced at the blond woman who had struck at Leach. Her clothes were threadbare, and her breasts jutted against the woolen shirt she wore. Worse than a whore, he decided, feeling his anger rise. He pictured the wagon aflame, the pagans pleading for mercy. But there should be no mercy for such as these, he resolved. Let them plead before the throne of the Almighty. Yes, they would die, he decided. Not the children, of course; he was not a savage.

Leach made the first torch and handed it to Aaron Crane. "By this act," shouted Crane, "may the name of the Lord be glorified!"

"Amen!" said the men grouped about him. Crane moved toward the first red wagon . . . and stopped. A tall man had stepped into view; he said nothing but merely stood watching Crane. The white-haired Oath Taker studied the man, noting two things instantly. The first was that the newcomer's eyes were looking directly into his own, and the second was that he was armed. Crane glanced at the two pistols in their scabbards at the man's hips. Acutely aware that his men were waiting, he was suddenly at a loss. The newcomer had made no hostile move, but he was standing directly before the wagon. To burn it, Crane would have to push past him.

"Who are you?" asked Crane, buying time to think.

"They have gaped upon me with their mouths, as a ravening and a roaring lion," quoted the man, his voice deep and low.

Crane was shocked. The quote was from the psalm he had asked the old Mover to recite, but the words seemed charged with hidden meaning.

"Stand aside," said Crane, "and do not seek to interfere with the Lord's work."

"You have two choices: live or die," said the tall man, his voice still low, no trace of anger in his words.

Crane felt a sick sense of dread in his belly. The man would kill him; Crane knew that with an ice-cold certainty. If he tried to fire the wagon, the man would draw one of those pistols and shoot him. His throat was dry. A burning cinder fell from the torch, scorching the back of his hand, but Crane did not move ... could not move. Behind him were fifteen armed men, but they might as well have been a hundred miles away, he knew, for all the good they could do him. Sweat dripped into his eyes.

"What's happening, Aaron?" called Leach.

Crane dropped the torch and backed away, his hands trembling. The tall man was walking toward him, and the Oath Taker felt panic surging within him.

Turning, he ran to his horse, scrambling into the saddle. Hauling on the reins, he kicked the beast into a gallop for almost half a mile. Then he drew up and dismounted.

Kneeling on the hard-packed earth, he tasted bile in his mouth and began to vomit.

* * *

Shannow's head was pounding as he walked toward the group of men. The Oath Taker was riding away, but his soldiers remained, confused and uncertain.

"Your leader is gone," said Shannow. "Do you have other business here?" The thickset man who had passed the burning torch to Crane was tense, and Shannow could see his anger growing. But Jeremiah stepped forward.

"You must all be thirsty after your long ride," he said. "Isis, fetch these men some water. Clara, bring the mugs from my wagon. Ah, my friends," he said, "in these troubled times such misunderstandings are so common. We are all people of the Book, and does it not tell us to love our neighbors and to do good to those who hate us?"

Isis, her face flushed and angry, brought forward a copper jug, while the pregnant Clara moved to the group, passing tin mugs to the riders.

The thickset man waved Isis away and stared hard at Shannow.

"What did you say to the Oath Taker?" he snarled.

"Ask him," said Shannow.

"Damn right I will," said the man. He swung on his comrades, who were all drinking. "Let's go!" he shouted.

As they rode away, Shannow returned to the fire and slumped down into Dr. Meredith's chair. Jeremiah and the doctor approached him.

"I thank you, my friend," said Jeremiah. "I fear they would have killed us all."

"It is not wise to stay here the night," Shannow told him. "They will return."

"There are those among us," said the Apostle Saul, the sunlight glinting on his long, golden hair, "who shed tears for the thousands who fell fighting against us in the Great War. And I tell you, Brothers, I am one of those. For those misguided souls gave their very lives in the cause of darkness while believing they were fighting for the light.

"But as the good Lord told us, narrow is the path and few

who will find it. But that Great War is over, my Brothers. It was won for the glory of God and his son, Jesus Christ. And it was won by you, and by me, and by the multitudes of believers who stood firm against the satanic deeds of our enemies, both pagan and Hellborn."

A great cheer went up, and Nestor Garrity found himself wishing he could have been one of those soldiers of Christ in the Great War. But he had been only a child then, attending the lower school and living in fear of the formidable Beth McAdam. All around him the men and women of Pilgrim's Valley had flocked to the Long Meadow to hear the words of the Apostle. Some of the other people present could still remember the sleek white and silver flying machine that had passed over Pilgrim's Valley twenty years before, bringing the Deacon and his Apostles to the people. Nestor wished he could have seen it in the air. His father had taken him to Unity eight years earlier, to the great cathedral at the city center. There, raised on a plinth of shining steel, was the flying machine. Nestor would never forget that moment.

"It may be over, my friends, but another battle awaits us," said the Apostle, his words jerking Nestor back to the present. "The forces of Satan are overthrown, but still there is peril in the land. For as it is written, the Devil is the great deceiver, the son of the morning star. Do not be misled, my brothers and sisters. The Devil is not an ugly beast. He is handsome and charming, and his words drip like honey. And many will be deceived by him. He is the voice of discontent whispering in your ears at night. He is the man—or woman—who speaks against the word of our Deacon and his holy quest to bring this tortured world back to the Lord.

"For was it not written, *by their works shall ye judge them?* Then I ask you this, brethren: Who brought the truth to this benighted world? Tell me!" Raising his arms, he stared down from the podium at the crowd.

"The Deacon!" they yelled.

"And who descended from the heavens with the word of God?"

"The Deacon!" Caught up in the hypnotic thrill of the moment, Nestor stood, his right fist punching the air with each answer. The voices of the crowd rolled like thunder, and Nestor found it hard to see the Apostle through the sea of waving arms. But he could hear him.

"And who did God send through the vaults of time?"

"The Deacon!"

The Apostle Saul waited until the roar died down, then spread his hands for silence. "My friends, by his work have you judged him. He has built hospitals and schools and great cities, and once more the knowledge of our ancestors is being used by the children of God. We have machines that will plow the land and sail the seas and fly through the air. We have medicines and trained doctors and nurses. And this tortured land is growing again, at one with the Lord. And He is with us through His servant in Unity.

"But everywhere sin waits to strike us down. That is why the Oath Takers move through the land. They are the gardeners of this new Eden, seeking out the weeds and the plants that do not bloom. No God-fearing family should fear the Oath Takers. Only those seduced by Satan should know the terror of discovery. Just as only brigands and lawbreakers should fear our new Crusaders, our fine young soldiers, like your own Captain Leon Evans."

Nestor cheered at the top of his voice, but it was lost within an ocean of sound.

As it died down, the Apostle Saul raised his voice one last time. "My friends, Pilgrim's Valley was the first settlement over which we flew when the Lord brought us from the sky. And for that reason the Oath Taker's role shall be a special one. The Deacon has asked me to fulfill that role, and I shall do so, with your blessing. Now let us pray . . ."

As the prayers were concluded, and the last hymn was sung, Nestor made his way back to the main street of Pilgrim's Valley, moving slowly within the crowd. Most of the people were returning to their homes, but a select few, Nestor among them, had been invited to a reception at the Traveler's Rest and the formal welcome for the new Oath Taker. Nestor felt especially privileged to be asked to attend, even though his role was only that of a waiter. History was being made there, and the young man could hardly believe that one of the Nine Apostles was actually going to live—if only for a month or two—among the people of Pilgrim's Valley. It was a great honor.

Josiah Broome, who now owned the Traveler's Rest, was waiting at the back of the inn as Nestor arrived. Broome was in his late sixties, a slender, bird-boned man, balding and near-sighted. Despite his tendency toward pompous speech Broome was a man with a heart, and Nestor liked him.

"Is that you, young Garrity?" asked Broome, leaning in close.

"Yes, sir."

"Good boy. There is a clean white shirt in the upper back room. And a new black necktie. Put them on and help Wallace prepare the tables."

Nestor said that he would and moved on through the rear of the inn, climbing the stairs to the staff quarters. Wallace Nash was pulling on his white shirt as Nestor entered the back room.

"Hi, Nes. What a day eh?" said the redheaded youngster. Two years younger than Nestor, he was an inch taller, standing almost six foot three and as thin as a stick.

"You look like a strong wind could blow you down, Wallace."

The redhead grinned. "I'd outrun it afore it could."

Nestor chuckled. Wallace Nash was the fastest runner he had ever seen. The previous year on Resurrection Day, when he was just fifteen, Wallace had raced three times against Edric Scayse's prize stallion, Rimfire, winning both short sprints and losing only a longer race. It had been a fine day. Nestor remembered it well, for it had been his first time drunk, an experience he had pledged to himself he would never repeat.

"You want to carry the drinks or the eats?" Wallace asked.

"Doesn't matter," said Nestor, pulling off his faded red shirt and lifting a clean white one from the dresser drawer.

"You take the drinks, then," said Wallace. "My hands ain't too steady today. Lord, who would have believed that an Apostle would come to our town?"

Nestor pulled on his shirt and tucked it into his black trousers. For a minute or so he fumbled with the necktie, then he moved to the mirror to see if the knot was in place.

"You think he'll perform any miracles?" asked Wallace.

"Like what?"

"Well, I guess he could try to raise the Preacher from the dead." The redhead laughed.

"That ain't funny, Wallace. The Preacher was a good man."

"That's not so, Nes. He spoke out against the Deacon during one of his sermons. Can you believe that? Right there in a church. It's a wonder God didn't strike him dead there and then."

"As I recall hearing it, he just said he thought it weren't necessary to have Oath Takers. That's all."

"Are you saying the Apostle Saul ain't necessary?" asked Wallace.

Nestor was about to make a lighthearted remark, but then he saw the shining glint in Wallace's eyes.

"Of course I'm not, Wallace. He's a great man," he said carefully. "Now come on, we'd better get to work."

The evening was long, and Nestor found his back aching as he stood against the wall holding the brass tray in his hands. Few were drinking now, and the Apostle Saul was sitting by the fire with Captain Leon Evans and Daniel Cade. The old prophet had been late arriving; most of the members of the welcoming party had long since gone to their homes before the old man had made his entrance. The Apostle had welcomed him warmly, but it seemed to Nestor that Daniel Cade was ill at ease.

"It is a privilege to meet you at last," said Saul. "Obviously I have read of your exploits against the Hellborn in the first war. Vile times, calling for men of iron, much as now. I am sorry to see that you have such difficulty with your movements. You should come to Unity; our hospital is performing miracles daily, thanks to the discoveries of our medical teams."

"The Daniel Stones, you mean," said Cade.

"You are well informed, sir. Yes, the fragments have been most helpful. We are still seeking larger stones."

"Blood and death is all they'll bring," Cade said. "Just like before."

"In the hands of the godly all things are pure," said Saul.

Excited as he had been earlier in the evening, Nestor was now tired and becoming bored. He was due at the lumber site soon after dawn to collate the orders for timber and issue working instructions to the men at the sawmill. Uncle Joseph was not an easy man to serve, and one yawn from Nestor would earn an hour's lecture at the end of the day.

"You knew the Jerusalem Man, I understand," remarked Saul to Cade. Instantly Nestor's weariness was forgotten.

"I knew him," grunted the old man. "And I never heard him say a word of prophecy. I don't reckon he'd be pleased to read what's said of him now."

"He was a holy man," said Saul, showing no sign of irritation, "and the words he spoke have been carefully gathered from sources all over the land. Men who knew him. Men who heard him. I regard it as a personal tragedy that I never met him."

Cade nodded solemnly. "Well, I did, Saul. He was a lonely man, heartsick and bitter, seeking a city he knew could not exist. As to his prophesying . . . as I said, I never heard it. But it's true to say that he brought you and the Deacon into this world when he sent the Sword of God thundering through the gates of time. We all know that's true."

"The ways of the Lord are sometimes mystifying," Saul said with a tight smile. "The world we left was a cesspool, owned by the Devil. The world we found had the potential for Eden, if only men would return to God. And by His grace we have conquered. Tell me, sir, why you have refused all invitations to travel to Unity and be honored for your work in the Lord's name."

"I don't need honors," Cade told him. "I lived most of my life, after the Hellborn War, in Rivervale. Had me a good woman and raised two tall sons. Both died in your wars. Lisa was buried last autumn, and I came here to wait for death. Honors? What are they worth?"

Saul shrugged. "A worthy point from a worthy man, Mr. Cade. Now tell me, do you think Pilgrim's Valley is a God-fearing community?"

"There are good people here, Saul. Some better than others. I don't think you can judge a man merely because three of his friends say he's a believer. We got farmers on the outskirts, newcomers who wouldn't be able to raise three men who know them that well. It doesn't make 'em pagans."

"You also had a church that welcomed Wolvers," Saul pointed out, "and a preacher who offered them the word of God. That was an obscenity, Mr. Cade. And it took outsiders to put an end to it. That does not reflect well on the community."

"What have you got against Wolvers?" Cade asked.

Saul's eyes narrowed. "They are not true creations, Mr. Cade. In the world I came from, animals were being genetically engineered to resemble people. This was done for medical reasons; it was possible then for a man with a diseased heart or lungs to have them removed and replaced. That was an abomination, Mr. Cade. Animals have no souls, not in the strictest sense of eternal life. These mutated creatures are like plague germs, reminding us all of the dangers and disasters of the past. We must not repeat the errors that led God to destroy the old world. Not ever. We are on the verge of a new Eden, Mr. Cade. Nothing must be allowed to halt our progress."

"And we're going to find this new Eden by hounding people from their homes, by killing Wolvers and anyone who doesn't agree with us?"

"Not the Deacon or any of his Apostles take any joy in

killing, Mr. Cade. But you know your Bible. The Lord God does not tolerate evil in the midst of his people."

Cade reached for his sticks and slowly, painfully pushed himself to his feet. "And the next war, Saul? Who is that going to be with?"

"The ungodly wherever we find them," answered Saul.

"It's late, and I'm tired," said Cade. "I'll bid you good night."

"May God be with you," said Saul, rising.

Cade did not reply as, leaning heavily on his sticks, he made his way to the door. Nestor stifled a yawn and was about to ask if he could be excused from his duties, when Saul spoke to Captain Evans.

"A dangerous man, Captain. I fear we may have to deal with him."

Nestor blinked in surprise. At that moment Leon Evans looked up and saw him, and the captain grinned. "Go on home, Nestor," he said, "otherwise you're going to keel over like a felled tree."

Nestor thanked him, bowed to the Apostle, and walked out into the night, where the old prophet was leaning against his buggy, unable to mount the steps. Nestor moved alongside him and took his arm. With an effort, he half lifted Cade to the seat. "Thank you, boy," grunted Cade, his face red from the exertion.

"It was a pleasure, sir."

"Beware the words of brass and iron, boy," whispered the prophet. He flicked the reins, and Nestor watched as the buggy trundled off into the night.

Alone now, Shannow waited among the rocks, his horse tethered some fifty paces to the north in a small stand of trees. Glancing to the east, he could make out the last of the wagons as they traveled farther into the mountains. The sky was lightening. Dawn was close.

Shannow settled down with his back against a rock and stared to the west. Maybe he had been wrong. Maybe the white-haired Oath Taker had decided against a punitive raid.

He hoped so. The night was cool, and he breathed deeply of the crisp mountain air. Glad to be alone, he let his mind wander.

Twenty years had passed since his name had been feared among the ungodly. Twenty years! Where have I been? he wondered. How did I live? Idly he began to review what he remembered of his life, the gunfights and the battles, the towns and settlements.

Yes, I remember Allion, he thought, and saw again the day Daniel Cade had led his brigands into the town. In the blaze of gunfire that had followed several of Cade's men had been shot from their saddles, while Cade himself had taken a bullet in the knee. Daniel Cade. Brother Daniel. For some reason that Shannow could never fathom, God had chosen Daniel to lead the war against the Hellborn.

But what then? Hazy pictures drifted into his mind, then vanished like mist in the breeze. A blond woman, tall and strong, and a young fighter, lightning-fast with a pistol . . . Cram? Glen?

"No," Shannow said aloud. "Clem. Clem Steiner."

It will all come back, he promised himself. Just give it time.

Then came the sound of horses moving slowly through the darkness, the creak of leather saddles, the soft clopping of hooves on the dry plain. Shannow drew his pistols and eased himself farther down into the rocks as the horses came closer. Removing his wide-brimmed hat, he risked a glance to the west; he could see them now, but not well enough to count them.

I don't want to kill again.

Aiming high, he loosed a shot. Some of the horses reared in fright, and several others stampeded. Shannow saw one man thrown from the saddle, and another jumped clear of his bucking mount. Several shots were fired in his direction, but the bullets struck the rocks and screamed off into the night.

Dropping to his belly, Shannow peered around the rocks. The riders had dismounted and were advancing on his position. From the east he heard the distant sound of gunfire.

The wagons! In that instant he knew that there were two groups and that the bloodletting had already begun. Anger surged within him.

Swiftly he pushed himself to his feet and stepped out from the rocks. A man reared up . . . Shannow shot him through the chest. Another moved to his right, and again his pistol boomed.

He walked in among the men, guns blazing. Stunned by this sudden attack, the raiders broke and ran. A man to Shannow's right groaned as the Jerusalem Man strode past him. A bullet whipped by Shannow's face, so close that he felt its passing, the sound ringing in his ears like an angry bee. Twisting, he triggered both pistols, and a rifleman was punched from his feet.

Two horses were standing close by. Shannow strode to the first and vaulted to the saddle. A man reared up from the undergrowth. Shannow shot him twice, then, kicking the animal into a run, headed east, reloading his pistols as the horse thundered across the plain. Anger was strong upon him now, a deep, boiling rage that threatened to engulf him. He did nothing to quell it.

Always it was the same, the evil strong preying on the weak, violence and death, lust and destruction. When will it end? he wondered. Dear God, when will it end?

The full moon bathed the land in silver, and in the distance the red of fire could be seen as one of the wagons blazed. The firing was sporadic now, but at least it suggested that some of the Wanderers were still fighting.

Closer still he came and saw five men kneeling behind a group of boulders; one of them had long white hair. A rifleman rose up, aiming at the wagons. Shannow loosed a shot that missed the man but ricocheted from the boulder, making the rifleman jerk back. The white-haired Oath Taker swung around, saw Shannow, and began to run. Ignoring him, Shannow trained his guns on the riflemen.

"Put down your weapons," he ordered them. "Do it now—or die!"

Three of the four remaining men did exactly as they were told and then raised their hands, but the last—the thickset man he had spoken to earlier—suddenly swung his rifle to bear. Shannow put a bullet into his brain.

"Jeremiah! It's me, Shannow," shouted the Jerusalem Man. "Can you hear me?"

"He's been shot," came the answering call. "We've wounded here—three dead, two badly hit."

Gesturing to the captured men, Shannow ordered them toward the wagons. Once inside, he gazed around. The pregnant Clara was dead, half her head blown away. A burly man named Chalmers was lying beside her. By Jeremiah's wagon lay the body of a child in a faded blue dress: one of Clara's two daughters. Shannow dismounted and moved to where Dr. Meredith was kneeling beside the wounded Jeremiah. The old man had taken two shots, one to the upper chest and a second to the thigh. His face was gray in the moonlight.

"I'll live," the old man whispered.

The wagons had been formed into a rough circle, and several of the horses were down. Isis and two of the men were battling to put out a fire in the last wagon. Guns in hand, Shannow strode back to the captured men, who were standing together at the center of the camp.

"The bellows are burned, the land is consumed of the fire; the founder melteth in vain, for the wicked are not plucked away." His guns leveled, and he eased back the hammers.

"Shannow, no!" screamed Jeremiah. "Let them be! Christ, man, there's been enough killing already."

Shannow took a deep, slow breath. "Help put out the fire," he ordered the men. They obeyed him instantly, and without another word he walked to his horse and stepped into the saddle.

"Where are you going?" called Dr. Meredith.

Shannow did not answer.

Aaron Crane and the survivors of the raid galloped into Purity and drew up before the long stone meeting hall. Crane, dust-covered and disheveled, dismounted and ran inside. The hall was crowded, the prayer meeting under way. On the dais Padlock Wheeler was reaching the midpoint in his sermon concerning the path of the righteous. He stopped as he saw Crane and inwardly groaned, but it was not wise to incur the wrath of the Oath Taker. The black-bearded minister fell silent for a moment, then forced a smile.

"You seem distraught, Brother," he said. Heads turned then, among them those of Captain Seth Wheeler and the twelve men of Purity's Crusaders. Crane drew himself up and ran a slender hand through his long white hair.

"The forces of the Devil have been turned against us," he said. "The Lord's riders have been cut down."

There was a gasp from the congregation, and several of the women began to shout out questions concerning the fate of their husbands, brothers, or sons.

"Silence!" thundered Padlock Wheeler. "Let the Oath Taker speak."

"As you all know," said Crane, "we came upon a band of pagan Wanderers. With them was a demonic force: I recognized the power of Satan instantly. We tried in vain to overcome it. Many are dead. A few of us escaped through the intervention of the Lord. We must have more men! I demand that the Crusaders ride out after these devils!"

Padlock Wheeler glanced down at his brother, Seth. The captain rose from his seat. He was a tall, slim man with a long face and a dour expression. "Let the women go to their homes," he said. "We'll discuss what's to be done."

"Where's my boy?" screamed a woman, rushing at Crane. "Where is Lemuel?"

"I fear he perished," Crane told her, "but he died in the Lord's work."

The woman's hand snaked out to slash across Crane's cheek. Two other women grabbed her, hauling her back.

"Stop this!" thundered Padlock Wheeler. "This is a house of God!" The commotion died instantly. Slowly the women filed from the hall, the men gathering around Crane.

Seth Wheeler moved forward. "Tell us of this demon," he ordered Crane.

"It is in the guise of a man, but it is Satan-inspired. He is a killer. A terrible killer!" Crane shivered. "He cast a spell on me that took all the power I had to overcome."

"How many are dead?" asked the Crusader captain.

"I don't know. We advanced on two fronts. The killer was waiting in the east and shot down four men: Lassiter, Pope, Carter, and Lowris. Then he rode west and slew . . . everyone but me. I managed to escape."

"You ran?"

"What else could I do?"

Seth Wheeler glanced at the men gathered in the hall. There were some twenty in all, plus his twelve Crusaders. "How many Wanderers were there?"

"Eleven wagons," Crane told him. "Perhaps thirty people. They must be destroyed. Utterly destroyed!"

Still on the dais, Padlock Wheeler saw the door at the back of the hall open and a tall man step inside. Dressed in a dust-stained black coat, patched on the left arm, he wore two long guns.

"Where are the lawmakers of this community?" he said, his voice, though not loud, cutting through the conversation at the center of the hall.

Crane saw him and screamed. "It's him! It's the Devil!" Backing away, the white-haired Oath Taker ducked down behind a line of benches.

"This is a house of the Lord," said Padlock Wheeler. "What do you want here?"

"Justice," answered the man. "You are sheltering a murderer, a killer of women and children."

"He tells it differently," said Padlock. "He claims you are demon-possessed."

The newcomer shook his head. "Twenty miles from here they are burying a woman named Clara. She was pregnant; half her head was shot away. They will bury one of her daughters beside her. The man Crane rode up to the wagons yesterday and demanded to hear Psalm 22. I gave him to understand that I knew it, as indeed I do. But he is an evil man and was determined to murder. So tell me this: How will you judge him?"

Padlock looked down at where Crane was cowering. The minister felt exultant. All along he had believed Crane to be a dangerous man, and this was an opportunity to bring him down. He would ask Seth for an inquiry, and he had no doubt that the Oath Taker would be shown to be a lawbreaker. But just as he was about to speak, he saw Crane draw a pistol from his belt and cock it.

Within a heartbeat all was chaos and confusion. "You lie!" screamed Crane, rearing up and pointing his pistol. The shot splintered the wood of the door by the stranger's head. The gathered men dived for cover, but the stranger calmly drew one of his pistols and fired once. Crane's head exploded.

The Oath Taker's body stood for a moment, his black coat drenched in blood and brain. Then it crumpled to the floor.

"I am the Jerusalem Man," said the stranger, "and I do not lie."

Sheathing his pistol, he left the hall.

One by one the watching men rose and moved back to view the body. Padlock Wheeler, his legs unsteady, climbed down from the dais. His brother, Seth, stood by the corpse and shook his head.

"What happens now?" asked Padlock.

"We'll send a message to Unity," said Seth. "They'll have to send another Oath Taker."

Padlock took his brother's arm and led him away from the other men. "He claimed to be Jon Shannow."

"I heard him. That was blasphemy! I'll take some men to the Wanderers tomorrow. We'll speak to them, find out what really happened."

"Crane was a wretch! I'll shed no tears for him. Why not let them go their way?"

Seth shook his head. "He claimed to be the Jerusalem Man. He took the saint's name in vain. Everyone heard it; he's got to answer for that."

"I don't want to see anyone else die for the sake of Crane's evil. Not even a blasphemer."

Seth smiled thinly. "I am a Crusader, Pad. What do you expect me to do?"

"Walk warily, Brother. You saw him shoot. He was under fire, but he calmly aimed and blew Crane's soul to hell. And if what the wretch said was true—and I don't doubt it was—he shot down a number of other armed men."

"I've no choice, Pad. I'll try to take him alive."

◇ 3 ◇

In a small section of the garden a tiny weed spoke to the blooms that grew there. "Why," he asked, "does the gardener seek to kill me? Do I not have a right to life? Are my leaves not green, as yours are? Is it too much to ask that I be allowed to grow and see the sun?" The blooms pondered on this and decided to ask the gardener to spare the weed. He did so. Day by day the weed grew, stronger and stronger, taller and taller, its leaves covering the other plants, its roots spreading. One by one the flowers died until only a rose was left. It gazed up at the enormous weed and asked: "Why do you seek to kill me? Do I not have a right to life? Are my leaves not green, as yours are? Is it too much to ask that I be allowed to grow and see the sun?"

"Yes, it is too much to ask," said the weed.

The Wisdom of the Deacon
Chapter VII

THEY HAD BURIED Clara and her daughter by the time Shannow returned to the wagons. Jeremiah was in bed in his wagon, his chest bandaged, his face gray with sorrow and pain. Shannow climbed in to sit beside the old man.

"You killed him?" asked Jeremiah.

"I did. I would have had it otherwise, but he fired upon me."

"That will not end it, Mr. Shannow, though I do not blame you. You did not inspire the evil. But you must go."

"They will come again, and you will need me."

"No. I spoke to the men you captured before I let them go.

Crane was the instigator." Jeremiah sighed. "There will always be men like Crane. Thankfully there will also always be men like Meredith and men like you. It is a balance, Mr. Shannow. God's balance, if you will."

Shannow nodded. "Evil will always thrive if men do not oppose it."

"Evil thrives anyway. Greed, desire, jealousy. We all carry the seeds of evil. Some are stronger than others and can resist it, but men like Crane will feed the seed." Jeremiah leaned back against his pillow, his eyes resting on Shannow's lean face. "You are not evil, my boy. Go with God!"

"I am sorry, old man," said Shannow, rising.

Back in the open he saw Isis coming toward him, carrying a bundle. "I gathered some ammunition from the dead, and there is a little food here," she said. He thanked her and turned away. "Wait!" She handed him a small pouch. "There are twelve Bartas here. You will need money."

Jeremiah heard the creak of saddle leather as Shannow mounted, then the steady clopping of hooves as he headed away from the wagons. The pain from his wound was strong, but the old man flowed with it. He felt sick and weaker than sin.

Isis brought him an herbal tisane, which settled his stomach. "I am happier with him gone," she said, "though I liked him."

They sat in companionable silence for a while, then Meredith joined them. "Riders coming," he said. "Look like Crusaders."

"Make them welcome and bring the leader here," said Jeremiah. Within minutes a tall, round-shouldered man with a long, dour face climbed into the wagon. "Welcome to my home," said Jeremiah.

The man nodded, removed his wide-brimmed gray hat, and sat alongside the bed. "I'm Captain Seth Wheeler," said the newcomer. "I understand you have a man with you who calls himself Jon Shannow."

"Will you not ask, sir, why there are fresh-dug graves outside and why I am lying here with a bullet in my chest?"

"I know why," muttered Wheeler, looking away. "But that was not my doing, Meneer, nor do I condone it. But there have been deaths on both sides, and the man who instigated them is among the dead."

"Then why hunt Jon Shannow?"

"He is a blasphemer and a heretic. The Jerusalem Man—of blessed memory—left this earth twenty years ago, taken up by God like Elijah before him in a chariot of fire."

"If God can lift him, which of course he can," said Jeremiah carefully, "then he can also bring him back."

"I'll not argue that point with you, Meneer. What I will say is this: If the good Lord did choose to bring back the Jerusalem Man, I don't think he'd arrive with singed hair and a patched coat. However, enough of this. Which direction did he take?"

"I cannot help you sir. I was in my wagon when he rode away. You will have to ask one of my people."

Wheeler rose and moved to the door, then he turned. "I have already said that I do not condone what happened here," he said softly. "But know this, Mover, I share Crane's view about the likes of you. You are a stain upon God's land. As the Deacon says, *'There is no place for the scavenger among us. Only those who build the cities of the Lord are welcome.'* Be gone from the lands of Purity by tomorrow night."

Shannow rode toward the high country, angling north. The horse was a bay gelding and strong, but it was tired after the exertions of the night and was breathing heavily. Shannow dismounted and led the horse into the trees, seeking a cave or a sheltered spot in the lee of the wind. He was cold, and his spirits were low.

The loss of memory was an irritation, but that he could bear. Something else was nagging at him from deep within the now-shuttered recesses of his mind. He had killed men this night, but that was nothing new for the Jerusalem Man. *I did not seek the battle,* he told himself. *They rode out in search of blood, and they found it. And it was their own. Such is the price of violence.* Yet the killings hung heavily upon him.

Shannow stumbled, his strength deserting him. His wounds were too recent for this kind of climb, he knew, but he pushed on. The trees were thicker now, and he saw a cleft in the rock face to his left. It will have to do, he thought. Taking a deep breath, he walked on. As he neared the cleft, he saw the flickering reflection of a fire on the rock face, just inside the cleft.

"Hello, the camp!" he called. It was not wise in the wilderness to walk uninvited into a campsite. With the fear of brigands everywhere, a sudden appearance could lead to a volley of shots from frightened travelers.

"Come on in," came a voice that echoed eerily up through the cleft. Shannow pushed his coat back over the butt of his right-hand pistol and, leading the horse with his left hand, approached the cleft. It was narrow only at the entrance and widened into a pear-shaped cave within. An old man with a waist-length white beard was sitting before the fire, above which a hunk of meat had been spitted. At the back of the cave a mule had been hobbled. Shannow led his horse to the rear and looped the reins over the beast's head, trailing them to the ground. Then he joined the white-bearded man.

"Welcome to my fire," said the man, his voice deep. He extended his hand. "You can call me Jake."

"Jon Shannow."

"You're welcome, Mr. Shannow. I kept looking at this meat and thinking, There's too much here for you, Jake. Now the Lord has supplied me with a dinner guest. Come far?"

Shannow shook his head. A great weariness settled on him, and he leaned back against a rock and stretched out his legs.

Jake filled a mug with a steaming brew and passed it to him. "Here, drink this, boy. It's a great reviver, and there's a ton of sugar in it."

Shannow sipped the brew. It was rich and bittersweet. "My thanks, Jake. This is good. Tell me, do I know you?"

"Could be, son; the world's a mighty small place. I've been here and there: Allion, Rivervale, Pilgrim's Valley, the Plague Lands. You name it, I've seen it."

"Rivervale . . . yes, I seem to remember . . ." He saw a beautiful woman and a young boy. The memory faded like a dream when one wakened, but a name slipped through the shutters. "Donna!" he said.

"You all right, boy?"

"Do you know me, Jake?"

"I've seen you. It's a fearsome name you carry. You sure it's yours?"

"I'm sure."

"You seem a mite young, if you don't mind me saying so. What are you . . . thirty-five . . . six?"

"I think I'll sleep now," said Shannow, stretching himself out beside the fire.

His dreams were fractured and anxious. He was wounded, and the lion-man Shir-ran was tending to him. A creature with scaled skin ran into the cave, a jagged knife held in its hand. Shannow's guns thundered, and the creature fell back, becoming a child with open, horrified eyes. "Oh, God, no! Not again!" cried Shannow.

His eyes opened, and he saw that Jake was kneeling beside him.

"Wake up, boy. It's just a dream." Shannow groaned and pushed himself to a sitting position. The fire had died down, and the old man handed him a plate on which strips of cold roast meat had been carved. "Eat a little. You'll feel better."

Shannow took the plate and began to eat. Jake took a pot from the dying fire and filled a tin mug. Then he added sticks to the coals. New flames flickered as Shannow shivered.

"It will soon warm up." Jake rose and walked to the rear of the cave, returning with a blanket, which he wrapped around Shannow's shoulders.

"You were in that gun battle last night," he said. "I can smell the powder on your coat. Was it a good fight?"

"Are there any good fights?" responded Shannow.

"It's a good fight when evil perishes," said Jake.

"Evil does not usually die alone," said Shannow. "They killed a young woman and her daughter."

"Sad times," agreed Jake.

The meat was good, and Shannow felt his strength returning. Unbuckling his gun belt, he laid it alongside him, then stretched his tired muscles. Jake was right. The heat from the fire was beginning to reflect back from the walls.

"What are you doing in the wilderness, Jake?"

"I like the solitude—generally speaking. And it is a good place to talk to God, don't you think? It's clean and open, and the wind carries your words to the heavens. I take it you were with the Movers."

"Yes. Good people."

"That's as may be, son, but they don't plant and they don't build," said Jake.

"Neither does the sparrow," responded Shannow.

"A nice biblical reference, Mr. Shannow, and I do enjoy a debate. But you are wrong. The sparrow eats many seeds, then he flies away. Not all the seeds are digested, and he drops them in other places. All the great forests of the world were probably started by birds' droppings."

Shannow smiled. "Perhaps the Wanderers are like the birds. Perhaps they spread the seeds of knowledge."

"That would make them really dangerous," said Jake, his eyes glinting in the firelight. "There's all kinds of knowledge, Mr. Shannow. Knew a man once who could identify every poisonous plant there was. Wanted to write a book on it. That's dangerous knowledge—you agree?"

"People reading the book would be able to tell what plants not to eat," said Shannow.

"Aye, and people wishing to learn of poisons would know what plants to feed their enemies."

"Did he write the book?"

"No. He died in the Unity War. Left a widow and five children. Did you fight in the war?"

"No. At least I don't think so."

Jake looked at him closely.

"You having trouble remembering things?"

"Some things," said Shannow.

"Like what?"

"Like the last twenty years."

"I saw the head wound. Happens sometimes. So what will you do?"

"I'll wait. The Lord will show me my past when he's good and ready."

"Anything I can do?"

"Tell me about the Deacon and his war."

The old man chuckled. "That's a tall order, boy, for one night around the fire." Leaning back, he stretched out his legs. "Getting too old to enjoy sleeping on rock," he said. "Well, then, where do we start? The Deacon." He sniffed loudly and thought for a moment. "If you are who you claim to be, Mr. Shannow, then it was you who brought the Deacon into this world. He and his brethren were in a plane that took to the skies on the day of Armageddon. It was then trapped, held by the power that also snared the Sword of God. You released them when you sent the sword into the past to destroy Atlantis."

Shannow closed his eyes. The memory was hazy, but he could see the sword hovering in the sky, the gateway of time opening. And something else . . . the face of a beautiful black woman. No name would come to him, but he heard her voice: *"It is a missile, Shannow. A terrible weapon of death and destruction."* Try as he would, Shannow could not pluck any more from his past. "Go on," he told Jake.

"The Deacon and his men landed near Rivervale. It was like the Second Coming. Nobody in this world knew about the decay and corruption that plagued the old cities, killers walking the streets, lust and depravity everywhere. The world, he said, was godless. The sins of Sodom and Gomorrah were multiplied a hundredfold in that old world. Before long the Deacon was a revered figure. His power grew. He said that the new world must never be allowed to make the mistakes of the old, that the Bible contained the seeds of man's future prosperity. There were those who argued against him, saying that his plans were an affront to their views of personal freedom and liberty. That led to the Great War and the Second Hellborn War. But the Deacon won both. Now he rules in Unity, and there is talk that he plans to build the New Jerusalem." Jake lapsed into silence and added more fuel to the fire. "Ain't much else I can tell you, boy."

"And the Jerusalem Man?" asked Shannow.

Jake grinned. "Well, you, if indeed that is you, were John the Baptist reborn, or maybe Elijah, or both. You were the herald to announce the new coming of God's word to the world. Until, that is, you were taken by God in a fiery chariot to a new world that needed your talents. You still remember nothing?"

"Nothing about a fiery chariot," said Shannow grimly. "All I know is who I am. How I came to be here or where I have been for the last twenty years is a mystery to me. But I sense I was living under another name, and I did not use my pistols. Maybe I was a farmer. I don't know. I will find out, Jake. Fragments keep coming back to me. One day they will form a whole."

"Have you told anybody who you are?"

Shannow nodded. "I killed a man in the settlement of Purity. I told them then."

"They'll come hunting you. You are a holy figure now, a legend. It'll be said that you've taken the Jerusalem Man's name in vain. Personally I think they'd be wise to leave you alone. But that's not the way it will be. In fact there could even be a terrible irony in all this."

"In what way?"

"The Deacon has a group of men close to him. One of them—Saul—has formed a group of riders called the Jerusalem Riders. They travel the land as judges and law bringers. They are skilled with weapons and chosen from the very best—or perhaps it is the worst—of the Crusaders. Deadly men, Mr. Shannow. Perhaps they will be sent after you." Jake chuckled and shook his head.

"You seem to find the situation amusing," said Shannow. "Is it because you do not believe me?"

"On the contrary, it is amusing simply because I *do* believe you."

Nestor Garrity took careful aim. The pistol bucked in his hand, and the rock he had set atop the boulder shivered as the bullet sliced the air above it. The sound echoed in the still mountain air, and a hawk, surprised by the sudden noise, took off from a tree to Nestor's left. Sheepishly Nestor looked around, but there was no one close, and he took aim again. This time he smashed fragments of stone from the boulder, low and to the right of the rock. He cursed softly, then angrily loosed the final four shots.

The rock was untouched. Nestor sat down, broke open the pistol, and fed six more shells into the chambers. It had cost him eighteen Bartas, almost a month's wages at the logging camp, and Mr. Bartholomew had assured him it was a fine, straight shooting piece created by the old Hellborn factory near Babylon.

"Is it as good as the Hellborn used to make?" Nestor had asked him.

The old man shrugged. "I guess," he said.

Nestor felt like taking it back and demanding the return of his money.

Sheathing the pistol, he opened the pack of sandwiches he had purchased from Mrs. Broome and took out his Bible. Then he heard the horse approaching and turned to see a rider coming over the crest of the hill. He was a tall, handsome man, dark hair streaked with silver, and he was wearing a black coat and a brocaded red waistcoat. At his hip was a nickel-plated pistol in a polished leather scabbard.

The rider drew up a little way from the youth and dismounted. "You'd be Nestor Garrity?" he asked.

"Yes, sir."

"Clem Steiner. Mrs. McAdam suggested I speak to you."

"In connection with what, sir?"

"The Preacher. She has asked me to find him."

"I fear he's dead, Mr. Steiner. I looked mighty hard. I seen blood and wolf tracks."

Steiner grinned. "You don't know the man as well as I do, Nestor. His kind don't die so easy." Nestor saw Steiner switch his gaze to the bullet-scarred boulder. "Been practicing?"

"Yes, sir, but I fear I am not skilled with the pistol. Safest place in these mountains is that rock yonder."

In one smooth motion Steiner's gun seemed to leap to his hand. At the first shot the rock leapt several feet into the air, and the second saw it smashed to powder. Steiner spun the pistol back into its scabbard. "Forgive me, Nestor; I never could resist showing off. It's a bad vice. Now, about the Preacher, were there any other tracks close by?"

Nestor was stunned by the display and fought to gather his thoughts. "No, sir. Not of a man afoot, anyway."

"Any tracks at all?"

"No . . . well, yes. There was wheel marks to the east. Big ones. I think they were Wanderers. The tracks were recent, though, sharp-edged."

"Which way were they heading?" Steiner asked.

"East."

"Any towns out there?"

"There's a new settlement called Purity. It's run by Padlock Wheeler. He used to be one of the Deacon's generals. I ain't . . . haven't been there."

Steiner walked to the boulder, selected another small rock, and placed it on the top. Strolling back to Nestor, he said, "Let's see how you shoot."

Nestor took a long, deep breath and wished he had the nerve to refuse. Drawing the pistol, he eased back the hammer and sighted along the barrel.

"Hold it," said Steiner. "You're tilting your head and sighting with your left eye."

"The right is not as strong," Nestor admitted.

"Put the gun away." Nestor eased the hammer forward and holstered the pistol. "All right, now point your finger at my saddle."

"What?"

"Just point at my saddle. Do it!" Nestor reddened, but he lifted his right hand and pointed. "Now point at the tree on your right. Good."

"I never had much trouble pointing, Mr. Steiner. It's the shooting that lets me down."

Steiner chuckled. "No, Nestor. It's the lack of pointing that lets you down. Now, this time draw the pistol, cock it, and point it at the rock. Don't aim. Just point and fire."

Nestor knew what would happen and wished with all his heart that he had chosen to stay home that day. Obediently he drew the long-barreled pistol and pointed at the rock, firing almost instantly, desperate to get the embarrassing moment over and done with.

The rock exploded.

"Wow!" shouted Nestor. "By damn, I did it!"

"Yes," agreed Steiner. "That's one rock that will never threaten innocent folks again."

Steiner moved to his horse, and Nestor realized the man was about to leave. "Wait!" he called. "Will you join me in some lunch? I got sandwiches and some honey biscuits. It ain't much, but you're welcome."

As they ate, Nestor talked of his ambition to become a Crusader and maybe even a Jerusalem Rider one day. Steiner listened politely, no hint of mockery in his expression. Nestor talked for longer than he ever had to one person at one time and eventually stumbled to a halt. "Gee, I'm sorry, Mr. Steiner. I think I near bored you to death. It's just, nobody ever listened so good before."

"I like ambition, Son; it's a good thing. A man wants something bad enough and he'll generally get it if he works at it and he's unlucky enough."

"Unlucky?" queried Nestor.

Steiner nodded. "In most cases the dream is better than the reality. Pity the man who fulfills all his dreams, Nestor."

"Did you do that, sir?"

"Certainly did." Steiner's face looked suddenly solemn, and Nestor switched the subject.

"You ever been a Crusader, Mr. Steiner?" he asked. "I never seen anybody shoot that good."

"No, not a Crusader."

"Not . . . a brigand?"

Steiner laughed aloud. "I could have been, Son, but I wasn't. I was lucky. I had me a curious ambition, though. I wanted to be the man who killed the Jerusalem Man."

Nestor's mouth dropped open. "That's a terrible thing to say."

"It is now. But back then he was just a man with a big, big name. I was working for Edric Scayse, and he warned me to change that ambition. I said, 'There's no way he can beat me, Mr. Scayse.' You know what he said? He told me, 'He wouldn't beat you, Clem, he'd kill you.' He was right. They broke the mold when they made Shannow. Deadliest man I ever knew."

"You knew him? Lord, you're a lucky man, Mr. Steiner."

"Luck certainly has played a part in my life," said Steiner. "Now I'd best be on my way."

"You're going to look for the Preacher?"

"I'll find him, Son," said Clem, easing himself to his feet. In that moment Nestor knew what he wanted to do, knew it with a certainty he had never before experienced.

"Could I come with you, Mr. Steiner? I mean, if you wouldn't mind."

"You've got a job here, boy, and a settled life. This could take some time."

"I don't care. Since my folks died I've been working for my uncle. But I think I could learn more from you, Mr. Steiner, than I ever could from him. And I'm sick of counting out Barta coin and docking wages for lost hours. I'm tired of counting timber and writing out orders. Will you let me ride with you?"

"I'll be riding into town to buy supplies, Nestor. You'll need a blanket roll and a heavy coat. A rifle would be handy."

"Yes, sir," said Nestor happily. "I've got a rifle. I'll get the other gear from Mr. Broome."

"How old are you, Son?"

"Seventeen, sir."

Clem Steiner smiled. "I can just remember what it was like to be seventeen. Let's go."

Josiah Broome pushed out his bare feet toward the hearth, trying to concentrate on the warmth of the flames while ignoring the constant stream of words coming from the kitchen. It was not easy: Else Broome was not a woman to be ignored. Broome stared into the fire, his thoughts gloomy. He had helped build Pilgrim's Valley back in the old days and then had been one of the leaders when the town had been rebuilt after the invasion from Atlantis. Josiah Broome had survived the assault by the scaled lizard warriors known as Daggers and had tried in his own small way to make Pilgrim's Valley a decent place for the families that settled there.

He abhorred men of violence, the hard-drinking, brawling warriors who had once peopled this land. And he loathed men like Jon Shannow, whose idea of justice was to slaughter any who crossed their path. Now, in these enlightened days, Jon Shannow was considered a saint, a holy man of God. Else's voice droned on, and he noticed a lilt at the end of the sentence. "I am sorry, my dear, I didn't catch that," he said.

Else Broome eased her vast bulk through the doorway. "I asked if you agreed that we should invite the Apostle Saul to the barbecue."

"Yes, dear. Whatever you think best."

"I was only saying to the widow Scayse the other day . . ." The words rolled on as she retreated to the kitchen, and Broome blanked them from his mind.

Jon Shannow, the saint.

The Preacher had laughed at it. Broome remembered their last evening together in the small vestry behind the church.

"It is not important, Josiah," said Jon Cade. "What I used to be is irrelevant now. What is important is that God's word should not be corrupted. The Book speaks of love as well as judgment. And I'll not be persuaded that the Wolvers are denied that love."

"I don't disagree with you, Preacher. In fact, of all men I hold you in the highest regard. You turned your back on the ways of violence and have shown great courage during these last years. You are an inspiration to me. But the people of Pilgrim's Valley are being seduced by the Deacon's new teachings. And I fear for you and the church. Could you not

minister to the Wolvers outside town? Would that not allow the anger to die down?"

"I expect that it would," agreed Cade. "But to do so would be like admitting to the ignorant and the prejudiced that they have a right to deny my congregation a service within my church. I cannot allow that. Why is it so hard for them to see the truth? The Wolvers did not seek to be the way they are; even the Deacon admits to that. And there is no more evil in them than in any race."

"I don't know what the Deacon thinks. But I have read the words of his Apostle Saul, and he claims they are not of God and are therefore of the Devil. A pure land, he says, needs pure people."

Cade nodded. "I don't disagree with that, and there is much good in what the Deacon has said in the past. I respect the man. He came from a world gone mad, depravity and lust, corruption and disease of the body and the spirit. And he seeks to make this world a better place. But no one knows better than I the dangers of living by iron rules."

"Come, come, my friend, are you not still living by those rules? This is but a building. If God—if there is a God—does care about the Wolvers, he will care about them in the mountains just as well as here. I fear there will be violence."

"Then we shall turn the other cheek, Josiah. A soft answer turneth away wrath. Have you seen Beth lately?"

"She came into the store with Bull Kovac and two of her riders. She looked well, Jon. It's a shame the two of you couldn't make a go of it. You were so well suited."

Cade smiled ruefully. "She was in love with the Jerusalem Man, not with the Preacher. It was hard for her, especially when the brigands raided and I did nothing to stop them. She told me I was no longer a man."

"That must have hurt."

Cade nodded. "I've known worse pain, Josiah. A long time ago I killed a child. I was being attacked; there were armed men all around me. I killed four of them, then heard a noise behind me, and I swung and fired. It was a boy, out playing. He haunts me still. What might he have been? A surgeon? A minister? A loving father and husband? But yes, losing Beth was a deep blow."

"You must have been tempted to take up your pistols during the raid."

"Not once. I sometimes dream that I am riding again, pistols by my side. Then I wake in a cold sweat." Cade stood and moved to a chest at the far end of the room. Flipping it open, he lifted clear a gun belt. "The weapons of Thundermaker." Broome stood and walked across to stand beside the Preacher.

"They look as they always did."

"Aye. Sometimes at night I sit here and clean them. It helps remind me of what once I was. And what, God willing, I will never become again."

"You're not listening to a word I say," said Else Broome, stalking back into the living room.

"What's that, my love?"

"What is the matter with you? I was asking if you would stand Oath for that McAdam woman."

"Of course. Beth is an old friend."

"Pah! She's a troublemaker, and we'd all be better off if she were sent from the valley."

"In which way does she cause trouble, my dear?"

"Are you soft in the head?" she stormed. "She shot at men hunting Wolvers. She speaks against the Deacon, and even her own son says she's been seduced by Satan. The woman is a disgrace."

"She's a good Christian woman, Else. Just like you."

"I take that as an insult," Else Broome snapped, her multiple chins quivering. "You have a store to run, and I don't think people will take it kindly if you are seen to support a woman of her kind. You'll lose business to Ezra Feard, you'll see. And I don't see why it should be you who gives Oath for her. Let her find someone else who doesn't mind being a laughingstock."

Broome turned his attention back to the fire.

"And another thing . . ." began Else Broome.

But her husband was not listening. He was thinking of five dead raiders on the road and the tortured spirit of the man who had killed them.

◊ **4** ◊

The world does not need more charismatic men. It does not need more intellectual men. No, and it does not need more caring men. What it cries out for is more holy men.
The Wisdom of the Deacon
Chapter II

SETH WHEELER PULLED the blanket up tight around his ears and settled his head against his saddle. The night air was cold, and it had been two years since he had slept out in the open. The blanket was thin. Either that or I'm getting old, he thought. No, it's the damn blanket. Sitting up, Seth held the blanket close to him as he moved to the fire. It was burning low, just a tiny flicker of flame above the coals. There were four sticks left, and they normally would have been left for the morning. Casting a nervous glance at his four sleeping comrades, he added the wood to the fire. It blazed instantly to life, and Seth shivered as the warmth touched him. God, he had almost forgotten just how good it felt to be warm.

There were no clouds in the night sky, and a ground frost was sprinkling the grass with specks of silvered white. The wind gusted, scattering ash across Seth's boots. He stared down at the sticks. Why did they have to burn so damned fast?

This high in the mountains there was little dead wood, and his men had gathered what there was close by. Seth had two choices: return to his cold bedroll or gather more wood. Rising with a softly whispered curse, he stepped across one sleeping body and walked to the thin line of trees.

It had been a long ride in search of the killer. They had

found his tracks soon enough and had followed him up into the mountains. But the pursuers had lost his trail twice after that, and four fruitless days had followed. Then they had picked up the wrong trail and come upon an old man and a mule. Strange old coot, thought Seth. Odd eyes; looked as if they could see right through you.

"We're hunting a man," Seth had told him. "We're Crusaders from Purity."

"I know that," the oldster had replied. "Spent the night in a cave yonder with the man you're looking for."

"Which way was he heading?"

"North. Into the wild lands."

"We'll find him," Seth had said.

"Hope you don't, Son. Strikes me you're good men. Shame to see such men die."

"Is he a friend of yours, this man?" Seth had asked.

The old man had shaken his head. "He only met me last night. But I'd say I like him. You best be careful, Crusader. Men like him don't offer second chances." The old man had grinned at them and without another word had ridden off.

Short on food and getting colder by the day, the Crusaders had finally found the killer's trail. The next day they would have him.

Seth gathered an armful of sticks and a thick broken branch and started back toward the fire. Something cold touched the back of his neck, and an even colder voice spoke. "You are making a mistake that will lead you to your death."

The Crusader swallowed hard. His legs felt shaky, and the gun barrel felt icy against his skin. But Seth was no coward, and he gathered himself.

"You are a blasphemer and a killer," he said.

"Take your men back to Purity," said the cold voice. "I do not wish to kill any of you. But if you are on my trail come daylight, none of you will ever see your families again. Had I so chosen, I could have walked into your camp tonight and slain you all. Now go."

The gun barrel withdrew. Seth blinked back the sweat that was dripping into his eyes. Strangely, he did not feel cold at all. He took a step, then another. Then he dropped the wood, threw aside the blanket, drew his pistol, and swiveled.

There was no one there.

For a minute or more he remained where he was. The cold came back into his bones. Sheathing the pistol, he gathered the fallen sticks and returned to the fire, banking it up until the flames were too hot to sit alongside. Returning to his bedroll, he thought of Elizabeth and his sons, Josh and Pad.

One of his men awoke with a cry. "Hell's bells, Seth, you trying to set us all ablaze?" The edge of the man's blanket was smoldering, and he beat at it with his palm.

The commotion woke the others.

"We're going home," said Seth. "We've no food, and the wild lands are just beyond the ridge."

"Are you all right, Seth?" asked Sam Drew, his lieutenant.

"Aye. But this man is too much for us, boys. Take my word on it. We'll send word to the Apostle Saul in Pilgrim's Valley. He can order out the Jerusalem Riders. Let them deal with him."

"This isn't like you, Seth. What changed your mind?"

"It's a funny thing, Sam. A little while ago I was cold and hated it. Now it feels good. It tells me I'm alive. I'd kind of like to stay that way."

It was near midnight, and the main street of Pilgrim's Valley was almost deserted as the five riders made their way to the house behind the Crusader compound. The first of the men, tall and broad-shouldered and wearing a full-length, double-shouldered topcoat, dismounted and turned to the others. "Get 'em stabled, then get some rest," he said.

Removing his wide-brimmed leather hat, he climbed the three steps to the porchway of the house and tapped on the front door. It was opened by a young woman in a long white gown. She curtseyed.

"God's greetings, Brother," she said. "Would you be Jacob Moon?"

"Aye. Where is the Apostle?"

"Would you follow me, sir?"

The dark-haired woman moved along the hallway, then opened a door on the right. Moon stepped past her and into the study where the Apostle Saul was sitting in a wide leather chair, reading a large gold-edged Bible. Putting it aside, he rose and smiled at the woman. "That will be all, Ruth. You may go." Ruth curtseyed once more and pulled shut the door. "God's greetings, Jacob."

"A pox on this religious bullshit," said Moon. "It's bad enough having to mouth it when people are around. Damned if I'll take it in private!"

Saul chuckled. "You are too impatient, Jacob. It is a bad failing in a man who seeks to rule."

"I don't want to rule," said the tall man. "I just want to be rich. The old fool is dead, just like you ordered."

Saul's smile faded, and his eyes took on a dangerous glint. "I chose you because you have talent. But understand this, Jacob: If you become a danger to me, I will have you cut down. And nothing is more dangerous than a loose tongue."

The tall man seemed unfazed by the threat. Tossing his hat to the floor, he removed his topcoat and draped it over the back of a chair. Unbuckling his gun belt, he sat down and stretched out his legs. "You have a drink here? It was a thirsty ride."

Saul poured a glass of red wine and handed it to the man. Moon downed it in a single swallow, holding out the glass for a refill. "Tell me of it!" Saul demanded.

Moon shrugged. "It was as you said. He rode alone to his cabin in the mountains, and I waited the twenty days, watching him all the time. Then a rider came from Unity. He saw the old man, then rode away. The following morning I shot the old man through the back of the head. Buried the body in the foothills. No one will find it."

"You're sure it was him?"

"I guess it might have been the angel Gabriel," sneered Moon. "Of course it was him. You can rest easy, Saul; the Deacon is dead. Question is: Who do you need dead now?"

Saul returned to his seat. "No one *today*, Jacob. But there will be trouble; I'm sure of that. There is some fine land to the west with good suggestions of silver—perhaps gold. The man who owns it is called Ishmael Kovac. There is also a farm which I believe has significant oil deposits; that is owned by a woman named Beth McAdam. Both will be refused the Oath; then we shall acquire the land legally."

"Then why call us down here? Sounds like it's all sewn up."

Saul sipped his wine. Then he said, "There is a complication, Jacob."

"There usually is."

"The burning of the church. There was a preacher who survived. He hunted down five of my men and killed them. Yesterday I had a long talk with a local man who knows the preacher—has known him for twenty years."

"Cut to the chase, Saul. I don't need the gift wrapping."

"I think you do. The Preacher came here twenty years ago, just after the blessed coming of our sainted Deacon. He was a young man, maybe twenty. But this local man told me an interesting story. He said that the Preacher was in fact much older and that he'd regained his youth through a Daniel Stone in a tower."

"Sounds like he's either drunk or an idiot," said Moon, draining his wine and reaching for the bottle.

"He's neither. And I know the Daniel Stone was in that tower, because the Deacon and I went there fifteen years ago. We saw what was left of it, its power gone. It was huge, Jacob, big enough to hold planes and ships in stasis for hundreds of years. Now, the man who took the last of its power, in order to become young again, was Jon Shannow."

Moon froze. "You've got to be joking!"

"Not at all, Jacob. The Jerusalem Man. The one and only. The new Elijah."

"And you think this preacher was Jon Shannow? Why the hell would he stay in this lousy backwater if he was the Jerusalem Man? He could have been rich beyond his dreams."

"I don't know his reasons, but I believe it to be the truth. He rode out and slew our comrades, and now he is somewhere out there." Saul waved his hand toward the window.

Moon glanced up. "Jesus, man, but couldn't he put the fox

in the henhouse? He could finish the myth of the Deacon right enough, prove him to be a pompous old windbag and a liar to boot."

"I don't think so," said Saul. "The Jerusalem Man is too much a part of myth now. People would expect to see the halo. No, that is only one part of the problem. First, we don't want the Deacon discredited, since I am his heir. And I want the kingdom united behind me as it is behind him. But second, Beth McAdam was once the man's mistress. There could well be residual good feeling between them. When she is dispossessed or killed, I don't want the likes of Jon Shannow hunting me."

"What about this man who knows the truth?"

"Well, he is another matter. At the moment he is useful to me, but he has promised to stand Oath for Beth McAdam in ten days. The night before the Oath Taking you will kill him."

"Has he got a pretty wife?"

Saul laughed aloud. "Pretty? Else Broome? She looks like an overweight sow that's been squeezed into a dress."

"Fat, eh? I like 'em fat," said Jacob Moon.

Dr. Meredith found the old stranger irritating beyond belief. Jeremiah, by contrast, seemed amused, but then, everyone knew that Jeremiah loved a good debate. Even Isis listened spellbound.

"How can you argue against the development of reason or science?" pressed the doctor.

"Easily," answered Jake. "Centuries ago a man in ancient Greece came up with the theory that all matter, however huge, from a planet down to a rock, is made up of tiny component parts. The tiniest of these he called 'atoms,' which is Greek for 'uncuttable.' Man being what he is, he just had to cut the uncuttable. And look where we are! Man is a hunting, killing animal. A predator. Every advance he makes is ultimately linked to destruction, either physical or moral."

"What of medicine?" Dr. Meredith persisted. "The world before the Fall made magnificent advances in the controlling of disease."

"Yes, they did," Jake agreed, "and they moved into genetic engineering in order that animal parts could be used for transplant into humans. Hence the Wolvers and the other poor mutated creatures who stalk this planet. Hence the awful buildup of chemical weapons, bacteria, and plague germs that were dumped into what was the Atlantic and have now poisoned vast areas of our present land."

Jake stood and moved to the water barrel, filling his tin mug. "You can pin it all on one example," he said. "Christ told people to love one another and to do good to them that hates you. He said that all men were brothers and that we should love our neighbors as ourselves. Within a few hundred years men were arguing about what this meant. Then they went to war over it and slaughtered one another in order to prove that their version of love thy neighbor was the best system."

Jeremiah laughed aloud. "Ah, Jake," he said, "you surely do have a way with words. You and the Deacon have a lot in common."

"Yep," said Jake. "Him in his ivory tower and me on my mule. We know how the world works, the Deacon and me."

"The Deacon is evil," said Meredith. "Plain and simple."

Jake shook his head. "Nothing in this godforsaken world is plain and simple, boy. Except death. That's the only sure thing you can guarantee: we're all going to die. Apart from that it's just a sea of complexity. But I would disagree with you about the Deacon. He's just a man who likes to see firm lines drawn. I was in Unity when he was chief magistrate; he made some good calls, to my mind."

"Ah, yes," sneered Meredith. "Like public murder. Dragging a man through the streets to be executed in front of his family."

"You're twisting it just a mite," said Jake. "You're talking about the villain meeting his punishment at the scene of his crime. I don't think that is too bad; it lets folk see that justice is done."

"That's not justice," stormed Meredith. "That's barbarity!"

"These are barbarous times, Doctor. But you could argue that it comes down to values. What value do we place on a life? The Deacon says that back in his time a killer could be walking the streets within a couple of years, sometimes less. Even mass killers could be released at some time. So the value they put on a human life was two years. Life was awful cheap in those days. At least with the Deacon a killer knows he will get just what his victim got. No more, no less."

"And what if the court is wrong?" asked Meredith. "What if an innocent man is found guilty?"

"What about it?" replied Jake. "It's sad, sure enough, but then, mistakes happen, don't they? It doesn't mean the system is wrong. A doctor once told a man I knew he was getting too fat and needed to exercise. He went on a diet and dropped dead. What are we supposed to do? Encourage everybody to get fat just in case there's another lardbelly with a weak heart?"

"That's an outrageous view!"

Jake grinned, and Jeremiah stepped in. "What about forgiveness, Jake? Didn't Christ talk about that, too?"

"Well, you can forgive a man and still hang him."

"This is too much!" hissed Dr. Meredith, rising from the fireside and stalking back to his wagon.

"Do you see everything so simply, Jake?" asked Isis. "Is it all black and white for you? Truly?"

The old man gazed at her, and his smile faded. "Nothing is simple, Isis, no matter how hard we try to make it so. I wish it was. Young Doctor Meredith is not wrong. Life is the greatest gift, and every man and woman has infinite possibilities for good or evil. Sometimes for both." The night breeze strengthened, fanning the flames of the fire. Jake shivered and pulled his old sheepskin coat more tightly around his shoulders. "But I suppose the question is really one of focus. For a society to succeed it must have strong rules to protect the weak and yet inspire the strong. You agree?"

"Of course," said Isis.

"Ah, but now the complications begin. In nature the weak perish, the strong survive. So then, if we protect the weak, they will flourish, growing like weeds within the society, needing more and more protection, until finally the weak so outnumber the strong that—in a democracy—they rule and make laws encouraging even more weakness. That society will sicken and die, slowly falling apart as it sows the seeds of its own destruction."

"How do you define weakness, Jake?" asked Jeremiah. "Do you mean the sick or the lame?"

Jake laughed. "As I said, this is where the complications begin. There are those who are weak in body but strong in mind and heart. There are those who have the physical strength of lions but who inside are cowardly and weak. Ultimately a society will judge its people on their ability to supply that society with what it needs to grow and be successful."

"Ah!" said Jeremiah. "But that brings us to the old, who have already worked for the society but can do so no longer. They become weak and therefore, by your arguments, useless. You are arguing against yourself, old man. You would have no place in a strong society."

"Not so," said Jake. "For if I have earned from my labors and amassed some savings, then I will use my money to buy food and clothing, which continues to help the society. For I will pay the tailor for my coat, enabling him to earn money. I still contribute."

"But what if you have amassed no savings?" asked Isis.

"Then, by my own definitions, I would be a fool—and therefore useless."

"It is a harsh image you paint, Jake," said Jeremiah.

"The world is a harsh place. But believe me, my friends, it is a lot less harsh than the one the Deacon left behind. As I said, it all becomes a sea of complexity. Out here, however, under God's stars you can still find simplicity. You Wanderers understand that. You hunt deer and wild sheep in order to eat, and you journey into towns in order to work for Barta coin to support the lifestyle you have chosen. If there are no deer, you will starve. Simple. And if there was one among you who refused to hunt or was incapable of hunting or working, you would cast him out."

"That's not true!" said Isis. "We would support him."

"For how long?" Jake asked. "And what if there was not

one but three, or five, or twenty-five? You can survive only for as long as you work together. A society is no different, child."

"But aren't you missing something, Jake, in all your equations?" insisted Isis. "Man is, I will agree, a hunting, killing animal. But he is also capable of love, of compassion, of self-lessness. A society must surely incorporate those values."

"You're a wise woman, Isis," Jake told her, "but your point also leaves out a number of man's vices, like the propensity for evil. Some men—and women—are just plain malicious. They wouldn't understand compassion or selflessness. They'd kill you for the price of a meal or just because they felt like it. When it comes down to basics, a society can prosper only as long as everyone in it is willing to work for its benefit. The word 'weak' is a coverall—maybe 'parasites' would be a better description. But then, I don't have all the answers. Neither does the Deacon."

"Tell me, Jake," said Isis, "even if I accept all the points you have made so far, what about the slaughter of the Hellborn? Men, women, and children were butchered by the Deacon's army. In their thousands. Were they all weak, Jake? Were the babies they murdered evil?"

Jake shook his head, and the smile faded from his face. "No, girl, they weren't evil. The Deacon was wrong, in my view. But in his defense, it was at the end of a terrible war and passions were running high. Two armies converged on Babylon . . ." He faded into silence, gazing into the fire.

"You were there?" whispered Jeremiah.

"I was there. I didn't go in when the city walls fell. I could hear, though. The screams! The Deacon heard them, too. He ran from his tent, scrambling over the walls and the bodies of the dead defenders. There was no stopping the slaughter. When the dawn came, the Deacon stumbled through the city, eyes red from weeping. And not a man in the Army of God failed to feel shame. But the war was over, right enough. And the Hellborn would never invade again."

Jeremiah leaned forward, placing his hand on Jake's shoulder. "I think that you, too, carry scars from that day."

Jake nodded. "The kind that never heal," he said sadly.

* * *

Shannow rode down the hillside and into the valley. There were plowed fields there and trees planted in lines as wind-breaks. To his right, about a half mile distant, was a farm-house, timber-built with a slate roof. There was a paddock beyond the two-story house and a barn beyond that. The setting was peaceful. Twisting in his saddle, Shannow glanced back. The mountains loomed high behind him, and there was no sign of pursuit.

The horse was tired and walked with a listless gait. "Not much farther, boy," said the rider.

Shannow rode up to the paddock and dismounted. The door of the house opened, and an elderly woman strode out into the yard. Tall and gaunt, her hair tied in a tight bun, she marched out to face the rider with a long rifle cradled in her arms, her right hand on the action, her finger resting on the trigger.

"If ye're a brigand, be warned," she said. "I'll tolerate no ructions here. And I can neuter a gnat from fifty paces with this rifle."

Shannow smiled. "Though I may look less than holy, lady, I am not a warmaker or a brigand. But I would be grateful for some water and to be allowed to rest my mount for a day. I'll chop wood or attend to any chores you set me."

Her eyes were bright, her face seamed with fine lines, her skin the texture of leather. She sniffed loudly and did not return his smile. "I'd turn no man away without a meal at least," she said. "Unsaddle the beast and come up to the house. But you can leave those pistols on the hook outside the front door. You'll have no use for them inside." So saying, she turned and walked back to the house. Shannow unsaddled the horse and led him into the paddock.

The front door led into a long, rectangular room elegantly furnished with carved wooden chairs, an elaborate folding table, and a long horsehide-covered couch. Even the cupboards on the walls boasted flourishes in carved pine. As she had requested, Shannow hung up his guns and moved to a chair by the empty hearth. His neck and back were aching from the ride, and he settled gratefully into the chair.

"I see you know how to make yourself at home," she said, striding in from the kitchen and laying a tray on a small table before him. There was a hunk of bread and a slab of cheese laid on plates of fine china.

"You have a beautiful house, lady."

"Aye, Zeb was a right handy man with wood and the like. And don't call me 'lady.' My name is Wheeler. Zerah Wheeler."

"The 'rising of the light,' " said Shannow.

"What?"

"The woman who raised me was called Zerah. It means 'the rising of the light' in one of the older tongues. Hebrew, I think."

Zerah sat down opposite him. "I kind of like that," she said. "You heading on for Domango?"

"How far is it?" asked Shannow.

"About three days west—if the weather is kind, and it usually is this time of year."

"I may." Shannow bit into the bread, but he was almost too tired to eat.

Zerah offered him a mug of cool water. "You been riding long?" she asked.

"Yes. All my life." Leaning back in his chair, he closed his eyes.

"Don't you go falling asleep in here!" she said harshly. "You're covered in dust. You go on out to the barn. There's a water butt, and you can wash the smell of travel and sweat from your body. If you're awake early enough, there'll be eggs and bacon. If not, it'll be stale bread. There's a fence out back you can mend in the morning if you're of a mind to earn your food."

Shannow pushed himself to his feet. "My thanks to you, Zerah Wheeler. May God bless your house."

"You got a name, young man?" she asked as he reached the door and looped his gun belt over his shoulder.

"Jon," he said, and stepped out into the dusk.

The barn was warm, and he slept on a bed of straw. His

dreams were many, but they ran together chaotically. He saw himself in a small church and then on a ship set on a mountain. Faces fled past his eyes; names danced in his mind.

He awoke with the dawn and washed in cold water. Locating a box of tools, he mended the broken fence, then replaced several tiles that had slipped from the slanting roof of the woodshed. The winter store was low, but there was a saw and an ax, and he set about preparing logs for the fire. He had been working for an hour when Zerah called him for breakfast.

"I like a man who knows how to work," she said as he sat down at the table. "I had three sons, and not one of them was lazy. How'd you get the wound to your head?"

"I was shot," he told her, spooning fried eggs and bacon onto his plate.

"Who by?"

"I don't know. I have no memory of it."

"I expect you shot back," she said. "You don't look the kind of man to be set upon and not smite them hip and thigh."

"Where are your sons?" countered Shannow.

"One died in the Unity War. Seth and Padlock are over in Purity. Seth's a Crusader now. It suits him; he's a man who likes order. You pass through there?"

"Yes."

"You know, it's strange. I'm sure I've seen you someplace. Just can't put a finger on where."

"If it comes to you, I'd be glad to hear it," said Shannow. Finishing the breakfast, he helped the old woman clear away the dishes and then returned to the wood store. The labor was tiring, but his muscles felt good, and the mountain air was fresh in his lungs. Zerah came out just after noon, bringing a mug of a hot, sweet tisane.

"I've been thinking," she said, "and it wasn't you, after all. There was a man back in Allion, where I grew up. He was a brigand slayer named Shannow. You look a little like him. Not as tall or as big in the shoulders. But you've a similar shape to the face. You planning to keep that beard?"

"No. But I have no razor."

"When you've finished what you're doing, come on over to the house. I still have Zeb's shaving blade. You're welcome to it."

◇ 5 ◇

There was a wolf who slew the lambs, the goats, and the geese. One day a holy man went to see the wolf and said to him: "My son, you are a wicked beast and a long way from God." The wolf thought about this for a while and realized that the man was right. He asked how he could come nearer to heaven. The holy man told him to change his ways and pray. The wolf did so and became known for his purity and the sweetness of his prayers. One summer the wolf was walking by the riverside, when a goose mocked him. The wolf turned and leapt, killing the goose with one bite from his terrible jaws. A sheep standing close by said: "Why did you kill it?"

The wolf replied: "Geese should not cackle at a holy wolf."

The Wisdom of the Deacon
Chapter XI

SHANNOW STARED INTO the oval mirror and wiped the last of the soap from his chin. He looked younger without the salt and pepper beard, but the sight of his clean-shaven face brought back no new memories. Disappointed, he stepped back, cleaned the razor, and returned it to its carved wooden box.

He was tired. The journey through the mountains had been long and hard, for the land was unfamiliar to him. Once convinced that the pursuit had ended, he had still to find a path through the peaks. He had tried many trails, but some of them had ended in box canyons or had led up to treacherous, narrow ridges where only bighorn sheep or mountain-bred mules could walk with safety. City dwellers had no conception of the vastness of the wild lands, the endless mountains, ridges, and hills stretching into eternity and beyond. On his journey Shannow had come across the rotted remains of a wagon, still packed with furniture and the beginnings of a home. It was in a boxed canyon, low down at the foot of a steep slope. Close to it he found a skull and a broken section of a thighbone. These people, too, had tried to cross the peaks and had found only a lonely, unmarked grave beneath the sky.

Back in the main room Zerah Wheeler looked at him closely. "Ye're not exactly a handsome lad," she said, "but it's a face that wouldn't curdle milk, neither. Sit at the table and I'll bring ye some lunch. Cold ham and fresh onions."

While he waited, he looked around the room. Every piece of furniture was lovingly carved, giving the home a tranquil quality. There was a triangular corner cabinet, inset with leaded-glass windows, containing beautifully painted and glazed tiny cups and saucers. Shannow walked to the cabinet and peered inside. Zerah saw him there as she returned with the food.

"Zeb found them on a ship in the desert. Beautiful, ain't they?"

"Exquisite," agreed Shannow.

"He liked beautiful things, did Zeb."

"When did he die?"

"More than ten years ago now. We were sitting on the couch watching the sunset. It was summer, and we used to move the couch out onto the porch. He leaned back, put his arm around me, then rested his head on my shoulder. 'Beautiful night,' he said. Then he just died." Zerah cleared her throat. "Best tuck into that ham, Jon. I don't want to get all maudlin. Tell me about yourself."

"There's not a great deal to tell," he said. "I was wounded, and some Wanderers found me. I know my name but precious little else. I can ride, and I can shoot, and I know my Bible. Apart from that . . ." He shrugged and cut into the ham.

"You might have a wife somewhere, and children," she said. "Have you thought of that?"

"I don't think so, Zerah." But as she spoke, he saw in his

mind a brief glimpse of a blond woman and two children, a boy and a girl ... Samuel? Mary? Yes, that felt right. But they were not his children. He knew that.

"So what do you remember about the wound?" she asked.

"There was a fire. I was ... trapped. I got out." He shook his head. "Gunshots. I remember riding up into the mountains. I think I found the men who caused the burning ..."

Were they ashamed when they had committed the abomination?

"You killed them?"

"I believe so." Finishing his meal, he made to rise.

"You sit there," she said. "I've got some cakes in the oven. Long time since I made cakes, and they may not be so grand. But we'll see."

So many brief memories were lying in the dust of his mind, like pearls without a string to hold them together. Zerah returned with the cakes; they were soft and moist, filled with fruit preserve.

Shannow chuckled. "You were wrong, Zerah. They are grand."

She smiled, then her expression became thoughtful. "If you're of a mind to stay awhile, you'd be welcome," she said. "The Lord knows I need help here."

"That is most kind," he said, seeing her loneliness, "but I must find out where I come from. I don't think it will come back to me here. But if I may, I'd like to stay a few days more."

"The stream that feeds my vegetable patch is silted up. That could be dug out," she said, rising and clearing away the dishes.

"That would be my pleasure," he told her.

As the dawn sun broke clear of the mountains, the Apostle Saul eased himself from the wide bed. One of the sisters stirred; the other remained deeply asleep. Saul rose and wrapped his robe about his shoulders. The golden stone lay on the bedside table. Gathering it up, he moved quickly from the room.

Back in his own quarters he stood before the long oval

mirror, surveying his square-chinned, handsome face and the flowing golden hair that hung to his broad shoulders. A far cry from the balding, slight, stoop-shouldered Saul Wilkins who had landed with the Deacon twenty years before. But then, Saul had almost forgotten *that* man. Now he stared hard at the tiny lines around the eyes, the almost imperceptible web marks of aging on his cheeks and throat. Gazing down at the coin-sized stone, he saw there were only four slender lines of gold in the black. The day before there had been five.

The sisters had not been worth it, he thought. Under the influence of the Daniel Stone they had obeyed his every desire, performing acts that would have shamed them to their souls if they could have remembered them. Inspiring their debauchery and then removing the memory had cost him a fifth of his power. Now, in the dawn light, it seemed a waste.

"Curse you, Deacon!" he hissed. Anger rose in him. The old fool knew where the Daniel Stones lay. Indeed, he had a score of them hidden in his palace in Unity. But did he use them for himself? No. What kind of an idiot could hold such power and not keep his body young and vibrant? It was unfair and unjust. Where would he have been without me? thought Saul. Who formed the Jerusalem Riders and led the final charge up Fairfax Hill? Me! Who organized the books and the laws? Me! Who created the great legend of the Deacon and made his dreams reality? Me. Always me. And what does he give me? One tiny stone.

From his window he could see the blackened earth where the church had stood, and the sight eased his anger.

"Fetch me the Preacher from Pilgrim's Valley," the Deacon had said.

"Why?"

"He's a very special man, Saul. The Wolvers respect him."

"They're just beasts. Mutated creatures!"

"They have human genes. And they are not a threat. I have prayed long and hard about them, Saul, and every time I pray, I see the Pillars of Fire. I believe the Wolvers could live in the lands beyond them. I believe that is where God intends them to be."

"And you will empower this preacher to lead them?"

"Yes. You and I are the only ones left now, Saul. I think this young man has a talent for leadership."

"What does that mean, Deacon? I am your heir; you know that."

The Deacon had shaken his head. "I love you, Saul, like a son, but you are not the man to lead a people. You follow the devices and desires of your heart. Look at you! Where is Saul Wilkins now? Where is the little man who loved God? You have used the stone on yourself."

"And why not? With them we can be immortal, Deacon. Why should we not live forever, rule forever?"

"We are not gods, Saul. And I am tired. Fetch me the Preacher."

Saul looked at the charred wood and the singed earth. Did the Deacon know that the anonymous Bible mouther was the Jerusalem Man? Saul doubted it. The one man on this new earth who could destroy the myth of the Deacon.

Well, that myth will only grow now that you are dead, you old bastard!

Saul would have liked to have seen the killing, the moment when the bullet smashed home. I wonder, he thought, what last thought went through your mind, Deacon? Was it a prayer? If it was, you finished it in person. How long, he wondered, before the Church realizes that its blessed Deacon will not be returning? Another ten days? Twenty?

Then they will send for me, for I am the last of the men from beyond the gates of time.

The first three Apostles had died long before the Unity Wars, killed by the radiation and pestilential chemicals that filled the air of this new world. Then the Deacon had found the stones and given the eight survivors one each to strengthen their bodies against the poisons in the atmosphere. One each! Saul found his anger rising again but fought it down. He had used his quite swiftly, making himself not just strong but also handsome. And why not? He had lived for forty-three years with an ugly face and a short, twisted frame. Did he not deserve a new life? Was he not one of the chosen?

Then the war had started. He and Alan had been given command of two sections of the Jerusalem Riders. Fairfax Hill had been the turning point. But Alan had died, shot to pieces as he had neared the summit. Saul had been the first to find the dying man.

"Help me!" Alan had whispered. Two of the shots had shattered his spine, cutting through his belt and separating it from his body. His stone was in a leather pouch; Saul had pulled it clear. It was almost totally gold, with only the thinnest of black strands. To heal Alan probably would have exhausted it. Indeed, the wounds were probably too great for his life to be saved. Saul had pocketed the stone and walked away. When he had returned an hour later, Alan was dead.

One month later Saul had met Jacob Moon, an old, grizzled former brigand. The man was a killer, and Saul had seen instantly the value of such a man. In giving him back his youth, he made an ally that would take him all the way to power.

Moon had killed the others one by one. And Saul had gathered the Stones of Power. Most were almost dry of magic.

Then only the Deacon was left . . .

Saul dressed and moved down to the ground floor. Moon was sitting at the breakfast table, finishing a meal of bacon and eggs.

"You had a good night, Brother Saul," Moon said with a sly grin. "Such noise!"

"What news of the Preacher, Jacob?"

Moon shrugged. "Be patient. I have men scouring the wild lands for news. I've also sent Witchell to Domango. We'll find him."

"He's a dangerous man."

"He doesn't even know he's being hunted. That will make him careless."

Saul poured a mug of fresh milk and was sipping it when he heard the sound of a walking horse in the yard outside. Going to the window, he saw a tall, square-bearded, broad-shouldered man in a long black coat dismount and walk toward the house. Moving to the door, Saul opened it.

"God's greetings, Brother," he said.

The man nodded. "God's greetings to you, Brother, and a blessing upon this fine house. I am Padlock Wheeler from Purity. Would you be the Apostle Saul?"

"Come in, Brother," said Saul, stepping aside. He remembered Wheeler as the Deacon's favorite general, a hard-riding martinet who drove his men to the edge of exhaustion and beyond. They followed him because he asked for nothing from them that he did not give himself. After the war, Saul recalled, Wheeler had returned to his own land and become a preacher. The man looked older, and two white streaks made a bright fork in his beard on either side of his chin. Wheeler removed his flat-crowned hat and stepped into the dining room.

"You looked different the last time I saw you, sir," said Padlock Wheeler. "You were thinner, I recall, and with less hair. Even your face seems now more . . . regular."

Saul was irritated. He did not like to be reminded of the man he once had been, the man he could become again if he ever lost the power of the stones.

"What brings you so far?" he asked, fighting to remain civil.

"Our Oath Taker has been shot dead," said Wheeler. "He was a verminous rascal and by all accounts deserved his fate. But the man who shot him is a blasphemer and a heretic. You will forgive me, sir, for speaking bluntly, but he claimed to be the Jerusalem Man."

Moon rose. "You apprehended him?"

Wheeler glanced at Moon and said nothing, appraising the man. "This is the Jerusalem Rider Jacob Moon," said Saul.

Wheeler nodded, but his dark eyes remained fixed on Moon for a moment. Finally he spoke. "No, we did not apprehend the man. Our Crusaders followed him but lost him in the mountains. He appeared to be heading into the wild lands near Domango."

Saul shook his head, his expression sorrowful. "You bring dreadful news, Brother Wheeler. But I am sure Brother Moon will know what to do."

"Indeed I do," said Jacob Moon.

* * *

There were many things twelve-year-old Oswald Hankin did not know, but of one he was sure: There was no God.

"I'm hungry, Oz," said his little sister, Esther. "When can we go home?"

Oz put his arm around the six-year-old's shoulder. "Hush now, I'm trying to think."

What could he tell her? She's watched Father being shot down, the bullets smashing into his head and chest, the blood exploding from his frame. Oz shut his eyes against the memory, but it remained locked in place in his mind's eye, bleak and harsh and terribly savage.

He and Esther had been playing in the long grass when the seven riders had come up to the house. There had been no indication of the murder to follow. The sky was clear, the sun was bright, and only that morning their father had read to them from an old leather-bound book with gold-edged pages. The tale of Lancelot and Guinevere.

For some reason Oz had decided to remain in the long grass, though Esther had wanted to run out and see the riders close up. His father had walked from the house to greet them. He had been wearing a white shirt, and his long fair hair had been golden in the sunlight.

"We told ye once," the leading rider had said, a bald man with a black trident beard. "We'll suffer no pagans around Domango."

"By what right do you call me a pagan?" his father had replied. "I do not accept your authority to judge me. I traveled far to buy this land, and where I came from I am well known as a man who loves the church. How can I be at fault here?"

"You were warned to leave," the rider had said. "What follows be on your own head, pagan."

"Get off my land!"

They were the last words his father had spoken. The leading rider produced a pistol and fired a single shot that hammered into the unarmed man's chest. Father staggered back. Then all the men began firing.

"Find the young'uns," shouted the trident-bearded leader.

Esther was too shocked to cry, but Oswald virtually had to drag her back into the long grass. They crawled for some way, then cut into the pines and up along the mountain paths to the old cave. It was cold there, and they cowered together for warmth.

What will I do? thought Oz. Where can we go?

"I'm hungry, Oz," said Esther again. She started to cry. He hugged her and kissed her hair. "Where's Poppa?"

"He's dead, Esther. They killed him."

"When will he come for us?"

"He's dead," Oz repeated wearily. "Come on, let's walk a little. It'll make you warmer and take your mind off your hunger."

Taking Esther's hand, he walked to the mouth of the cave and peered out. Nothing moved on the mountain trails, and he listened for the sound of horses. Nothing. Nothing but the wind whispering through the trees.

Leading Esther, he began to walk toward the east, away from his home.

His mother had died back in Unity just a year after Esther had been born. Oz did not remember much about her except that she had had red hair and a wide, happy smile. His one clear memory was of a picnic by a lake when he had fallen in and swallowed some water. His mother had hurled herself in after him, dragging him back to the bank. He recalled her red hair, wet and dripping, and her green eyes so full of love and concern.

When she had died he had cried a lot and had asked his father why God had killed her.

"God didn't kill her, Son. A cancer did that."

"He's supposed to work miracles," argued the seven-year-old Oswald.

"And he does, Oz. But they're His miracles. He chooses. Everybody dies. I'll die one day. It's wrong to blame God for death. Maybe we should be thanking Him for the gift of what life we have."

Oz adored his father and put his lack of faith on hold.

But today he knew the truth. There was no God—and his father was dead. Murdered.

Esther stumbled over a jutting tree root, but Oz was holding her hand and hauled her up. She started to cry again and refused to go on. Oz sat with her on a fallen tree. He had not been that far along the mountain path before and had no idea where it led, but he had nowhere else to go. Behind them the killers would be searching.

After a while Esther calmed down, and they walked on, coming to a steep trail that led down into a valley. In the distance Oz could see a house and a barn. He stopped and stared at the house.

What if trident-beard lived there? Or one of the others?

"I'm really *very* hungry, Oz," said Esther.

Oz took a deep breath. "Let's go down, then," he said.

Zerah Wheeler sat in the chair by the fire and thought about her sons not as men but as the children they once had been. Oz Hankin and Esther were asleep now in the wide bed Zeb had built more than forty years earlier, their pain and loss shrouded in the bliss of sleep. Zerah sighed as she thought of Zachariah. In her mind he was always the laughing child, full of pranks and mischief that no amount of scolding could forbid. Seth and Padlock had always been so serious. Just like me, she thought, gazing at the world through cynical, suspicious eyes, ever wary and watchful.

But not Zak. He gloried in the sunshine or the snow and gazed about him with a wide-eyed sense of wonder at the beauty of it all. Zerah sniffed and cleared her throat. "Did you believe them?" she asked her mysterious guest.

He nodded solemnly. "Children can lie," he said, "but not this time. They saw what they saw."

"I agree," said Zerah. "They witnessed a murder. You'll have to ride to Domango and inform the Crusaders. It was their territory. I'll keep the children here with me."

Jon remained silent for a moment. "You're a good woman, Frey Wheeler. But what if they come here when I'm gone?"

Zerah's gray eyes took on a frosty gleam. "Son, I'm a

known woman. There have been those who sought to take advantage. I buried them out back. Don't you worry none about this old girl." She gave him directions to Domango, advising him of various landmarks to watch out for.

"I'll ride out now," he said, rising from his chair. "I thank you for the meal."

"You don't have to stay so formal, Jon," she told him. "I'd look on it kindly if you stopped calling me Frey and started to use my given name."

He smiled then, and it was good to see, for his eyes seemed less cold. "As you wish . . . Zerah. Good night."

She rose and walked to the door, watching him gather his guns from the hook and stroll to the paddock. And, not for the first time, she wondered who he was. Turning back into the house, she extinguished one of the lamps. Oil was short now, and soon she would have to ride into Domango for supplies. There had been a time when the farm had supported three hired men, when cattle had roamed in the pasturelands to the south. But those days were gone, just like the cattle. Now Zerah Wheeler survived by growing vegetables in the plot out back and by breeding a few pigs and many chickens.

Twice a year Padlock would visit, arriving in a wagon laden with boxes, tins of peaches canned in Unity, sacks of flour, salt and sugar, and—most precious of all—books. Most of them were Bible studies printed by the Deacon Press, but occasionally there were gems from the old world. One she had read a score of times, savoring every sentence over and over. It was the first part of a trilogy. Pad had not realized that when he had bought it for her; to him it was just an antique tome his mother might enjoy. And she had. At first she had been irritated by the fact that there was no record of any of the other books in the series. But during the last seven years she had thought and thought about the story, inventing her own endings, and this had given her immense pleasure in the long, lonely evenings.

She heard the soft sounds of sobbing begin in the bedroom and walked swiftly through to sit on the bed alongside the little girl. Esther was crying in her sleep. "Hush now, child; all is safe. All is well," she crooned, stroking the child's auburn hair. "All is safe, all is well," Esther murmured, then began sucking her thumb. Zerah was not a great believer in thumb sucking, but there was a time and a place for admonishments, and this was not it.

"Always wanted a girl-child," whispered Zerah, still stroking the child's head. Then she saw that Oswald was awake, his eyes wide and fearful. "Come join me for a glass of milk," she said. "Always have one before sleeping. Move soft, now, so as not to wake little Esther."

Oswald padded out after her. He was a strongly built boy, reminding her of Seth, with serious eyes and a good jaw. Pouring two glasses from the stone jug, she passed one to Oswald, who hunkered down by the dying fire.

"Having trouble sleeping, boy?"

He nodded. "I dreamed of Poppa. He was walking around the house calling for us. But he was all covered with blood, and his face wasn't there anymore."

"You've seen some hard, hard times, Oz. But you're safe here."

"They'll come for us. You won't be able to stop them."

Zerah forced a chuckle. "Me and Betty will stop them, Oz. Count on it." She walked to the fire and lifted the long rifle from its rack. "She fires four shots, and every shell is thicker than your thumb. And I'll tell you a little secret: I ain't missed with this gun for nigh on seventeen years."

"There was more than four of them," said Oz.

"I'm glad you mentioned that, Oz," she said, laying aside the rifle and moving to a handsomely carved chest of drawers. From it she produced a small nickel-plated revolver and a box of shells. "This here pistol belonged to my son, Zak. She's small, but she's got stopping power. It was made by the Hellborn thirty years ago." Flipping open the breech, she put the pistol on half cock, freeing the cylinder, and fed in five shells, lowering the hammer on the empty chamber. "I'm giving this to you, Oz. It is not to play with. This is a gun. It will kill people. You fool with it and it's likely to kill you or your sister. Are you man enough to deal with that?"

"Yes, Frey Wheeler. I am man enough."

"I didn't doubt it. Now between us, Oz, we're going to look after little Esther. And we're going to see justice done. My man, Jon, is riding now to Domango to report the ..." She hesitated as she saw the look of anguish in his eyes. "To report the crime to the Crusaders."

Oswald's face twisted then, and his eyes shone. "The man who first shot Poppa *was* a Crusader," he said.

Zerah's heart sank, but she kept her expression neutral. "We'll work things out, Oz; you see if we don't. Now you best get back to bed. I'll need you fresh and clear of eye in the morning. Put the pistol by your bedside."

The boy padded off, and Zerah returned to the chest of drawers. From the third drawer she pulled a scabbard and belt, then a short-barreled pistol. For some time she cleaned the weapon. Then she loaded it.

Despite the dangers, Shannow loved night riding. The air was crisp and clean, and the world slept. Moonlight gave the trees a shimmering quality, and every rock glistened with silver. He rode slowly, allowing the horse to pick its way carefully over the trail.

The loss of memory no longer caused him irritation. It would come back or it would not. What did concern him were the problems such a loss could cause the Jerusalem Man. If his worst enemy of the last twenty years were to ride up in plain sight, Shannow feared he would not recognize the danger.

Then there was the question of aging. According to Jeremiah, the Jerusalem Man had ridden through the Plague Lands twenty years before and had then been a man in his late thirties or early forties. That would make him around sixty now. Yet his hair was still dark, his skin virtually unlined.

He rode for almost three hours, then made camp in a hollow. There was no water nearby, and Shannow did not bother with a fire but sat with his back to a tree, his blanket wrapped around his shoulders. The head wound gave him no pain now, but the scab itched.

Sitting in the moonlight, he traced over his life in his mind, piecing together tiny fragments as they came to him. *I am Jon Shannow.*

Then a face leapt to his memory, a thin, angular face with deep brooding eyes. A name came with it: Varey. Varey Shannow. Like a key slipping sweetly into a lock, he saw again the brigand slayer who had taken the young man under his wing. *I took his name when he was murdered.* And his own name slipped into his mind: Cade. Jon Cade. The name settled on his mind like water on a parched tongue.

The world had gone mad, with preachers everywhere talking of Armageddon. But if Armageddon was true, then the New Jerusalem would exist somewhere. The new Jon Shannow had set out to find it. The journey had been long, with many perils. Varey Shannow had taught him never to back away from evil:

"Confront it wherever you find it, Jon. For it will thrive when men cease to fight it."

Shannow closed his eyes and remembered the conversations around many campfires. *"You are a strong man, Jon, and you have tremendous hand-eye coordination. You have speed, and yet you are cool under fire. Use those skills, Jon. This land is full of brigands, men who would lie, steal, and kill for gain. They must be fought, for they are evil."* Shannow smiled at the memory. *"It used to be said that you can't stop a man who keeps on going and knows he's right. It just ain't true, Jon. A bullet will stop any man. But that's not the point. Winning is not the point. If a man only fought when he believed there was a chance to win, then evil would beat him every time. The brigand relies on the fact that when he rides in with his men, all armed to the teeth, the victim will—realizing he has no chance—just give in. Trust me, Jon, that's the moment to walk out with guns blazing."*

Just before the fateful day, as the two men had ridden into the small town, Varey Shannow had turned to the youngster beside him. *"Men will say many things about me when I'm gone. They could say I got angry too fast. They could say I wasn't none too bright. They'll certainly say that I was an ugly cuss. But no man ever will be able to say that I abused a woman, stole or lied, or backed down in the face of evil. Ain't too bad an epitaph, is it, Jon?"*

Varey Shannow had been cut down in his prime, backshot by villains who had feared he was hunting them.

Jon Shannow opened his eyes and gazed up at the stars. "You were a good man, Varey," he said.

"Talking to yourself is a sure sign of madness, they say," said Jake, "and I hope you don't fire that pistol." Shannow eased back the hammer and holstered the gun. At the first sound he had drawn and cocked the weapon in one swift, fluid move. Despite the speed of his response, he was nettled by the old man's silent approach.

"A man could be killed approaching a camp that way," he said.

"True, boy, but I reckoned you weren't the type to shoot before looking." Jake moved opposite Shannow and hunkered down. "Cold camp. You expecting trouble?"

"Trouble has a way of happening when you least expect it," said Shannow.

"Ain't it the truth." The old man's beard was shining silver in the moonlight. Shucking off his sheepskin topcoat, he gave a low whistle, and his mule came trotting into the camp. Swiftly Jake removed the saddle and blanket roll, then patted the beast's rump. The mule moved out to stand alongside Shannow's horse. "She's an obedient girl," Jake said fondly.

"How did you find me?"

"I didn't. The mule must have picked up the scent of your stallion. You heading for Domango?"

Shannow nodded but said nothing.

"A sight of activity there in the last few days," continued Jake. "Riders coming in from all over. Tough men, by the look of them. Ever heard of Jacob Moon?"

"No."

"Jerusalem Rider. Killed fourteen men that I heard of. Can you guess who he's asking about?"

"Who are you, Jake?" countered Shannow.

"Just an old man, Son. Nothing special. I take it you aren't interested in Moon."

"At the moment I'm more interested in you. Where are you from?"

Jake chuckled. "Here and there. Mostly there. I've been over the mountain a few times. You think I'm hunting you?"

Shannow shook his head. "Perhaps. Perhaps not. But you are hunting something, Jake."

"Nothing that need worry you, Son." Shaking loose his blanket, Jake wrapped it around his shoulders and stretched out on the earth. "By the way, those Wanderers you helped—they're on the way to Domango, too. You'll probably see them."

"You do get around, old man," said Shannow, closing his eyes.

Shannow awoke with the dawn to find that the old man had gone. He sat up and yawned. He had never known anyone who could move as quietly as Jake. Saddling his horse, he rode out onto a broad plain. There were ruins to his left—huge pillars of stone, shattered and fallen—and the horse's hooves clattered in the remains of a wide stone road. The city must have been vast, Shannow considered, stretching for several miles to the west.

He had seen many such on his travels, cold stone epitaphs to the glory that once had been Atlantis.

Another memory came to him then, of a man with a golden beard and eyes the color of a clear summer sky.

Pendarric. The king.

And he recalled with great clarity the day when the Sword of God had torn across the curtain of time. Reining in his horse, he gazed with fresh eyes on the ruins.

"I destroyed you," he said aloud.

Time's portals had been opened by Pendarric, the ruler of Atlantis, and Shannow had closed them by sending a missile through the gateway. The world had toppled, tidal waves roaring across the continent. The words of Amaziga Archer floated up from the hidden depths.

"You are not the Jerusalem Man any longer, Shannow. You're the Armageddon Man!"

Shannow turned his back on the ancient city and headed southwest. It was not long before he saw the Hankin house. There was no body outside, but there was fresh blood on the dust of the yard. As he rode in, a tall man with a sandy beard came walking from the house, a rifle cradled in his arms.

"What do you want here?" he asked.

"Nothing, friend. I am on my way to Domango and thought I'd stop for a little water, if it is not inconvenient to you." Shannow could not see the second man at the window, but he saw a rifle barrel showing at the edge of the curtain.

"Well, be quick about it. We don't like Movers here."

"Is that so? When last I stopped here, there was a man with two children. Has he moved on?"

The man's eyes narrowed. "Yes," he said at last. "He moved on."

"Do you own the property now?"

"No, I just been told to watch over it. Now get your drink and be gone."

Shannow dismounted and led his horse to a trough by the well. Loosening the saddle girth, he wandered back to where the man stood. "It is a fine place," he said. "A man could raise a family here and never tire of looking at the mountains."

The sandy-haired rifleman hawked and spit. "One place is pretty much like another."

"So where did he move on to ... my friend with his children?" asked Shannow.

"I don't know anything about it," said the rifleman, growing more uneasy.

Shannow glanced down at the dust and the stains that peppered the ground.

"Slaughtered a pig," said the man swiftly. The second man moved from the house. He was powerfully built, with a bull-like neck and massive shoulders.

"Who the hell is he, Ben?" asked the newcomer, his right hand resting on the butt of his scabbarded pistol.

"Stranger riding for Domango. He's just watering his horse."

"Well, you've done that," he told Shannow. "Now be on your way."

Shannow stood silently for a moment, holding back his anger. There was no movement in the house, and he guessed that these two men alone had been left to guard the property. All his life he had known such men: hard, cruel killers with no understanding of love or compassion. "Were either of you party to the murder?" he asked softly.

"What?" responded the rifleman, eyes widening. The big-shouldered man took a step back and made a grab for his pistol. Shannow shot him in the head; he stood for a moment, eyes wide in shock, then toppled to the bloodstained earth. The Jerusalem Man's pistol swung, the black eye of the barrel halting directly before the other man's face.

"Jesus Christ!" said the rifleman, dropping his weapon and raising his hands.

"Answer the question," said Shannow. "Were you party to the murder of Meneer Hankin?"

"No . . . I never shot him, I swear to God. It was the others."

"Who led the killers?"

"Jack Dillon. But Hankin, he never had no Oath papers, and no one would stand up and speak for him. It was the law. He was told to leave; he brung it on himself. If he'd just gone, none of this would have happened. Don't you see?"

"And this Dillon has now laid claim to the property?"

"No. It's held for Jacob Moon. Please, you're not going to kill me, are you?" The man fell to his knees and began to weep.

"Did Meneer Hankin weep and beg?" asked Shannow. He knew he should kill this man. More than that, he knew that the old Jon Shannow would have done so without a second thought. Holstering his pistol, he moved to his horse.

"You son of a bitch!" the man screamed, and Shannow turned to see that he had gathered up his rifle, which was now pointed in Shannow's direction. "You bastard! Think you're so tough? Think you can just ride in here and do as you like? Let's see how tough you act with a bullet in your guts."

Smoothly Shannow stepped to the right, palming his pistol as he moved. The rifle shot slashed past him on the left, cutting through his coat. Shannow fired, and the rifleman pitched backward, the weapon flying from his hands. Hitting the ground hard, the man grunted once; then his leg twitched, and he was still.

"You have become a fool, Shannow," said the Jerusalem Man.

The land to the east was vast and empty, the plain dry, the grass yellow-brown. He could see where once there had been rivers and streams, but they were long gone, evaporated by the searing heat of the sun. After an hour of riding he saw the broken hull of a rusted ship jutting from the desert that stretched away to the horizon and beyond, grim evidence that this had once been the ocean floor.

Shannow skirted the edge of the desert and after another hour began the long climb up into the higher country. Here there were green trees, and grass, and a wide, well-used road that angled down toward the distant town of Domango.

The sun was high in the sky, and Clem was enjoying the freedom of the ride. Meg was a gentle woman and a fine wife, but he had felt trapped at the ranch in Pernum. The thought made him feel guilty. His life at the ranch had brought him everything he thought he had ever wanted: security, status, and love. So why had it not been enough? When the locusts had wiped out his crop five years earlier, he could have worked on, laboring through the long hours of daylight. The merchants in town all liked him, and they would have extended his credit. Instead, he had run away and taken to the road.

The first robbery had been easy: two men carrying a shipment of Barta notes to Pernum. Clem had ambushed them on the mountain road, shooting the first through the shoulder. The second had thrown away his gun. Twelve thousand he had made that day.

After that everything had gone to hell in a bucket. Half the cash had been sent to the banker in Pernum who held the mortgage on the farm. The rest had gone to Meg.

Nothing had been easy from that moment on.

"What was he like?" asked Nestor, the words cutting

through Clem's thoughts. They were no more than an hour's ride from the settlement of Purity, and Clem could already see the smoke from the town's factories drifting lazily into the blue sky.

"What's that, lad? Did you say something?"

"The Jerusalem Man. What was he like?"

Clem thought about the question. "He was grim, Nestor. Mighty grim. Unpredictable and deadly. Pilgrim's Valley was a new settlement then. There was no Deacon, no natural unified government. Settlers just headed out into uncharted lands and built their farms. Merchants followed them, and soon there were towns. We stopped in Pilgrim's Valley, just short of the Great Wall. Now, that was a sight to behold."

"I seen it," said Nestor. "But what about Jon Shannow?"

Clem laughed. "By God, boy, I do so like the young. That wall was built twelve thousand years ago, and beyond it there was a city where men became lions. And in the sky, shining bright, there was the Sword of God. Hell of a thing, Nestor. Anyways, the demons of the pit were released around then, walking snake-men."

"I seen one of those, too," said Nestor. "They got one down in Unity, on display. And several skeletons."

"I've seen that, too," Clem mimicked, growing irritated by the interruptions. "But what you won't know is that the king of these demons sent three special men to kill Shannow. Great warriors, fearless and lightning-fast with pistols. Shannow killed the first, but the other two kidnapped Frey McAdam and took her to where the sword was hanging in the sky."

"Why'd they take the headmistress?"

"God's blood, Son, will you just listen?"

"I'm sorry, sir."

"They kidnapped Beth because she was close to Shannow. They wanted to bring him to them. And they did just that. But it didn't take 'em long to wish they hadn't. I'd been wounded, but I followed them anyway. I come on the scene just as Shannow had given himself up. Suddenly there was guns blazing. I took down one, but the best of them was facing up to the Jerusalem Man. Shannow just stood there like he didn't have a care in the world—calm, powerful. Then it was over. I tell you, boy, I wouldn't want to face him."

"He was that fast?"

"Oh, it wasn't the speed. I'm faster than ever he was. It's the sureness. Strange man—holds himself in chains of iron." He glanced at Nestor. "You know why he hates brigands and killers?" The boy shook his head. "Because deep down he is one. A natural. You see, most men hesitate when it comes to killing. I think that's a good thing, generally. Life is precious, and you don't want to take it away from someone over a whim. I mean, even a brigand can change. Look at Daniel Cade. There wasn't a more murderous bastard than him, but he saw the light, boy. And he fought the Hellborn. So, like I said, life is precious. But Shannow? Cross him and you die. It's that simple. That's why brigands fear him. He deals with them just like they deal with others."

"You talk about him like he's alive. But he ain't, is he? He went up to heaven years back."

Clem hesitated, anxious to share the secret he had kept hidden for twenty years. "He is alive to me," he said. "I never saw him die, and I never saw no fiery chariot, neither. But I watched him tame a wild town. You've never seen the like."

"Wish I had," said Nestor. "I'd love to have met him—just once."

Clem laughed again. "If wishes were fishes, poor men wouldn't starve. How long have you known the Preacher?"

"All my life. Quiet man. He used to live with Frey McAdam, but she threw him out. Then he had a little place behind the church. He gave some good sermons ... always kept you awake in church. Well, until he started letting Wolvers in, that is. Most people stopped going then. If he'd been a stronger man, he'd have kicked those Wolvers out. Then there would've still been a church."

"What's strength got to do with it?"

"Well, everybody in town got mighty sick of it, and they told him so. But I guess he just didn't have the nerve to order the Wolvers away. Some men just don't take to confrontation."

"I guess not," said Clem. "Did you like him?"

Nestor shrugged. "Didn't like him or dislike him. Felt sorry for him mostly. Shem Jackson hit him once, knocked him into the mud. The Preacher just got up and went on his way. I was ashamed for him then. I still can't believe how he shot down all them raiders. Guess he must have surprised them."

"A surprising man," agreed Clem.

◇ **6** ◇

Evil will always rise like scum to the surface, for an evil man will seek to impose his power on others. All the governments in history have seen evil men gain ascendancy. How, then, do we ensure that the rule of evil is forever banished from this new land? We cannot. All we can do is strive for holiness and seek out, individually, the will of God. And we can pray that when evil rises, there will be men, aye, and women, who will stand against it.

The Wisdom of the Deacon
Chapter XXII

ISIS STOOD BEFORE the broad desk and stared at the Crusader, trying to hold on to her temper. The man had small, bright eyes and a face that seemed to her to show cruelty and arrogance. "You have no reason to lock up our doctor," she said.

"When the Oath Taker gets here, we'll see what's right," he said. "We're not partial to Movers here. We don't like thieves and skulkers in Domango."

"We are not thieves, sir. We came into town looking for work. I am a seamstress, our leader Jeremiah is a tailor, and Doctor Meredith is a physician."

"Well, now he's a prisoner."

"Of what is he accused?"

"Begging. Now be on your way or I'll find a nice cell for you." His eyes raked her figure. "Maybe you'd like that," he said, leering.

113

"I doubt that she would," said a cold, deep voice, and Isis turned to see Jon Shannow standing in the doorway. Moving inside, he walked past her without a word and stood before the broad desk. "I am here to report a murder," he said.

The Crusader leaned back in his chair, linking his hands behind his head. "A murder, you say? Where and when?"

"About three hours' ride northeast of here. A man named Hankin. Shot to death by a group of riders."

Isis saw the change of expression on the Crusader's face. The man sat up straight. "How do you know there was a murder?" he asked. "Did you see it?"

"His children saw it," said Shannow.

"And where are they now?"

"Safe," Shannow told him.

"You saw the body?"

"No. But I believe the children."

The man fell silent, but the fingers of his right hand began tapping nervously on the desktop. "All right," he said at last, "this'll have to wait until the captain gets back sometime this afternoon. Why not get yourself something to eat and come back later."

"Very well." Shannow swung and left the office, and Isis followed him.

"Wait!" she called as he stepped off the boardwalk. "They've got Doctor Meredith in there!"

"It would be better for you to avoid me," said Shannow. "There is evil here, and it will draw unto me."

Isis was about to reply, but he walked away across the wide street toward an eating house on the far side.

"You know that man?" asked the Crusader, moving alongside her.

"No," she said. "He rode by our wagons some days back, that's all."

"Well, steer clear of him. He's trouble."

"Yes, I will," said Isis.

Inside the small eating house Shannow sat with his back to the wall. There were three other diners: a thin, balding man who was reading a book, having finished his meal; a thickset young miner with his left arm in a sling; and a slim, dark-eyed black man who was nursing a hot mug of Baker's. Dismissing the other two from his mind, Shannow concentrated on the young black man. He was wearing a coat of dark gray wool over a white shirt, and Shannow could see the enameled butt of a revolver in a shoulder holster on his left side.

A tall black woman approached Shannow's table. "We got good steaks, some fresh-laid eggs, and new bread from the oven this morning," she said. "Or else there's what's printed on the board."

Shannow glanced up at the blackboard and the dishes and drinks scribbled in chalk. "I'll have bread and cheese and some warmed milk, if you please."

"You want honey in the milk?" she asked him.

"That would be pleasant."

As she walked away, his thoughts returned to the meeting in the office. The Crusader's reactions had been wrong. There had been no surprise when Shannow had mentioned the murder, and the man's twin concerns had been the whereabouts of the children and whether Shannow had seen the body. When the waitress returned with a mug of sweetened milk, Shannow thanked her, then asked in a low voice, "There is a man in this area named Jack Dillon. How will I know him?"

"Best if you don't," answered the woman, walking away. As she passed the table of the slim black man, Shannow saw her bend her head and whisper something to him. The man nodded, then rose and walked toward Shannow's table. Reversing a chair, he sat down opposite the Jerusalem Man.

"Dillon's big and he's bald, and he sports a thick beard," said the newcomer. "Is that a help?"

"Where will I find him?"

"If you are looking for him, my friend, he will find you. Seeking to work for him, are you?"

"What would make you think so?"

"I know your kind," said the black man. "Predator."

"If that is the case," said Shannow with the briefest of smiles, "then are you not walking a perilous path by insulting me?"

The man chuckled. "All life involves risk, friend. But I think it is minimal in this situation. For you see, I am armed—and facing you." His dark eyes were gleaming, and the fact that he held Shannow in contempt was all too obvious. "What do you say to that?"

"A fool uttereth all his mind, but a wise man keepeth it in," Shannow told him. "Beware, boy; it can be fatal to make hasty judgments."

"You calling me a fool?" The black man's hand was hovering over the enameled pistol butt beneath his jacket.

"I am stating a fact," said Shannow, "and if you listen very closely, you will hear the sound of a pistol being cocked." The double click of the drawn-back hammer sounded from below the table. "You seem very anxious to cause trouble, young man," continued Shannow. "Could it be you have been sent to kill me?"

"No one sent me. I just despise your kind," the man answered.

"The young are always too swift to judge. Did you know a farmer named Hankin?"

"I know him. Men like you forced him off his place. Couldn't find three people to give Oath for him."

"He was murdered," said Shannow. "Shot to death, his children hunted like animals. I am waiting to see the captain of the Crusaders; then I shall file a complaint against Jack Dillon."

The black man leaned forward, elbows on the table. "You really don't know anything about Dillon, do you?"

"I know that he—and other men—shot an unarmed man in cold blood. And I will see him brought to justice."

The black man sighed. "I guess I may have been wrong about you, friend. But I'm not the only one who's being foolish. I think you should just ride out now—far and fast."

"Why would I wish to do that?"

The black man leaned in close. "Jack Dillon *is* the captain of the Crusaders. Appointed last month by the Apostle Saul himself."

"What kind of settlement is this?" asked Shannow. "Are there no honest men?"

The black man laughed. "Where have you been living, friend? Who is going to speak against an anointed Crusader? There's forty of them—and Jacob Moon and his riders. No one is going to go against them."

Shannow fell silent, and the black man heard the welcome sound of the pistol hammer being eased forward. "My name is Archer, Gareth Archer." He extended his hand.

"Leave me, boy. I have much to think on."

Archer moved away, and the waitress returned with a second mug of sweetened milk. This time she smiled. Shannow gazed out the window at the settlement's main street. Beyond the buildings to the west he could see the mines on the distant hillsides, and beyond them the smoke from smelting houses and factories. So much dirt and darkness from the soot and smoke.

A face leapt unbidden to his mind, a slender man in late middle age, balding and sharp-featured with soft brown eyes.

"It's progress, Preacher. Ever since the planes landed and we found out what once we were, things changed. The planes carried engineers and surgeons, all sorts of skilled people. Most of them died within the year, but they passed on a lot of knowledge. We're building again. Soon we'll have good hospitals and fine schools and factories that can manufacture machines to help us till the land and gather the harvest. Then there'll be cities and roads to those cities. It will be a paradise."

"A paradise built on belching smoke and foul-smelling soot? I see the trees have all died around the canning plant, and there are no fish now in the Little River."

Shannow sipped the sweetened milk and sought a name for the face. Brown? Bream? Then it came to him: Broome. Josiah Broome. And with it came another face, strong female features surrounded by corn-blond hair.

Beth.

The memory struck him like a knife in the heart.

"Jesus Christ! You used to be a man. Now you let scum like Shem Jackson strike you in front of a crowd. Knock you down in the dirt! God's teeth, Jon, what have you become?"

"The blow lessened him more than me. I have done with killing, Beth. I have done with the ways of violence. Can't you understand that there must be a better way for men to live?"

"What I understand is I don't want you here anymore. I just don't want you!"

The sound of approaching horses jerked Shannow back to the present as four riders drew up in front of the Crusader offices. Shannow stood, left a half silver on the table, then walked to the door.

Gareth Archer moved alongside him. "Don't be a fool, man! Dillon is a dead shot, and those others with him are no angels."

"If thou faint in the day of adversity, thy strength is small," said Shannow. Stepping out, he moved from the wooden sidewalk down the three short steps to the dusty street.

"Jack Dillon!" he called. The four men dismounted, and the tallest of them, dark-bearded and powerfully built, swung around to face him.

"Who wants me?" he replied. People who had been moving along the street stopped and watched the two men.

"I am Jon Shannow, and I name you as a murderer and a brigand." Shannow could hear the sharp intake of breath from the crowd and saw the bearded man redden.

Dillon blinked and licked his lips, then recovered some of his bluster. "What? This is nonsense!"

Shannow walked slowly toward him, and his voice carried to all the observers. "You shot down a farmer named Hankin, murdered him in cold blood. Then you hunted his children. How do you answer this accusation, villain?"

"I don't answer to you!"

The big man's hand swept down toward his pistol, and the crowd scattered. Dillon drew first, a bullet slashing past Shannow's cheek. Shannow's guns boomed in reply, and Dillon, struck in the chest and belly, staggered back, triggering his revolver into the dust. A second man loosed a shot at Shannow, the bullet passing high and wide. Sighting his right-hand pistol, Shannow shot the man in the chest; he fell back over a guardrail and did not move. The other two Crusaders were standing stock-still. Dillon was on his knees, blood drenching his vest.

Shannow strode to where the dying man waited. *"Whoso diggeth a pit shall fall therein, and he that rolleth a stone, it will return upon him."*

"Who . . . are . . . you?" Dillon fell sideways, but his pain-filled eyes continued to stare up at his killer.

"I am retribution," Shannow told him. Kicking away the man's pistol, he scanned the crowd. "You have allowed evil to prosper here," he said, "and that is a shame upon you all." To his left he saw Gareth Archer move into sight, leading Shannow's horse.

Keeping the two remaining Crusaders in sight, Shannow mounted.

"Ride southeast for an hour," Archer whispered, "then turn west by the fork in the stream."

"She is there?"

Archer was shocked, but he nodded. "You knew?"

"I see her in you," said Shannow.

And turning the horse, he rode slowly from the town.

Amaziga Archer was waiting for him by the stream. The black woman had changed little since Shannow had last seen her, and like himself, she seemed untouched by the passage of the decades. Her hair was still jet-black, her face unlined, her almond-shaped eyes dark and lustrous. She was wearing a gray shield shirt and a riding skirt of leather. Her horse was a gray gelding of some sixteen hands.

"Follow me," she ordered him, then headed up over rocky ground, her mount splashing along the shallow stream. They rode in the water for almost half an hour before she turned the gelding to the right, urging him up a steep bank. Shannow followed, his mount struggling on the greasy slope.

"They will see where we emerged," he said. "A skilled tracker will not be fooled by our route. The stream is not swift-running, and the hoof marks will be there for some days."

"I am aware of that, Shannow," she said. "Grant me a little respect. I spent the last hour before your arrival moving back and forth in the water, emerging at no fewer than seven banks. Added to that, where we are about to go no man—save one—could follow."

Without another word she rode on, heading toward a high wall of rock. The ground was hard, and glancing down, Shannow saw that they were moving along an ancient road paved with slabs of granite.

"This was the road to Pisaecuris," she told him, "a major city of the Akkadians. They were descended from the peoples of the Atlantean empire and flourished thousands of years ago."

Ahead of them was a series of ruined buildings, and beyond that a circle of great stones. Amaziga Archer rode through the ruins and dismounted at the center of the circle. Shannow stepped from the saddle. "What now?" he asked.

"Now we go home," she said. From a deep pocket in her skirt she took a small golden stone. The air shimmered with violet light, and Shannow's horse reared, but he calmed him swiftly. The light faded. Beyond the circle there was now a two-story house built of red brick and painted timbers with a slanted roof of black slate. Before it was a garishly painted and highly elaborate carriage; it had windows all around and rested on four thick black wheels.

"This is home," she said coldly, interrupting his examination of the object. "I wish I could say you were welcome, but you are not. There is a paddock behind the house. Release the horses there. I will prepare some food." Tossing him the reins to her gray, she walked into the house. Shannow led the horses to the rear of the building, unsaddled them, and freed them in the paddock. Then he returned to the front door and tapped lightly on the wood. "For God's sake," she said, "you don't need to observe the niceties here."

Stepping inside, he saw a remarkable room. It was fully carpeted in thick gray wool on which stood four padded armchairs and a couch covered with soft black leather. From the ceiling hung a curious lamp of glass, no larger than a wine goblet, from which came a light so bright that it hurt his eyes to stare at it. There was a fire blazing in a stone hearth, but the coals, though they glowed, did not burn. On a desk by the far wall was a curious contraption, a box, gray on three sides but with one black side facing a chair. Wires extended from the rear, running down to a small block set in the wall.

"What is this place?" asked Shannow.

"My study," said Amaziga. "You should be honored, Shannow. You are only the third man to see it. The first was my second husband; the second was my son, Gareth."

"You married again. That is good."

"What would you know about it?" she snapped. "My first husband died because of you. He was the love of my life, Shannow. I don't suppose you'd understand that, would you? And because of you and your demented faith, my home was destroyed and I lost my first son. I didn't think there was much more you could do to hurt me. Yet here you are, large as life. The new Elijah, no less, and your twisted values have become enshrined in the laws of your bizarre new world."

"Is that why you brought me here, lady?" he asked softly. "So that you could blame me for all the evils of man? Your husband was killed by an evil man. But your people died because they followed Sarento, and he was behind the Hellborn War. It was he, not I, who turned the Daniel Stones to blood and brought destruction on the Guardians. But then, you know all this. So unless you want to blame me for every storm and drought, every plague and pestilence, pray tell me why you asked your son to guide me to you."

Amaziga closed her beautiful eyes and drew in a deep breath, which she released slowly. "Sit down, Shannow," she said at last, her voice more mellow. "I'll make some coffee, then we'll talk." She moved to a cupboard on the far wall and removed a brightly colored packet. Shannow watched as she tipped the contents—small dark stones—into a glass jug. She flicked a switch, and the jug whirred, grinding the stones to powder. This she poured into a paper container set atop a second, larger jug. Seeing him watching her, she smiled for the first time. "It's a drink that is popular in this world," she told him. "You may prefer it sweetened with milk and sugar. It will take a little time."

"Where are we?" he asked.

"Arizona," she said, leaving him none the wiser.

Crossing the room, she sat opposite him. "I am sorry," she said, "for my angry words. And I do know that you are not *wholly* at fault. But equally, had you not entered my life, my first husband would still be alive and so would Luke. And I cannot forget that I saw you destroy a world, perhaps two worlds. Millions upon millions of people. But Beth was right. You were not seeking to detonate the Sword of God; you did not even fully know what it was." Hot water began bubbling into the jug, and Amaziga rose and stood by it. "I am not religious, Shannow. If there is a God, then he is capricious and willful and I want no part of him. So I find myself disliking you on too many counts to be able to handle."

The bubbling noises from the jug abruptly ceased, and Amaziga poured the black liquid into two ornate mugs. She passed one to Shannow, who sniffed it apprehensively. When he sipped it, the taste was acrid and bitter, similar to Baker's but with more body. "I'll get the sugar," said Amaziga.

Sweetened, the drink was almost bearable. "Tell me what you want of me, lady," he said, putting aside the mug.

"You are so sure I want something?"

He nodded. "I am not seeking another angry dispute, but I already knew that you hold me in contempt. You have made that clear on a number of occasions. So the fact that I am here means you need me. The question is, For what purpose?"

"Perhaps it was just to save your life."

He shook his head. "No, lady. You despise me and all that you believe I stand for. Why would you save me?"

"All right!" she snapped. "There is something."

"Name it, and if it is possible, I will attempt it."

She rubbed her face and looked away. "You give your promises so easily," she said, her voice low.

"And when I do, I keep them, lady. I do not lie."

"I know that!" she said, her voice rising. "You are the Jerusalem Man! Oh, Christ . . ."

"Just tell me what you want," he urged her.

"I will tell you what I need from you, Shannow. You will think I am mad, but you must hear me out. You promise that?" He nodded, and for a moment she said nothing. Then she looked directly into his eyes. "All right. I want you to bring Sam back from the dead."

He stared at her in silence.

"It is not as crazy as it sounds," Amaziga went on. "Trust me on that, Shannow. The past, the present, and the future all coexist, and we can visit them. You know that already, because Pendarric's legions crossed the vault of time to invade our lands. They crossed twelve thousand years. It can be done."

"But Sam is dead, woman!"

"Can you think only in straight lines?" she stormed. "Supposing you were to go back into the past and prevent them from killing him?"

"But I didn't. I do not understand the principles behind such journeys, but I do know that Sam Archer died, because that is what happened. If I went back and changed that, then it would already have happened and we wouldn't be having this conversation."

Suddenly she laughed and clapped her hands. "Bravo, Shannow. At last a little imagination! Good. Then think on this: If I journeyed back into the past and shot your father before he met your mother and then returned here, would I be alone? Would you have ceased to exist?"

"One would suppose so," he said.

"No," she said triumphantly. "You would still be here. That is the great discovery."

"And how would I be here without having had a father?"

"There are infinite universes existing alongside our own, perhaps in the same space. Infinite. Without number, in other words. There are thousands of Jon Shannows, perhaps millions. When we step through the ancient gateways, we cross into parallel universes. Some are identical to our own, some fractionally different. With an infinite number it means that anything the mind can conceive *must* exist somewhere. So somewhere Sam Archer did not die in Castlemine. You see what I am saying?"

"I hear the words, lady. Understanding is something else entirely."

"Think of it in terms of the grains of sand in a desert. No two are exactly identical. The odds against finding twin grains would be, say, a hundred million to one. But then, the number of grains is finite. It may be thirty trillion. But supposing there was no limit to the number of grains? Then a hundred million to one would be small odds. And within infinity there would be an infinite number of twins. That is a fact of life within the multiverse. I know. I have seen it."

Shannow finished his coffee. "So you are saying that in some world, somewhere, there is a Sam Archer waiting to be taken to Castlemine? Yes?"

"Exactly."

"Then why do you not go back and find him? Why is it necessary to send a messenger?"

Amaziga moved to the jug and refilled the mugs. This time Shannow sipped the brew appreciatively. She sat down and leaned back in the leather chair. "I did go back," she said, "and I found Sam and brought him home. We lived together here for almost a year."

"He died?"

She shook her head. "I made a mistake. I told him everything, and one morning he was gone, searching for what he termed *his* own life. What he didn't know was that I was already pregnant with Gareth. Perhaps that would have changed his mind. I don't know. But this time I'll get it right, Shannow. With your help."

"Your son must be around twenty years old. How is it you have waited this long to try again?"

Amaziga sighed. "He is eighteen. It took me two years to find Sam again, and even in that I was lucky. I have spent the last decade in research, studying clairvoyance and mysticism. It came to me that clairvoyants cannot *see* the future, for it does not exist yet. What they can do is to glimpse other *identical* worlds, which is why some of their visions are so ludicrously wrong. They see a future that exists on another world and predict that it will happen here. But all kinds of events can change the possible futures. Finally I found a man whose powers were incredible. He lived in a place called Sedona— one of the most beautiful lands I have ever seen, red rock buttes set in a magnificent desert. For a time I lived with him. I used my Sipstrassi Stones to duplicate his powers and imprint them on a machine." She stood and walked to the black-faced box on the desk by the wall. "This machine. It resembles a computer, but it is very special." Amaziga pressed a button, and the screen flickered to life, becoming the face of a handsome man with red-gold hair and eyes of startling blue.

"Welcome home, Amaziga," it said, the voice low and smooth and infinitely human. "I see you found the man you were seeking."

"Yes, Lucas. This is Jon Shannow."

Shannow rose and approached the box. "You trapped the man in there?" he said, horrified.

"No, not the man. He died. I was away on research, and he collapsed with a heart attack. Lucas is a creation that holds all the man's memories. But he is also something different. He is self-aware in his own right. He operates as a kind of timescope, using both the power of Sipstrassi and the magic of the ancient gateways. Through his talent we can view alternative worlds. Show him, Lucas."

"What would you like to see, Mr. Shannow?" asked Lucas.

He wanted to say "Jerusalem," but he could not. Shannow hesitated. "You choose," he told the machine.

The face disappeared, and Shannow found himself staring at a city on a hill, a great temple at the center. The sky above was deep blue, and the sun shone with unbearable brightness. A man was standing outside the temple, arms raised, and a great crowd was listening to him; he was dressed in golden armor with a burnished helm on his head. Sounds came from the machine, a language Shannow did not know, but the armored man's voice was low and melodious. Lucas's voice cut in: "The man is Solomon, and he is consecrating the great temple of Jerusalem." The scene faded and was replaced instantly by another; this time the city was in ruins, and a dark-bearded figure stood brooding over the broken stones. Again Lucas cut in: "This is the king of the Assyrians. He has destroyed the city. Solomon was slain in a great battle. There is, as you can see, no temple. In this world he failed. Do you wish to see other variations?"

"No," said Shannow. "Show me the Sam Archer you wish me to find."

The screen flickered, and Shannow saw a mountainside and a collection of tents. Several people were gathering wood. One of them was the tall, broad-shouldered man he remembered so well: Sam Archer, archaeologist and Guardian. He had a rifle looped over his shoulder and was standing on a cliff edge, staring down over a plain. On the plain was an army.

"The day following this scene," said Lucas, "the army sweeps into the mountains, killing everyone."

"What war is it?"

"It is the Hellborn. They have conquered and are now sweeping away the last remnants of the defeated army."

The screen changed once more, becoming the handsome face with the clear blue eyes. "Do I exist in this world?" asked Shannow.

"You did, as a farmer. You were killed in the first invasion. Sam Archer did not know you."

"Who rules the Hellborn? Sarento? Welby?"

"Neither. The Bloodstone rules."

"Someone must control it, surely."

"No, Shannow," said Amaziga. "In this world the Bloodstone lives. Sarento drew it into himself and in doing so created a demon with awesome powers. Thousands have died since to feed the Bloodstone."

"Can it be killed?"

"No," said Lucas. "It is impervious to shot or shell and can create a field around itself of immense force. The Sword of God could have destroyed it, but in this world there is no missile waiting."

"The Bloodstone is not your problem, Shannow," put in Amaziga. "All I want is for you to rescue Sam and bring him back. Will you do it?"

"I have a problem," he said.

"Yes, with your memory. I can help you with that. But only when you get back."

"Why wait?"

She hesitated before answering. "I will tell you the truth and ask you to accept it. You would not be the same man if I returned your memory to you. And the man you will become—though more acceptable to me—would have less chance of success. Will you take that on trust?"

Shannow sat silently, his pale gaze locked to her dark eyes. "You need Shannow the killer."

"Yes," she whispered.

He nodded. "It lessens us both."

"I know," she answered, her eyes downcast.

The main street of Purity was bustling with people as Nestor and Clem rode in; miners, their weekend pay burning holes in their pockets, were heading for the taverns and gambling houses, while the locals moved along packed sidewalks to restaurants and eating houses. Shops and stores were still open even though dusk was long since past, and three lamplighters were moving along the street carrying ladders and tapers. Behind them, in double lines, the huge oil lamps gave off a yellow glow that made the mud of the main street shine as if it were streaked with gold.

Nestor had never been to Purity, though he had heard that the silver mines had brought great prosperity to the community.

The air stank of smoke and sulfur, and music was playing all along the street, discordant and brash as many melodies vied for the ear.

"Let's get a drink," shouted Clem. "My throat feels like I'm carrying half the desert caked around it." Nestor nodded in reply, and they drew up outside a large tavern with ornate stained-glass windows. Some twenty horses were hitched to the rail, and Nestor had difficulty finding a place to leave their mounts. Clem ducked under the rail and strode into the tavern. Inside there were gaming tables and a long bar served by five barmen. A band was playing brass instruments, a pianist accompanying them. Above the gaming hall a gallery ran around the room, and Nestor saw gaudily dressed women moving along it, arm in arm with miners or local men. The boy frowned. Such behavior was immoral, and it surprised him that any Deacon township would tolerate such displays.

Clem eased his way to the bar and ordered two beers. Nestor did not like the taste of beer but said nothing as the glass was pushed toward him.

The noise in the tavern was deafening, and Nestor drank in uncomfortable silence. What pleasure, he wondered, can men draw from these places? He wandered across to a card table where men were pushing Barta notes into the center of the table. He shook his head. Why work all week and then throw your money away in a single night? It was incomprehensible.

Nestor turned away and collided with a burly man carrying a pint of beer. The liquid splashed down the man's shirt, and the glass fell from his grasp to shatter on the sawdust-strewn floor.

"You clumsy bastard!" the man shouted.

"I'm sorry. Let me buy you another."

A fist hit Nestor square in the face, hurling him back over a card table, which toppled, spilling Barta notes to the floor. Nestor rolled and tried to come upright but, dizzy, stumbled back to his knees. A booted foot cracked into his side, and he rolled away from the blow but came up against a table leg. The man reached down and dragged him up by the lapels of his jacket.

"That will be enough," Nestor heard Clem Steiner say.

The man glanced around. "It will be enough when I say it is. Not before," retorted his attacker.

"Let him go or I'll kill you," said Clem.

The music had ceased when Nestor had been struck, but now the silence was almost unbearable. Slowly the man let him go, then pushed him away. He turned toward Clem, his hand hovering over the holstered gun at his hip. "You'll kill me, dung breath? You know who I am?"

"I know you're a lardbelly with all the speed of a sick turtle," Clem said with an easy smile. "So before you make an attempt to pull that pistol, I should call on what friends you have to stand beside you."

The man swore and made a grab for the gun, but even as his hand closed on the butt, he found himself staring down the barrel of Clem's nickel-plated revolver. Clem walked forward until the barrel rested on the man's forehead. "How did anyone as slow as you live to get so ugly?" he asked. As he finished speaking, he stepped forward and brought his knee up hard into the other's groin. With a groan the man slumped forward, and Clem's pistol landed a sickening blow to the back of his neck. He hit the floor face first and did not move.

"Friendly place," said Clem, holstering the pistol. "You finished fooling around, Nestor?"

The boy nodded glumly. "Then let's find somewhere to eat," said Clem, clapping the younger man on the shoulder.

Nestor stumbled forward, still dizzy, and Clem caught him. "By God, boy, you are a trouble to be around."

An elderly man approached them. "Son, take a little advice and leave Purity. Sachs won't forget that beating. He'll be looking for you."

"Where's the best eating house in town?" Clem countered.

"The Little Marie. Two blocks down toward the south. On the right."

"Well, when he wakes up, you tell him where I've gone. And tell him to bring his own shovel. I'll bury him where he lands."

Clem steered Nestor out of the tavern and half lifted him to the saddle. "Cling on there, boy," he said. "The pain'll pass."

"Yes, sir," mumbled Nestor. Clem mounted and led Nestor north. "Ain't we going the wrong way, sir?"

Clem just chuckled. Several blocks farther along the street they came to a small restaurant with a painted sign proclaiming "The Unity Restaurant." "This will do," said Clem. "How are you feeling?"

"Like a horse walked over me."

"You'll survive. Let's eat."

The restaurant boasted just five tables, only one of which was occupied. The diner was a tall man wearing the gray shield shirt of a Crusader. Clem hung his hat on a rack by the door and walked to a table. A slender waitress with honey-blond hair approached him. "We got steak. We got chicken. We got ham. Make your choice."

"I can see the reason for the restaurant's popularity," said Clem. "I hope the food is warmer than the welcome."

"You won't find out till you make a choice," she said without a change of expression. "We got steak. We got chicken. We got ham."

"I'll have steak and eggs. So will he. Medium rare."

"Er, I prefer mine well done," said Nestor.

"He's young, but he'll learn," put in Clem. "Make it two, medium rare."

"We got local wine. We got beer. We got Baker's. Make your choice."

"How good is the wine?" She raised one eyebrow. "Forget I asked. We'll take the beer."

As she walked away, Nestor leaned forward. "What kind of a town is this?" he asked Clem. "Did you see what they were doing in that tavern? Gambling and consorting with . . . with . . ." The young man stumbled to a halt.

Clem chuckled. "You mean the women? Ah, Nestor, you've got a lot to learn, boy."

"But it's against the Deacon's laws."

"There are some things you can't legislate against," said

Clem, his smile fading. "Most men need the company of a woman from time to time. In a mining community, where men outnumber women maybe twenty to one, there's not enough to go around. That sort of situation leads to trouble, Nestor. A good whore can help keep the peace."

"Your friend is a wise man," said the Crusader, easing back his chair and wandering over to their table. He was tall and stoop-shouldered with a drooping mustache. "Welcome to Purity, boys," he said. "I'm Seth Wheeler, local captain of the Crusaders."

"Those are the first pleasant words we've heard," said Clem, offering his hand.

Wheeler shook it and pulled up a chair. "Just visiting?" he asked.

"Passing through," Clem said, before Nestor could speak.

Wheeler nodded. "Don't judge us too harshly, young man," he told Nestor. "Your friend is right. Once the silver mines opened up, we got every kind of villain here and some four thousand miners. Hard men. At first we tried to uphold the laws regarding gambling and the like, but it went on just the same. Tricksters and con men fleeced the workers. That led to killings. So we opened up the gambling houses and tried to keep them fair. It ain't perfect, but we do our best to keep the peace. It ain't easy."

"But what about the law?" said Nestor.

Wheeler gave a weary smile. "I could make a law that says a man can only breathe on a Sunday. You think it would be obeyed? The only laws men will follow are those that they agree with or that can be enforced by men like me. I can make the miners and the rogues stay away from the decent folk here. I can do that. But Unity needs silver, and this is the richest strike ever. So we got special dispensation from the Apostle Saul to operate our . . . places." It was obvious that Wheeler did not like the situation, and he struck Clem as a decent man. "So where you heading?" he asked Nestor.

"We're looking for someone," replied the youngster.

"Anyone in particular?"

"Yes, sir. The Preacher from Pilgrim's Valley."

"Jon Cade? I heard he was killed after his church was burned down."

"You knew him?" asked Clem.

"Never seen him, but word spread that he was friendly to Wolvers—even had them in his church. No wonder it got blazed. He's alive, then, you reckon?"

"Yes, sir, we think so," said Nestor. "He killed some of the raiders, but he was wounded bad."

"Well, he's not been here, Son. I can assure you of that. Still, give me a description and I'll see it's circulated."

"He's around six feet two, dark hair, a little gray at the temples. And he was wearing a black coat and a white shirt, black trousers and shoes. He's sort of thin in the face, with deep-set eyes, and he don't smile much. I'd say he was around thirty-five, maybe a little older."

"This wound he took," said Wheeler softly. "Was it in the temple . . . here?" he added, tapping the right side of his head.

"Yes, sir, I believe so. Someone seen him riding out, said he was bleeding from the head."

"How would you know that if you haven't seen him?" put in Clem.

"Oh, I've seen a man who answers that description. What else can you tell me about him?"

"He's a quiet man," said Nestor, "and he doesn't like violence."

"You don't say? Well, for a man who doesn't like it he's mighty partial to it. He shot our Oath Taker to death. Right there in the church. I have to admit that Crane—the dead man—was an odious little runt, but that ain't hardly the point. He was also involved in an earlier gun battle when Crane and some other men attacked a group of Wanderers. Several men—and a woman—were killed. I think the wound must have scrambled your preacher's brains, Son. You wouldn't believe who he's claiming to be."

"Who?" asked Nestor.

"The Jerusalem Man."

Nestor's mouth dropped open, and he swung a quick glance to Clem. The older man's face was expressionless. Wheeler leaned back in his chair. "Don't seem to have surprised you none, friend."

Clem shrugged. "Head wounds can be very tricky," he said. "I take it you didn't catch him."

"Nope. To be honest, I hope we don't. That's a very sick man. And he was provoked. I'll tell you this, though: he can surely handle a pistol. That's a surprising gift for a preacher who don't like violence."

"He's a surprising man," said Clem.

Jacob Moon was thinking of other, more weighty matters as the mortally wounded man crawled painfully across the yard, trying to reach the fallen pistol. He was considering his prospects. The Apostle Saul had treated him fairly, giving him back his youth and supplying a plentiful share of wealth and women. But Saul's day was passing.

Saul might think he could take the Deacon's place, but Moon knew it would not happen. For all his bluster and his willingness to kill for power, there was a weakness in Saul. Others had not apparently noticed it. But then, they were blinded by the brilliance of the Deacon and failed to see the flaws in the man who stood beside him. Let's face it, thought Moon, Saul casts a mighty thin shadow.

The wounded man groaned. He was close to the pistol now; Moon waited until his hand closed over the butt, then shot him twice in the back. The last shot severed the spine just above the hip, and the man's legs were useless. Moon's victim, the pistol in his hand, was trying to roll over to aim at his assailant. He could not. The legs were dead weight now.

Moon moved to the right. "Over here, Kovac," he said. "Try this side."

Gamely, the injured Bull Kovac pushed against the ground, his powerful arms finally twisting him far enough to be able to see the tall assassin. With trembling fingers Bull eased back the hammer of his pistol. Moon drew and fired, the bullet entering Kovac's head just above the bridge of the nose.

"By God, he was game," said one of the two Jerusalem Riders accompanying Moon.

"Game doesn't get it done," said Moon. "You boys get back to Pilgrim's Valley and report the attack on Kovac's farm. You can say that I'm out hunting the killers. If you need me, I'll be in Domango. And Jed," he called as the riders turned their mounts.

"Yes sir, Jacob?"

"I haven't the time to deal with the storekeeper. You handle it."

"When?"

"In two days," Moon told him. "The night before the Oath Taking."

As the men rode away, Moon stepped across the corpse and strolled into the house. The log walls were well crafted and neatly fitted, the dirt floor hard-packed and well swept. Bull Kovac had traced a series of motifs into it, making it more homey. There were no pictures on the wall, and all the furniture was handmade. Moon pulled up a chair and sat down. A jug of Baker's was still sitting on the old iron stove, gently steaming. Reaching out, he filled a mug, his mind returning to the problem of Saul.

The Apostle was right. Land was the key to wealth. But why share it? Most of what they had gathered was already in Moon's name. With Saul dead I will be doubly rich, he thought.

A small black and white cat moved out of the shadows and rubbed against Moon's leg. It jumped to his lap and began to purr. Moon stroked its head, and the animal gratefully curled up, its purrs increasing.

When to kill him was the question now.

Stroking the cat, Moon found his inner tension subsiding, and he remembered a line from the Old Testament, something about for every thing there is a season, a time to plant, a time to reap, a time to live, a time to die. That sounded right.

It was not the season on Saul just yet . . .

First there was the Jerusalem Man. Then the woman, Beth McAdam.

Moon finished his mug of Baker's and stood, the cat dropping to all fours on the floor. As he strode from the building, the cat followed and stood in the doorway meowing.

Moon turned and fired in one flowing motion. Then, reloading his pistol, he mounted his horse and set off for Domango.

◇ 7 ◇

People say we no longer live in an age of miracles. It is not so. What has been lost is our ability to see them.

The Wisdom of the Deacon
Introduction

JOSIAH BROOME PUT aside his Bible. He had never been a believer, not in the fullest sense, but he valued the sections of the New Testament that dealt with love and forgiveness. It always amazed him how people could be so quick to hate and so slow to love. But then, he reasoned, the first seemed so much easier.

Else was out for the evening at the Bible study group held every Friday at Frey Bailey's home on the outskirts of town, just beyond the meeting hall, and Josiah Broome was enjoying the unnatural silence. Friday night produced an oasis of calm in his tidy home. Replacing the Bible on the bookshelf, he moved to the kitchen and filled the kettle. One mug of Baker's before retiring, heavily sweetened with honey, was his one luxury on a Friday night. He would carry it out onto the porch and sip it while watching the distant stars.

Tomorrow he would give Oath for Beth McAdam, and Else would scold him for the entire evening. But tonight he would enjoy the silence. The kettle began to vibrate. Taking a cloth from a peg on the wall, he wrapped it around the handle and lifted the kettle from the range. Filling the mug, he added the powdered Baker's brew and three heaping spoonfuls of honey. As he was stirring it, he heard a tapping at the front door. Annoyed by the interruption, he carried the drink

136

through the kitchen and across the main room. "Come in!" he called, for the door was never locked.

Daniel Cade eased his way inside, leaning heavily on his sticks, his face red from exertion. Josiah Broome hurried to his side, taking hold of the Prophet's arm and guiding him to a deep chair. Cade sank down gratefully, laying his sticks on the floor.

Leaning his head back, the Prophet took several deep breaths. Broome laid the mug of Baker's on a table to his visitor's right. "Drink that, sir," he said. "It will help restore your strength." Hurrying back to the kitchen, he made a second mug and returned to the fireside. Cade's breathing had eased, but the old man looked tired and worn out, with dark circles beneath his eyes and an unhealthy pallor replacing the fiery red of his cheeks.

"I'm about all done in, Son," he wheezed.

"What brings you to my home, sir ... not that you are unwelcome, you understand!"

Cade smiled. Lifting the Baker's with a trembling hand, he sipped the brew. "By God, that is sweet!" he said.

"I could make you another," offered Broome.

Cade shook his head. "It will do, Son. I came to talk, not to drink. Have you been noticing the new arrivals?"

Broome nodded. More than a score of riders had come into Pilgrim's Valley during the past week, all of them tough men, heavily armed. "Jerusalem Riders," he said. "They serve the Deacon."

Cade grunted. "Saul, more like. I don't like it, Broome. I know their kind. God's blood, *I am their kind.* Brigands, take my word for it. I don't know what game Saul is playing, but I don't like it, Broome."

"I understand that Jacob Moon called them in after the murder of poor Bull Kovac," said Broome.

Cade's pale eyes narrowed. "Yes," he said softly. "The man you and Beth were to stand Oath for. Now two of those same Jerusalem Riders have moved into Bull's house. There's something very wrong here, but no one else can see it."

"What do you mean?"

"It started with the burning of the church. Why were no Crusaders present? And how did the raiders know that there would be no one to stand against them? There were at least twenty masked killers around that building, yet only five left the town. Take away the dead man outside the church, and that leaves fourteen unaccounted for in the raid. Curiously, that is the same number of Crusaders who rode out to the supposed attack on Shem Jackson's farm."

"You're not suggesting . . . ?"

"I'm suggesting that something is beginning to smell bad in Pilgrim's Valley."

"I think, if you'll pardon my directness, that you are overreacting. I have spoken to the Apostle Saul, and he assures me that Jacob Moon and his riders will soon apprehend the brigands who murdered poor Bull. These men are carefully chosen for their skills and their dedication, as indeed are the Crusaders. I have known Leon Evans since he was a boy; I cannot believe he would have taken part in such a . . . such a dreadful business."

"You've more faith than I have," said Cade wearily. "Something is happening, and I don't like it. And I don't like that Saul, can't understand what the Deacon sees in him save that he's the only one of the Apostles still living."

"I'm sure he is a fine man. I have spoken to him on many occasions and always found him to be courteous and caring," said Broome, beginning to be uncomfortable. "He knows all the Scriptures by heart, and he spends his day in prayer and communion with the Lord."

Cade chuckled. "Come, come, Broome, you don't need to pull no wool over these old eyes. You ain't a Christian, though you're a damn sight closer to it than many others. But that's by the by. Jon told me that you were one of the few who knew of his past. He trusted you . . . and I will, too. I'm heading for Unity tomorrow. I'm going to try to see the Deacon and find out just what the hell is happening."

"Why come to me?"

"I think Saul knows how I feel, and he may try to stop me

from reaching the capital. If I don't make it, Broome, I want you to tell Jonnie what I said. You understand?"

"But . . . but he's dead. Lost in the desert."

"He ain't dead. Don't you listen to the gossip? A man claiming to be the Jerusalem Man shot the Purity Oath Taker to death. He ain't dead, Broome. Goddamn, he's alive again! And he'll be back."

A movement came from the doorway, and Broome glanced up to see a tall, wide-shouldered man standing there, a gun in his hand. "What do you want?" he asked, rising.

"Been told to kill you," the man said amiably, "but no one said a goddamn thing about this old fart. Still, orders is orders." The gunman smiled. His pistol thundered, and Broome was smashed back against the wall. He fell heavily, pain flaring in his chest, and collided with the small table by his chair. It tipped, and he felt the mug of Baker's strike his back, the hot liquid soaking through his shirt. Despite the pain, he stayed conscious and stared up at the man who had shot him.

"Why?" he asked, his voice clear.

The gunman shrugged. "I don't ask questions," he said.

"Neither do I," said Daniel Cade.

Broome's eyes flicked to the Prophet. His voice sounded different, colder than the grave. The gunman swung his pistol, but he was too late and Cade shot him twice in the chest. The man fell back into the door frame and tried to lift his weapon, but it fired into the floor. He sagged down, his fingers losing hold of the pistol.

"You're . . . supposed to . . . be a . . . man of God," said the gunman, coughing blood.

"Amen to that," said Cade. His gun came up, and a third shot smashed through the man's skull. "Rot in hell," said the Prophet. Broome struggled to his knees, blood staining his shirt, his left arm hanging uselessly at his side.

"Come on, Jed," shouted a voice from outside, "what the hell is keeping you?"

"If you can walk, Broome," whispered Cade, "I suggest you

go out back. You'll find my buggy. Make for Beth McAdam's place."

"What about you?"

"Go now, Son. There's no more time for talk."

Cade had broken open his pistol and was feeding shells into the cylinder. Broome stood, staggered, then backed away through the kitchen. The glass of the front window shattered, and a man pushed the curtains aside. Cade shot him. Another gunman leapt through the doorway. Broome saw him fire twice, both bullets hammering into the Prophet. Cade's gun boomed, and the gunman flew back, blood spraying the wall behind him.

Broome staggered out into the night, hauling himself up onto Cade's buggy. Grabbing the reins with his good hand, he kicked free the brake and lashed the reins down on the horse's back. The beast lurched into the traces, and the buggy picked up speed.

A shot sounded from behind him, then another. He heard a bullet thud into the wooden frame and ducked down. Then the buggy was clear and racing away into the night.

"I'd like to know what is going on," Nestor Garrity told Clem Steiner once the two men were alone. Clem looked away and cut into his steak. "Who is he? Really?" Nestor persisted.

Clem pushed away his plate and wiped his mouth with a napkin. "He's who he says he is."

"The Jerusalem Man? He can't be! I know him! He's the Preacher, for God's sake!"

"Times change, Nestor. Men change. He fought the Daggers, and he'd had enough. Think of it, boy. He was a sad, bitter man, searching for a city that didn't exist. Then he sent the Sword of God through time and destroyed a world. Maybe two worlds. He was in love with Beth. He wanted a different life. The last ounce of power in the Daniel Stone gave him back his youth. It was a new start. As far as I know, only two people recognized him when he came back from the Wall: Josiah Broome and Edric Scayse. Scayse took the secret to the grave—and Broome? He's a peaceful man and a dreamer.

He liked what Shannow was trying to become. That's all, Nestor."

"But the books? The chariot to heaven? Is it all lies?"

"Mostly," Clem said, with a wry grin. "But then, legends are like that, Son. We misremember them. We don't do it intentionally most of the time. Take me, for example. When I was a kid, I had a teacher who told me that I would be a brigand or a warmaker. He expelled me from school and told my folks there was no good in me. Now I own three hundred thousand acres and I'm a rich, powerful man. I saw that teacher last year; he came to live in Pernum. Know what he said? 'Clem, I always knew you had the seeds of greatness in you.' He wasn't lying. Understand?"

The young man shook his head. "I don't understand any of it. It's all built on lies. The Deacon, everything. It's all lies! All that Bible shit. All the studying. Lies!"

"Whoa, Son! Don't lump it all in together!" warned Clem. "We all need heroes, and Shannow was—is—a good man. No matter what other people may write about him, he always did what he thought was right, and he would never pass by and let evil have its way. And some of the things he did can't be disputed. He fought the Hellborn, and he destroyed the Guardians who were behind the war. Nestor, he is a good man; it is not his fault that others—of a more political mind—chose to take his name in vain."

"I want to go home," said Nestor. "I don't want to do this anymore."

"Sure, Son," said Clem. "I understand that."

Clem paid for the meal and stood. Nestor rose also, his shoulders hunched, his eyes distant. Clem felt for the boy. The iron hooves of reality had ground his dreams to dust. "Let's go," said the older man, and together they walked out onto the street. A shot sounded, and shards of wood exploded from the post beside Clem's head; he ducked, drew his pistol, and dived forward. A rifleman stepped into sight, and Clem fired, the bullet striking the man in the shoulder and spinning him, the rifle falling from his hands. Nestor stood transfixed; then he saw the man from the tavern.

Sachs was aiming a pistol at Clem's back. Without thinking, Nestor drew his pistol and triggered it, the shell hammering home into Sachs's chest. Suddenly all of Nestor's anger welled up, and, walking toward the wounded man, he fired again. And again. Each shot thundered home, and Sachs was hurled back against the wall of a building.

"You bastard!" screamed Nestor, continuing to pull the trigger even after the gun was long empty and the lifeless would-be assassin was dead at his feet. Clem came alongside him, gently pulling the pistol clear. Nestor was crying, his body racked by deep, convulsive sobs. "It's all lies!" he said.

"I know," said Clem.

Seth Wheeler appeared, a long-barreled pistol in his hands. "What in Hades is happening here?" he asked Clem.

"We had an argument earlier with ... him," he said, pointing down at the corpse. "When we left the eating house, they opened fire on us. There's a man back there with a busted shoulder; I guess he'll tell you more."

"Well," said Wheeler, "it's for damned sure that Sachs ain't going to tell us anything. You boys better walk with me to the office. I'll need to make a report for the town elders."

"He was a damn fool," Clem said bitterly. "He's dead over a spilled beer."

"He's killed others for less, I reckon," muttered Wheeler. "But there was never any proof."

Later, when Seth Wheeler had painstakingly written out his report, he put down his pen and looked up at Nestor. The young man's face had a ghostly pallor, and his eyes were distant. "You all right, Son?" asked the Crusader. Nestor nodded but said nothing, and Wheeler looked at him closely. "I guess you've never been in a killing fight before." Nestor just stared at the floor. Wheeler turned his attention to Clem. "I think you should both ride out. Sachs wasn't popular, but he had drinking friends. Tough men. They may feel the need to ... well ... you know."

Clem nodded. "We were leaving anyway in the morning. But now's as good a time as any."

Wheeler nodded. "I take it you'll be traveling toward Domango. It's where your friend was last seen."

"I guess so," agreed Clem.

"Then I'd take it as a kindness if you'd stop by and see that my mother is well. She has a farm just over the mountains. You take the Domango trail and you won't miss it. An old place in a valley east of the trail. She'll fix you a good meal and give you a roof for the night."

"Any message?"

Wheeler shrugged and gave a boyish grin. "Just tell her that Seth and Pad are fine and we'll be coming by at summer's end."

Wheeler lifted Nestor's empty pistol and opened the side drawer of his desk, taking out a box of shells. Swiftly he loaded the revolver and handed it to Nestor. "An empty gun is no good to anyone," he said. "And you might as well keep these," he added, tossing the box to Clem.

"It might be better if all the guns were empty," replied Clem, reaching out to shake the Crusader's hand.

"Amen to that," said Seth Wheeler.

Shannow lay awake in the spare bedroom, staring out of the window at the bright stars. He and Amaziga had talked into the early hours, then she had shown him through to this curious room. The bed had a metal frame and a thick mattress, but instead of blankets there was a single down-filled covering. Beside the bed was a small table on which sat one of the strange lamps that burned brightly without oil. It was lit and extinguished by what appeared to be a coat button attached to the base. Beside this was a small box, which at first bore the glowing numbers 03:14. When Shannow next glanced at it, the numbers had changed: 03:21. He watched it and soon worked out that it changed at regular intervals. A timing device!

Climbing from his bed, he walked naked to the window and opened it. The night air was fresh but not cool. Indeed, it was considerably warmer outside than in. A humming sound began, coming from the wall by his bed. There was a metal grille there, and he moved to it. Cold air was spilling from the vent.

Shannow walked across the room and entered the second room Amaziga had shown him. Stepping inside the tall glass box, he turned the small steel wheel as she had demonstrated. Cold water streamed from a dish above him. Taking a tablet of soap, he began to scrub the dust of travel from his body. But the water grew steadily more hot until at last he had to leap from the box. Kneeling down, he examined the wheel. There were painted arrows on it pointing to two colored circles, one blue and one red. The colored circles were repeated on the faucets at the sink beside the glass box. Shannow pressed each: one hot and the other cold.

Returning to the shower, he twisted the metal wheel back toward the blue. Gradually, the steam subsided and the water cooled. Satisfied, he stepped back into the box and rinsed the soap from his body.

Refreshed, he toweled himself down and wandered back to his bed. The humming was still sounding from above him, and he found the noise irritating, like making camp close to a beehive. Standing on the bed, he stared into the vent, seeking some way to close it. There was a lever, and just as he was about to press it, he heard Lucas's voice echoing in the vent. ". . . too dangerous, Amaziga. It has already all but destroyed a world. Why take such a terrible risk?"

Shannow could not hear her response, but Lucas cut in swiftly: "Nothing, as you know, is certain. But the probabilities are too high. Let me show you the data."

Stepping down from the bed, Shannow walked to the door, easing it open and moving into the carpeted hallway. Now the voices were louder, and he could hear Amaziga: ". . . probabilities are high; they are bound to be. But they would be high regardless of whatever action I take. Sarento has become the Bloodstone, and with the power it gives him and with his extraordinary intelligence, he is almost bound to discover gateways. Is that not so?"

"That is not the point," came the reasoned voice of the

machine man. "By your actions you will increase the probabilities."

"By a fraction," said Amaziga.

"And what of Shannow? The risks to him are great. He might die on this quest of yours."

"Hardly the greatest loss to the culture of a planet." Amaziga sneered. "He is a killer, a man of violence. Whereas the rescue of Sam would mean so much. He was . . . is . . . a scientist and a humanitarian. Together we may even be able to stop this world from falling. You understand? At least on this version of earth we might prevent the apocalypse. That alone is worth the risk to Shannow's life."

The Jerusalem Man stepped back into his room and lay down.

There was truth in the harsh words he had heard. From somewhere deep in his memory he remembered Josiah Broome saying: *"I dread to think of people who look up to men like Jon Shannow. What do they give to the world? Nothing, I tell you."*

His guns were hanging over the back of a chair. The weapons of Thundermaker.

What peace have they ever brought? he wondered. What good have you ever done?

It was not a question he could answer, and he fell into an uneasy sleep.

"Lie back and rest," the voice told him, but Josiah Broome could not obey it. His shoulder ached abominably, and he felt a painful throbbing in the fingers of his left hand. Nausea swept over him in waves, and tears squeezed through his closed eyelids, flowing to his thin cheeks. Opening his eyes, he saw an old man with a long white beard.

"I've been shot," he said. "They shot me!" Even as he spoke, he realized how stupid it must sound. Of course the man knew he had been shot. Broome could feel the bandage around his chest and up over his shoulder. "I'm sorry," said Broome, weeping and not knowing what he was apologizing for. The pain flared in his wound, and he groaned.

"The bullet glanced up from a rib," said the old man softly, "then broke your collarbone before digging deep to rest under your shoulder blade. It's nasty but not fatal." Broome felt the man's warm hand on his brow. "Now rest like I told you. We'll talk in the morning."

Broome took a deep breath. "Why did they do it?" he asked. "I have no enemies."

"If that's true," said the old man, his voice dry, "then at least one of your friends doesn't like you too much."

The humor was lost on Josiah Broome, and he drifted into a nervous and disturbed sleep punctuated by appalling nightmares. He was being chased across a burning desert by riders with eyes of fire. They kept shooting at him, every bullet smashing into his frail body. But he did not die, and the pain was terrible. He awoke with a start, and fresh agony bloomed in the wound. Broome cried out, and instantly the old man was beside him. "Best you sit up, Son," he said. "Here, I'll give you a hand." The old man was stronger than he looked, and Broome was hoisted to a sitting position, his back against the cave wall. There was a small fire, and meat was cooking in a black iron pot. "How did I get here?" asked Broome.

"You fell off a buggy, Son. You were lucky—the wheel just missed you."

"Who are you?"

"You can call me Jake."

Broome stared hard at the man. There was something familiar about him, but he could not find the connection. "I am Josiah Broome. Tell me, do I know you, Jake?"

"You do now, Josiah Broome." Jake moved to the cook fire and stirred the broth with a long wooden spoon. "Coming along nicely," he said.

Broome gave a weak smile. "You look like one of the prophets," he said. "Moses. I had a book once, and there was a picture of Moses parting the Red Sea. You look just like him."

"Well, I ain't Moses," said Jake. As he shrugged off his coat, Broome saw the butts of two pistols scabbarded at the old man's hips. Jake glanced up. "Did you recognize any of the men?"

"I think so . . . but I'd hate to be right."

"Jerusalem Riders?"

Broome was surprised. "How did you know?"

"They followed you and found the buggy. Then they back-tracked. I listened to them talking. They were mad fit to bust, I can tell you."

"They didn't . . . see you?"

"Nobody sees me unless I want them to," Jake told him. "It's a talent I have. Also, you'll be relieved to hear that I know a little about healing. Where were you heading?"

"Heading?"

"Last night, in the buggy?"

"Oh, that was Daniel Cade's vehicle. He . . . Oh, dear God . . ."

"What is it?"

Broome sighed. "He was killed last night. He saved me by shooting the . . . the assassin. But there were others. They rushed the house and killed him."

Jake nodded. "Daniel would have taken at least two of them with him. Tough man." He chuckled. "No one ever wants to leave this life, Son, but old Daniel, given a choice, would have plumped for a fight against the ungodly."

"You knew him?"

"Back in the old days," said Jake. "Not a man to cross."

"He was a brigand and a killer," Broome said sternly. "Worthless scum. But he saw the light."

Jake laughed, the sound rich and merry. "Indeed he did, Meneer Broome. A regular Damascus road miracle."

"Are you mocking him?" Broome asked, as Jake spooned the broth into a wooden bowl and passed it to the wounded man.

"I don't mock, Son. But I don't judge, either. Not anymore. That's for the young. Now eat your broth. It'll help replace some of that lost fluid."

"I must get word to Else," said Broome. "She'll be worried."

"She certainly will," agreed Jake. "From what I heard of the riders' conversations, she thinks you killed the Prophet."

"What?"

"That's the word, Son. He was found dead in your house, and when the Jerusalem Riders went to find out what the shooting was about, you shot two of them dead. You're a dangerous man."

"But no one would believe that. I have stood against violence all my life."

"You'd be amazed what people will believe. Now finish the broth."

"I'll go back," Broome said suddenly. "I'll see the Apostle Saul. He knows me. He has the gift of discernment; he'll listen."

Jake shook his head. "You're not a fast learner, are you, Broome?"

The man called Jake sat quietly at the mouth of the cave as the wounded man groaned in his sleep. He was tired, but this was no time to enjoy the bliss of a dark, dreamless sleep. The killers were still out there, and a greater evil was waiting to seep into this tortured world. Jake felt a great sadness flow over him, and rubbing his eyes, he stood and stretched his weary legs. A little to the left, on a stretch of open ground, the mule raised her head and glanced at him. An owl swooped overhead, banking and turning, seeking its rodent prey. Jake took a deep breath of the mountain air, then sat again, stretching out his long legs.

His mind wandered back over the long, long years, but his eyes remained alert, scanning the tree line for signs of movement. It was unlikely that the killers were closing in; they would be camped somewhere, waiting to follow the tracks in the morning. Jake drew one of his pistols and idly spun the chamber. How long since you fired it? he wondered. Thirty-eight years? Forty?

Returning the pistol to its scabbard, he dipped a hand into the wide pocket of his sheepskin coat and drew out a small golden stone. With its power he could be young again. Flexing his knee, he felt the arthritic pain flare up. Use the stone, you old fool, he told himself.

But he did not. The time was coming when the power would be needed, and it would need to serve a far greater purpose than repairing an age-eroded joint.

Could I have stopped the evil? he thought. Probably, if only I'd known how.

But I didn't, and I don't. All I can do is fight it when it arrives.

If you have the time!

It had been weeks since the last paralyzing chest pain, the dull ache in his right bicep, and the pins and needles in his fingertips. He should have used the stone then, but he had not. Against the power that was coming, even this pure and perfect fragment of Sipstrassi might not be enough.

The night was cool. Josiah Broome was sleeping more peacefully as Jake walked silently back into the cave and added fuel to the dying fire. Broome's face was wet with perspiration and streaked with the gray lines of pain and shock.

You're a good man, Broome, thought Jake. The world deserves more like you, with your hatred of violence and your faith in the ultimate nobility of man. Returning to his sentry post, Jake felt the sorrow growing. Glancing up at the velvet sky, he gave a rueful smile. "What do you see in us, Lord?" he asked aloud. "We build nothing and smother everything. We kill and we torture. For every man like Broome there are hundreds of Jacob Moons, scores of Sauls." He shook his head. "Poor Saul," he whispered. "Treat him gently when you see him, Lord, for he was once a man of prayer and goodness."

Was he?

Jake remembered the balding, stooped little man who had organized the church's finances, arranging fetes and gatherings, fund-raisers and parties. There were thorns in his flesh even then, but he controlled them. Nature helped him there, for he was short and ugly. Not now! I should have seen it, thought Jake, when he used the stone to make himself golden and handsome. I should have stopped it then. But he had not. In fact he had been pleased that Saul Wilkins had at last found a form that brought him happiness.

But the joy had been so transient, and Saul had gone searching for the bodily pleasures his life, his ugliness, and his faith had denied him for so long.

"I can't hate him, Lord," said Jake. "It's just not in me. And I'm to blame for putting the power in his hands. I tried to make a holy world, and I failed." Jake stopped talking to himself and listened. The night breeze was low, whispering through the leaves of the nearby trees. Closing his eyes, he drew in a long slow breath through his nostrils. There was the scent of grass—and something else.

"Come out, little Pakia," he said, "for I know you are there."

"How do you know me?" came a small voice from the undergrowth.

"I am old, and I know many things. Come out and sit with me."

The little Wolver emerged and shuffled nervously forward, squatting down some ten feet from the old man. Her fur shone silver in the moonlight, and her dark eyes scanned the weather-beaten face and the white beard. "There are men with guns in the woods. They found the trail of your mule. They will be here at first light."

"I know," he said softly. "It was good of you to seek me out."

"Beth asked me to find Meneer Broome. I smell blood."

"He is inside . . . sleeping. I will bring him to Beth. Go and tell her."

"I know your scent," she said, "but I have no knowing of you."

"But you know you can trust me, little one. Is that not so?"

The Wolver nodded. "I can read your heart. It is not gentle, but you do not lie."

Jake smiled. "Sadly, you are right. I am not a gentle man. When you have seen Beth, I want you to go to your people. Tell them to move away from here with all haste. There is an evil coming that will tear through the land like a burning fire. The Wolvers must be far away."

"Our holy one has told us this," said Pakia. "The Beast is coming from beyond the Wall. The spiller of blood, the feaster of souls. But we cannot desert our friend Beth."

"Sometimes," said Jake sadly, "the best thing we can do is to desert our friends. The Beast has many powers, Pakia, but the worst of them is to change that which is good into that which is evil. Tell your holy man that the Beast can turn a heart to darkness and cause a friend to rip out the throat of his brother. He can do this. And he is coming soon."

"Who shall I say has spoken these words?" asked Pakia.

"You tell him they are the words of the Deacon."

Clem Steiner was worried about the youngster. Nestor had said little since they had ridden from Purity and had seemed unconcerned at the prospect of pursuit. Twice Clem had swung off the trail, studying the moonlit land, but there was no sign that they were being followed. Nestor rode with his head down, obviously lost in thought, and Clem did not try to pierce the silence until they were camped in a natural hollow with a small fire burning. Nestor sat with his back against a thick pine, his knees drawn up.

"It wasn't your fault, boy," said Clem, misunderstanding the youngster's anguish. "He came looking for us." Nestor nodded but did not speak, and Clem sighed. "Speak to me, Son. There's nothing to be gained by brooding."

Nestor looked up. "Didn't you ever believe in anything, Meneer Steiner?"

"I believe in the inevitability of death."

"Yeah," said Nestor, looking away.

Clem cursed inwardly. "Just tell me, Nestor. I never was much at guessing."

"What's to tell? It's all just horseshit." Nestor laughed. "I believed it all, you know. Jesus, what a fool! The Deacon was sent by God; the Jerusalem Man was a prophet like in the Book. We were God's chosen people! I've lived my life chasing a lie. Don't that beat all?" Nestor took up his blanket and spread it on the ground.

Clem stayed silent for a moment, gathering his thoughts, before he spoke. "If you need to hear something sage, Nestor, you're camped out with the wrong man. I'm too old to even remember what it was like to be young. When I was your age, I just wanted to be known as the greatest shootist in the known world. I didn't give a cuss about God or history. Never thought about anything much except maybe getting a little faster. So I can't advise you. But that doesn't mean that I don't know you're wrong. You can't change the world, Son. There'll always be serpents. All you can do is to live your own life in the way you feel is right."

"And what about the truth?" asked Nestor, his eyes angry.

"The truth? What the hell is the truth? We're born, we live, and we die. Everything else is just shades of opinion."

Nestor shook his head. "You don't understand, do you? I guess your kind never will."

The words stung Clem, but he tried to bite back his anger. "Maybe you'd like to tell me what my kind is, boy."

"Yeah, I'll do that. All your dreams have always been selfish. The fastest shootist. To make a name for yourself by killing the Jerusalem Man. To own land and be rich. So why would you care if the Deacon proves to be a fraud or if hundreds of kids like me are lied to? It doesn't mean anything to you, does it? You just act like all the rest. You lied to me. You didn't tell me the Preacher was Shannow—not until you had to."

"Put not your faith in princes, Nestor," said Clem, all too aware of the bitter truth in the boy's words.

"What's that supposed to mean?"

Clem sighed. "There was an old man used to work for Edric Scayse. He read old books all the time, some of them just fragments. He told me the line. And it's true, but we do it all the time. Some leader rises up, and we swear to God that he's the best man since Jesus walked on water. It ain't so. Because he's human, and he makes mistakes, and we can't forgive that. I don't know the Deacon, but a lot of what he's done has been for the good. And maybe he truly believed Shannow was John the Baptist. Seems to me a lot of would-be holy men get led astray. It's got to be hard. You look up at the sky, and you say, 'Lord, shall I go left or shall I go right?' Then you see a bird flying left, and you take it as a sign. The Deacon and his people were held in time for three hundred years. The Jerusalem Man released them. Maybe God did send him; I don't know. But then, Nestor, the sum of all I don't know could cover these mountains. But you're right about me. I won't deny it—I can't deny it. But what I'm saying is that the truth—whatever the hell it is—doesn't exist outside of a man. It exists in his heart. Jon Shannow never lied. He never claimed to be anything other than what he was. He fought all his life to defend the light. He never took a backward step in the face of evil. It didn't matter what men *said* was right. And there isn't a man alive who could have dented his faith. Because he didn't hand that faith over to men. It was his, his alone. You understand? And as for the truth, well . . . I once asked him about that. I said, 'Supposing all that you believe in is just so much dust on the wind. Suppose it ain't true. How would you feel?' He just shrugged and smiled. You know what he said? 'It wouldn't matter a damn, because it ought to be.' "

"And I'm supposed to understand that?" stormed Nestor. "All I know is that all my life I've been taught to believe something that was just made up by men. And I don't intend to be fooled again. Not by the Deacon and not by you. Tomorrow I head for home. You can go to hell in a bucket!"

Nestor lay down, turning his back on the fire. Clem felt old and tired and decided to let the matter rest. The next day they would talk again.

Your kind never will!

The boy was sharp, no doubt about that. Over the years Clem had gathered a band of robbers to him, and their raids had been daring and brilliantly executed. Exciting times! Yet men had been killed or crippled, good men for the most part. Clem remembered the first of them, a young payroll guard who against all odds had refused to lay down his rifle. Instead he had fired a shot that had clipped the top of Clem's shoulder and killed the man behind him. The guard had gone down in a volley of fire. One shot had come from Clem's gun. The young man haunted him now; he was only doing his duty, earning an honest day's pay.

Your kind never will!

Clem sighed. You want to know *my kind*, boy? Weak men governed by their desires yet without the strength of purpose to work for them.

When the ambush had come, the bullets ripping into the gang, Clem had spurred his horse over a high cliff face and fallen a hundred feet into a raging torrent. He had survived, whereas all his men had died. With nowhere to go he had headed back to Pilgrim's Valley, where any who remembered him would recall a gallant young man by the name of Clem Steiner, not a brigand who rode under the name Laton Duke. By what right do you preach to this boy? he wondered. How could you tell him to live his life the way he thinks is right? When did you do that, Clem?

And what had the stolen money bought him? A fine red waistcoat and a nickel-plated pistol, several hundred faceless whores in scores of nameless towns. Oh, yes, Clem, you're a fine teacher!

Picking up a handful of twigs, he leaned toward the fire. The ground trembled, the little blaze spitting cinders into the air. The hobbled horses whinnied in fear, and a boulder was dislodged from the slopes above them, rolling and bouncing down into the valley below. Nestor came to his knees and tried to stand, but the ground shifted under his feet, hurling him off balance. A bright light shone on the hollow. Clem glanced up. Two moons hung in the sky, one full and the other like a crescent. Nestor saw it, too.

A jagged rip tore across a narrow hillside, swallowing trees. Then the full moon faded from sight, and an eerie silence settled on the land.

"What's happening?" asked Nestor.

Clem sat back, the fire forgotten. All he could think of was the last time he had seen such a vision and felt the earth tremble beneath him, when the terror of the lizard warriors had been unleashed on the land.

Nestor scrambled across to him, grabbing his arm. "What's happening?" he asked again.

"Someone just opened a door," Clem said softly.

◇ 8 ◇

Two wise men and a fool were walking in the forest when a ravening lion leapt out at them. The first wise man estimated the size of the charging lion as some eight feet from the nose to the tip of its tail. The second wise man noted that the beast was favoring its left front leg, indicating that it was lame and thus had, through hunger, been forced to become a man-eater. As the beast reared, the fool shot it. But then, he didn't know any better.

The Wisdom of the Deacon
Chapter XIV

SHANNOW AWOKE EARLY and looked for his clothes. They were gone, but in their place he found a pair of black trousers of heavy twill and a thick woolen cream-colored shirt. His own boots were beside them. Dressing swiftly, he swung his guns around his hips and walked through to the main room. Amaziga was not there, but the machine had been switched on, with the calm, handsome face of the redheaded Lucas pictured on the screen.

"Good morning," said the face. "Amaziga has driven into town to fetch some supplies. She should be back within the hour. There is coffee, should you desire it, or some cereal." Shannow glanced suspiciously at the coffee maker and decided to wait.

"Would you care to listen to music?" asked Lucas. "I have over four thousand melodies on hand."

"No, thank you." Shannow sat down in a wide leather chair. "It is cold in here," he said.

"I'll adjust the AC," said Lucas. The soft whirring ceased, and within moments the room began to feel warmer. "Are you comfortable with me here?" asked Lucas. "I can remove this visual and leave the screen blank if you prefer. It does not matter to me. Amaziga created it and finds it comforting, but I can understand how disconcerting it might be to a man from another time."

"Yes," agreed Shannow, "it is disconcerting. Are you a ghost?"

"An interesting question. The man from whom my memory and thought patterns were duplicated is now dead. I am therefore a copy, if you like, of his innermost being and one which can be seen though not touched. I would think my credentials as a ghost would be quite considerable. But since we co-existed, he and I, I am therefore more like a cerebral twin."

Shannow smiled. "If you want me to understand you, Lucas, you'll have to speak more slowly. Tell me, are you content?"

"Contentment is a word I can describe, but that does not necessarily mean that I understand it. I have no sense of discontent. The memories of Lucas the man contain many examples of his discontent, but they do not touch me as I summon them. I think that Amaziga would be better equipped to answer such questions. It was she who created me. I believe she chose to limit the input, eliminating unnecessary emotional concepts. Love, hate, testosteronal drives, fears, jealousies, pride, anger—these things are neither helpful nor useful in a machine. You understand?"

"I believe that I do," Shannow told him. "Tell me of the Bloodstone and the world we are to enter."

"What would you wish to know?"

"Start at the beginning. I usually find I can follow stories better that way."

"The beginning? Very well. In your own world you fought the Guardian leader Sarento many years ago, destroying him in the catacombs beneath the mountains which held the broken ship. In the world to which Amaziga will take you there was no Jon Shannow. Sarento ruled, but then he was struck down with a crippling and terminal illness. Having corrupted the Sipstrassi boulder, creating a giant Bloodstone, he could no longer rely on its powers to heal him. He searched everywhere for a pure stone that could take away the cancer. Time was against him, and in desperation he turned to the Bloodstone; it could not heal, but it could reshape. He drew its power into himself, merging with the stone, if you will. The energy flowed through his veins, changing him. His skin turned red, streaked with black veins. His power grew. The cancer shriveled and died. There was no going back; the change was irrevocable. He could no longer take in food and drink; all that could feed him was contained in blood: the life force of living creatures. He hungered for it, lusted for it. The Guardians saw what he had become and turned against him, but he destroyed them, for he was now a living Bloodstone with immense power. With the Guardians slain or fled, he needed to feed and journeyed to the lands of the Hellborn. You know their beliefs, Mr. Shannow. They worship the Devil. What better Devil could they find? He strode into Babylon and took the throne from Abaddon. And he fed. How he fed! Are you a student of ancient history, Mr. Shannow?"

"No."

"But you know your Bible?"

"Indeed I do."

"Then you will recall the tales of Molech, the god fed by souls upon the fire. Citizens of cities where Molech was worshiped would carry their firstborn children to furnaces and hurl them alive into the searing depths. All for Molech. The Hellborn do that for Sarento, though there are no flames. The children are slaughtered, and at first Sarento would bathe in the blood of victims. Every citizen carried a small Bloodstone—a demonseed. These are corrupted Sipstrassi Stones, the pure power long used up. They are fed with blood and thereby acquire a different kind of power. They can no longer heal wounds or create food. Instead they give great strength and speed to their bearers while feeding the baser human instincts.

An angry man in possession of a Bloodstone becomes furious and psychopathic. Honest desire becomes lustful need. They are foul creations. Yet with them Sarento can control the people, swelling their lusts and desires, reducing their capacity for compassion and love. He rules a nation founded on hatred and selfishness. *Do as thou wilt is the whole of the law.* But his need for blood grows daily. Hence the war, where his legions sweep across the land. And before them go the Devourers. He has mutated the Wolvers, making them larger, more ferocious, huge beasts that move with great speed and kill without pity. He no longer needs to bathe in blood, Mr. Shannow. Every time a Devourer feeds, it swells a Bloodstone embedded in its skull. This transmits power to Sarento, the ultimate Bloodstone.

"Samuel Archer is—at the point where you will enter the story—one of the few rebels still alive. But he and his people are trapped in the high country, surrounded. Soon the Devourers will stalk them."

Shannow stood and stretched his back. "Last night you and Amaziga spoke of probabilities. Would you explain them to me in a way that I might understand?"

"I hardly think so, yet I will try. It is a question of mathematics. There are doorways we can use to cross what has been believed to be the thresholds of time. But it is not really time we cross. There are millions of worlds. An infinite number. In the world of the Bloodstone no one yet knows of the gateways. By opening one, therefore, we increase the mathematical possibilities that our actions will alert the Bloodstone to their existence. You follow?"

"So far."

"So then, by rescuing Sam Archer, we risk the Bloodstone finding other worlds. And that would be a disaster of colossal proportions. Do you know anything about hummingbirds, Mr. Shannow?"

"They're small," said the Jerusalem Man.

"Yes," agreed the machine. "They are small, and their metabolism works at an astonishing rate. The smallest weighs less than a tenth of an ounce. They have the highest energy output per body weight of any warm-blooded animal, and to survive they must consume half their body weight in nectar every day. Sixty meals a day, Mr. Shannow, just to survive. The need for a plentiful supply of food makes them extraordinarily aggressive in defending their areas. The Bloodstone is identical. It needs to feed; it *lives* to feed. Every second of its existence it suffers enormous pangs of hunger. And it is insatiable, Mr. Shannow. Insatiable and ultimately unstoppable. Any world it finds it will ultimately devour."

"You do not think that saving Sam is a risk worth taking," observed Shannow.

"No, I do not. And neither do you. Amaziga points out that Sarento is a man with high intelligence and that intelligence is now boosted by corrupted Sipstrassi power. She maintains, perhaps rightly, that he will discover the gateways regardless of any action on our part. Therefore, she is adamant that the quest will continue. But I fear she is guided by emotion, not by reason. Why are you helping her?"

"She would go without me. It may be arrogance on my part, but I believe she will have a better chance of success with me. When do we set out?"

"As soon as Amaziga returns. Are your pistols fully loaded?"

"Yes."

"Good. I fear they will need to be."

The roar of angry lions came from outside, and Shannow moved from the chair, his right-hand pistol pointing toward the door. "It is only Amaziga," said Lucas, but the Jerusalem Man was already moving out onto the porch. There he saw the bright-red four-wheeled carriage swing from the dirt track to draw up outside the house in a trail of dust and noise. The noise subsided, then died.

Amaziga pushed open a side door and stepped out. "Help me with these boxes, Shannow!" she called, moving to the rear of the vehicle and opening another door. This one swung out and up, and Shannow watched her lean inside. Holstering the pistol, he walked toward her. A strange and unpleasant smell came from the vehicle, acrid and poisonous. It made his nostrils itch.

Amaziga was pulling a large box toward her, and Shannow leaned in to help. "Be careful. It's heavy," she said. Shannow lifted it and turned toward the house, happy to be clear of the fumes from the vehicle. Once inside, he laid the box on the table and waited for the black woman.

The voice of Lucas sounded: "It may interest you to know, Mr. Shannow, that your reflexes are five point seven percent higher than normal."

"What?"

"The speed at which you drew the pistol shows that you are faster than the average man," explained Lucas.

Amaziga entered and heaved a second box alongside the first. "There's one more," she told Shannow, who left reluctantly to fetch it. This was lighter, and with no room on the tabletop, he set it down alongside the table.

"Did you sleep well?" she asked him. He nodded. She was wearing a soft long-sleeved shirt with no collar. It was dark blue, and a portrait of a leaping black man had been painted on the chest.

"Is that Sam?" he asked.

Amaziga laughed, the sound good-humored. "No, it's a basketball player. A sportsman in this world." She laughed again. "I'll explain it later," she said. "But now let's unpack the shopping." Glancing at a dial on her wrist, she turned to Lucas. "Six and a half hours, yes?"

"An adequate approximation," responded the machine.

Amaziga pulled a small folding knife from her pocket and opened the blade. Swiftly she ran it along the top of the first box, then placed it on the table. Opening the flaps, she lifted clear a squat black weapon shaped, to Shannow's eyes at least, like the letter T. More weapons followed: two automatic pistols and twelve clips of ammunition. Discarding the empty box, she opened the second, drawing from it a short rifle with a pistol grip and two barrels. "This is for you, Shannow," she said. "I think you'll like it." Shannow did not, but he said nothing as she laid boxes of shells alongside the gun.

Leaving her to unpack the other box, he walked to the door and stared out over the landscape. The sun was high, the temperature soaring. Heat shimmers were rising from the front of the vehicle. To the left he saw a movement from within a giant cactus. Narrowing his eyes, he stared at the hole in the central stem. A tiny buff-colored owl appeared, launched into the air, and flew in a tight circle around the cactus before disappearing back into the hole. Shannow guessed the bird to be around six inches in height with a wingspan of around fourteen inches. He had never seen an owl so small.

Amaziga moved out alongside him, handing Shannow the ugly rifle with the pistol grip. "It's a shotgun, and it takes six shells," she said. "It is operated by a pump under the barrels. Try it out on that cactus."

"There's a nest there," said Shannow.

"I don't see a nest."

"A small owl in that hole. Let's move farther out." Shannow strode away. The desert sun was riding high, the temperature searing. Some way to the right he saw what could have been a small lake but was more likely to be a mirage. He pointed it out to Amaziga.

"There's nothing there," she said. "During the last century scores of settlers died here, taking their tired oxen down into the valley, expecting water. It's a harsh country."

"It is one of the greenest deserts I've seen," observed Shannow.

"Most of the plants here can live for up to five years without rainfall. Now, how about that saguaro? See any nests?"

Shannow ignored the sarcasm and hefted the weapon, aiming from the hip at a small barrel cactus close by. He pulled the trigger, and the cactus exploded; the sound of the shot hung in the air for several seconds. "It's grotesque," said the Jerusalem Man. "It would tear a man's arm off."

"I would have thought you would have loved that," put in Amaziga.

"You have never understood me, woman, and you never will."

The words were not spoken with anger, but Amaziga reacted as if struck. "I understand you well enough!" she stormed. "And I'll not debate my thoughts with the likes of you." Swinging, she aimed her own squat weapon at a saguaro and pulled the trigger. A thunderous wall of sound erupted from the gun, and Shannow was peppered with bright brass shell cases. The saguaro leaned drunkenly to one side, its thick body showing gaping holes halfway up the central stem, then fell to the desert floor.

Shannow turned and headed back to the house. He heard Amaziga ram another clip home, and a second burst followed the first. Inside, he dropped the shotgun to the table.

"What did she shoot?" asked the machine.

"A tall cactus."

"A saguaro," the machine told him. "How many arms did it have?"

"Two."

"It takes around eighty years before a saguaro grows an arm. And less than a second to destroy it."

"Is that regret?" Shannow asked.

"It is an observation," answered the machine. "The bird you saw is called an elf owl; they are quite common here. The desert is home to many interesting birds. The man Lucas used to spend many long hours studying them. His favorite was the gilded flicker. It probably made the nest hole the elf owl now inhabits."

Shannow said nothing, but his eyes strayed to the shotgun. It was an obscene weapon.

"You will need it," said Lucas.

"You read minds?"

"Of course. My clairvoyant abilities are what caused Amaziga to create me. The Devourers are powerful creatures. Only a shot to the heart with a powerful rifle or pistol will stop them. The skulls are thick and will resist your weapons. What are they, thirty-eights?"

"Yes."

"Amaziga has purchased two forty-fours, Smith and Wesson, double-action. They are in the box on the floor." Shannow knelt by it and opened the flaps. The guns were long-barreled and finished in metallic blue, the butts white and smooth. Lifting them clear, he hefted them for weight and balance. "Each weighs just under two and a half pounds," Lucas told him. "The barrels are seven inches long. There are three boxes of shells on the table."

Shannow loaded the weapons and stepped out into the sunlight to see Amaziga walking back toward the house. There was a small sack hanging on a fence post some thirty feet from the Jerusalem Man. Moving to it, she pulled out four empty cans, which she stood on the fence rail around two feet apart. Stepping aside, she called to Shannow to try out the pistols.

His right arm came up. The pistol thundered, and a can disappeared. The left arm rose, but this time his shot missed. "Put them close together," he ordered Amaziga. She did so, and he fired again. The can on the left flew from the rail. "More cans," he called. Reloading the pistols, he waited as she set out another six.

This time he fired swiftly, left and right. All the targets were smashed from the fence.

"What do you think of them?" asked Amaziga, approaching him.

"Fine weapons. This one pulls a fraction to the left. But they'll do."

"The salesman assured me they would stop a charging rhino . . . a very large animal," she added, seeing his look of puzzlement.

He tried to drop the pistols into his scabbards, but they were too bulky. "Don't worry about that," Amaziga told him. "I picked up a set of holsters for you at Rawhide." She chuckled, but Shannow could not see the reason for humor.

Back inside the house she unwrapped a brown parcel, handing Shannow a black hand-tooled gun belt with two scabbards. The leather was thick and of high quality, the buckle highly polished brass. There were loops all around it, filled with shells. "It is very handsome," he said, swinging it around his hips. "Yes, very handsome. My thanks to you, lady."

She nodded. "They do suit you, Shannow. Now I must leave you again. We'll be back at dusk. Lucas will brief you."

"*We'll* be back?" queried Shannow.

"Yes, I'm going to meet Gareth. He'll be coming with us."

Without another word she left the house. Shannow watched her move to the circle of broken stones. There was no bright light; she merely faded and disappeared from sight.

Inside once more, Shannow gazed at the calm, tranquil face on the screen. "What did she mean, *brief* me?"

"I shall show you the route you will travel and the landmarks you must memorize. Sit down, Mr. Shannow, and observe."

The screen flickered, and Shannow found himself staring out over a range of mountains thickly covered with pine.

Jacob Moon watched as the painted wagons moved slowly out of sight, the tall, slender blond woman riding the last of them. He hawked and spit. On another day he would have extracted a price for freeing the sandy-haired young man . . . Meredith? And the price would have been the woman Isis. Mostly Jacob Moon liked his women fat, but there was something about this girl that excited him. And he knew what it was: innocence and a fragile softness. He wondered if she was consumptive, for her skin was unnaturally pale and she had had, he noticed, difficulty climbing into the wagon. Turning away, he focused on more important matters.

Dillon's body lay in the undertaker's parlor, and the Jerusalem Man rode free somewhere in the mountains. The trackers had followed him but had lost the trail in the desert. Shannow and a companion had ridden their horses into a circle of stones and vanished. Moon shivered.

Could the man be an angel? Could the whole sorry Bible fairy tale be fact? No. He could not believe that. If God exists, then why does he not strike me down? Christ alive, I've killed enough people! He was quick enough to strike down Jenny, and she had never harmed anyone.

It's all random, he thought. A game of chance.

The strong survive; the weak die.

Bullshit! We all die someday.

The town was unnaturally quiet. The previous day's shooting had astonished them. True, Dillon had been a feared man, but more than that he had been full of life. A loud, powerful bull of a man radiating strength and certainty. Yet in the space of a few heartbeats he had been cut down by a stranger who had stood in the street and named their sins.

Jacob Moon had arrived in Domango three hours after the killing, when the hunters had just been returning. Then a rider had come in from the Hankin farm. Two more men dead. The Jerusalem Man? Probably, thought Moon.

Still, sooner or later he would have Shannow in his sights. Then that problem would be over.

Moon smiled and recalled the woman. With Dillon's blood still staining the street, she had walked into the Crusader office and approached him. "I understand, sir, that you are a Jerusalem Rider." Moon had nodded, his hooded eyes raking the slender lines of her body. "My name is Isis. I have come to you for justice, sir. Our doctor, Meredith, has been wrongly imprisoned. Would you release him?"

Moon had leaned back in his chair and thrown a glance at the stocky Crusader standing by the gun rack. The man cleared his throat. "They're Movers," he said. "They come in beggin'."

"That is not true," said Isis. "Doctor Meredith merely erected a sign saying that he was a doctor and inviting people to visit him."

"We already got a doctor," snapped the Crusader.

"Let him go," said Moon.

The Crusader stood silent for a moment, then lifted a ring of keys from a hook by the gun rack and moved back through to the rear of the building.

"I thank you, sir," said Isis. "You are a good man."

Moon smiled then, but he said nothing. He glanced up as the Crusader brought out Meredith, a tall young man with sandy hair and a weak face. Moon wondered if he was the girl's lover and idly pictured them coupling. "They knew Dillon's killer," said the Crusader. "That's a fact."

Moon turned his stare to the woman. "He was wounded," she said. "We found him near to death and nursed him. Then, later, when we were attacked, he fought off the raiders." Moon nodded but remained silent. "Then he killed the Oath Taker from Purity. After that he rode away. I don't know where."

"Did he say his name?" asked Moon.

"Yes. He said he was Jon Shannow. Our leader, Jeremiah, thinks the wound to his head has confused him. He has no memory, you see. He cannot remember who shot him or why. Jeremiah believes he has taken refuge in the identity of the Jerusalem Man."

The sandy-haired young man stepped alongside Isis, putting his arm around her shoulder. The action annoyed Moon, but he remained silent. "The mind is very complex," said Meredith. "It is likely that his memories of childhood included many stories about Shannow. Now that he is an amnesiac, the mind is trying to piece together those memories. Hence his belief that he is the fabled Jerusalem Man."

"So," said Moon softly, "he does not remember where he is from?"

"No," said Isis. "He struck me as a lonely man. Will you treat him with understanding when you find him?"

"You can rely on that," promised Jacob Moon.

Shannow watched the screen, noting landmarks and listening as Lucas talked of the lands of the Bloodstone. Mostly the terrain was unfamiliar to Shannow, but occasionally he would see in the distance the shape of a mountain that seemed to strike a chord in his memory.

"You must remember, Mr. Shannow, that this is a world gone mad. Those disciples who follow the Bloodstone receive great gifts, but for the vast majority the future is only to die to serve his hunger. We will not have long to find Samuel Archer. The jeep will get us within range within a day. We will then have perhaps another twenty-four hours to save him."

"Jeep?" queried Shannow.

"The vehicle outside. It can travel at around sixty miles per hour over difficult terrain. And no Devourer or horseman will catch it."

Shannow said nothing for a moment. Then: "You can see many places and many people."

"Yes, I have extensive files," agreed Lucas.

"Then show me Jon Shannow."

"Amaziga does not wish you to see your past, Mr. Shannow."

"The lady's wishes are not at issue. I am asking *you* to show me."

"What would you like to see?"

"I know who I was twenty years ago, when I fought the lizard-men and sent the Sword of God through to destroy Atlantis. But what happened then? How did I use those years? And why am I still relatively young?"

"Wait for a moment," said Lucas. "I will assemble the information."

Shannow immediately felt a sensation he had long forgotten, and it surprised him. His stomach trembled, and he could feel his heart beating wildly. In that moment nameless terrors seemed to be clawing at him from deep within his mind, and he realized with a sickening certainty that he did not want to know. His mouth was dry, and he found himself breathing too quickly, becoming dizzy. The desire rose in him to stop the machine, to command it to silence. "I will not be a coward," he whispered. Gripping the arms of the chair, he sat rigid as the screen flickered and he saw himself on a tower of rock, the Sword of God blazing across the sky. The man on the rock slumped down, his black and silver beard darkening.

"That," came Lucas's voice, "is the moment when you regained youth. The last fractions of Sipstrassi power seeping through the tower, regenerating aging tissue." The scene shifted to Pilgrim's Valley, and Shannow watched as the preacher Jon Cade gave his first sermon, listened to the words and the message of hope and peace. Beth McAdam was sitting in the front row, her eyes on the speaker, the light of love shining in them.

Sadness engulfed the Jerusalem Man . . . the sadness of love, the grief of bereavement. His love for Beth came roaring from his subconscious to rip at his heart. Forcing himself to stare at the screen, he watched the passing of the years, saw himself struck down by Shem Jackson, and felt again the numbing shame that came from having the strength to walk away. He heard once more the man's scornful laughter behind him.

At the last he saw the burning of the church and the murder of the Wolvers. "Enough," he said softly. "I want to see no more."

"You remember it?" asked the machine.

"I remember it."

"You are a man of extremes, Mr. Shannow, and great inner strength. You cannot walk the middle ground, and you have never learned how to compromise. You became a preacher, and you preached of love and understanding—at its best a gentle doctrine. You could not be a man of violence and preach such a doctrine; therefore, you put aside your guns and *lived* it, using the same iron control that you enjoyed as a brigand slayer."

"But it was a fraud," said Shannow. "I was living a lie."

"I doubt that. You gave it everything you could—even to losing the woman you loved. That is a commitment beyond most men. Even iron, however, can be ripped apart. When the raiders burned the church, the iron gave way. You pursued them and slew them. The mind is a very sensitive creature, Mr. Shannow. To all intents and purposes you had betrayed everything you had stood for during those twenty years. So the mind, in self-protection, threw the memories of those years into a box and held it from your view. The question is, Now that the box has been opened, who are you? Are you Jon Cade, preacher and man of God, or are you Jon Shannow, fearless killer?"

Shannow ignored the question and rose. "Thank you, Lucas. You have been of great service to me."

"It was my pleasure, Mr. Shannow."

Outside the light was beginning to fade, the desert heat abating. Shannow wandered to the paddock and climbed to the fence, watching the four horses cropping grass. They were standing in two pairs, nose to tail, protecting each other's faces from the swarms of flies that surrounded them.

He drew one of the long, blue-barreled pistols.

The question is, Now that the box has been opened, who are you? Are you Jon Cade, preacher and man of God, or are you Jon Shannow, fearless killer?

As Nestor Garrity and Clem Steiner were riding toward Purity and Jon Shannow stood alone on the streets of Domango, the Apostle Saul urged his tired mount toward the ruined city.

Saul was seething with suppressed fury. Word had reached him that the Deacon had survived Moon's attack, that the man killed had been Geoffrey, the Deacon's secretary. The council in Unity was in turmoil. The Deacon was missing.

Missing! My God, thought Saul, what if he knows it was me?

A mosquito stung Saul's right leg, and he slapped it angrily, the sound causing the horse to shy. He swore. The heat was unbearable, and stinking horse sweat had seeped through his trousers. His back ached from hours in the saddle, and the ancient city seemed no closer. He swore again.

The Deacon was alive! Josiah Broome was alive! Jon Shannow was alive! It was all coming to nothing, all the years of careful planning unraveling before his eyes.

I've always been cursed, he thought, remembering his childhood in Chicago, the taunts he had taken from his fellow schoolchildren over his lack of size and his weasel features, the mockery from girls who would not be seen dead with a "runt like you." And always in his work there were others who would succeed, moving past him on the promotional ladder, men and women with far less talent. Always it was Saul Wilkins who was overlooked. Little Saul.

It was not as if he did not play the game. He sucked up to those above him, laughed at their jokes, supported their endeavors, and worked hard to be as good as anyone. Yet never did he gain the recognition he craved.

Now it was happening again, this time to the tall, hand-some, golden-haired Apostle Saul. Overlooked by the Deacon, he had for the first time in his life planned for the great gamble. And he was failing.

As he had always failed . . .

No, not always, he thought. There had been the golden time at the tabernacle when he had first found God. Laid off from his job in the north, Saul had moved to Florida. One Thursday afternoon late in February he had been driving along I-4 West and had pulled in for a coffee at a fast-food outlet. There had been a trailer parked there, and several young people had been handing out leaflets. A girl had offered one to Saul. It was an invitation to a Bible picnic being held near Kissimmee the following Sunday. The girl's smile had been radiant, and she had called him "Brother."

That Sunday Saul had attended the picnic with some three hundred other people. He had enjoyed himself, and the sermon from the fat preacher had touched a chord in him with its emphasis on the meek and the lowly. God's love was very special for them.

Short of friends, his layoff money running out, Saul had joined the small church. It had been the happiest time of his life, especially after the Deacon had arrived and appointed him as full-time church treasurer. Jason had been set for the role, had coveted it, and he was tall and handsome. Saul had been convinced that yet again he would be overlooked. But no. The Deacon had called him in and calmly offered him the post. Jason, bitter and vengeful, had quit the church.

Good days. Great days, Saul realized.

Then had come the fateful flight and the end of the world he had known. Even then there were joys ahead, the gifts of the Sipstrassi, a handsome body, endless women.

I had it all, thought Saul. But the Sipstrassi was running out, the Deacon was getting older, and soon it would all end. Without the Sipstrassi I would be little Saul Wilkins again, bald and bent, peering at the world through watery eyes. Who would take me seriously? What would I do?

The answer was simple. Become rich in this new world. Take control like the hard, ruthless men of the old world.

Control land and resources, oil, silver, gold. And all the while search for Sipstrassi.

The Deacon had found his hoard soon after arriving. He had ridden off into the wild lands and returned with a bag of stones.

Oh, God, thought Saul, there must have been thirty of them! He had asked him where he had found them.

"On my travels," the Deacon had answered with a smile.

Then, the previous year, a man had come to Unity who claimed to know the Deacon. He had been ushered into Saul's office. He was an old prospector who said he had met the Deacon during his wanderings in the land beyond the Wall. "Whereabouts?" Saul had asked.

"Near Pilgrim's Valley—you know," the man had said, "where the Lord guided your flying machine to land."

Somewhere near here the Deacon had discovered the stones of power.

There must be more! Please God, let there be more!

With enough Sipstrassi he could still gain power. Just five stones! Three. Dear God, help me find them!

He was close enough to see the towering columns of stone that marked the southern gate of the Atlantean city. One was taller than the other, reaching almost sixty feet. Once there had been a lintel stone between them, but it had fallen to the paved area below, shattering into fragments.

For several moments Saul forgot his mission as he gazed over the miles and miles of what had once been a magnificent city. There were statues in marble, mostly toppled and broken, but some remaining still on their plinths, stone eyes staring at this latest observer of their silent grief. Many of the buildings were still standing, seemingly untouched by thousands of years on the ocean floor. Saul rode on, his horse's hooves clattering on the paved streets, the sound echoing eerily.

The Deacon had told him that there was an ancient king of Atlantis named Pendarric. It was he who had brought about the doom of his people, the earth toppling, drowning the empire under a tidal wave of colossal proportions.

Saul rode his tired mount up a long hill, toward a multi-turreted palace. The horse was breathing heavily, its flanks white with foaming sweat. At the top he dismounted and tethered the poor creature in the sunshine. The horse stood with its head hung low. Ignoring the beast's discomfort, Saul strode into the palace. The floor was covered in thick dry dust that had once been silt. Close to the windows, where the wind had blown away the dust, Saul could see evidence of an elaborate mosaic on the floor, deep blues and reds in shifting patterns. There was no furniture or any sign of wood. That had long since been destroyed, probably adding to the dust. But there were statues of warriors in breastplates and helms, reminding Saul of pictures he had seen of Greek soldiers during the battle for Troy.

He walked on through many doorways until he came to a vast, round hall at the center of which stood a circle of beautifully crafted rectangular stones standing vertically. The dust was everywhere, and as he walked, it rose up around him, drying his throat and causing him to cough.

Slowly he searched the hall but found nothing except the golden hilt of a ceremonial dagger, which he dropped into the pocket of his coat. Returning to the horse, he took a drink from his canteen. From there he could see even more powerfully the vastness of this ancient city. Ruins as far as the eye could see, stretching in all directions.

Despair touched him. Even if the stones are here, how will I find them?

Then an idea came to him. It was brilliant in its simplicity, and although he did not know it, Saul Wilkins had arrived at a conclusion that had evaded thousands of brilliant men in the past. He licked his lips and fought to control his rising excitement.

Sipstrassi power could do anything! Could it not therefore be used like a magnet, calling upon other stones, drawing them to it or at the very least guiding him to where they lay hidden?

Saul delved into his pocket, pulling clear the stone. Only three threads of gold remained. Would they be enough? And where to test his theory?

The stones were too powerful to have been owned by many people in the city. Only the rich would have had access, and the man who had owned this palace must have been rich indeed.

The circular hall was at the very center of the building. That is where to begin, thought Saul. Hurrying back through the empty palace, he made his way to the center of the circle of stones. There he paused. How to use the power? Think, man!

Clenching the stone tightly in his fist, he pictured a full golden stone and willed it to come to him. Nothing happened. The stone in his fist did not grow warm, as was usual when power was drawn from it. What he could not know was that there was no Sipstrassi left in that ancient ruin. He tightened his grip. A small, sharp fragment of the stone bit into his palm. Saul swore and opened his fingers. A tiny bead of blood swelled there, touching the stone. The bright yellow threads darkened, turning red-gold in the dim light.

But now the stone was warm. Saul tried again. Holding up his fist, he willed the stone to seek out its fellows. And the new Bloodstone obeyed, sending its power through the gateway of the circle.

Violet light filled the air around him. Saul was exultant: it was working! The light was blinding, and when it cleared, he saw a strange scene. Some thirty yards away a powerful man was sitting on a huge golden throne, staring directly at Saul. The man's skin was deep red and seemed to be decorated with thin black lines. Saul glanced over his shoulder. Behind him everything was as it should be, the stone circle and the dust-covered hall. But ahead was this curious man.

"Who are you?" asked the tattooed man, his voice rich and deep.

"Saul Wilkins."

"Saul . . . Wilkins," echoed the man. "Let me read your mind, Saul Wilkins." Saul felt a curious warmth creep into his head, flowing through him. When it finally receded, he felt lost and alone. "I don't need you, Saul Wilkins," said the tattooed man. "I need Jacob Moon."

A shape reared up before Saul, obscuring his view. He had

a fraction of a second to register sleek gray fur, bloodred eyes, and yellow-stained fangs in a gaping maw. There was no time to scream. Talons ripped into his chest, and the terrible mouth opened before him, the fangs closing on his face.

◇ **9** ◇

A wise man and a fool were lost in the desert. The one knew nothing of desert life and soon became thirsty and disoriented. The other had grown up in the desert. He knew that often a man could find water by digging at the lowest point of the outside bend of a dry streambed. This he did, and the two drank.

The one who had found the water said to his companion, "Which of us is the wise man now?"

"I am," said the other. "For I brought you with me into the desert, whereas you chose to travel with a fool."

The Wisdom of the Deacon
Chapter VI

AMAZIGA MET HER son at the crossroads outside Domango. She smiled as he rode up and waved. He was a handsome man, more slender than his father but with a natural grace and confidence that filled Amaziga's heart with pride.

"You have him safe?" asked Gareth, leaning across his saddle to kiss Amaziga's cheek.

"Yes. And ready."

"You should have seen him, Mother, striding out onto the street and calling out Dillon. Amazing!"

"He's a killer. A savage," snapped Amaziga, irritated by the admiration she saw in Gareth.

Gareth shrugged. "Dillon was the savage. Now he's dead. Do not expect me to mourn for him."

"I don't. What I also do not expect is for a son of mine to hero-worship a man like Jon Shannow. But then, you are a

176

strange boy, Gareth. Why, with your education in the *modern* world, would you choose to live here of all places?"

"It is exciting."

She shook her head in exasperation and swung her horse. "There's not much time," she said. "We had better get moving."

They rode swiftly back to the stone circle. Amaziga lifted her stone, and violet light flared around them.

The house appeared, and the two riders moved down toward the paddock. Shannow was sitting on the fence as they approached. He looked up and nodded a greeting.

Amaziga swung down and opened the paddock gate. "Unsaddle the horses," she ordered Gareth. "I'll load up the jeep."

"No jeep," said Shannow, climbing down from the fence.

"What?"

"We will ride through."

"That jeep can move three times as fast as the horses. Nothing in the world of the Bloodstone can catch it."

"Even so, we don't take it," said the Jerusalem Man.

Amaziga's fury broke clear. "Who the hell do you think you are? I am in command here, and you will do as I say."

Shannow shook his head. "No," he said softly, "you are not in command here. If you wish me to accompany you, then saddle fresh horses. Otherwise be so kind as to return me to the world I know."

Amaziga bit back an angry retort. She was no fool; she heard the iron in his voice and swiftly changed tack. "Listen, Shannow, I know you do not understand the workings of the . . . vehicle, but trust me. We will be far safer with it than on horseback. And our mission is too vital to take unnecessary risks."

Shannow stepped closer and gazed down into her dark brown eyes. "This entire enterprise is an unnecessary risk," he said, his voice cold, "and were I not bound by my word, I would leave you to it without a moment's hesitation. But understand this, woman. I will lead; you and your son will follow that lead. You will obey without question . . . and that begins now. Choose your horses."

Before Amaziga could respond, Gareth spoke up. "Is it all right if I keep this mount, Mr. Shannow?" he asked. "She's a stayer and is still fresh."

Shannow's eyes raked the buckskin, then he nodded. "As you will," he said, and without another word he moved away, walking toward the open desert.

Amaziga swung on her son. "How could you side with him?"

"Why keep a dog if you are going to bark yourself?" answered Gareth, stepping down from the saddle. "You say he is a killer and a savage. Everything I know about the Jerusalem Man tells me that he is a survivor. Yes, he is hard and ruthless, but where we are going we will need a man like that. No disrespect, Mother. You are a fine scientist and a wonderful dinner companion. But on this venture I guess I would sooner follow the tall man. Okay?"

Amaziga masked her anger and forced a smile. "He's wrong about the jeep."

"I'd sooner ride, anyway," said Gareth.

Amaziga strode into the house and on to her room. From a closet by the far wall she removed a shoulder rig to which two small silver and black boxes were attached. Swinging it over her shoulder, she clipped it to her black leather belt, then attached two leads to the first box, which nestled against her waist on the left-hand side. Connecting the other ends of the leads into the second box, she clipped this to the back of her belt, alongside a leather scabbard containing four clips of ammunition for the nine-shot Beretta holstered at her hip. Returning to the outer room, she pulled a fresh set of leads from the drawer beneath the computer and attached them first to the back of the machine and then to the small box at her belt.

"You are angry," said Lucas.

"The batteries should last around five days. Long enough, I think," she said, ignoring the question. "Are you ready for transfer?"

"Yes. You are of course aware that I cannot load all my files into your portable? I will be of limited use."

"I like your company," she said with a wide smile. "Now, are you ready?"

"Of course. And you have not connected the microphone."

"It's like living with a maiden aunt," said Amaziga, looping a set of headphones around her neck. The transfer of files took just under two minutes. Lifting the headphones into place, she flipped out the curved stick of the microphone. "Can you hear me?" she asked.

"I dislike not being able to see," came Lucas's voice, as if from a great distance.

Amaziga adjusted the volume. "One thing at a time, dear heart," she said. The fiber-optic camera had been designed to fit neatly into a black headband; the leads connected to a set of tiny batteries contained in the shoulder rig. Settling it into place, she engaged the batteries.

"Better," said Lucas. "Move your head to the left and right." Amaziga did so. "Excellent. Now, will you tell me why you are angry?"

"Why should I tell you something you already know?"

"Gareth was correct," said Lucas. "Shannow is a survivor. He is an untutored clairvoyant. His gift lies in reading signs of danger before that danger has materialized."

"I know about his skills, Lucas. That's why I am using him."

"Look down," Lucas told her.

"What? Why?"

"I want to see your feet."

Amaziga chuckled and bent her head low. "Aha," said Lucas. "As I thought, trainers. You would be advised to wear boots."

"I am already hip-deep in wires and leads. The trainers are comfortable. Now, do you have any other requests?"

"It would be nice if you were to walk to the saguaro where the elf owl is nesting. The camera on the roof cannot quite traverse far enough for a good study."

"When we get back," she promised. "For now I'd like you to concentrate on the lands of the Bloodstone—if it is not too much trouble. You'll need to rethink the route and the place and the time of entry. Without the jeep it'll take a damn sight longer."

"I never liked jeeps," said Lucas.

Josiah Broome awoke to see the old man cleaning two long-barreled pistols. Pain lanced through Broome's chest, and he groaned.

Jake glanced up. "Despite how you feel, you will live, Josiah," he said.

"It wasn't a dream?" whispered Broome.

"It surely wasn't. Jersualem Riders tried to kill you and shot Daniel Cade in the process. Now you are a wanted man. Shoot on sight, they've been told." Broome struggled to a sitting position. Dizziness swamped him. "Don't do too much now, Josiah," insisted Jake. "You've lost a lot of blood. Take it slow and easy. Here . . ." Jake laid aside the pistol and lifted a steaming jug from the coals of the fire. Filling a tin mug, he passed it to Broome, who took it with his left hand. The old man returned to his place and lifted the pistol, flipping out the cylinder and loading it.

"What am I going to do?" asked Broome. "Who will believe me?"

"It won't matter, Son," said Jake. "Trust me on that."

"How can you say that?" asked Broome, astonished.

Jake returned the pistols to two deep shoulder holsters and reached for a short-barreled rifle, which he also began to load, pressing shell after shell into the side gate. When he had finished, he pumped the action and laid the weapon aside.

"Sometime soon," he said, his voice low, "people will forget all about the shooting; they'll be too concerned with just staying alive. And against what's coming that won't be easy. You were there when the Daggers invaded. But they were an army of soldiers. They had orders. They were disciplined. But a terror is about to be unleashed that is almost beyond understanding. That's why I'm here, Josiah. To fight it."

Josiah Broome understood none of it. All he could think of was the terrible events of the previous day, the murder of Daniel Cade, and the pain-filled flight into the night. Is the old man insane? he wondered. He seemed rational. The pain in his chest settled to a dull, throbbing ache, and the dawn breeze chilled his upper body. He shivered. The bandages around his thin chest were caked with dried blood, and any movement of his right arm sent waves of nausea through him.

"Who are you?" he asked the old man.

"I am the Deacon," said Jake, emptying out the jug and stowing it in a cavernous pack.

For a moment all Broome's pain was forgotten, and he stared at the man with undisguised astonishment. "You can't be" was all he could say, taking in the man's threadbare trousers and worn boots, the ragged sheepskin coat, and the matted white hair and beard.

Jake smiled. "Don't be deceived by appearances, Son. I am who I say I am. Now, we've got to get you to Beth McAdam's place. I need to speak to the lady." Jake hoisted the pack to his shoulders, hefted his rifle, then moved over to Broome and helped him to his feet. Wrapping a blanket around the wounded man's upper body, Jake steered him out into the open, where the mule was hobbled. "You ride, I'll lead," said the old man. With great difficulty Broome climbed to the saddle.

An eerie howl echoed in the trees, and Jake stiffened. It was answered by another some way to the east . . . then another.

Broome noted the sound, but compared with the pain from his chest wound and the pounding that had begun in his head, it seemed unimportant. Then he heard two gunshots in the distance, followed by a piercing scream of terror, and he jerked in the saddle. "What was that?" he asked.

Jake did not reply. Slipping the hobble from the mule's forelegs, he took the reins in his left hand and began the long descent down into the wooded valley.

The Deacon moved on warily, leading the mule and glancing back often at the wounded man. Broome was semidelirious, and the man called Jake had lashed his wrists to the pommel of the saddle. The day was bright and clear, and there was no discernible breeze. The Deacon was thankful for that. The pack was heavy, as was the rifle, and he was mortally tired. The descent into the valley was slow, and he paused often, listening and scanning the trees.

Death stalked the mountains now, and he knew the Devourers were fast and lethal. He would have little time to bring the rifle to bear. Every now and then the Deacon glanced at the mule. She was a canny beast and would pick up their scent much faster than he could. At the moment she was moving easily, head down, ears up, contentedly following his lead.

With luck they would make Beth McAdam's farm by sunset. But what then?

How do you defeat a god of blood?

The Deacon did not know. What he did know was that the pain in his chest was intense and that his old and weary body was operating at the outer edge of its limits. For the first time in years he was tempted to use the stone on himself, rejuvenating his ancient muscles, repairing the time-damaged heart.

It would be so good to feel young again, full of energy and purpose, infused with the passion and belief of youth. And the speed, he realized. That could be vital.

The mule stopped suddenly, jerking the Deacon back. He swung and saw her head come up, her eyes widen in fear. Slipping the pack from his shoulders, he hefted the rifle and moved back to stand beside the mule's head. "It's all right, girl," he said, his voice soft and soothing. "Steady, now!"

He noticed that an easterly breeze had picked up. The mule had caught the scent of the man-wolves. Leaving the pack where it lay, the Deacon scrambled up behind Broome and kicked the mule into a run. She needed no further encouragement and set off down the slope at breakneck speed. As Broome swayed to his left, the Deacon's left arm caught him, hauling him upright.

The mule thundered on. When a gray shape reared from the right of the trail, the Deacon lifted the rifle like a pistol and loosed a shot that caught the beast high on the shoulder, spinning it. Then the mule was past and onto level ground, racing out into the valley.

They crossed the gateway at midnight, the air cool, the stars glittering above them, and emerged seconds later into the bright sunshine of an autumn morning. The stone circle into which they had traveled was almost completely overgrown by dense bush, and they were forced to dismount and force a way through to open ground some fifty yards to the left.

Amaziga spoke softly into the microphone. Shannow could not hear the words, but he saw her lift the timepiece on her wrist and make adjustments. She saw him watching her. "Lucas says it is 8:45 A.M., and we have two days to reach the Mardikh mountains, where Sam and his group are holding out. It is forty-two miles from here, but the ground is mostly level."

Shannow nodded and stepped into the saddle. Gareth rode alongside him. "I am grateful to you, Mr. Shannow," he said. "It is not every day that a man is given the opportunity to bring his father back from the dead."

"As I understand it," said Shannow, "he is not your father, merely a man who carries the same face and name."

"And an identical genetic structure. Why did you come?"

Shannow ignored the question and rode toward the north, Amaziga and Gareth falling in behind. They pushed on through the day, stopping only once to eat a cold meal. The land was vast and empty, the distant blue mountains seeming no nearer. Twice they passed deserted homes, and in the distance, toward dusk, Shannow saw a cluster of buildings that had once made up a small town on the eastern slopes of a narrow valley. There was no sign of life, no lanterns burning, no movement.

As the light began to fade, Shannow turned off the trail and up into a stand of pine, seeking a place to camp. The land rose sharply, and ahead of them a cliff face ran south to north. A narrow waterfall gushed over basaltic rock, the fading sunlight casting rainbows through the spray and a rippling stream flowing on toward the plain.

Shannow dismounted and loosened the saddle cinch. "We could make at least another five miles," said Amaziga, but he ignored her, his keen eyes picking up a flash of red in the undergrowth some sixty yards beyond the falls. Leaving the horse with trailing reins, he waded across the narrow stream and climbed the steep bank beyond. Gareth followed him.

"Jesus Christ!" whispered Gareth as he saw the crushed and ruined remains of a red jeep.

"Do not take His name in vain," said Shannow. "I do not like profanity."

The jeep was lying on its back, the roof twisted and bent. One door had been ripped clear, and Shannow could see the marks of talons scoring through the red paint and the thin steel beneath it. He glanced up. Torn and broken foliage on the cliff above the jeep showed that it had fallen from the cliff top and bounced several times against sharp outcrops before landing there. Ducking down, he pulled aside the bracken and peered into the interior. Gareth knelt alongside him.

Inside the jeep was a crushed and twisted body. All that could be seen was an outflung arm, half-severed. The arm was black, the blood-soaked shirtsleeve olive-green with a thin gray stripe. Gareth's shirt was identical.

"It's me," said Gareth. "It's me!"

Shannow rose and moved to the other side of the wreck. Glancing down, he saw huge paw prints in the soft earth and a trail of dried blood leading into the undergrowth. Drawing a pistol and cocking it, he followed the trail and twenty yards farther on found the remains of a grisly feast. Lying to the left was a small box, twisted, torn wires leading from it. Easing the hammer forward, he holstered his pistol, then picked up the blood-spattered box and walked back to where Gareth was still staring down at the body.

"Let's go," said the Jerusalem Man.

"We've got to bury him."

"No."

"I can't just leave him there!"

Hearing the anguish in the young man's voice, Shannow moved alongside him, laying a hand on his shoulder. "There are hoof marks around the vehicle as well as signs of the Devourers. If any of the riders return and find the corpses buried, they will know that others have passed this way. You understand? We must leave them as they are."

Gareth nodded, then his head flicked up. "Corpses? There is only one, surely."

Shannow shook his head and showed Gareth the blood-spattered box.

"I don't understand . . ." the young man whispered.

"Your mother will," Shannow said, as Amaziga strode to join them. He watched her as she examined the jeep, her face impassive. Then she saw the box, identical to the one she had strapped to her belt, and her dark eyes met Shannow's gaze.

"Where is her body?" she asked.

"There is not much of a body left. The Devourers lived up to their name. A part of the head remains, enough to identify it."

"Is it safe to remain here?"

"Nowhere in this land is safe, lady. But it offers concealment for the night."

"I take it the twin of your body is not here, Mr. Shannow?"

"No," he said.

She nodded. "Then she chose to undertake the mission without you, obviously a mistake which she paid for dearly."

Amaziga turned away and returned to the horses as Gareth approached Shannow. "That's the closest she'll ever come to saying you were right about the jeep," said the young man, attempting a smile. "You're a wise man, Shannow."

The Jerusalem Man shook his head. "The wise man was the Jon Shannow who *didn't* travel with them."

Gareth took the first watch, a thick blanket around his shoulders against the cool night breeze. He was sitting on a wide branch that must have snapped in a recent storm. The sight of the body in the jeep had unnerved him as nothing else had in his young life. He *knew* the dead man better than he knew anyone, understood the hopes and dreams and fears the man had entertained or endured. And he could not help wondering what had gone through his twin's mind as the jeep had crashed over the cliff. Despair? Terror? Anger? Had he been alive after the fall? Had the Devourers forced their way in and torn at his helpless body?

The young black man shivered and glanced to where Shannow slept peacefully beneath a spreading elm. This quest had seemed like an adventure to Gareth Archer, yet another exciting experience in his rich, full young life. The prospect of danger had been enticing. But to see his own corpse! Death was something that happened to other people . . . not to him. Nervously he glanced across at the ruined jeep.

The night was cold, and he noticed that his hands were trembling. He glanced at his watch: two more hours before he woke his mother. She had seemed unfazed by the tragedy that had befallen their twins, and just for a moment Gareth found himself envious of her calm. Amaziga had spread out her blanket, removed the boxes and headphones, and passed them to her son. "Lucas's camera has an infrared capacity," she had said. "Don't leave it on for long. We must conserve the batteries. Two minutes every half hour should be sufficient." Now she, too, seemed to be sleeping.

Gareth pressed the button on the box. "You are troubled," whispered Lucas's voice, sounding tinny and small through the earphones.

Gareth flipped the microphone into place. "What can you see?" he asked, turning his head slowly, giving the tiny camera on the headband a view of the plain below.

"Move your head to the right—about an inch," ordered Lucas.

"What is it?" Gareth's heart began to pound, and he slipped his Desert Eagle automatic from its shoulder holster.

"A beautiful spotted owl," said Lucas. "It's just caught a small lizard." Gareth swore. "There is nothing on the plain to concern you," the machine chided him. "Calm yourself."

"Easy for you to say, Lucas. You haven't seen your own corpse."

"As a matter of fact, I have. I watched the original Lucas collapse with a heart attack. However, that is beside the point. Your resting heartbeat is currently 133 beats per minute. That is very close to panic, Gareth. Take some long, slow deep breaths."

"It is 133 beats faster than the poor son of a bitch in the jeep," snapped the young man. "And it is not panic. I've never panicked in my life. I won't start now."

A hand touched his shoulder, and Gareth lurched upright. "One hundred sixty-five beats," he heard Lucas whisper, and he spun around to see Amaziga standing calmly behind him.

"I said use the machine," she told him, "not get into an argument with it." She held out her hand. "Let me have Lucas, and then you can get some sleep."

"I've another two hours yet."

"I'm not tired. Now do as you're told."

He grinned sheepishly and carefully removed the headband and boxes. Amaziga laid aside her Uzi and clipped the machine to her shoulder rig. Gareth moved to his blanket and lay down. The Desert Eagle dug into his waist, and easing it clear, he laid it alongside him.

Amaziga turned off the machine and walked to the edge of the trees, staring out over the moonlit landscape. Nothing moved, and there were no sounds except the rustling of leaves in the trees above her. She waited until Gareth was asleep and then waded back across the stream, past the ruined jeep, and onto the scene of the feast. The body—or what was left of it— was in three parts. The head and neck were resting against a boulder with the face—thankfully—turned away. Amaziga flicked on the machine.

"What are we looking for?" asked Lucas.

"I am carrying a Sipstrassi Stone. There is little power left. She should have an identical stone. Scan the ground."

Slowly she turned her head. "Can you see anything?"

"No. Nothing of interest. Traverse to the left . . . no . . . more slowly. Was it in the trouser pocket or the shirt?"

"Trouser."

"There's not much left of the legs. Perhaps one of the beasts ate the stone."

"Just keep looking!" snapped Amaziga.

"All right. Move to the right . . . *Amaziga!*" The tone in his voice made her blood grow cold.

"Yes?"

"I hope the weapon you are holding is primed and ready. There is a beast some fifteen meters to your right. He is around eight feet tall . . ."

Amaziga flipped the Uzi into position and spun. As a huge, gray form hurtled toward her, the Uzi fired, a long thunderous roar of sound exploding into the silence of the night. Bullets smashed into the gray chest, blood sprayed from the wounds, but still it came on. Amaziga's finger tightened on the trigger, emptying the long clip. The Devourer was flung backward, its chest torn open.

"Amaziga!" shouted Lucas. "There are two more!"

The Uzi was empty, and Amaziga scrabbled for the Beretta at her hip. Even as she did so, the beasts charged.

And she knew she was too slow . . .

"Down, woman!" bellowed Shannow.

Amaziga dived to her right. The booming sound of Shannow's pistol was followed by a piercing howl from the first Devourer, which pitched backward with half its head blown away. The second swerved past Amaziga and ran directly at the tall man at the edge of the trees. Shannow fired once; the creature slowed. A second shot ripped into its skull, and Amaziga was showered with blood and brains.

Shannow stepped forward, pistols raised.

Amaziga turned her head. "Are there any more of them?" she whispered to Lucas. There was no answer, and she saw that one of the leads had pulled clear of the right-hand box. She swore softly and pressed it home.

"Are you all right?" Lucas asked.

"Yes. What can you see?" asked Amaziga, turning slowly through a full circle.

"There are riders some four kilometers to the north, heading away from us. I can see no beasts. But the cliff face is high; there may be others on the higher ground. Might I suggest you reload your weapon?"

Switching off the machine, Amaziga rose unsteadily to her feet. Shannow handed her the Uzi just as Gareth came running onto the scene, his Desert Eagle automatic in his hand.

"Thank you, Shannow," said Amaziga. "You got here very fast."

"I was here all the time," he told her. "I followed you across the stream."

"Why?"

He shrugged. "I felt uneasy. And now, if you'll excuse me, I'll leave you to your watch."

"Son of a bitch," said Gareth, staring down at the three dead beasts. "They're huge!"

"And dead," Shannow pointed out as he strode past.

Gareth moved alongside Amaziga, who was pressing a full clip into the butt of the Uzi. "Jesus, but he's like an iceman . . ." He stopped speaking, and Amaziga saw his gaze fall on the moonlit head of the other Amaziga. "Oh, my God! Sweet Jesus!"

His mother took him by the arm, leading him away. "I'm alive, Gareth. So are you. Hold to that! You hear me?"

He nodded. "I hear you. But Christ . . ."

"No buts, my son! They are dead—we are not. They came to rescue Sam. They failed; we will not. You understand?"

He took a long, deep breath. "I won't let you down, Mother. You can trust me on that."

"I know. Now go get some sleep. I'll resume the watch."

Samuel Archer was not a religious man. If there was a God, he had long since decided, he was either willful or incompetent. Perhaps both. Yet Sam stood now on the crest of the hill and prayed. Not for himself, though survival would be more than pleasant, but for the last survivors of those who had followed him in the war against the Bloodstone. Behind him were the

remaining rebels, twenty-two in all, counting the women.
Before and below them on the plain were the Hellborn elite.
Two hundred warriors, their skills enhanced by the demonseeds embedded in their foreheads. Killers all! Sam glanced
around him. The rebels had picked a fine setting for their last
stand, high above the plain, the tree line and thick undergrowth
forming a rough stockade. The Hellborn would be forced to
advance up a steep slope in the face of withering volleys. With
enough ammunition we might even have held, thought Sam.
He glanced down at the twin ammunition belts draped across
his broad chest; there were more empty loops than full. Idly
he counted the remaining shells. From the breast pocket of
his torn gray shirt he drew a strip of dried beef, the last
of his rations.

There would be no retreat from there, Sam knew. Two hundred yards behind them the mountains fell away into a deep
gorge that opened out on to the edge of the Mardikh desert.
Even if they could climb down, without horses they would die
of thirst long before reaching the distant river.

Sam sighed and rubbed his tired eyes. For four years he had
fought the Bloodstone, gathering fighters, battling against
Hellborn warriors and Devourers. All for nothing. His own
small store of Sipstrassi was used up, and without it they could
not hope to hold off the killers. An ant crawled onto Sam's
hand. He brushed it away.

That's what we are, he thought, ants standing defiantly
before an avalanche.

Despair was a potent force and one Sam had resisted for
most of these four years. It had not been hard back at the
beginning. The remnants of the Guardians had gathered
against Sarento and had won three battles against the Hellborn. None had proved decisive. Then the Bloodstone had
mutated the Wolvers, and a new, terrible force had been
unleashed against the human race. Whole communities had
fled into the mountains to escape the beasts. The flight meant
that the Guardian army, always small, was now without supplies as farming communities disappeared in the face of the
Devourers. Ammunition was in short supply, and many fighters

left the army to travel to their homes in a vain bid to protect their families.

Now twenty-two were left. Tomorrow there would be none.

A young, beautiful olive-skinned woman approached Sam. She was tall and wore two pistols in shoulder holsters over a faded red shirt. Her jet-black hair was drawn tightly into a bun at the nape of her neck. He smiled as he saw her.

"I guess we've come to the end of a long, sorrowful road, Shammy. I'm sorry I brought you to this."

Shamshad Singh merely shrugged. "Here or at home . . . what difference? You fight or you die."

"Or do both," Sam said wearily.

She sat down beside him on the boulder, her short-barreled shotgun resting on her slim thighs. "Tell me of a happy time," she said suddenly.

"Any particular theme?" he asked. "I've lived for 356 years, so there is a lot to choose from."

"Tell me about Amaziga."

He gazed at her fondly. She was in love with him and had made it plain for the two years she had been with the rebels. Yet Sam had never responded to her overtures. In all his long life there had been only one woman who had opened the doors to his soul, and she was dead, shot down by the Hellborn in the first months of the war.

"You are an extraordinary woman, Shammy. I should have done better by you."

"Bullshit," she said with a wide smile. "Now tell me about Amaziga."

"Why?"

"Because it always cheers you up. And you need cheering."

He shook his head. "It has always struck me as particularly sad that there will come a point in a man's life where he has no second chances. When Napoleon saw his forces in full retreat at Waterloo, he knew there would never be another day when he would march out at the head of a great force. It was over. I always thought that must be hard to take. Now I know that it is. We have fought against a great evil, and we have been unable to defeat it. And tomorrow we die. It is not a time for happy stories, Shammy."

"You're wrong," she said. "At this moment I can still see the sky, feel the mountain breeze, smell the perfume of the pines. I am alive! And I luxuriate in that fact. Tomorrow is another day, Sam. We'll fight them. Who knows? Maybe we'll win. Maybe God will open up a hole in the sky and send His thunderbolts down on our enemies."

He chuckled then. "Most likely he'd miss and hit us."

"Don't mock, Sam," she chided him. "It is not for us to know what God intends."

"It baffles me, after all you've seen, how you can still believe in Him."

"It baffles me how you can't," she responded. The sun was dropping low on the horizon, bathing the mountains in crimson and gold.

Down in the valley the Hellborn had begun their campfires, and the sound of raucous songs echoed up in the mountains.

"Jered has scouted the gorge," said Shamshad. "The cliff face extends for around four miles. He thinks some of us could make the descent."

"That's desert down there. We'd have no way of surviving," said Sam.

"I agree. But it is an option."

"At least there are no Devourers," he said, returning his stare to the Hellborn camp.

"Yes, that is curious," she replied. "They all padded off late yesterday. I wonder where to."

"I don't care as long as it's not here," he told her with feeling. "How many shells do you have?"

"Around thirty. Another twenty for the pistol."

"I guess it will be enough," said Sam.

"I guess it will have to be," she agreed.

Amaziga watched as Gareth lifted the coils of rope from his saddle. The cliff face was sheer and some six hundred feet high, but it rose in a series of three ledges, the first around eighty feet above them, its glistening edge shining silver in the bright moonlight.

"What do you think?" asked Amaziga.

Gareth smiled. "Easy, Mother. Good hand- and footholds all the way. The only problem area is that high overhang above the top ledge, but I don't doubt I can traverse it. Don't worry. I've soloed climbs that are ten times more difficult than this." He turned to Shannow. "I'll go for the first ledge, then lower a rope to you. We'll climb in stages. How is your head for heights, Mr. Shannow?"

"I have no fear of heights," said the Jerusalem Man.

Gareth looped two coils of rope over his head and shoulder and stepped up to the face. The climb was reasonably simple until he reached a point, just below the ledge, where the rock had been worn away by falling water. He considered traversing to the right, then saw a narrow vertical crack in the face some six feet to his left. Easing his way to it, Gareth pushed his right hand high into the crack, then made a fist, wedging his hand against the rock. Tensing his arm, he pulled himself up another few feet. There was a good handhold to the left, and he hauled himself higher. Releasing the hand jam hold, he reached over the edge of the ledge and levered himself up. Swinging, he sat on the edge staring down at the small figures below. He waved.

Climbing was always so exhilarating. His first experience of it had been in Europe, in the Triffyn mountains of Wales. Lisa had taught him to climb, shown him friction holds and hand jams, and he had marveled at her ability to climb what appeared to be surfaces as smooth as polished marble. He remembered her with great affection and sometimes wondered why he had left her for Eve.

Lisa wanted marriage; Eve wanted pleasure. The thought was absurd. Are you really so shallow? he wondered. Lisa would have been a fine wife, strong, loyal, and supportive. But her love for him had been obsessive and, worse, possessive. Gareth had seen what such love could do, for he had watched his mother and lived with her single-minded determination all his life. I don't want that kind of love, he thought. Not ever!

Pushing such thoughts from his mind, Gareth stood and moved along the ledge. There was no jutting of rock to which he could belay the rope, providing friction to assist him in helping Shannow make the climb, but there was a small vertical crack. From his belt he unclipped a small clawlike object of shining steel. Pushing it into the crevice, he pulled the knob at its center. The claw flashed open, locking to the walls of the crack. Lifting one coil of rope clear, he slid the end through a ring of steel in the claw and lowered it to the waiting Shannow. Once the Jerusalem Man had begun the climb, Gareth looped the rope across his left shoulder and took in the slack.

Shannow made the climb without incident and levered himself over the ledge.

"How did you find it?" whispered Gareth.

Shannow shrugged. "I don't like the look of those clouds," he replied, keeping his voice low. Gareth tied the rope to his waist. Shannow was right. The sky was darkening, and they had still a fair way to go.

Lowering the rope once more, Gareth helped his mother make the climb. She was breathing heavily by the time she pushed herself up alongside them.

During the next hour the three climbers inched their way up to the last ledge. They were only forty feet from the top, but darkness had closed in around them and a light drizzle had begun, making the rock face slick and greasy. Gareth was worried. It had not been possible to see from the ground the slight overhang at this point. Climbing it would be difficult at the best of times, but in darkness, with the rain increasing?

For the third time Gareth prowled along the ledge, gazing up, trying to judge the best route. Nothing he could see filled him with encouragement. The rain slowed. He glanced down at the tiny, insect-sized shapes of the hobbled horses. To come this far and not be able to complete his mission—Jesus, Amaziga would never forgive him. He had long known that his mother did not love him, and he accepted her pride in him as a reasonable substitute. She would—could—never love anyone as she did her husband. That love was all-encompassing, all-consuming. As a child this had hurt Gareth, but in manhood he had come to understand the complexities and the bewildering brilliance of the woman who had borne him. If her pride was all he could have, then it would have to suffice. He stepped up to the face and reached up for the first handhold; it was no more than a groove in the rock, but he found a small foothold and levered himself up. Friction holds were vital on an overhang, but the young man's fingers were tired, the rock face slippery. Gareth's mouth was dry as he struggled to climb another fifteen feet. His foot slipped. He locked the fingers of his right hand to a small jutting section of rock and swung out over the six-hundred-foot drop. Panic touched him. He was hanging by one hand and unable to reach a second hold. Worse, he had moved out onto the overhang, and if he fell now, he would miss the first ledge. The drop to the second was more than eighty feet ... he would be smashed to pulp. Gareth's heart was pounding so hard that he could feel the pulse thudding at his temple. Twisting his body, he looked up at the face. There was a small hold around eighteen inches above the tiny piece of rock to which he clung. Taking a long, deep breath, he prepared himself for the surge of effort needed to reach it.

If you miss, you will be dislodged! Christ! Don't think like that! But he could not help it. His mind flew back to the other Gareth, dead in a crushed jeep.

And he knew he did not have the courage to make that last effort.

Oh, God, he thought. I'm going to die here!

Suddenly something pressed hard against the underside of his foot, taking the weight. Gareth looked down and saw that Shannow had climbed out onto the overhang. Now the two of them were out on the face, and if Gareth fell, he would carry the Jerusalem Man to his death.

Shannow's voice drifted up to him, calm and steady. "I can't hold you like this all night, boy. So I suggest you make a move."

Gareth lunged up, catching the hold and swinging his foot to a small ridge in the stone. Above there the holds were infinitely easier, and he gratefully hauled himself over the summit.

For a moment he lay back with eyes closed, feeling the rain on his face. Then he sat up, looped the rope over his shoulder, and tugged it twice, signaling Shannow to start the climb. The rope went tight. Gareth leaned back to take the strain.

Something cold touched his temple.

It was a pistol . . .

A hand moved into sight. It held a razor-sharp knife, which sliced through the rope.

Shem Jackson was sitting in the front room of his house, his booted feet resting on a table. His brother, Micah, idly shuffled a pack of dog-eared cards. "You wanna game, Shem?"

"For what?" responded the older man, lifting a jug of spirits and swigging from it. "You lost everything you got."

"You could lend me some," Micah said, reproachfully.

Shem slammed the jug down on the tabletop. "What the hell is the point of that? You play cards when you got money—it's that simple. Can't you get it into your head?"

"Well, what else is there to do?" whined Micah.

"And whose fault is that?" snapped Shem, pushing a dirty hand through his greasy hair. "She wasn't much to look at, but you had to go and thrash her, didn't you?"

"She asked for it!" replied Micah. "Called me names."

"Well, now she's run off. And this time it's for good, I'll bet. You know the trouble with you, Micah? You never know when you're well off."

Shem stood and stretched his lean frame. Rain could not be far away; his back was beginning to ache. Walking to the window, he stared out at the yard and the moonlit barn beyond. A flash of movement caught his eye, and, leaning forward, he rubbed at the grimy glass. It merely smeared, and Shem swore.

"What is it?" asked Micah.

Shem shrugged. "Thought I saw something out by the barn. It was probably nothing." He squinted, caught a flash of silver-gray fur. "It's Wolvers," he said. "Goddamn Wolvers!" Striding across the room, he lifted the long rifle down from its pegs over the mantel and, grinning, swung on Micah. "Damn sight more fun than playing cards with a loser like you," he said, pumping a shell into the breech. "Come on, get your weapon, man; there's hunting to be had."

Good humor flowed back to him. Little bastards, he thought. They won't get away this time. No Beth McAdam to save you now!

Stepping to the front door, he wrenched it open and walked out into the moonlight. "Come on, you little beggars, show yourselves!" he called. The night was quiet, the moon unbearably bright to the eye, a hunter's moon. Shem crept forward with the gun raised. He heard Micah move out behind him and stumble on the porch. Clumsy son of a bitch!

On open ground now, Shem angled to the right, toward the vegetable patch and the corral. "Show yourselves!" he shouted. "Old Uncle Shem's got a little present for you!"

Behind him Micah made a gurgling sound, and Shem heard the clump of something striking the ground. Probably his rifle, Shem thought as he turned.

But it was not a rifle. Micah's head bounced twice on the hard-packed earth, the neck completely severed by a savage sweep from a long-taloned hand. Micah's body toppled forward, but Shem was not looking at it. He was staring in paralyzed horror at the creature towering before him, its silver fur shining, its eyes golden, a bright red stone embedded in its forehead.

Shem Jackson's rifle came up, and he pulled the trigger. The bullet smashed into the creature's chest, sending up a puff of dust. But it did not go down; it howled and leapt forward, its talons flashing down. Shem felt the blow on his shoulder and staggered back. The rifle was on the ground. He blinked and then felt a rush of blood from his shoulder. There was no pain, not even when his arm fell clear, thumping against the ground and draping across his boot.

The Devourer lashed out once more . . .

Shem Jackson's face disappeared.

From the shadows scores more of the beasts moved forward. Several stopped to feed.

Most loped on toward the sleeping town of Pilgrim's Valley.

◇ **10** ◇

*The greatest folly is to believe that evil can be overcome
by reason. Evil is like gravity, a force that is beyond
argument.*

The Wisdom of the Deacon
Chapter XXVII

JACOB MOON WAS not given to hearing voices. Such gifts
were for other men. No visions, no prophecies, no mystic
dreams or revelations. Jacob Moon had only one real gift, if
such it could be called: he could kill without emotion. When
the voice did come, Moon was utterly astonished. He was sitting by his campfire in the lee of the Great Wall some twenty
miles from Pilgrim's Valley. Having heard nothing from the
Apostle Saul, Moon had left Domango and made the long ride
across the mountains. A flash flood had diverted him from his
course, delaying him, but he was now less than a three-hour
ride from the town. His horse was exhausted, and Moon made
camp beside the Wall.

The voice came to him just before midnight, as he was settling down to sleep. At first it was a whisper, like a breath of
night winds. But then it grew. *"Jacob Moon! Jacob Moon!"*

Moon sat up, pistol in hand. "Who's there?"

"Behind you," came the response, and Moon spun.

One of the great rectangular blocks had apparently disappeared, and he found himself facing a red-skinned man with
what appeared to be painted black lines across his face and
upper body. The man was seated on an ebony throne. Moon
cocked his pistol. "You will not need that," said the man on

the throne. The image drifted closer until the strange face filled the hole in the Wall: the eyes were the red of rubies, the whites bloodshot. "I need you, Moon," said the vision.

"Well, I don't need you," was Moon's response as the pistol bucked in his hand, the bullet lancing through the red face. There was no mark to show its passing, and a wide smile appeared on the face.

"Save your ammunition, Moon, and listen to what I offer you—riches beyond your dreams and life eternal. I can make you immortal, Moon. I can fulfill *your wildest desires*."

Moon sat back and sheathed his pistol. "This is a dream, isn't it? Goddamn it, I'm dreaming!"

"No dream, Moon," the red man told him. "Would you like to live forever?"

"I'm listening."

"My world is dying. I need another. A man known to you as Saul opened the gateway for me, and I have now seen your world. It is to my liking. But it would help me to have a lieutenant here to direct my . . . troops. From the few thoughts I could extract from the dying Saul, I gathered that you were that man. Is that so?"

"Tell me about the life eternal," said Moon, ignoring the question.

"That can begin now, Moon. Is it what you desire?"

"Aye." Moon reeled back as a terrible burning sensation erupted on his forehead. He cried out and lifted his hand to his head. The pain subsided as suddenly as it had appeared, and Moon could feel a small stone embedded in his brow.

"As long as you serve me, Moon, you will be immortal. Can you feel the new strength in your limbs, the power . . . the life?"

Jacob Moon felt more than that. His long-held bitterness was unleashed, his anger primal. As the vision had promised, he felt strong, no longer tired from his journey, no longer aching from long hours in the saddle. "I feel it," he admitted. "What do you want from me?"

"Ride to the ruined city north of Pilgrim's Valley. There I shall greet you."

"I asked what you wanted from me," said Moon.

"Blood," responded the vision. "Rivers of blood. Violence and death, hatred and war."

"Are you the Devil?" asked Moon.

"I am better than the Devil, Moon. For I have won."

Unknown to Gareth, it was his mother who had chosen to climb next, leaving Shannow on the ledge. When the rope suddenly gave, she was dislodged from the face. Many people faced with such a moment would have panicked, screamed, and fallen to their deaths. Amaziga was different.

She lived for only one prize—finding Sam.

In the moment the rope gave way and she slipped, her hand snaked out, fingers scrabbling against the wet stone. The first hold she grasped was not large enough to hold her, and she slipped again. Her fingers scraped down the rock, one fingernail tearing away, then her hand clamped over a firm hold and the descent ceased. She was hanging on the lower part of the overhang, her legs dangling below the curve of the rock. Her arm was tiring fast, and she could feel her grip loosening.

"Shannow!" she called. "Help me!"

A hand grabbed at her belt just as her fingers lost their grip, and she fell, but he dragged her back to the ledge. Slumping to her haunches, she leaned her head against the rock face and closed her eyes. The pain from her damaged hand was almost welcome: it told her she was alive.

Shannow hauled in the rope and examined the end.

"Someone cut it," he said.

Fear coursed through her. "Gareth!" she whispered.

"Maybe they took him alive," said Shannow, keeping his voice low. "The question is, What do we do now? We have enemies above and horses below."

"If they look over the edge, they will not be able to see us," she said. "They will assume we have fallen. I think we should make the climb." She saw Shannow smile.

"I don't know if I can, lady. I know you cannot—not with that injured hand."

"We can't just leave Gareth." She glanced at her watch.

"And there is only an hour left before they will kill Sam. We have no time to climb down and go around."

Shannow stood and prowled along the ledge. There was nowhere that he could climb. Amaziga joined him, and together they examined the face. Long minutes passed; then the sound of gunfire came from above them, heavy and sustained.

"You are right," she said at last, her voice heavy with despair. "There is nothing we can do."

"Wait," said Shannow. Lifting a pistol from his belt, he pushed the end of the rope through the trigger guard and tied it in place. Stepping to the edge of the ledge, he let out the rope, then began to swing it around and around. Amaziga looked up. Some twenty-five feet above them, at the narrowest point of the overhang, there was a jutting finger of stone. Shannow let out more rope and continued to swing the weighted end. Finally he sent it sailing up; the pistol clattered against the rock face, then dropped, looping the rope over the stone. Shannow lowered it, removed the pistol, and holstered it.

"You think it will take your weight?" asked Amaziga.

Shannow hauled down on the doubled rope three times. "Let us hope so," he said.

And he began to climb.

Gareth's anger was mounting. The olive-skinned woman had cut the rope and then ordered him to rise with his hands on his head. "Listen to me," he said, "I am here to—"

"Shut it!" she snapped, and he heard the pistol being cocked. "Walk forward and be aware I'm right behind you and have killed before." She did not rob him of his weapons, which spoke of either confidence or stupidity. Gareth guessed it to be confidence. He obeyed her and walked toward the clearing, where he could see around a score of men and women kneeling behind rocks or fallen trees, rifles in their hands. A tall black man turned as they approached.

"I found this *creature*," sneered the woman, "climbing the cliff face behind us. There were others, but I cut the rope."

"Indeed she did," said Gareth, "and probably killed one of the few friends you had in this world, Sam."

The black man's eyes widened. "Do I know you, boy?"

"In a manner of speaking." The sky was lightening with the predawn, and the rain had cleared. "Look at me closely, Sam. Who do I remind you of?"

"Who are you?" asked Samuel Archer. "Speak plainly."

Gareth could tell by his surprised expression that he had, at least in part, guessed the truth. "My mother's name is Amaziga," he said.

"You lie!" shouted Sam. "I've known Amaziga all her life. She had no other sons."

"My mother is stuck back there on that rock face. She crossed a world to find you, Sam. Ask her yourself."

At that moment a volley of shots came from Gareth's right. Several men and a woman fell screaming. Then the Hellborn rushed the camp, firing as they came, tall men in tunics of black leather and ram-horned helms. Sam swung away, reaching for his pistol. Gareth flipped the Uzi into position, and the sound of rolling thunder exploded in the clearing. The first line of Hellborn warriors went down as if scythed. Gareth ran toward the rest with the machine pistol shuddering in his hands. Other shots sounded from all around him as the rebels opened fire. He snapped clear the empty clip and rammed home another. But the first attack having failed, the Hellborn had faded back into the trees and were firing from cover. A bullet slashed past Gareth's head, and another kicked up dirt at his feet. Ducking, he sprinted to a boulder and crouched down behind it. A dead young woman lay to his left, a small dark hole oozing blood from her temple. A shot glanced from the boulder above Gareth's head. Risking a glance, he saw a rifleman in the upper branches of a nearby tree. Lifting the Uzi, he squeezed off a quick burst. The sniper tipped back and fell through the tree, crashing into the undergrowth below.

Across the clearing Sam was lying behind a fallen log. He cursed himself for a fool for not realizing that the Hellborn would try a sneak attack under cover of the dawn mist. The young man's arrival with the multifiring rifle had saved them. He glanced at Gareth. In profile he could see even more clearly the resemblance to Amaziga, the fine high cheekbones, the pure sleek brow. Gareth saw him and grinned, and that was the final proof. Sam did not understand how such a thing was possible, but it was true!

A volley came from the left, and some thirty Hellborn leapt from cover, firing as they came. Sam saw several of the rebels fall. The Uzi thundered, but the charge continued. Raising his pistol, Sam shot into the charging group. Bullets ripped the air around him, one grazing his skull and knocking him from his feet. He rolled and saw Shammy, a pistol in each hand, running toward the invaders. Her life seemed charmed until a shot caught her in the upper thigh, spinning her to the floor. Jered, firing his shotgun from the hip, leapt to her aid. Just as he reached her, his face disappeared in a spray of crimson.

Sam came to his knees and emptied his pistol into the last of the attackers. Gareth's Uzi fired again, and the clearing was still. Shammy crawled to where he lay. Blood was soaking her leggings. "I'll get a tourniquet on that," said Sam.

"No point," answered Shammy.

Sam looked around. There were maybe 40 Hellborn dead, leaving at least another 150. But of the rebels only he and Shammy were still alive—and the young stranger.

Gareth joined them, moving across the ground in a commando crawl. "My rope is still back there," he said. "We'd at least have a chance if we pulled back."

"No time," answered Shammy, lifting her reloaded pistols just as the next wave of Hellborn rushed them. Gareth rolled to his knees and emptied the last clip into the warriors. At least ten of them were hurled from their feet, but the others came on.

Then a second roll of thunder scythed through the attackers, and Gareth saw Amaziga run forward, her own Uzi blazing. Behind her was Shannow, his long pistols firing steadily. The Hellborn broke and fled back into the undergrowth.

"Let's get out of here!" said Gareth. He and Sam lifted the injured Shamshad and staggered across the clearing. Shots sounded around them, but then they were into the cover of the trees. Swiftly Gareth tied his last rope to a slender tree trunk. "You first, Sam," he said. "There's a ledge below, and you'll

find another rope. There are horses at the foot of the cliff."
Sam seemed not to hear. He was staring at Amaziga. "Questions later, okay?" said Gareth, grabbing the man's arm. "For now ... the rope! When you are on the ledge, flick the rope twice. Then the next to come will follow you."

Sam grabbed the rope and slithered over the edge as Gareth moved alongside his mother. "You have any more clips for the Uzi?"

"One more," she said, handing it to him.

A Hellborn moved into sight with his rifle aimed. Shannow shot him twice through the body. Gareth glanced back at the rope. "Come on, man!" he whispered. As if obedient to his thoughts, the unseen Sam reached the ledge and the rope flicked twice. "You next, Mother," he said. "Give the Uzi to Shannow." Tossing the weapon to the Jerusalem Man, she moved to the rope and disappeared from sight.

Shots sliced the air around them. Shannow fired the Uzi, and all was suddenly silent.

The rope flicked. "Now you, Shannow!"

"I'll come last," he said. "Get yourself down." Gareth handed his Uzi to Shammy and moved to the edge.

There was silence for a while, then Shannow saw the rope jerk twice. "Better join them," he told the young woman.

She smiled and shrugged. "Lost too much blood, friend. No strength left. You go. I'll hold them for a while."

"I'll carry you," he announced.

"No. The artery is cut in the groin. I'm bleeding to death. I've probably only minutes left. Save yourself—and Sam. Get Sam away."

Two Hellborn reared up. A bullet ricocheted from the tree by Shannow's head. Twisting, he emptied the Uzi, then cast it aside. Shammy was lying down now, a second wound in her chest. Shannow crawled to her.

"Well," she whispered, "that one took the pain away."

"You are a brave woman. You deserved better."

"You'd better go," she said. "Sit me up first. I may yet get off another few rounds."

Shannow lifted her to a sitting position with her back to a

tree, the Uzi in her hands. Then he slithered back to the edge and dropped from sight.

As he reached the ledge, he heard a burst of firing.

Then silence . . .

Sam sat on the hillside above the small cluster of deserted buildings, his mind still reeling from the shocks of the day. Shammy was dead. They were all dead: Jered, Marcia, Caleb . . . And Amaziga was alive. He was filled with a sense of unreality, a pervading numbness that blocked all emotion. They had climbed down to the foot of the cliff, the Hellborn firing down on them, the bullets kicking up puffs of dust but none coming near. He and Amaziga had shared the lead horse, the young black man and the grim warrior following behind. They had ridden for hours, stopping at last at this deserted hamlet, its residents long since slain by the forces of the Bloodstone, the few homes empty, dust-filled reminders of a community that had vanished forever.

Amaziga had led him into one of the houses, sitting him down and kneeling before him. There she had explained it all. But her words had drifted around in his mind without meaning. He had reached out and touched her face; she had leaned in to him and kissed his fingers, just as she had always done. His tears flowed then, and he rose and staggered from the house, brushing past the young man and breaking into a run that carried him far up the hill.

Shammy was dead. Loyal, steadfast Shammy who asked for nothing except to fight beside him.

Yet where was the grief? Amaziga, whom he had loved more than life, was back. Not his Amaziga, she said, but another woman from another world. It made no sense, and it made no difference. On the ride he had sat behind her, the scent of her hair filling his nostrils, the feel of her body against him.

Samuel Archer struggled to marshal his thoughts. He had studied the principle of multiple universes back at the Guardian Center, had indeed theorized that other Samuel Archers might exist. Then Sarento had mutated into the Blood Beast, and all

Sam's studies had been forgotten in the savage wars that had followed.

Amaziga had died, cut down by a hail of bullets, her beautiful face shattered and torn.

Amaziga was alive!

Oh, God!

It was all too much. Sam stared up at the sky. Not a single bird flew, and as far as the eye could see not one living creature roamed the land. The Bloodstone had sucked the world dry. The sun was shining, the sky powder-blue and dappled with clouds. Sam lay back on the grass, his thoughts haphazard, chaotic. Amaziga came walking up toward him, and his eyes drank in her lithe movements, the swaying, unselfconscious sexuality, the lightness of step. God, she was the most beautiful woman he had ever known.

I don't know her!

"We need to talk, Sam," she said softly, sitting beside him.

"Let's talk about our shared memories," he said, more harshly than he had intended. "You recall the summer in Lost Hawk, near the lake?"

She shook her head sadly. "You and I have shared no summers, though I don't doubt that some of our memories will be linked. That's not the point, Sam. I crossed the universe to find you and save you from death. I could not save my own Sam any more than you could protect the Amaziga you knew. But we are each the identical copies of the originals. Everything I loved about my Sam you share, and that is why I can say—without fear of contradiction—that I love you, Sam. I love you, and I need you."

"Who is the boy?" asked Sam, knowing the answer but needing the confirmation.

"Your son, the son you would have sired. Whichever."

"He's a fine man, brave and steady. I could be proud of a son like that."

"Then *be* proud, Sam," she urged him. "Come with us. Together we can try to stop a world from falling. It won't be our own, but it will be a world just like the one that almost died. We can save it, Sam. We can fulfill the dreams of the Guardians."

"And what of the Bloodstone?"

She spread her hands. "What of him, Sam? He has killed a world. He will not be able to feed. He is finished, anyway."

Sam shook his head. "Sarento was no fool. What is to stop him from finding other worlds? No, I have pledged myself to destroy him, and that I must do."

Amaziga was silent for a moment. "This is foolish, Sam; we both know it. His powers are beyond us. You have a plan? Or is this just a quixotic impulse that will not allow you to know when you are beaten?"

"*My* Amaziga would not have asked that," he said.

"Yes, she would, Sam, and you know it. You are a romantic and an idealist. She never was. Was she?"

He sighed and turned his face away from her, staring down at the small cluster of buildings and the two men who waited there. "Who is the cold killer?" he asked, avoiding the question.

"His name is Shannow. In his own world they call him the Jerusalem Man. He, too, had an impossible dream, but he learned the folly of such fantasies."

"He does not look like a dreamer. Nor does he look like a man who has lost hope." Swinging back toward her, he smiled. "You are right: my Ziga would have asked the same question. What interests me is how you will react to what I am about to say. Or can you predict it?"

"Oh, I can predict it, Sam," she told him. "You are going to say that running away would destroy you, for it would mean turning your back on everything you believe in. Or something like it. You are going to tell me that you will continue the battle against the Bloodstone even if I say we will leave without you. Am I right?"

"I can't deny it."

"And you are wrong, Sam. Oh, I admire you for your courage, but you are wrong. Before coming here we studied the Bloodstone. Sarento cannot be harmed by any weapon in our possession. He is invulnerable. We cannot shoot him, starve him, or burn him. We could pack him in a thousand tons of ice, and it would have no effect on him. So tell me, Sam, how will you fight this monster?"

Sam looked away. "There has to be a way. God knows, there has to be."

"If there is, my love, we will not find it here. Perhaps in the world before the Fall we can find something—and then come back."

Sam thought about it for a while, then slowly nodded. "You are right, as always. How do we get to your world?"

Amaziga laughed. "Don't look so crestfallen. There is so much we can do together for the good of all mankind. You are alive, Sam! And we are together."

"And the Bloodstone is triumphant," he whispered.

"Only for now," she assured him.

Shannow glanced up at the two of them, watching their embrace.

Gareth moved alongside him. "Well, we did it, Mr. Shannow. We brought the lovers back together."

Shannow nodded but said nothing, turning his gaze to the distant mountains and the fringe of the desert to the north.

"You think they will follow us?" asked Gareth.

"Count on it," Shannow told him. "According to Lucas, it would take them most of a day to find a path down for their horses. Even so, I don't like the idea of sitting here and waiting. Four people with three tired horses? We won't outrun them, that's for sure." He stood and wandered back to a brick-built well to the rear of the first house. Lowering the bucket, he dunked it below the surface, then hauled it back to the top. The water was cool and clear, and he drank deeply. The death of the olive-skinned girl had touched him: she had been so young, with untold paths lying before her. Now she would walk none of them, her life snuffed out by a murdering band of killers serving an abomination.

Not for the first time he wondered how men could descend to such barbarism. He remembered the words of Varey Shannow: *"Jon, man is capable of greatness, love, nobility, compassion. Yet never forget that his capacity for evil is*

*infinite. It is a sad truth, boy, that if you sit now and think of
the worst tortures that could ever be inflicted on another
human being, they will already have been practiced somewhere. If there is one sound that follows the march of
humanity, it is the scream."*

Gareth led the horses to the well and filled a second bucket.
"You look far away, Mr. Shannow," said the young man.
"What were you thinking?"

Shannow did not reply. Turning, he saw Amaziga and Sam
approaching hand in hand.

"We're ready to go," she said.

"The horses will need to rest for tonight," said Shannow.
"They're worn out. We'll make use of one of these houses and
leave at first light. I'll take the first watch."

To his surprise, Amaziga offered no argument. Removing
the headband and silver boxes that contained Lucas, she
handed them to him, pointing out how to engage the machine
and warning him of the need to limit the use to conserve the
energy.

Sam and Amaziga went into the first house. Gareth
remained for a moment with Shannow; he grinned. "I think
I'll sleep in the next house," he said. "I'll relieve you in four
hours."

Removing his hat, Shannow slid the headband into place
and then looped the shoulder rig across his right shoulder and
pressed the button on the first box. Seconds later he heard
Lucas's soft voice. "Is everyone safe?"

"Yes," said Shannow.

"I can't hear you, Mr. Shannow. Engage the microphone. It
eases from the headband. Once in position, it will activate
automatically."

Shannow twisted the slender rod into place. "Yes, we are
safe. Amaziga has Sam."

"There is sadness in your voice. I take it there was some
tragedy?"

"Many people died, Lucas."

"Ah, yes . . . I see her now. Young and beautiful. You did
not want to leave her. Oh, Mr. Shannow. The world can be so

savage." Lucas was silent for a moment. "What a lonely place this is," he said at last. "No birds, no animals. Nothing. Would you turn your head, Mr. Shannow? There is a camera in the headband. I will scan the countryside." Shannow did as he was asked. "Nothing," said Lucas. "Not even an insect. Truly this is a dead place. Wait . . . I am picking up something . . ."

"What? Riders?"

"Shhh. Wait, please." Shannow scanned the distant mountains, seeking any sign of movement, but there was nothing that he could see in the fading light. Finally the voice of Lucas drifted back. "Tell Amaziga that we will be traveling back through the stone circle in Babylon; it is closer."

"You want us to ride to the Hellborn city?" asked Shannow, astonished.

"It will save half a day."

"There is the matter of an enemy nation to consider," observed Shannow.

"Trust me," said Lucas. "Ride northeast tomorrow. Now, Mr. Shannow, please cut the power. I have seen all I want to see."

Shannow flicked the switch, then removed the headband.

Else Broome could not sleep. Her enormous body tossed and turned on the rickety bed, the springs creaking in protest at the weight. She was angry. Her husband had lost his mind and shot down the Prophet, ending in one miserable moment all her dreams of status and respect. He had always been useless, weak, and spineless, she thought. I should never have married him. And she would not have if Edric Scayse had not rejected her. Men! Scayse would have been a considerable catch: rich, handsome, respected. He had also died young, which would have left Else as the grieving widow, heir to his fortune and able to live a life of luxury, perhaps even in Unity. The widow Scayse. It was a delicious thought. Yet despite every inducement she could offer, Scayse had remained immune to her advances, and she had been forced to settle for second best. Second best? She almost laughed at the thought. Josiah Broome was the runt of the litter. But through good fortune—

and the benefit of a sensible wife—he had risen to a place of eminence among the people of Pilgrim's Valley.

Now even that small gain was gone for good. Today, on the main street, in front of everyone, several women had crossed the road to avoid Else Broome. Eyes had been downcast as she had passed—all except for Ezra Feard, Josiah's main competitor. He had smiled broadly, and his thin witch of a wife had hurried out to stand beside him, gloating in Else's downfall.

And it would get worse. The Jerusalem Riders would bring her husband back, probably sniveling and crying, and lock him up in the Crusader jail before the public trial that would see him hang. Oh, the shame of it!

Squeezing shut her eyes, she said a prayer aloud. "Oh, Lord, you know what trials I have been through with that wretched man. It is said that he was shot trying to escape. Let him die in the mountains. Let his body be devoured and never found."

Maybe, after a few years, the memory of her mad husband would diminish in the eyes of the townsfolk. Or she could marry again.

A sudden noise downstairs caused her eyes to jerk open. Someone was moving around the house. "Dear God, don't let it be Josiah! Anything but that!" she whispered.

There was a small pistol in the bedside table. Else sat up. If she crept down and killed him, she would become a hero, all her status restored. Opening the drawer, she pulled out the weapon. It seemed tiny in her fat fist. Flicking open the revolver's side gate, she checked that it was loaded; then, easing her vast bulk from the bed, she moved out to the doorway and the stairs beyond. The belt of her cavernous white flannel nightgown caught on the door handle. Shaking it loose, she stepped onto the first stair, which creaked loudly.

"Is that you, Josiah, dear?" she called as she moved down into the darkness. Then she caught a flicker of movement to the left. Cocking the pistol, she stepped from the stairs. The moon emerged from behind the clouds, silver light streaming through the window and the open door. A huge shape reared up before her.

Else Broome had time for one piercing scream . . .

It was heard by the Crusader Captain Leon Evans as he made his nightly rounds. The sound chilled him. A figure moved from the shadows, and Leon spun, his gun flashing into his hand.

"It's only me, sir," said Samuel McAdam, stepping out to join him. "Did you hear it?"

"Damn right. It came from West Street."

"You want me to come with you?"

Leon smiled and clapped the boy on the shoulder. "You're not a Crusader yet, Sam. Wait until you get paid for it." Holstering his pistol, he moved along the street. A silver shape ran at him from the shadows, but Leon was moving past the alleyway and failed to see it. Samuel blinked. He could not believe his eyes. No Wolver could possibly be that big.

"Captain!" he shouted, at the same time dragging out his pistol. His first shot missed the beast. But Leon Evans swung, drew, and fired in one smooth motion. Samuel saw the beast stagger, its head snapping back as blood sprayed from a cut to the scalp. Samuel fired again. Dust kicked up from the beast's hide just above the hip, and blood pumped from the wound. Leon Evans stepped in close and triggered two shots into the Devourer's chest. With a terrible howl it sank to its haunches. Movement came from the far end of the street, and screaming began in several of the houses to Samuel's right. High above, a window smashed and a man's body hurtled down, smashing through the slanting wooden roof that protected the sidewalk. He landed headfirst. Leon ran to the body, Samuel following. It was Ezra Feard, his chest ripped open.

People came running from their homes, converging at the center of the main street. A huge beast climbed from Ezra Feard's window and leapt down among them. Samuel saw a woman dragged screaming to the ground. A man ran to her aid, but talons ripped into his chest. Panic swept through the crowd, and they began to run. From the far end of the street came a score more of the creatures, their howls echoing above the screams of the crowd.

"Get to the Crusader building!" yelled Leon Evans, trying to make himself heard above the sounds of terror that were rending the night. Pistol in hand, Samuel forced his way through the crowd, trying to reach the law officer. The Crusader captain was standing his ground with arm extended, coolly firing at the charging beasts. The hammer clicked down on an empty chamber. Leon Evans broke open the pistol and began to reload, but a beast bore down on him and leapt. Samuel was some yards back. He fired and missed. Talons ripped into Leon Evans's cheek, tearing his face away. The Crusader captain fell back, dropping his pistol. As the creature leapt again, the mortally wounded man drew a hunting knife and lunged out, but the blade did not even pierce the hide. Talons tore into his body, and he fell in a spray of blood. Samuel backed away, trembling, then turned and ran for his life.

Many people were crowding into the stone-built Crusader building, while others continued to run along the main street. As a horse came bolting from a side street, Sam jumped at it, grabbing the mane and trying to vault onto the animal's bare back. He missed and was dragged for some thirty yards before falling to the dust. Scrambling up, he gazed around him. A huge Wolver was running at him. When Samuel's hand swept down to his holster, it was empty.

A shotgun blast came from the right and above. Hit full in the chest, the creature staggered back, letting out a bellow of pain. Samuel glanced up to see the youngster Wallace Nash leaning out of a window above him. "Better get in here, Sam!" shouted Wallace. Samuel ran up the three short steps to the main door and swiftly moved inside. Out on the street the wounded beast bounded forward to hurl itself at the door, which broke into two pieces as it burst open. Samuel fled for the stairs, taking them two at a time, the beast just behind him. Wallace Nash appeared at the top. "Drop, Sam!" shouted the youngster.

Samuel threw himself down as the shotgun blasted, and he

heard the body of the beast tumbling back behind him. Scrambling up, he joined the redheaded youngster at the top of the stairs. He did not know Wallace well, but remembered that the boy was a sprinter who had once outrun Edric Scayse's racing horse, Rimfire.

"Thanks, Wallace," he said as the youngster thumbed two shells into the double-barreled gun.

"We got to get out of here," said Wallace. "This old bird gun ain't going to hold them, that's for damn sure. Where's your pistol?" he asked, glancing down at the empty scabbard.

Samuel was embarrassed. "Dropped it out on the street. I panicked."

Wallace nodded, then reached into his belt to pull clear an old single-action Hellborn pistol.

Fresh screaming erupted from the street, and the two young men ran through to the upper front room and looked out the window. A young woman carrying a baby was hammering on the door of the Crusader building, but the people inside were too frightened to let her in.

A beast loped toward her.

"Over here!" shouted Samuel. The woman spun, and Samuel could see her gauging the distance against the speed of the Wolver. She would never make it . . .

But she tried.

Wallace leveled the shotgun and let fly with both barrels, taking the beast high in the shoulder and spinning it. Regaining its balance, it lurched after the woman. Samuel pushed open the window and climbed out. To the eternal regret of his mother, Beth, he had never been blessed with great courage or stamina. Samuel believed he had failed her in almost everything. Taking a deep breath, he jumped, landing heavily and twisting his ankle. The woman was almost at the steps, the beast just behind her, as Samuel moved left and fired, his first bullet smashing into the creature's open mouth. His second took it in the throat, and blood sprayed from the exit wound. Still it came on.

In that instant Samuel McAdam knew he was going to die, and an icy calm settled on him.

The woman ran by him without a glance, her baby screaming. Other beasts were gathering now. The first creature loomed above Samuel, and he fired twice more, straight into the heart. The Wolver slumped—then its taloned hand slashed out.

"Get back, Sam!" he heard Wallace shout. The beast fell dead. Something hot and sticky was drenching Sam's shirt. He glanced down. It was blood gushing from a gaping wound in his throat.

Samuel fell to his knees, all strength seeping from him. As he toppled sideways, his face struck the hard-packed dirt of the street. There was no pain. I'm dying, he thought dispassionately. This is it. A great weariness settled over him, and an old nursery prayer drifted into his mind. Samuel tried to say it, but there was no time.

This was the day Dr. Julian Meredith had long dreaded. Isis lay in the wagon, unconscious, her pulse weak and fluttering erratically, her eyelids tinged with blue, her cheeks sunken. With hindsight he knew this day had been coming for several weeks. Her energy was low, and it was becoming an effort even to talk.

Meredith sat by the bedside as Jeremiah drove the wagon. How long, he wondered, before the end? Leaning forward, he kissed her cold brow. His eyes misted, and a warm tear splashed to the pale cheek below him. When the wagon creaked to a stop, Meredith rose and opened the rear door, climbing down to the ground. Jeremiah looped the reins around the brake handle and joined him.

"Is she any better?" asked the old man.

Meredith shook his head. "I think it will be tonight."

"Oh, dear," whispered Jeremiah. "She's such a sweet lass. There's no justice, is there, Doctor?"

"Not in cases like hers," Meredith agreed.

Jeremiah built a fire and carried two chairs down from the wagon. "I still don't understand what's killing her," he said. "Cancer I can understand, or a weak heart. Not this."

"It's very rare," explained Meredith. "In the old world it used to be called Addison's disease. We all have a defense system inside our bodies which can isolate germs and destroy them. In the case of Isis the system malfunctioned and began to turn on itself, destroying the adrenal glands, among others."

"Then she is killing herself," said Jeremiah.

"Yes. The old race found cortisonal substitutes, and these kept Addisonians alive. These days we do not know how they were manufactured."

Jeremiah sighed and glanced around at the vast, empty prairie. They had left the other wagons outside Domango when Isis had fallen sick and were heading now for Pilgrim's Valley, searching for a miracle. The Apostle Saul was the last of the Deacon's disciples, and it was said that he had performed miracles in Unity years before. When they had heard he was in Pilgrim's Valley, Jeremiah had left the others and headed the wagon across the prairie.

They were only two days from the valley now, but those two days might just as well be two centuries. For Isis was dying before their eyes.

Jeremiah lapsed into silence and fed the blaze as Meredith returned to the wagon. Isis lay so still, he thought she had passed away, but he held a small mirror beneath her nostrils, and the merest ghost of vapor appeared on the surface. Taking her hand, he began to talk to her, saying the words he had longed to speak. "I love you, Isis. Almost from the first day I saw you. You had a basket of flowers, and you were walking down the main street offering them for sale. The sun was shining, and your hair was like a cap of gold. I bought three bunches. They were daffodils, I think." He fell silent and squeezed her fingers; there was no answering pressure, and he sighed. "And now you are going to leave me and journey where I cannot follow." His voice broke, and the tears flowed. "I find that hard to take. Terribly hard."

When Meredith climbed down from the wagon, Jeremiah had a pot of stew on the fire and was stirring it with a wooden spoon. "Thought I saw a Wolver," said the old man, "over there in the trees." Meredith squinted but could see nothing except the breeze flickering over the top of the grass, causing the stems to imitate the action of waves on an ocean.

From the distance came an eerie howling. "Do you have a gun?" asked Meredith.

"Nope. Gave it to Malcolm. Said I'd pick it up when next we met."

Meredith sat down and extended his fingers to the blaze. Camped in the open, there was little heat to be felt, for the breeze dispersed it swiftly. Normally they would have found a sheltered place to set the fire, against a rock or even a fallen tree. But the oxen were tired, and there was good grass here.

"I don't suppose we'll need a weapon," said Meredith. "I have never heard of a single instance of Wolvers attacking humans."

"What will you do, Doctor, when . . . ?" Jeremiah stumbled to silence, unable to finish the sentence.

"When she dies?" Meredith rubbed his hand over his face. His eyes were tired, his heart heavy. "I shall leave the Wanderers, Jeremiah. I'll find a little town that has no doctor, and I'll settle there. I only joined you to be close to Isis. You?"

"Oh, I'll keep traveling. I like to see new land, fresh scenery. I love to bathe in forgotten streams and watch the sun rise over unnamed mountains."

A silver-gray form moved out from the grass and stood unnoticed some twenty yards from the wagon. Meredith was the first to see the Wolver, and he tapped Jeremiah on the shoulder.

The old man looked up. "Come join us, little friend," he said.

The Wolver hesitated, then loped forward to squat by the fire. "I am Pakia," it said, head tilting to one side, long tongue lolling from its mouth.

"Welcome, Pakia," said Jeremiah. "Are you hungry? The stew is almost ready."

"No hunger. But very frightened."

Jeremiah chuckled. "You have nothing to fear from us. I am Jeremiah, and this is my friend, Doctor Meredith. We do not hunt your people."

"I fear you not," said the Wolver. "Where do you go?"

"Pilgrim's Valley," answered the old man.

The Wolver shook her head vehemently. "No go there. Much evil. Much death. All dead."

"A plague?" asked Meredith. Pakia tilted her head, her eyes questioning the word. "A great sickness?"

"Not sickness. The Blood Beasts come, kill everyone. I smell them now," she added, lifting her long snout into the air. "Far away but coming closer. You have guns?"

"No," said Meredith.

"Then you will die," said Pakia, "and my Beth will die."

"Who is Beth?" asked Jeremiah.

"Good friend. Farms land south of here. You go to her; she has guns. Maybe then you live. She live."

Pakia stood and loped away without another word. "Curious creature," said Meredith. "Was it a male or a female?"

"Female," said Jeremiah, "and she was jumpy. I've traveled these lands for years, and I know of no Blood Beasts. Maybe she meant lions or bears. I shouldn't have given Malcolm my rifle."

"What do you think we should do?"

Jeremiah shrugged. "We'll finish the stew and then head for the farm." The howling came again, and Jeremiah shivered. "Let's forget the stew," he said.

Beth McAdam was dozing when Tobe Harris tapped lightly on the door frame. She came awake instantly and rubbed her eyes. "Been a long day, Tobe," she said.

The workman doffed his cap and grinned. "There's still some old bulls up in the thickets. Take a sight of work to move 'em out."

Beth stretched her back and rose. Tobe Harris had arrived two weeks before on a worn-out horse that was in better condition than he was. A small wiry man with a stoop, he had worked as a miner in Purity and as a horse breaker on a ranch near Unity and had been a sailor for four years before that. On an impulse he had decided to ride into what used to be termed the wild lands and make his fortune. When he had arrived at Beth McAdam's farm, he had been out of food, out of Barta coin, and just about out of luck. Beth had taken an instant liking to the little man; he had a cheeky grin that took years from his weather-beaten face and bright blue eyes that sparkled with humor.

Tobe ran a hand through his thinning black hair. "I seen a wagon heading this way," he said. "Wanderers, most like. Guess they'll stop by and beg a little food."

"How many?" asked Beth.

"One wagon, all brightly painted. Ox-drawn. Two men riding it."

"Let's hope one of them's a tinker. I've some pots that need repairing and some knives that are long overdue for a sharpening. Tell them they're welcome to camp in the south meadow; there's a good stream there."

Tobe nodded and backed out of the door as Beth took a long, deep breath. With winter coming, she had needed a good workman. Her few cattle had wandered high into the hills, deep into the thickets and the woods. Driving them out was at least a four-man job, but Tobe worked as hard as any three workmen she had employed before. Samuel used to help, but he now spent all his time in the settlement, studying to be a Crusader. Beth sighed; they could not meet now without harsh words.

"I raised him too hard," she said aloud.

Tobe reappeared. "Begging your pardon, Frey McAdam, but there's a rider coming. Two to be precise. Riding double on an old mule. I think one of them's ill—or drunk."

Beth nodded, then moved to the mantel, lifting down the old rifle. Levering a shell into the breech, she stepped out into the fading light. The riders were coming down from the mountains, and even from there she could see the sweat-streaked flanks of the mule. In the waning light she could just make out a white beard on one of the riders; the other looked familiar, but his head and upper body were bent low across the mule's neck, the old man holding him steady. The mule pounded up, and the old man slid from its back, turning to support his companion. Beth saw that it was Josiah Broome and, laying the rifle aside, ran forward to help.

"He's been shot," said White-beard.

"Tobe!" yelled Beth. The wiry workman came forward, and together they lowered the wounded man. Broome was unconscious, his face pale, the gleam of fever sweat on his brow. "Get him to my room," said Beth, leaving the two men to carry Broome into the house.

"Pick up your rifle, Frey McAdam," said White-beard. "There's killers close by."

They laid Broome in Beth's wide bed and covered him with a thick blanket. White-beard moved outside. "What killers?" she asked.

"The most terrible creatures you'll ever see," he told her. "Huge Wolvers. Right about now they'll be moving in on Pilgrim's Valley. I hope the Crusaders there are good, steady men."

"Wolvers would never attack anyone," said Beth suspiciously.

"I agree with you, but these aren't just Wolvers. Is that rifle fully loaded?"

"Be pretty useless if it wasn't!" she snapped. The old man was tall and commanding, but there was about him an unconscious arrogance that nettled Beth McAdam. If there were such beasts as he described, she certainly had never seen one, and she had lived near Pilgrim's Valley for twenty years. "How did Josiah get his wound?" she asked, changing the subject.

"Shot down in his home. They killed Daniel Cade, too."

"The Prophet? My God! Why?"

"The same reason Bull Kovac was killed. Broome was going to give Oath for you."

"That makes no sense," she said. "What difference could it make?"

"This is rich land, Frey McAdam. Saul has taken to gathering such land to himself through Jacob Moon and his men. I should have seen what was happening. But I had other, more pressing problems on my mind. I'll deal with Saul—if we survive what is coming."

"*You'll* deal with Saul. By what right?"

White-beard turned, his gaze locking to hers. "I made him, Beth; he is my responsibility. I am the Deacon."

"This is insane," stormed Beth. "Giant Wolvers and supposed murders are bad enough. You're obviously deranged."

"Begging your pardon, Frey McAdam," said Tobe, "but he *is* the Deacon. I seen him at Unity Cathedral last year; it's him, all right."

The Deacon smiled at Tobe. "I remember you," he said. "You worked with horses, and you brought in the young rider with the broken back. He was healed, I recall."

"Yes, sir, Deacon. Then he got killed in a flash flood."

Beth's anger flared. "If you are the Deacon, then you are not welcome in my house," she said icily. "Because of you a good man saw his church burned, his people slaughtered. And he's out there now, suffering. By God, you should be ashamed of yourself."

"And I am, lady," he said softly. "I gave orders that the Wolvers should be moved back away from human settlements. My reasons will be all too clear within days. There is an enemy coming with powers you could not dream of; he has mutated Wolvers into creatures of colossal power. But yes, I am ashamed. It does not matter that I did what I thought was right. Whatever evil was done in my name is my responsibility, and I will live with that. As to not being welcome . . ." He spread his hands. "I can do nothing about that save ask you to bear with me. Only I can fight what is coming."

"Why should I believe that?" countered Beth. "Everything you have is built on lies. The Jerusalem Man never predicted your coming. Shall I tell you how I know?"

"I'll tell you," he said mildly. "Because Jon Shannow, after sending the Sword of God through to destroy Atlantis, came back here to live a life as Jon Cade, a preacher. He lived with you for many years, but you tired of his purity and cast him out. Now understand this: Nothing was built on lies. Shannow brought me down from the sky, but more than that, he is my reason for being! He is why I am here, at this time, to fight this enemy. It is not necessary that you believe me, Beth. It is only necessary that you put aside your disbelief."

"I have a friend out looking for him," she said, her words cold. "He'll come back. Then you can explain it to him!"

An eerie howl echoed in the valley. It was answered by several others.

"I saw a wagon to the north," said the Deacon. "I suggest you invite the occupants to join you. They may not survive the night if you don't."

◇ 11 ◇

When the farmer seeds his field with corn, he knows that the weeds will grow also. They will grow faster than his crop, the roots digging deep, drawing the nutrients from the land. Therefore, if he is wise, he patrols his field, uprooting the weeds. Every human heart is like that farmer's field. Evil lurks there, and a wise man will search out the weeds of evil. Beware the man who says, "My heart is pure," for evil is growing within him unchecked.

The Wisdom of the Deacon
Chapter XIV

THE CITY WAS vast and silent, the shutters on open windows flapping in the early-morning breeze, open doors yawning and creaking. The only other sound to break the silence was the steady clopping of the horses. Shannow was in the lead, Amaziga and Sam sharing the horse behind, with Gareth bringing up the rear.

The great south gate of Babylon was open, but there were no guards, no sentries patrolling the high walls. The silence was eerie, almost threatening.

The streets were wide and elegantly paved, the houses built of white rock, many boasting colorful mosaics. Statues lined the avenues, heroic figures in the armor of Atlantis. Although Babylon was a relatively new city, many of the statues and ornaments had been looted from an Atlantean site, as had much of the stone used in the buildings. The riders moved on through an open market square with rotting fruit displayed in the stalls: brown, partly collapsed apples, oranges covered with blue-gray mold. Slowly they rode on, passing a tavern. Several bench tables were set outside the main doors, and on them were goblets and plates of mildewed bread and cheese.

Not a dog or a cat moved in the silence, and no flies buzzed around the decomposing food. In the clear sky above them no bird flew.

Gareth eased his horse alongside the mount carrying his mother and Sam. "I don't understand," he said.

"You will," she promised him.

On they rode, through narrow streets and out onto broad avenues, the hoofbeats echoing through the city. Shannow loosened his pistols in their scabbards, his eyes scanning the deserted homes. Ahead of them was a huge coliseum five stories high, colossal, demonic statues surrounding it, images of demons, horned and scaled. Shannow drew back on the reins. "Where now?" he asked Amaziga.

"Lucas says that beyond the coliseum's arena is a wide tunnel leading into the palace. The grounds beyond that contain the remnants of the stone circle."

Shannow gazed up at the enormous building. "It must hold thousands," he said.

"Forty-two thousand," said Amaziga. "Let's go on."

The central avenue led directly to the bronze gates of the main entrance; they were open, and Shannow rode through into an arched tunnel. Many doorways opened onto stairs to the left and right, but the trio rode on and down, emerging at last into what had been a sand-covered arena.

Now it boasted a new carpet. Corpses lay everywhere, dried husks that once had been human. Shannow's horse was reluctant to move on, but he urged it forward. The gelding stepped out gingerly, its hoof striking a corpse just below the knee; the leg snapped and fell away.

Shannow looked around as the horse slowly picked its way across the center of the arena. Row upon row of seats, in tier upon tier, ringed the circle. Corpses filled every seat.

"My God!" whispered Gareth Archer.

"No," said Shannow, "*their* god."

"Why would he kill them all? All his people?"

"He had no more use for them," said Amaziga, her voice flat, cold, and emotionless. "He found a gateway to a land of plenty. What you see here is the result of his last supper."

"Sweet Jesus!"

With great care they moved across the arena of death, and Gareth kept his eyes fixed on the distant entrance to yet another tunnel, wincing as dried bones broke beneath his mount's hooves. At last they reached the far side, and Gareth swung in his saddle, looking back over the coliseum and its silent audience.

Forty-two thousand people, their bodies drained of moisture. He shuddered and followed the others down into the second tunnel.

The palace gardens were overgrown with weeds and bracken, and only three of the old stones were still standing. One of them had slipped to the right, showing a jagged crack on its side. Shannow dismounted and forced his way through the undergrowth. "Will the circle still ... work?" he asked as Amaziga joined him.

"The stones are not important in themselves," she told him. "They were merely placed by the ancients at points of great natural power." Amaziga flicked the microphone into place and switched on the computer. Shannow wandered away, eyes raking the wall surrounding the garden and the balconies that overlooked what once had been a series of rose beds. He felt uncomfortable there, exposed. One rifleman creeping along behind those balcony walls could kill them all.

Samuel Archer approached him. "I have had no time to thank you properly, Mr. Shannow. I am grateful for your courage."

Shannow smiled at the tall black man. "I knew another Sam Archer once," he said. "I could not save him, and I have always regretted that." He glanced to the left, where Gareth Archer was sitting quietly lost in thought, his face a mask of sorrow. "I think you should speak to him," said the Jerusalem Man. Archer nodded.

Gareth looked up as the older man sat down on the marble bench beside him. "Soon be home," said Gareth. "You'll like Arizona. No Bloodstone."

"It is always hard to gaze on the fruits of evil," Sam said softly.

Gareth nodded agreement. "Forty-two thousand people. Son of a bitch!"

"Do you study history, Gareth?"

"Battle of Hastings, A.D. 1066; Second World War, A.D. 1939; War of Liberation, A.D. 2016," said Gareth. "Yes, I studied history."

"I didn't mean the dates, son. You've just seen a multitude of the dead, yet Genghis Khan killed ten times as many people and Stalin murdered a hundred times more. Man's history is hip-deep in Bloodstones. The dead that you saw *chose* to worship Sarento. They fed him their children and the children of other races. Lastly they fed him themselves. I mourn for their stupidity, but there is nothing new about a leader who leads his people to destruction."

"There's a cheering thought," said Gareth.

Amaziga joined them. "Lucas says that we must wait four hours for a window home. It's almost over, Sam."

Samuel Archer stared at her intently, noting the lines of anguish on her beautiful face. "There is something else," he said.

She nodded and glanced around to look for Shannow, but the Jerusalem Man was gone. "The Bloodstone is now in Shannow's world," she said.

Gareth swore. "Did we open the gate?" he asked bitterly.

"Lucas says not. Yet the fact remains that it is free to reduce another world to dust and death."

"You once told me about Sarento," said Gareth, anger in his voice. "You told me he wanted to see a return to the old world, hospitals and schools, care, love and peace. How could you be deceived by such a monster?"

Sam cut in. "He did want all those things," he said. "He was a man in love with the past. He adored all aspects of twentieth- and twenty-first-century life. And he *did* care. Thirty years ago there was a plague. The Guardians went out among the people with medicines and vaccines we hoped would eradicate it. We were wrong. Many of us died. Yet still Sarento went out until he himself succumbed. He almost died, Gareth, trying to help others. It was the Bloodstone that corrupted him. He is no longer the human Sarento we knew."

"I don't believe that," snapped Gareth. "There must have been evil in him to begin with. You just couldn't see it."

"Of course there was," said Amaziga. "As there is in all of us, in our arrogance, in our belief that we know best. But the Bloodstone enhances such feelings at the same time it drowns the impulses toward good. You have no idea of the influence of such stones. Even a small demonseed will drive a bearer to violence, unleashing the full force of the beast within man. Sarento took into himself the power of an entire *boulder*."

Gareth rose and shook his head. "He knew the Bloodstone was evil even before he did that. I'll not listen to excuses for him. I just want to know how we can kill him."

"We can't," said Sam, "not while he has power. I used to believe that if we could deprive him of blood until he was weak and then attack him, we would have a chance to destroy him. Yet how would it have been possible? Whoever approached him would only feed him. You understand? He is invulnerable. He might have died here, on a planet drained of life. But now he is free to wander the universe, growing in power."

"There must be a way," urged Gareth.

"If there is, we'll find it, Gareth," said Amaziga. "I promise you that."

Jon Shannow wandered through the deserted halls of Babylon, past columns fashioned from human bones and mosaics depicting scenes of torture, rape, and murder. His footsteps echoed, and he came out at last onto a balcony overlooking the garden. From there could be seen the original layout of the grounds, the walkways shaped like intertwined serpents, forming the number of the Beast. Nature had conspired to cover most of the walkways, and vines grew up over the repulsive statues that ringed the six small pools. Even these were stagnant, and the fountains were silent.

Shannow felt burdened by it all, the evidence of man's stupidity laid out before him like an ancient map. Why is it, he thought, that men can be inspired to evil more swiftly and powerfully than they can be inspired to good?

His heaviness of heart deepened. Look at yourself, Jon Shannow, before you ask such questions. Was it not you who put away the guns, pledging yourself to a life of pacifism and religion? Was it not you who took to the pulpit and reached out your mind to the king of heaven?

And what happened when evil men brought death and flames?

"I gunned them down," he said aloud.

It always had been thus. From his earliest days, when he and Daniel had seen their parents slain, he had been filled with a great anger, a burning need to confront evil head to head, gun to gun. Through many settlements and towns, villages and communities the Jerusalem Man had passed. Always behind him there were bodies to be buried.

Did it make the world a better place, Shannow? he asked himself. Has anything you have done ensured a future of peace and prosperity? These were hard questions, but he faced them as he faced all dangers—with honesty.

No, he told himself. I have made no difference.

Twice he had tried to put aside the mantle of the Jerusalem Man, once with the widow Donna Taybard and then with Beth McAdam. Believing him to be dead, Donna had married another man. Beth had grown tired of Jon Cade's holiness.

You are a man of straw, Shannow, he chided himself. A year before, when Daniel Cade had first moved to Pilgrim's Valley, he had visited the Preacher in the small vestry behind the church.

"Good morning, Brother Jon," he said. *"You are looking well for a man of your years."*

"They do not know me here, Daniel. Everything has changed."

Daniel shook his head. "Men don't change, Brother. All

that happens is that they learn how best to disguise the lack of change. Me, I'm still a brigand at heart, but I'm held to goodness by the weight of public opinion and the fading strength of an age-weakened body."

"I have changed," said the Preacher. "I abhor violence and will never kill again."

"Is that so, Jonnie? Answer me this, then: Where are your guns? In a pit somewhere, rusted and useless? Sold?" His eyes twinkled, and he grinned. "Or are they here? Hidden away somewhere, cleaned and oiled?"

"They are here," admitted the Preacher. "I keep them as a reminder of what once I was."

"We'll see," said Cade. "I hope you are right, Jon. Such a life is good for you."

The sun broke clear of the clouds above Babylon, and Jon Shannow felt the weight of the pistols at his side. "You were right, Daniel," he said softly. "Men don't change."

Gazing down on the garden, he saw Amaziga, Gareth, and Sam sitting together. The first Samuel Archer had been a man of peace, interested only in researching the ruins of Atlantis. He had been beaten to death in the caverns of Castlemine. In this world the black man was a fighter. In neither had he won.

Amaziga said there existed an infinity of universes. Perhaps in one of them Samuel Archer was still an archaeologist who would slowly and with great dignity grow old with his family. Perhaps in that world or in another Jon Shannow did not see his family gunned down. He was a farmer, maybe, or a teacher, his sons playing around him, happy in the sunshine, a loving wife beside him.

A whisper of movement came from behind, and Shannow hurled himself to the left as a bullet ricocheted from the balcony, screaming off into the air. Spinning as he fell, Shannow drew his right-hand pistol and fired. The Hellborn warrior staggered, then tipped over the balcony wall. Drawing his left-hand gun, Shannow rose and ran back to the hall entrance.

Two Hellborn warriors were crouching behind pillars. The first, shocked by his sudden appearance, fired too swiftly, the bullet slashing past Shannow's face. His own left-hand gun boomed, and the man was flung back. The second warrior reared up, a knife in his hand. Shannow's pistol slammed down, the barrel cracking home against the man's cheekbone, and the warrior fell heavily.

Shots sounded from the garden. As Shannow ran through the hall, a rifleman leaned over the gallery rail above him. Shannow fired but missed, the bullet chipping wood from the rail. He ducked into a corridor and turned left down a stairway and right into another corridor. There he stopped and waited, listening for sounds of pursuit.

Footsteps sounded on the stairs, and two men ran down. Stepping out, Shannow shot them both, then ran for the garden. Halting in a shadowed archway, he reloaded his pistols. There were no sounds from the garden.

Guns in hand, he moved swiftly out into the sunshine, scanning the balconies.

No one was in sight.

Creeping silently through the undergrowth, he approached the circle of stone. The sound of voices came to him as he neared the circle.

"The Lord has left us," said a deep voice, "and you are to blame. We were ordered to kill you, and we failed. Now that we have you, he will come back for us."

"He's not coming back," Shannow heard Amaziga tell them. "Can't you understand what has happened? He's not a god; he's a man—a corrupted, ruined man who feeds on life. Have you not seen the coliseum? He's killed everyone!"

"Silence, woman! What do you know? The Lord has returned to his home in the valleys of hell, and there he has taken our people to enjoy the rewards of service. This is what he promised. This is what he has done. But my comrades and I were left here because we failed him. When your bodies bleed upon the high altar, he will return for us, and we shall know the joy of everlasting death-life."

Sam's strong, steady voice cut in. "I understand that you *need* to believe. Yet I also see that the demonseeds embedded in your brows are black now and powerless. You are men again, with free will and intelligence. And deep down you are already questioning your beliefs. Is that not true?"

Shannow heard the sound of a vicious slap. "You black bastard! Yes, it is true, and all part of the test we face because of you. We will not be seduced from the true path."

Shannow edged to the right to a break in the undergrowth and stepped out onto the walkway some fifteen yards from the Hellborn group. There were five in all, and each held a weapon pointed at his three companions. The Hellborn leader was still speaking. "Tonight we shall be in hell, with servants and women and fine food and drink. Your souls will carry us there."

"Why wait for tonight?" asked Shannow.

The Hellborn swung to face him, and Shannow's guns thundered. The Hellborn leader was hurled back, his face blown away; another man spun back, his shoulder shattered. Shannow stepped to his right and continued to fire. Only one answering shot came his way; it passed a few feet to his left, smashing into the stone head of a statue demon and shearing away a horn.

The last echoes faded away. Shannow cocked his pistols and moved to join the trio. Amaziga was kneeling beside Gareth. Blood was staining the olive-green shirt he wore as Shannow knelt beside him.

"Jesus wept, Shannow!" whispered the young man. "You really are death on wheels." Blood frothed at his lips, and he choked and coughed. Amaziga pulled out her Sipstrassi Stone, but Gareth's head sagged back.

"No!" screamed Amaziga. "Please, God, no!"

"He's gone," said Shannow.

Amaziga reached out and stroked the dead boy's brow, then turned her angry eyes on the Jerusalem Man.

"Where were you when we needed you?" she stormed.

"Close by," he said wearily, "but not close enough."

"May God curse you, Shannow!" she screamed, her hand lashing out across his face.

"That's enough!" roared Sam, reaching down and hauling her away from him. "It is not his fault. How could it be? And if not for him we would all be dead." He glanced at Shannow. "Are there more, do you think?"

"There were two inside I did not kill." He shrugged. "There may be others."

Sam took Amaziga by the shoulders. "Listen to me, Ziga. We must leave. What will happen if we activate the gateway early?"

"Nothing, save that it uses more Sipstrassi power. And I have little left."

"Is there enough to get us back?"

She nodded. A shot ricocheted from the walkway, and Sam ducked, dragging Amaziga down with him. Shannow returned the fire, his bullets clipping stone from a balcony.

"Let's go," said Shannow calmly.

Amaziga reached down to touch her son's face for the last time, then stood and ran for the stone circle. Sam followed. Shannow backed after them, eyes scanning the balconies. A rifleman reared up; Shannow fired, and the man ducked down.

Inside the circle Amaziga knelt behind one of the stones and engaged the computer. Shots peppered the ground around them. "They're circling us," said Shannow.

Violet light flickered around them . . .

Shannow holstered his pistols and strode out onto the hillside above Amaziga's Arizona home.

Shannow sat on the paddock fence for more than an hour, oblivious to the blazing sunshine. The desert here was peaceful on the eye, the giant saguaros seemingly set in place by a master sculptor. His thoughts swung back to the rescue of Samuel Archer. So much death! The girl Shammy and all the other nameless heroes who had followed Sam. And Gareth. Shannow had liked the young black man; he had had a zest for life and the courage to live it to the full. Even the sight of his twin's corpse had not kept him from his path, a path that had led to a bullet fired by a Hellborn warrior who had seen the destruction of his race and had not understood its meaning.

Amaziga's unjust anger was hard to take, but Shannow

understood it. Every time they met it seemed that someone she loved had to die.

Sam strolled out. "Come inside, my friend. You need to rest."

"What I need is to go home," Shannow told him.

"Let's talk," said Sam, avoiding Shannow's gaze. The Jerusalem Man climbed down from the fence and followed the black man into the house. It was cool inside, and the face of Lucas shone from the computer screen. Amaziga was nowhere in sight. "Sit down, Mr. Shannow. Amaziga will be with us shortly."

Unbuckling his guns, Shannow let the belt fall to the floor. He was mortally tired, his mind weary beyond words. "Perhaps you should clean up first," suggested Sam, "and refresh yourself."

Shannow nodded. Leaving Sam, he walked through the corridor to his own room and removed his clothes. Turning on the faucets, he stepped under the shower, turning his face up to the cascading water. After some minutes he stepped out and moved to the bed, where he sat down, intending to gather his thoughts, but he fell asleep almost instantly.

When Sam woke him, it was dark, the moon glinting through the clouds. Shannow sat up. "I didn't realize how tired I was," he said.

Sam sat down alongside him. "I have spoken to Ziga. She is distraught, Shannow, but even so she knows that Gareth's death could not be laid at your door. She is a wonderful woman, you know, but headstrong. She always was incapable of being wrong. I think you know that from past experience. But she is not malicious."

"Why are you telling me this?"

Sam shrugged. "I just wanted you to know."

"There is something else, Sam."

"That's for her to tell you. I brought some clean clothes. Amaziga will be in the lounge when you are ready." Sam stood and left the room.

Rested and refreshed, Shannow rose and walked to the chair where Sam had laid the fresh clothes: a blue plaid shirt, a pair of heavy cotton trousers, and a pair of black socks. The chest of the shirt was overlarge and the sleeves too short, but the trousers fitted him well. Pulling on his boots, he walked out into the main room, where Amaziga was sitting at the computer, speaking to Lucas. Sam was nowhere in sight.

"He went for a walk," said Amaziga, rising. Slowly she approached him. "I am very sorry," she said, her eyes brimming with tears. Instinctively he opened his arms, and she stepped into his embrace. "I sacrificed Gareth for Sam," she said. "It was my fault."

"He was a brave lad" was all Shannow could think to say.

Amaziga nodded and drew away from him, brushing her sleeve across her eyes. "Yes, he was brave. He was everything I could have wished for. Are you hungry?"

"A little."

"I'll prepare you some food."

"If it is all the same to you, lady, I would like to go home."

"Food first," she said. "I'll leave you with Lucas for a moment."

When she had left the room, Shannow sat down before the machine. "What is happening?" he asked. "Sam out for a walk, Amaziga playing hostess. Something is wrong."

"You came through the window earlier than anticipated," said Lucas. "It drained her stone."

"She has others, surely."

"No. Not at the moment."

"Then how will she send me back?"

"She can't, Mr. Shannow. I have the capacity to hack into . . . to enter the memory banks of other computers. I have done so, and in the next few days papers will begin to arrive giving you a new identity in this world. I will also instruct you in the habits and laws of the United States. They are many and varied."

"I cannot stay here."

"Will it be so bad, Mr. Shannow? Through my . . . contacts, if you like . . . I have amassed a large fortune for Amaziga. You will have access to those funds. And what is there left behind you? You have no family and few friends. You could be happy in America."

"Happy?" Shannow's eyes narrowed. "Everything I love is lost to me, and you speak of happiness? Damn you, Lucas!"

"I fear I am already damned," said the machine. "Perhaps we all are for what we have done."

"And what is that?" asked Shannow, his voice hardening. "What is there that is still unsaid?"

Amaziga returned at that moment, carrying two cups of coffee. "I have some food in the oven. It will not take long," she said. "Has Lucas spoken to you?"

"He has. Now you tell me."

"Tell you what?"

"No games, lady. Just the truth."

"I don't know what you mean. The power is gone. Until I find more Sipstrassi, we are trapped in this version of the old world."

"Tell him," said Sam from the doorway. "You owe him that."

"I owe him nothing!" stormed Amaziga. "Don't you understand?"

"No, I don't understand, but I know how you feel, Ziga. Tell him."

Amaziga moved to an armchair and sat, not looking at Shannow or Sam but staring down at the floor. "The Bloodstone found a gateway through to your world, Shannow. That's where he is now. It wasn't our fault. Truly it wasn't. Someone else opened a gateway—Lucas will vouch for that."

"Indeed I will," said the machine. "Amaziga transferred the files from the portable. I know everything that happened back in Babylon. Sarento passed through the gateway while we were in the hills, camping at that deserted town. All I can tell you is that the Bloodstone is in the time of the Deacon. Your time."

Shannow slumped down in a chair. "And I can't get back there, back to Beth?"

"Not yet," said Lucas.

The Jerusalem Man looked up at Amaziga. "What will I do

here in the meantime, lady, in this world of machines? How will I live?"

Amaziga sighed. "We have thought of that, Shannow. Lucas has arranged papers for you under a new name. And you will stay here while we teach you the ways of this world. There are many wonders for you to see. There is Jerusalem, for this world is still twenty-one years from the Fall."

"Twenty years, four months, and eleven days," said Lucas.

"We have that amount of time to try to prevent it from happening," said Amaziga. "Sam and I will search for Sipstrassi. You will do what you did in Pilgrim's Valley—become a preacher. There is a church in Florida, a small church. I have friends there who will make you welcome."

Shannow's eyes widened. "A church in Florida? Is that not where the Deacon is from?"

Amaziga nodded.

"And my new name?" he said, his voice harsh.

"John Deacon," she told him, her voice barely above a whisper.

"Dear God!" said Shannow, pushing himself from the chair.

"We did not know, Shannow," said Amaziga, "and it won't be the same. Sam and I will find Sipstrassi, and then you will be able to return."

"And if you don't?"

Amaziga was silent for a moment, then looked up into his angry eyes. "Then you must take your disciples and be on that plane on the day the earth falls."

The Deacon stood outside the farm building and watched as Beth McAdam and Tobe Harris led the horses from the paddock into the barn. You are still beautiful, Beth, he thought. And you did not know me. That hurt him. But then, why should she? he asked himself. Only weeks before she had seen a relatively young man giving sermons. Now a long-haired ancient stood in her home, his features obscured by a thick white beard. Understanding did nothing to help the pain.

Shannow felt alone in that moment and terribly weak.

Amaziga and Sam had kept in touch with him, keeping him up to date on their journeys and their search for the stones. Sometimes they had believed themselves to be close, only to face terrible disappointment. With eleven days left before the Fall, they had telephoned Shannow.

"Have you arranged the tickets?" asked Sam.

"Yes. Why don't you come also?"

"Ziga has found evidence of a circle in Brazil. The architecture of the surrounding ruin is different from other Aztec finds. We will journey there and see what is to be found."

"May God go with you, Samuel."

"And with you, Deacon."

Shannow remembered the day the plane had emerged from time's dungeon and soared above the ruined tower of Pendarric. He had looked down, trying to make out the tiny figures below, hoping to see himself and Beth and Clem Steiner, but the plane was too high and flew on, making a landing near Pilgrim's Valley.

The temptation had been great in those early years to seek out Beth. But the shadow of the Bloodstone remained with him, and he gathered to himself clairvoyants and seers in a bid to pierce the veils of time.

Shannow had grown used to leadership during his days in Kissimmee, but the demands of forming rules and laws for a world took their toll. Every decision seemed to lead to discord and disharmony. Nothing was simple. Banning the carrying of weapons in Unity led to protests and violent disagreements. Every community had evolved its own laws, and unifying the people proved a long and bloody affair. The Unifier Wars had begun when three communities in the west had refused to pay the new taxes. Worse, they had killed the tax collectors. The Deacon had sent a force of Crusaders to arrest the offenders. Other communities joined the rebels, and the war spread, growing more bloody with each passing month. Then, after two savage years, with the war almost over, the Hellborn had invaded. Shannow remembered his reaction with deep regret. He and Padlock Wheeler had routed the enemy in three pitched battles, then had entered the lands of the Hellborn, burning settlements and slaughtering civilians. Babylon was razed to the ground. No surrender was accepted. The enemy was butchered to a man—not just to a man, Shannow remembered.

The Deacon had won. In doing so he had become a mass murderer.

Estimates of the dead in the two wars reached more than eighty thousand. Shannow sighed. What was it Amaziga called you once, "the Armageddon Man"?

After the wars the Deacon's laws grew more harsh, Shannow's rule being governed more by fear than by love. He felt increasingly alone. All but one of the men who had traveled with him through time were dead. He alone knew of the terrible evil waiting to be unleashed on the world; it was an awful burden, dominating his mind and blinding him to the beginnings of Saul's betrayal. It would have been so different if Alan had survived.

Alan had been the best of his disciples, calm, steady, his faith a rock. He had died on Fairfax Hill in one of the bloodiest battles of the Unity War. Saul had been with him. They never recovered Alan's stone. One by one they died, three from disease and radiation sickness left over from the Fall and the others cut down in battles or skirmishes.

Until only Saul was left. All those years of wondering where the Bloodstone would strike, and had he but known it, the answer lay with Saul.

Who else in this area had the use of Sipstrassi? Who else could have opened the gateway?

"You were a fool, Shannow," he told himself.

Something moved beyond the fence! The Deacon's rifle came up, and he found himself aiming at a hare that had emerged from a hole in the ground. Slowly he scanned the valley and the distant hillsides. The moon was bright, but there was no sign of movement.

They will come, though, he told himself. Tobe Harris moved alongside him. "All the animals is locked away, Deacon. Save for my horse, like you ordered. What now?"

"I want you to ride to Purity," Shannow told him. "Padlock Wheeler is the man to see. Tell him the Deacon needs him and every man with a rifle he can bring. Miners, farmers, Crusaders—as many as can be gathered. Tell him not to ride into the town but to meet us here."

"Yes, sir."

"Go now, Tobe."

Beth McAdam, her rifle cradled in her arms, came alongside in time to hear the order. "We've seen nothing yet," she said. "What makes you so sure they are coming?"

"I've seen them, lady. Not here, I'll grant you. But I've seen them."

The Deacon had been leaning on the fence rail. Now he straightened and staggered, weariness flowing over him. As he almost fell, Beth caught his arm. "You're all in," she said. "Go and get some rest. I'll stand watch."

"No time for rest," he said. Tobe galloped away into the night. The Deacon drew a deep breath, then climbed to the fence and sat, resting his rifle on a post.

"Someone coming," said Beth. The Deacon followed her pointing finger, but his old eyes could see nothing.

"Is it silver-gray?" he asked.

"No, it's a young man leading a woman. She's carrying a baby."

They waited together as the two approached. As they neared, Beth said, "It's Wallace Nash and Ezra Feard's daughter. What the hell are they doing walking out here at this time of night?"

The Deacon did not answer. Instead he said, "Look beyond them. Is anything following?"

"No ... Yes. Christ! It's a monster! Run, Wallace!" she screamed.

Shannow felt helpless, but he watched as Beth's long rifle came up. She sighted and fired. "Did you hit it?" he asked.

Beth sighted again, and the rifle boomed. "Son of a bitch," whispered Beth. "Got it twice, but it's still coming!"

Jumping from the fence, the Deacon stumbled toward the fleeing couple, straining to see the creature beyond them. His chest was tight, and pain flared in his left arm as, heart pounding, he ran on. He saw the young man release his hold on the woman's arm and swing around to face whatever was chasing them. Shannow saw it at the same time Wallace Nash did. It was huge, over seven feet tall, with blood flowing from two wounds in its chest. Nash fired his shotgun. The creature fell back. A second lunged out of the darkness, and Shannow fired three times, smashing it from its feet.

"Get back!" yelled Beth. "There are more of them!"

Shannow's legs felt like lead, and all energy seemed to vanish. Wallace grabbed his arm. "Come on, old man! You can make it!"

With the young man's help he backed away to the fence as Beth's rifle thundered. "Into the house," he wheezed. "The house!"

Something hard struck him in the side. His body hit the fence rail, snapping the wood. Hitting the ground hard, he lost hold of his rifle but instinctively drew a pistol and rolled. A huge form bore down on him, and he could feel hot, fetid breath on his face. Thrusting up with all his strength, he pushed the gun barrel into the creature's mouth and pulled the trigger. The head snapped back as the bullet passed through the skull. Beth took hold of his arm, dragging him clear of the dead beast.

All was quiet now.

The Deacon gathered up his fallen rifle, and together they backed to the house.

The woman with the baby was sitting slumped in an armchair. Shannow pushed shut the door, dropping a thick bar into place to lock it. "Check the windows upstairs," he told the redheaded youngster. "Make sure the shutters are in place."

"Yes, sir," said the boy. Shannow glanced around.

"Where are the people from the wagon?"

"Oh, my God, I forgot them," said Beth.

Jeremiah's wagon was some two hundred yards from the farm buildings when the shots sounded. The old man ducked, thinking at first that the shots were aimed at them. Meredith stood up on the driver's seat. "I think they must be shooting

rabbits," he said. "I can see a blond woman with a rifle and an
old man . . . damn, I think it's that reprobate Jake."

"I like the old boy," said Jeremiah. "Lively company."

Meredith said nothing. The four oxen were tired and
moving slowly, heads low. The ground beneath the wheels
was soft from the heavy overnight rain, and they were making
little headway. Isis was still clinging to life, but she could not
last much longer now, he knew, and he dreaded the moment
when she would be gone forever.

He saw Jake jump from the fence and run off, but his view
was masked by the stone-built farm building. More shots followed. The wagon entered the yard, then one wheel sank into
a deep mud hole. Jeremiah swore. "I guess we're close enough,"
he said.

A young woman came into sight, carrying a baby. She
ducked behind the fence rails and ran on toward the house. A
redheaded youngster came next, supporting Jake. Meredith
would never forget the next sight. A huge beast reared up
alongside Jake, an enormous arm clubbing the old man against
the fence, which shattered under his weight. As he fell, Jake
drew a pistol, but the creature leapt on him. In the fading light
Meredith heard the muffled shot and saw blood spray up like a
crimson mushroom from the creature's head. The woman
pulled Jake clear of the corpse, and they made it to the house.
The door slammed shut.

Several more of the creatures came into sight.

Only in that moment did Meredith realize the seriousness
of their plight. It had been like watching a tableau, a piece of
theater.

"Get back inside," hissed Jeremiah, twisting in his seat and
opening the front hatch to the inner cabin. The old man
scrambled back, Meredith followed him. The hatch lock was a
small brass hook.

"It won't hold them," Meredith whispered.

"Stay silent," urged Jeremiah.

A terrible scream rose from the oxen, and the wagon rocked
from side to side, the air filled with the sounds of howling and
snarling. Meredith risked a glance through the narrow slit in

the hatch—and wished that he had not. The still-struggling oxen were engulfed in a writhing mass of blood-spattered silver-gray fur.

The rocking of the wagon continued for several minutes, then the two men sat quietly, listening to the beasts feed. Meredith began to tremble, jerking with every snap of bone. Jeremiah put his hand on the doctor's shoulder. "Be calm now," he whispered.

Moonlight shone through the cabin's wide windows. Meredith and Jeremiah crouched on the floor beneath the left window, listening to the sounds of their own breath. Meredith glanced up. Moonlight was shining directly onto the still, pale face of Isis as she lay on the bed, one arm outside the coverlet.

A grotesque face appeared at the window above her. Steam clouded the glass, but Meredith could see the long fangs and the oval eyes and what appeared to be a red stone on the creature's brow. The snout pressed against the window, and both men heard the snuffling as it sought the smell of flesh.

The wagon rocked again as a second beast came up on the right, pushing at the wood.

Meredith's mouth was dry, and his hands continued to tremble so badly that he felt that the movement must be obvious.

Suddenly the window was smashed to shards, glass peppering the cabin. A taloned hand gripped the frame, hauling on it as the creature slowly pulled itself half into the cabin, directly over Isis. Its snout lowered, and its nose snuffled over the face of the unconscious woman. A low growl sounded, then it dropped back to the yard.

A shot sounded, making both men jerk. The creatures outside howled, and Meredith heard the padding of their paws as they moved away from the wagon.

"What are we going to do?" whispered Meredith.

"Stay still, boy. Wait."

"They'll come back. They'll tear us apart."

Jeremiah eased himself to his knees and looked through the hatch. With great care he moved back alongside the panic-stricken doctor. "They've gorged on the oxen, Doctor. I think that's why it left Isis." Stepping over his companion, Jeremiah risked a glance from the right window. Meredith rose alongside him. The yard was empty.

"We've got to try for the house," said Jeremiah.

"No!" The thought of going out into the open was more than Meredith could consider.

"Listen to me, Son. I know you are frightened. So am I. But you said it yourself: to stay here is to die. The house looks solid, and there are people with guns inside. We have to risk it."

Meredith looked down at the comatose woman. "We can't leave her!"

"We surely can't carry her, Meredith. And she is beyond this world now. Come on, my boy. Just follow me, eh?"

Jeremiah moved silently to the rear of the cabin and unfastened the door latch. As usual it gave out with a creak as it opened. Gingerly he lowered himself to the ground, and Meredith scrambled after him.

"Don't make any noise," warned Jeremiah. "We'll walk across and hope to God the people inside are watching for us. You understand?" Meredith nodded.

The night was silent, and there was no sign of the creatures as Jeremiah drew in a deep breath and began to make his way across the thirty yards of open space that separated the wagon from the house. Meredith was behind him. Then the young doctor started to run, and Jeremiah set off after him.

"Open the door!" screamed Meredith.

A creature emerged from behind the barn, howled, and set off after them, covering the ground with immense speed. Meredith managed to reach the raised walkway around the house, then stumbled and fell on the steps. Jeremiah came up behind him and grabbed for his arm, trying to haul him upright.

The creature was close, but Jeremiah did not look back.

The door opened.

Jake stepped into sight with two pistols in his hands. Meredith lunged upright, colliding with Jake and knocking the old man aside. Jeremiah was just behind him. Something struck him in the back, and a terrible pain tore through him.

Recovering his balance, Jake fired twice. The creature was smashed back from the walkway. Jake hauled Jeremiah inside, and a woman slammed the door behind him. Meredith swung to see Jeremiah lying facedown on the dirt floor with blood streaming from a terrible wound in his back. "Why the hell did you shout, boy?" stormed Jake, grabbing Meredith by his shirt.

"I'm sorry! I'm sorry!" Meredith pulled himself clear and knelt by Jeremiah, his hands trying to cover the gaping wound.

Jeremiah sighed and rolled to his side. Reaching up, he took hold of the doctor's blood-drenched hand. "Don't . . . blame . . . yourself. You're a good . . . man."

And then he was gone. "You pitiful son of a bitch!" said Jake.

◇ 12 ◇

Nothing that lives is without fear. It is a gift against reck-
lessness, a servant against complacency in the face of
danger. But like all servants it makes a bad master. Fear
is a small fire in the belly to warm a man in the coldness
of conflict. Let loose, it becomes an inferno within the
walls which no fortress can withstand.

The Wisdom of the Deacon
Chapter XXI

ESTHER HAD FALLEN asleep, and Oz was manfully trying
to hold her steady in the saddle. Zerah Wheeler glanced
back and smiled at the boy. "We'll rest soon," she promised,
leading the horse higher into the hills and cutting toward the
west. There were many caves close by, hidden in the trees, and
only a very good tracker could have followed the trail she had
left. The rifle was heavy in her hands, and the holstered pistol
was beginning to chafe her leg. It's been too long since I
strolled these hills, thought Zerah. I'm getting old and useless.

A cave mouth beckoned, but it was narrow and south-
facing, the wind whistling into the opening, stirring up dust.
Zerah moved on, leading the old buckskin along a narrow
ledge that widened into a deep pear-shaped cave. At first the
buckskin was reluctant to enter the dark, but Zerah coaxed her
in with soft words and a firm pull on the rein. Inside it was as
large as the biggest room back at the house, with a long natural
chimney opening out onto the stars. Zerah looped the reins
over the buckskin's head, leaned the rifle against the rock

wall, and moved back to lift Esther. The little girl moaned in her sleep, then looped her arms around Zerah's neck.

"You get down by yourself, boy. Untie the blanket roll before you do."

Oz untied the rawhide strips that held the roll, then lifted his leg over the saddle and jumped to the ground. "You think they'll find us?" he asked.

"They'll wish they hadn't if they do," said Zerah. "You still got that pistol safe?"

"Yes, Frey," he answered, patting the pocket of his black broadcloth jacket.

Zerah ruffled his fair hair. "You're a good boy, Oz. Your father would be proud of you. Now, you wait here with Esther while I gather some wood for a fire." Oz spread the blanket roll, and Zerah knelt and laid Esther on it. The six-year old turned to her side, her thumb in her mouth. She did not wake.

"Want me to come with you, Frey?"

"No, Son. You stay here. Look after your sister."

Gathering up the rifle, she passed it to the boy. "It's a mite long for you, Oz, but it'll do no harm to get used to the feel."

Zerah left the cave and walked back along the ledge. From that height, more than a thousand feet, she could see a .vast area of the plains below. There was no sign of pursuit. But then, she reasoned, they could be in the trees over the vast dense carpet of green that stretched far away to the east.

Leaning back, she stretched the muscles around her lower spine. They ached like the devil, but she took a good deep breath and walked back into the shadows of the trees. Night was falling fast, and the temperature would soon drop. Zerah gathered an armful of dead wood and walked back to the cave, returning for five more loads before weariness called her to a halt. From the pocket of her old sheepskin coat she took a pouch of tinder and carefully built a small fire.

Oz moved in close to her. "They won't find us, will they, Frey?" he asked again.

"I don't know," she told him, putting her thin arm around his shoulders and drawing him to her.

One of the men who had killed Oz's father had ridden up to

the house and stopped at the well for water. He had seen Oz and Esther playing by the back fence. Zerah, not knowing the man, had walked from the house to greet the newcomer.

"Nice kids," he had said. "Your grandchildren?"

"They surely are," she had told him. "You passing through?"

"Yep. Well, thank you for the water, Frey," he had said, reaching for the pommel of his saddle.

Esther, looking up and seeing him, had screamed and jumped to her feet. "He shot my daddy!"

The man had dropped to the ground, but in that moment Zerah had dragged her pistol clear and pulled the trigger, the shell hammering into his thigh. His horse had reared and run, and he had grabbed for the pommel and had been dragged for thirty yards. Zerah had fired twice more but missed. She had watched him haul himself into the saddle and ride off.

Knowing he would return, Zerah had packed some food and supplies and taken the children back into the mountains, heading for Purity. But the pursuers had cut her off and were camped across the trail as she had reached the last rise. Luckily Zerah had not ridden over the rise but had left the buckskin with Oz and had crawled to the lip to check the road.

Now they were deep in the mountains, and Zerah was pretty sure they had lost their pursuers.

With the fire blazing Zerah rose and moved outside the cave mouth, checking to see if any reflected light was flickering there. A carelessly laid campfire could be seen for miles. However, once outside the cave, no light could be seen, and high above, what little smoke there was had been dissipated by the undergrowth and trees on the cliff top.

Satisfied, Zerah walked back inside. Oz was curled up alongside Esther, and both were fast asleep.

"Makes you feel young again, woman," Zerah said aloud, covering the two children. She felt a sense of pride. She had saved them from killers. "You're not so useless," she whispered.

Tomorrow they would be safe in town, and the Crusaders would be hunting the villains.

It had been a long time since she had visited Pilgrim's Valley, and she wondered what changes she would see.

In the distance a wolf howled. Zerah settled down to sleep alongside the children.

Sarento strolled through the wooded hills above the Atlantean ruin, enjoying the cloudless blue sky and the sounds of early-morning birdsong. The wind was cool on his red-gold skin, and for the first time in years he had no sense of hunger. With a thrill of intense pleasure he recalled the gathering in the coliseum, the anticipation, and, at the last, the inflow of life. Rich and fulfilling and infinitely warming. . .

Below him was the camp of his elite, the five hundred Hell-born warriors he had sent through ahead of him. With them and men like Jacob Moon he would feed in this new world and dream.

The gateway was a desperately needed boon. His hunger in the old world had been painful, agonizing, its clawing demands dominating his days. But here he could appreciate once more the beauty of a blue sky. His golden eyes focused on the ruined city. This was no fit place for a god, he thought as he gazed upon the derelict palace. Before it were two fallen pillars and a smashed lintel.

"Up!" he said. The distant stones groaned and raised themselves, powdered sections re-forming into shaped stone, the shards of the lintel flowing back into a whole and rising through the air to settle into place. Tiny remnants of paint grew, spreading out over the motifs on the lintel: fierce reds, vibrant blues, golden yellows. Golden tiles reappeared on the roof of the palace, catching the sunlight.

Trees flowered in the palace gardens, and rosebushes sprouted. Cracked and broken walkways repaired themselves, with fallen statues climbing back to their plinths, their stone limbs as supple as the warriors who in ages past had inspired them.

Gold leaf decorated the windows of the palace, and long-dry fountains sent sprays of water high into the air in the gardens.

Sarento gazed down on the city and smiled . . . Then the smile faded.

The hunger had returned. Not great as yet, but a gnawing need. Glancing down at his naked torso, he saw that the thin black lines across his skin had thickened; the red-gold was fading. Raising his arms, he reached out with his mind.

The birds of the forest flew around him, foxes awoke and emerged from their holes, and squirrels ran down from their treetop homes. A huge bear let forth a roar and padded from his cave. Sarento was almost hidden from sight by the fluttering birds and the scrambling mass of furred creatures scurrying around his feet.

Then, in an instant, all was silent. The birds fell lifeless to the ground, and the bear collapsed in on itself to crumble like ancient parchment.

Sarento walked across the corpses, which cracked underfoot like long-dead twigs.

His hunger was almost gone.

But the seed of it remained.

His Devourers were roaming the countryside, and he could feel the steady trickle of sustenance. Not enough to satisfy yet adequate for the present. Reaching out, he sought other Wolvers, ready to draw them to him for the Change. But there were none within the range of his power. Curious, he thought, for he knew such beasts existed in this world; he had plucked their image from the dying memories of Saul Wilkins and read them again in the sadistic mind of Jacob Moon. A tiny flicker of concern touched him. Without new Devourers his task in this new world would be more difficult. Then he thought again of the gateway. If there was one, there must be more.

He pictured the teeming cities of the old world: Los Angeles, New York, London, Paris.

In such places he would never know hunger again.

Beth covered the dead man with a blanket and took hold of the weeping Meredith's shoulders. "Come on," she said gently. "Come away."

"It's my fault," he said. "I don't know why I shouted. I just . . . panicked."

"Damn right!" said the Deacon.

"Leave it alone," Beth told him icily. "Not everyone is like you, and thank God for it. Yes, he panicked. He was frightened. But even his friend told him not to blame himself." She patted Meredith's shoulder and stepped in closer to the Deacon. "Blood and death is all you know, Deacon. Murder and pain. Now leave it be!"

At that moment there was a splintering of wood upstairs and the sound of a rifle booming. "Are you all right, Wallace?" shouted Beth.

The young man appeared at the head of the stairs. "One of them jumped up to the window. It's all right now. There's more coming across the meadows, Frey McAdam. Maybe fifty of them."

"The shutters won't hold them," said the Deacon. He drew a pistol, then winced and fell against the wall. Beth moved alongside him. His face was gray with exhaustion and pain. Reaching out, she put her arm around him and led him to a chair. As he sat, she saw that her hand was smeared with blood.

"You're hurt," she said.

"I've been hurt before."

"Let me see it." He half turned in the chair. The back of his old sheepskin coat had been ripped open, the flesh beneath it gashed and torn, and she remembered the snapping of the fence rail as his frail body had been hurled against it. "You may have broken a rib or two," she said.

"I'll live. I have to."

Meredith leaned over her. "Let me look to it," he said. "I am a doctor." Together they helped the Deacon rise, removing his coat and torn shirt. Gently Meredith probed the wound. The old man made no sound. "Two ribs at least," said Meredith. In the background the baby began to cry.

"Needs feeding," said Beth, but the young woman slouched in the chair made no movement. Beth moved to her and saw that her eyes were vacant. She undid the buttons of the girl's sweat-stained blouse, then lifted the baby to the swollen breast. As it began to suck, the girl moaned and started to cry. "There, there," said Beth. "Everything is all right now. Look at her feed. She was real hungry."

"He's a boy," whispered the mother.

"Of course he is. What a fool I am!" Beth told her. "And a handsome boy he is. Strong, too."

"My Josh was strong," said the girl. "They tore his head off." Tears welled in her eyes, and she began to tremble.

"You just think of the babe," said Beth swiftly. "He's all that matters now. You understand?" The girl nodded, but Beth saw that she was once more drifting away, and with a sigh she returned to Meredith and the Deacon. The young doctor had cut up a tablecloth to make bandages. The old man reached up as Meredith completed his work.

"I am sorry, Son," he said. "I hope you'll forgive my harsh words."

Meredith nodded wearily. "It's easier to forgive you than to forgive myself. I have never been more frightened, and I am ashamed of my actions."

"It's in the past, boy. You've been to the edge and looked in the pit. Now you can be either stronger or weaker. It's a choice, but it's your choice. In life a man has to learn to be strong in the broken places."

"They're moving on the barn," Wallace shouted.

"Keep your voice down!" ordered Beth.

From across the yard came the sound of wood being splintered and broken, followed by the terrified neighing of horses. In the chair by the fire the young mother began to weep.

Beth lit two more lanterns, hanging them on hooks by the wall. "It is going to be a long night," she said. The screaming of the trapped animals went on for some minutes, then there was silence. Beth sent Meredith through to the back room to check on Josiah Broome. The girl in the chair had fallen asleep, and Beth lifted the babe from her arms and sat with it on the old rocker.

Wallace Nash came down the stairs and stood in front of her.

"What is it, Wallace?"

The redheaded youngster was ill at ease. "I'm sorry, Frey McAdam. There's no other way to tell it but to go at it straight out. Samuel, well, he died saving the girl yonder and the child. Jumped from a window as one of them creatures was bearing down on her. Calm as you like. He killed it sure enough, but it got him, too. I'm terrible sorry, Frey."

"Best get back upstairs, Wallace," she said, hugging the baby to her. "Best keep a good watch."

"I'll do that," he said softly. "You can rely on me, Frey."

Beth closed her eyes. She could smell the burning oil in the lamps, the seasoned cedarwood on the fire, and the milky, newborn scent of the child in her arms.

Outside a beast howled.

Shannow reached into his pocket, his arthritic fingers curling around the golden stone. I don't want to live forever, he thought. I don't want to be young again. The pain in his chest was intensifying, linking and merging with the agony of his fractured ribs. You have no choice, he told himself. Gripping the stone, he willed away the pain in his heart and felt new strength and vitality pounding through his veins. The ribs, too, he healed, drawing on the strength of the stone.

Opening his hand, he gazed down at the golden pebble. Only the faintest thread of black showed where the power had been leached. Rising, he moved to the window. The aching pain was gone from his shoulder and knees, and he moved with a spring in his step. Glancing through the gap in the shutters, he saw Devourers clambering over Jeremiah's wagon, moving into the cabin and up through the hatches. The barn was silent, but he could see gray shapes lying on the hard-baked dirt of the yard or squatting near the fence.

Stepping back, he looked at the shutters. The wood was less than an inch thick; it could not withstand the explosive power in the taloned arms of the Devourers. Delving into his coat, he produced a box of shells, which he tipped onto the tabletop. Twenty-three remained, plus the twelve in his pistols.

Meredith returned. "The wounded man is sleeping," said the doctor. "His color is good, and his pulse is steady."

"He's tougher than he knows," said Shannow.

"Where did these creatures come from?" Meredith asked. "I have never heard of anything like them."

"They're Wolvers," answered Shannow, "but they've been changed by . . . sorcery, if you will." He started to speak but became aware that the young man was staring at him with what Shannow took to be blank disbelief. "I know it is hard to understand," he said. "Just take me on trust, Son. There is a creature—"

"Beth called you Deacon," Meredith said, interrupting him, and Shannow realized that the young man had not been listening to a word of his explanation.

"Yes," he said, his voice weary. "I am the Deacon."

"I have always hated you," said Meredith. "You have been the cause of great evil."

Shannow nodded. "I don't argue with that, Son. The butchery in the lands of the Hellborn was unforgivable."

"Then why did you do it?"

"Because he's a killer and a savage," said Beth, her voice flat and without anger. "Some men are like that, Doctor. He came to power by deceit and held on to it by fear. All who opposed him were killed; it was all he knew."

Meredith swung to Shannow. "Is that how it was?"

Shannow did not answer. Rising, he moved back through the house, pausing at Josiah Broome's bedside.

Is that how it was?

Broome stirred and opened his eyes. "Hello, Jake," he said sleepily.

Shannow sat on the edge of the bed. "How are you feeling?"

"Better," said the wounded man.

"That's good. You rest now." Broome closed his eyes.

Shannow remained where he was, remembering the two armies converging on the lands of the Hellborn, remembering his fury at the Hellborn betrayal and his fears about the coming of the Bloodstone. Many of the men who had fought under him had lost family and friends to the Hellborn, and hatred ran strong in their veins. And in mine, he thought sadly.

Padlock Wheeler and the other officers had come to him on that fateful morning outside Babylon, when the Hellborn leaders were begging to be allowed to surrender.

"What orders, Deacon?"

There were many things he could have said in that moment about the nature of evil or the wisdom of forgiveness. As he had stared at them he could think only of the terror that was coming and the fact that in his previous world the Bloodstone had used the Hellborn to wreak destruction and death. And in the space of a single heartbeat he had made a decision that still haunted him.

"Well, Deacon?"

"Kill them all."

Zerah awoke before dawn and groaned. A small stone was digging into her hip, and her shoulders ached abominably. Another groan followed her attempt to sit up, and she swore bitterly.

"That's not nice," said little Esther.

"Neither is the rheumatics," grunted Zerah. "How long you been awake, child?"

"Ever since the howling," said Esther, sitting up and rubbing her eyes. "There's lots of wolves about."

Zerah had heard nothing. Pushing herself to her feet, she stretched, then walked to the buckskin, lifting her water canteen from the saddle pommel. After a long drink she returned to the children and the dead fire. "Wolves won't attack us," she said. "Now you see if you can find a spark in them ashes, and I'll cook us up some breakfast."

With a yawn she stepped outside. The air was fresh and cool, and Zerah could smell the dew on the leaves and the musky scents of the forest. The sky was lightening in the east, and early birdsong greeted her as she walked under the trees. Despite the rheumatic pain in her back and shoulders, she felt good, glad to be alive.

It's the youngsters, she thought; they make everything seem

fresh and new again. Zerah had not realized how much she missed company until the stranger had arrived. It saddened her that he had not come back. Jon was a good man and quiet company. But the young ones were a joy even when they squabbled. It brought back memories of her own children, back in the days of her youth, when the sky was more blue and the future was a golden mystery yet to be discovered.

Zeb had been a handsome man with a ready wit that had endeared him to everyone. And he had been kind and loving. Everybody had liked Zeb, because Zeb had liked everybody. "Never knew a man could see so much good in people," she said aloud.

When he had died, she remembered Padlock coming home. He had put his arms around her and said, "You know, Ma, there's no one in this world that he would ever need to say sorry to."

Seemed like that was a good epitaph for a kind man.

Folks had come from far and wide for the funeral, and that had pleased Zerah. But after he had died, the visitors had stopped coming. I never was the popular one, she thought. Old Zerah with her sharp tongue and her sharper ways.

She glanced up at the sky. "Sometimes I wonder what you saw in me, Zeb," she said.

Turning to go back to the cave, she saw a paw print in the soft earth. Kneeling, she ran her hand over it, opening her fingers to measure the span. It was enormous. Not a bear, though it was the right size. Not a lion. Her mouth was dry as she stood. It was a wolf print but larger than any she had ever seen.

Zerah hurried back to the cave. "What's for breakfast?" asked Oz. "Esther's got the fire going."

"I think we'll wait until we reach town," said Zerah. "I think we should move on."

"But I'm hungry," complained Esther. "Really starving!"

Zerah chuckled. Good God, woman, she thought, why the panic? You have a fire and a good pistol. "All right," she agreed. "We'll eat first and then travel."

Walking to the back of the cave, she approached the buckskin. The horse was trembling, its ears tucked flat against its skull. "It's only me, girl," said Zerah. "Calm down, now." As she spoke, Esther screamed, and Zerah spun around.

In the mouth of the cave stood a monstrosity. Eight feet tall, with huge shoulders and long arms, the fingers ending in curved talons, the beast was covered with silver-gray fur. Its massive head was lowered, its tawny eyes fixed on the two children cowering by the small fire. The buckskin reared and whinnied, catching the creature's attention.

Zerah Wheeler drew her old pistol and wondered whether a bullet could bring the giant Wolver down. "You stay calm, now, kids," she said, her voice steady. Cocking the pistol, she walked forward. "I don't know if you can understand me," she said, keeping her eyes on the beast, "but this here pistol has six charges. And I hit what I goddamn aim at. So back off and we'll all be happier."

The beast howled, the sound reverberating like thunder in the cave. Zerah glanced at the fire. Beside it lay a thick branch festooned with long-dead leaves. Keeping the pistol steady, she reached down with her left hand and lifted the branch, touching the leaves to the little blaze. They caught instantly, flames searing out. Zerah stood and walked toward the creature. "Back off, you son of a bitch!" she said.

The beast backed up but then sprang forward. Zerah did not give an inch. Thrusting the flames into its face, she shot it in the throat. The huge Wolver went down and rolled. Zerah jumped to the mouth of the cave and shot it again as it tried to stand.

"Jesus wept!" she whispered.

Outside the cave there were more of the beasts. "Kids," she called, "I want you to climb that chimney at the back. I want you to do it *now*."

Still holding the branch, she backed into the cave. A creature sprang at her, but she calmly shot it in the chest. Another ran from the right; a shot came from the back of the cave, shearing half the beast's head away. Zerah glanced back to see that Oz had her rifle in his hands and was standing his ground.

Pride flared in her then, but her voice was sharp and commanding. "Get up that goddamn chimney!" she ordered.

The beasts were advancing cautiously. With only three shells left, Zerah knew she could not hold them all, nor would she have time to turn and climb out of their reach. "Are you climbing?" she called, not daring to glance back.

"Yes, Frey," she heard Oz shout, his voice echoing from within the chimney.

"Good boy."

Suddenly the buckskin bolted past her, scattering the beasts as it made a dash for the freedom of the forest. In that moment Zerah turned and sprinted for the chimney. Slamming the pistol into her holster, she grabbed a thin ledge of rock and levered herself up, her boots scrabbling on the stone. Swiftly she climbed until she could see Oz just above her, helping Esther. It was narrow in the chimney, but there was just enough room for the children to squeeze up onto a wider ledge below the cliff top.

Pain flashed through her foot. Zerah screamed and felt herself being dragged down. Oz pushed the rifle over the edge, barrel down, and fired. Zerah dragged out her pistol and put two shots into the Wolver below. It fell, its talons tearing off Zerah's boot. Oz grabbed her, and with the boy's help she eased her skinny body through the gap. Blood was seeping from a wound in her ankle, and a six-inch talon was embedded in her calf. Zerah prized it loose. "You are brave kids," she said. "By God, I'm proud of you!"

From the pocket of her coat Zerah took a folding knife and opened the blade. "If you'd be so good as to give me your shirt, Oz, I'll make some bandages and try to stop this bleeding."

"Yes, Frey," he said, pulling off his coat and shirt. As she worked, she told the boy to count the shells left in the rifle. It did not take long: there were two.

"I still have the little gun you gave me," said Oz.

She shook her head. "That'll do you no good against these creatures. Still, the noise might frighten 'em, eh?" The boy forced a smile and nodded. Zerah bandaged her ankle and then delved into the pocket of her coat, producing a strip of dried beef. "It's not much of a breakfast," she said, "but it will have to do."

"I'm not hungry," said Esther. "Are we going to die?"

"You listen to me, child," said Zerah. "We're alive, and I aim for us to stay that way. Now, let's climb out of here."

"Is that wise, Frey?" asked Oz. "They can't get us here."

"That's true, boy. But I don't think that strip of beef is going to hold us for the rest of our lives, do you? Now, we can't be more than six, maybe seven miles from Pilgrim's Valley. We'll be safe there. I'll go first; you follow."

Zerah forced herself to her feet and climbed toward the patch of blue some twenty feet above her.

Shannow climbed the stairs to the second level and found the redheaded youngster kneeling by a window, staring out over the yard. "What are they doing now?" he asked the boy.

Wallace put down his rifle and stood. "Just sitting. Can't understand it, Meneer. One minute they're tearing up everything in sight, the next they're lying like hounds in the moonlight."

"They fed," explained Shannow. "The question is, How long before their hunger brings them against us? You be ready now."

"This is a strong-built house, Meneer, but the windows and doors ain't gonna hold 'em, I can tell you that. Back in town they was ripping them apart like they was paper. And they can jump, too, by God! I saw one spring maybe fifteen feet up onto the side of a building."

"They can jump," agreed Shannow, "and they can die, too."

Wallace grinned. "They can at that." As Shannow turned to move away, the boy reached out and took hold of his arm. "You saved my life. I didn't even know that thing was close. I won't forget it."

Shannow smiled. "You settled that debt when you half carried me back. I was all finished. You're a good man, Wallace. I'm proud to know you." The two men shook hands, and Shannow walked back to the narrow hallway, checking the other two adjoining rooms on the upper floor. Both were bedrooms, one decorated with lace curtains that were yellowed with age. Children's drawings and sketches were still pinned to the walls, stick men in front of box houses with smoke curling from chimneys. In the corner, by the closed window, was a stuffed toy dog with floppy ears. Shannow remembered when little Mary carried it everywhere. The other room was Samuel's. The walls were lined with shelves that carried many books, including a special gold-edged edition of *The New Elijah*. Shannow sighed. Another of Saul's little vanities. When it had been published, Shannow had read the first chapter, outlining God's call to the young Jerusalem Man, then had sent for Saul.

"What is this . . . garbage?"

"It's not garbage, Deacon. Everything in that book is fact. We got most of it from primary sources, men who knew the Jerusalem Man, who heard his words. I would have thought you would have been pleased. He predicted your coming."

"He did no such thing, Saul. And half the names in the first chapter never came within a hundred miles of Shannow. Several others have let their imaginations run riot."

"But . . . how would you know that, Deacon?"

"I know. How is no concern of yours. How many have been printed?"

Saul smiled. "Forty thousand, Deacon. And they've sold so fast, we're going for a second printing."

"No, we are not! Let it go, Saul."

Shannow lifted the book from the shelf and flipped it open. In the center was a black and white engraving showing a handsome man on a rearing black stallion, silver pistols in the rider's hands, and a sleek black hat on his head. All around him were dead Hellborn. "At least they didn't say I killed ten thousand with the jawbone of an ass," whispered Shannow, tossing the book to the pine bed.

Carefully he opened the shutter and leaned out. Below him was Jeremiah's wagon, the roof ripped apart. Several Wolvers were asleep within it; others were stretched out by the ruined barn.

What are you going to do, Shannow? he asked himself.

How do you plan to stop the Beast?

Fear touched him then, but he fought it down.

"What are you doing here?" asked Beth. "This is my son's room."

Shannow sat on the bed, remembering the times he had read to the boy. "I don't need your hatred, Beth," he said softly.

"I don't hate you, Deacon. I despise you. There is a difference."

Wearily he stood. "You ought to make up your mind, woman. You despise me because I gave no ground and saw my enemies slain; you despised your lover, Jon Cade, because he wouldn't slay his enemies. What exactly do you require from the men in your life?"

"I don't need to debate with you," she said stonily.

"Really? Then why did you follow me here?"

"I don't know. Wish I hadn't." But she made no move to leave. Instead she walked farther into the room and sat down on an old wicker chair by the window. "How come you knew about me and Jon? You have spies here?"

"No ... no spies. I knew because I was here, Beth. I was here."

"I never saw you."

"You still don't see me," he said sadly, rising and walking past her. The pine steps creaked under his weight, and Dr. Meredith turned as Shannow approached.

"It's terribly quiet," said the younger man.

"It won't stay that way, Doctor. You should ask if Frey McAdam has a spare weapon for you."

"I am not very good with guns, Deacon. I never wanted to be, either."

"That's fine, Doctor, as long as there is someone else to do your hunting for you. However, you won't need to be good. The targets will be close enough to rip off your face. Get a gun."

"What does it take to make a man like you, Deacon?" asked Meredith, his face reddening.

"Pain, boy. Suffering, sorrow, and loss." Shannow pointed at Jeremiah's blanket-covered corpse. "Today you had a tiny taste of it. By tomorrow you'll know more. I don't mind you judging me, boy. You couldn't be harder on me than I am on myself. For now, though, I suggest we work together to survive."

Meredith nodded. "I guess that is true," he said. "You were starting to tell me about the gateways. Who made them and why?"

Shannow moved to the armchair and gazed down at the sleeping woman. Beth had found a small, beautifully carved crib and had placed the babe in it, beside the chair. "No one knows," he said, keeping his voice soft. "A long time ago I met a man who claimed they were created in Atlantis twelve thousand years before the Second Fall. But they may be older. The old world was full of stories about gateways and old straight paths, dragon trails, and ley lines. There are few facts but scores of speculative theories."

"How are they opened?"

Shannow moved silently away from the mother and child and stood by the door. "I couldn't tell you. I knew a woman who was adept at such matters. But she remained behind on the day of the Fall and I guess was killed with the rest of the world. She once took me through to her home in a place called Arizona. Beautiful land. But how she did it . . ." He shrugged. "She had a piece of Sipstrassi, a Daniel Stone. There was a burst of violet light, and then we were there."

"Ah, yes," said Meredith, "the stones. I've heard of them but never seen one. A hospital in Unity used them to cure cancer and the like. Astonishing."

"Amen to that," said Shannow. "They can make an old man young, or heal the sick, or create food from molecules in the air. It is my belief that Moses used them to part the Red Sea, but I cannot prove it."

"God had no hand in it, then?" asked Meredith with a smile.

"I don't try to second-guess God, young man. If He created the Sipstrassi in the first place, then they are still miracles. If He gave one to Moses, you could still say that God's power parted the waves. However, this is not the time for biblical debate. The stones make imagination reality. That's all I know."

"Be nice to have one or two at this moment," said Meredith. "With one thought we could kill all the wolves."

"Sipstrassi cannot kill," Shannow told him.

Meredith laughed. "That's your problem, Deacon. You lack the very imagination you say the stones need."

"What do you mean?"

Meredith stood. "Take this chair. It is of wood. Surely a stone could transform it into a bow and arrows. Then you could shoot something and kill it. Sipstrassi would have killed it, albeit once removed. And these gateways you speak of, well, perhaps there is no technique. Perhaps the woman you knew was not adept at all, merely imaginative."

Shannow thought about it. "You think she merely *wished* herself home?"

"Quite possibly. However, it is all academic now."

"Yes," agreed Shannow absently. "Thank you, Doctor."

"It is a pleasure, Deacon." Meredith moved to the window and leaned down to peer through the gap in the shutters. "Oh, God!" he said suddenly. "Oh, my dear God!"

Isis floated back to consciousness on a warm sea of dreams, memories of childhood on the farm near Unity: her dog, Misha, unsuccessfully chasing rabbits across the meadow, barking furiously in his excitement. His enjoyment was so total that when Isis gently merged with his feelings, tears of joy flowed from her eyes. Misha knew a happiness no human except Isis could ever share. He was a mongrel, and his heritage could be seen in every line of his huge body. His head was wolflike, with wide tawny eyes. But his ears were long and floppy, his chest powerful. According to Isis's father, Misha was quite possibly the worst guard dog ever born; when strangers approached, he would rush up to them with tail wagging and wait to be petted.

Isis loved him.

She had been almost grown when he had died. Isis had been walking by the stream when the bear had erupted out of the thicket. Isis had stood her ground and mentally reached out to the beast, using all her powers to calm its rage. She was failing, for the pain within it was colossal. The young girl had even had time to note the cancerous growth that was sending flames of agony through the bear's belly even as it bore down on her.

Misha had charged the bear, leaping to fasten his powerful jaws on the furred throat. The bear had been surprised by the ferocity of the attack but had recovered swiftly, turning on the hound and lashing out with its talons.

A shot had rung out, then another and another. The bear had staggered and tried to lumber back into the thicket. A fourth shot had made it slump to the ground, and Isis's father had run up, dropping his rifle and throwing his arms around his daughter. "My God, I thought you were going to die," he had said, hugging her to him.

Misha had whimpered then. Isis had torn herself loose from her father's embrace and thrown herself down alongside the dying hound, stroking its head, trying to draw away its pain. Misha's tail had wagged weakly even as he died.

Isis had wept, but her father had drawn her upright. "He did his job, girl. And he did it well," he said gently.

"I know," Isis had answered. "Misha knew it, too. He was happy as he died."

The sadness was still with her as she opened her eyes in the wagon. She blinked and found herself staring at the stars. Half the roof was missing, and she could see great tears in the wooden canopy. Her right side was warm, and she reached out, her hand touching fur. "Oh, Misha," she said, "you mustn't get on the bed. Daddy will scold me."

A low rumbling growl sounded, but Isis drifted off to sleep again, the terrible strength-sapping power of her illness draining her of energy. A weight came down over her chest, her eyes opened, and she saw a huge face above hers, a long lolling tongue and sharp fangs. Her hand was still touching the fur, and she could feel the warmth of flesh beneath it. "I can't stroke you," she whispered. "I'm too tired."

She sighed and tried to turn to her side. At least the pain is gone, she thought. Maybe death will not be so very bad, after all. Isis wanted to sit up but did not have the strength. Opening her eyes again, she saw that the side of the wagon was also partially destroyed. Something had happened! Some calamity.

"I must get up," she said. Lifting her hand, she looped her arm over Misha's neck and pulled. He growled, but she succeeded in raising her body. Dizziness swamped her, and she fell toward Misha, resting her head on his shoulder.

A second growl came from below the bed, and a monstrous creature loomed up from the floor of the cabin. Isis looked at it and yawned. Her head was spinning, and her thoughts were fragmented. Misha felt so warm. Reaching out, she touched his mind. There was anger there, a poisonous fury held in check only by . . . by what? Memories of a hollow by a lake, young Wolvers running around his feet. A . . . wife?

"You're not my Misha," said Isis, "and you are in pain." Softly she stroked the fur.

The second beast lunged at her. The first hit it with a back-hand blow, sending it smashing against the cabin wall.

"Stop it! Stop it!" said Isis wearily. "You mustn't fight." She sagged against the beast. "I'm thirsty," she said. "Help me up." Pulling once more, she rose on trembling legs, pushing past the Devourer and stumbling to the rear of the cabin, where she almost fell down the steps and out into the yard.

The moon was high, and she was almost at the end of her strength. There was no sign of Jeremiah, Meredith, or the others. No wagons camped in a circle. No fires burning. Her vision swam, and she swayed, catching hold of the left rear wheel.

The yard was full of hounds, big hounds.

She saw the house, bars of golden light showing through the closed shutters. Everyone must be there, she thought. But I can't reach it.

I must! I don't want to die here, alone. Drawing in a deep breath, she let go of the wheel and took two faltering steps.

Then she fell.

* * *

The Deacon saw Meredith stumble away from the window. Shannow stepped up to the shutters, peering out through the crack. He saw a young woman in a dress of faded blue, her blond hair shining white in the moonlight, lying stretched out on the ground. Before he could speak, he heard the door open. "No!" he hissed.

But Meredith was already moving out into the yard.

With a muttered curse Shannow followed him, drawing his pistols. The beasts were everywhere, most lying quietly under the stars, their bellies full, but a few prowling at the edge of the barn or gnawing on the bloody bones of the butchered horses, milk cows, and oxen. Shannow cocked the pistols and stood in the doorway, watching the young doctor make his way across to the fallen girl. Meredith was moving slowly, and for the moment the beasts seemed to be ignoring him.

A Devourer moved from the rear of the wagon and saw the walking man. A deep growl sounded, and it ambled forward. Several others looked up. One stretched and howled, the sound chilling. Meredith faltered but then walked on and knelt beside Isis. Reaching down, he took hold of her wrist. The pulse was weak and fluttering. Pushing his hands under her shoulders, he hauled her into an upright position, then twisted down to lift her legs. Her head fell to his shoulder.

A Devourer reared above him, saliva dripping from its fangs. Isis moaned as Meredith backed away, the beast following.

In the doorway Shannow aimed his pistol, but now other beasts were closing in on the doctor. Meredith turned his back on them and started to walk back toward the house. Shannow's mouth was dry, his palms greasy with sweat. The doctor stumbled but righted himself and walked on. Shannow stepped aside as he climbed the porch steps and entered the house. Swiftly Shannow followed him, slamming shut the door and dropping the bar into place.

Outside a great howl went up. The shutters on the window exploded inward, and a beast thrust its upper body through the frame. Shannow shot it through the head. Another clambered over the body of the first; Shannow fired twice into its huge chest, and it slumped forward, leaking blood to the dirt floor.

The young mother lurched to her feet, screaming. "Don't let them get me! Don't let them get me!"

Talons raked at the door, splintering the wood. Wallace Nash ran halfway down the stairs and leveled his shotgun. A section of timber on the door was torn away as a taloned arm lunged through. Wallace fired both barrels. The arm jerked as blood sprayed from it. Shannow shot through the door.

The sounds of gunfire echoed away. Shannow moved to the window, seeing that the beasts had pulled back.

"I've never seen anything like it," said Wallace Nash. "Son of a bitch! Man, that took some nerve."

Meredith was not listening. He was kneeling over the unconscious Isis, his tears falling to her face.

Shannow pushed closed the shutters. The locking bar had been snapped in half, but he wedged it by ramming a knife down into the windowsill. It would not hold against a Devourer, but it gave the illusion of security.

He could scarcely believe what he had seen. Meredith, the man whose panic had killed Jeremiah, had just performed an act of complete heroism. Beth came downstairs. The baby was crying, and she lifted it from the crib. When the young mother snatched it away and fled upstairs, Beth moved alongside Meredith. There were no signs of wounds on the body of the young blond girl he was attending. "What's the matter with her, Doctor?" Beth asked.

"She has an illness which has corrupted her immune system. It is very rare; even in the old world it affected only a handful in every million." He glanced up and saw that Beth did not understand him. Meredith sighed. "Our bodies are equipped with a . . . defense mechanism. When illness strikes, we make antibodies to fight it. Like measles. A child generally will succumb only once, because the body identifies the invading organism, then makes defenses to stop it from happening again. You understand? Well, in the case of Isis, her defense mechanism has targeted organs in her own body and is slowly destroying them. It was called Addison's disease."

"And there is nothing that can be done?" asked Wallace.

"Nothing. The elders used medicines called steroids, but we don't know how they were made."

"Where did she come from?" asked Wallace. "How did she get here, through all them creatures?"

"We brought her with us," said Meredith. "She was in the wagon. We thought she was on the verge of death, and to my eternal shame I left her there."

"Jesus!" said Wallace. "But why didn't they kill her? They was all over the wagon."

Meredith shrugged. "I have no answer to that."

"No, but she does," said the Deacon softly. Kneeling beside her, he laid his hand on her brow. "Come back to us, Isis," he said. Meredith watched amazed as color seeped back into the pale face. Beneath his fingers the pulse became steadier, stronger.

Isis opened her eyes and smiled. "Hello, Jake," she said.

"How are you feeling?"

"Wonderful. Rested." She sat up and looked around. "Where is this place?"

"It's a farm near Pilgrim's Valley," said Shannow.

"Where's Jeremiah?"

Shannow helped her to her feet. "Do you remember the beasts in the wagon?" he asked, ignoring her question.

"Yes. Big, aren't they? Are they yours, Jake?"

"No. They are savage. They killed Jeremiah and many others. The question is, Why did they not kill you?"

"Jeremiah is dead?" Then she saw the blanket-covered body. "Oh, no, Jake!" Isis moved to the body, pulling back the blanket and gazing down on the old man's face.

Meredith moved alongside Shannow. "Is she . . . healed?"

Shannow nodded. "Completely. But I must know about the beasts."

"Let it rest, for God's sake," protested Beth. "She's been through enough."

"We cannot let it rest," said Shannow. "When those beasts make a concerted attack, we will be dead. If Isis knows a way to control them or render them harmless, I must learn it. You hear me, child?" he asked the weeping Isis.

She nodded and covered Jeremiah's face once more. Rising, she faced the Deacon. "I don't know why they didn't harm me," she said. "I can't help you."

"I think you can, my love," said Meredith. "Animals never attack you, do they? You once told me it was because you liked them. But it is more than that, isn't it? You can . . . communicate with them. Remember when you told Jeremiah about the lung disease that was crippling his lead oxen?"

"I . . . can't talk to them or anything," Isis told him. "I just . . . merge with their minds."

"What do you remember of *their* minds?" asked the Deacon, pointing toward the window.

"It's very hazy. It's like their thoughts are full of angry wasps, stinging them all the time."

"Here they come!" yelled Wallace.

Oz Hankin was more tired than frightened as they crossed the ridge and began the long descent into Pilgrim's Valley. They had walked for most of the day, and there had been no sign of the wolf creatures. The wind had been at their backs for most of the journey, and it seemed now that they would escape the beasts. Esther was being carried by Frey Wheeler, and that annoyed Oz. Little girls always got the best treatment. It was the same back at the farm with Dad; if their room was a mess or if the chores were not completed, it was Oz who got it in the neck.

Now it was Esther who was being carried. The fact that he was ten pounds heavier than Esther and three inches taller made little difference to the twelve-year-old. Life just was not fair.

And he was hungry. As he walked, he remembered the taste of apple pie and powdered sugar and the sweet honey cakes his father had made after they had found the hive in the woods.

Frey Wheeler halted and swung Esther to the ground. "Need to rest a mite, child," she said. The woods were close, and Oz saw Zerah studying them. She sniffed, then spit. It surprised Oz; ladies were not supposed to spit. Esther immediately copied her, and Zerah laughed. "Don't imitate me, Esther," she warned. "There's things people will tolerate in the old that they won't in the young."

"Why?" Esther asked.

"It just ain't done, child." She turned toward Oz. "You got sharp eyes, young Oz. What can you see in the trees yonder?"

"Nothing, Frey. Looks clear."

"Then we'll chance it," she said, hefting her rifle. Slowly the trio set off across the last stretch of open ground. The land dropped sharply to their right, and as they walked they saw a trail leading west across the mountains. "Logging road," said Zerah as they scrambled down it. At the foot Zerah stopped again, her ancient face showing purple streaks under the eyes and beside the mouth. She was breathing heavily, and Oz became concerned.

"You feeling okay, Frey?" asked Oz. The old lady was sweating, and her eyes seemed more sunken than usual, lacking their normal brightness. She smiled, but Oz could see the effort behind it.

"Just tired, boy. But I ain't done yet. Just give me a minute to catch my breath."

Oz sat back on a rock, while Esther ran off into the bushes at the side of the road.

The sound of horses' hooves came to him. Oz was about to warn Esther, but the riders appeared around a bend in the road. At first Oz was pleased, for if they were men from Pilgrim's Valley, it would mean a pleasant ride in comparative safety. His joy was short-lived as he recognized the man on the lead horse: he was one of those who had shot his father. The men saw them and spurred their horses forward. There were seven in the group, but Oz recognized only the first as they reined in before Zerah.

"Well, well, what have we here?" asked the lead rider, a thin man with long sideburns and deep-set dark eyes. In his hands was a squat, black pistol that was pointed at Zerah. Oz saw that Zerah's rifle was still resting against the rock. There would be no time to lift it and fire. And even if she could, there were only two shots left.

"Don't harm these children," the old lady said wearily.

"Where's the girl?" asked the leader.

Oz slipped his hand in his pocket, curling it around the butt of the little pistol. Only the lead rider had a gun in his hand; the rest were merely sitting on their horses, watching the exchange.

"You should just ride on," said Zerah. "Killing children is no work for grown men."

"Don't lecture me, you hag! We was told to find them and get rid of them. That's what we aim to do. Now tell me where the girl is and I'll kill you clean. One shot. Otherwise I'll blow away your kneecaps and make you scream for an hour or two."

"You always was a low creature, Bell," said a voice. "But by God, I swear you could walk under a door without bending your knees."

Oz looked to the right, where two riders had arrived unnoticed. The man who spoke was wide-shouldered, wearing a dust-stained black coat and a red brocade waistcoat. His hair was dark, though there was silver at the temples. Beside him was a younger man.

"By heaven," said Bell, "you're a long way from home, aren't you, Laton? Heard that they butchered your gang and that you ran off with your tail between your legs. I always knew you weren't so salty. Now be on your way; we've business here."

"Threatening women?" taunted the rider. "That's about all you're worth, Bell."

Bell laughed and shook his head. "Always one for words, Laton," he said.

Oz saw the killer suddenly swing the black pistol toward the rider. Laton swayed to the side, a nickel-plated pistol seeming to leap into his hand. Bell fired and missed. Laton returned the shot, and Bell pitched from his saddle. Seizing the chance, Oz pulled the little pistol clear and fired at the closest man. He saw the shot strike home as a puff of dust came from the man's jacket and he sagged in the saddle. Horses reared, and shots exploded all around him. Oz tried to aim, but Zerah dived at him, dragging him down and covering him with her body.

He heard the thunder of hooves and saw the three remaining hunters fleeing. One horse was down, and there were four bodies lying on the logging road. The other three horses had run off a little way and were standing some fifty yards distant. "It's all right, Frey, they've gone," he said.

The man in the brocade waistcoat knelt by them, lifting Zerah from him. "Are you hurt, lady?" he asked.

"Only my pride," she said, allowing Laton to help her rise. "Don't know how I let them get so close."

Laton grinned. A groan came from the left, where Bell was pushing himself to his knees, his right hand gripping his belly, blood pouring through his fingers. Oz watched as their rescuer approached the wounded man.

"By damn, Bell, you are a hard man to kill," he said. His pistol came up and fired, and Bell pitched backward and lay still.

"He was one that needed killing," said Zerah, struggling to rise. Oz helped her, then recovered his pistol from the road.

"I should have done it a long time ago," said Laton. Turning away, he called out to his friend, "Hey, Nestor, catch those horses yonder and we'll offer these folks company on the road."

Esther peeped out from the bushes. Zerah called to her, and she scampered across to the old lady, hugging her leg. Zerah leaned down and kissed the top of the child's head.

As the younger man rode off for the riderless horses, the older one turned to Oz. "You did right well there, Son. I like a lad with spirit."

"Are you Laton Duke, sir?" asked Oz.

The man grinned and extended his hand. "The name is Clem. Clem Steiner."

"But he called you . . ."

"Just a case of mistaken identity. I never saw him before," he said with a wink.

Oz shook the man's hand as Zerah gathered up her rifle. "I don't much care who you are," she said. "I'd have welcomed the Devil himself with open arms just to see that piece of scum go to hell."

"Your grandma is one tough lady," observed Clem.

"Yes, sir!" agreed Oz. "You don't know the half of it."

The attack was short-lived, with only four of the creatures charging the house. Wallace took out the first with a double-barreled blast while it was still in the yard. Shannow shot down two others as they tore the shutters away from the window. The last leapt to the porch awning and tried to enter an upstairs window. Beth ran into the room and fired three shots into the beast's chest, catapulting it back to the yard, where Wallace killed it as it tried to rise.

The downstairs rooms stank of cordite, and a haze of blue smoke hung in the air. Dr. Meredith approached the Deacon. "You have a stone, don't you?" he said as the Deacon reloaded his pistols.

"Yes. One small stone."

"Surely, with its power, you could block all the windows and the doors."

"I could," the Deacon agreed, "but I don't know how long the power would last, and I need that stone, Doctor, for when the real evil shows up."

Meredith's eyes widened. "The real evil? These beasts are not the *real* evil?" Quietly Shannow told him about the Blood-stone and how it had destroyed its own world. He told him of the coliseum and the forty thousand dead, of the absence of birds, animals, and insects.

"Oh, God . . . you really saw this?" asked Meredith.

"I saw it, Doctor. Trust me. I wish I hadn't."

"Then what can stop him?"

The Deacon gave a weary smile. "That is a problem that has haunted me for twenty years. I still have no answer."

Isis joined them. Leaning forward, she kissed the Deacon's cheek, and the old man smiled up at her. "A kiss from a beautiful girl is a wonderful tonic."

"It must be working," said Isis, "for I'm sure your beard is darker, Jake, than when first I saw you."

"That's true," agreed Meredith. "How is your wound?"

"I healed it," said Shannow.

"I think you did more than that," said Meredith. "Isis is right: your skin is looking less wrinkled and ancient. You're getting younger." He sighed. "Good Lord, what wonders could be achieved if we had more of those stones!"

The Deacon shook his head. "The Guardians had them, but the stones were corrupted—just like everything man touches. Sipstrassi has its dark side, Doctor. When it is fed with blood, the result is terrifying. Look at the creatures yonder, the Bloodstones in their brows. Once they were Wolvers, gentle and shy. Look at them now. Consider the Bloodstone himself. Once he was a man with a mission: to bring back the earth to a Garden of Eden. Now he is a destroyer. No, I think we would all be better off without any stones of power."

Beth called out to Meredith, to come and help her prepare food. The doctor moved away, and Isis sat beside Shannow.

"You are sad," she said.

"You see too much," he told her with a smile.

"I see more than you think," she said, her voice low. "I know who you are."

"Best to say nothing, child."

"I felt as if I were floating on a dark sea. Then you came to me. We merged when you drew me back. We were one, as we are one now." She took his hand and squeezed it, and he felt a sudden warmth in his mind, a loss of loneliness and sorrow. He heard her voice inside his head: "I know all your thoughts and concerns. Your memories are now mine. That's why I can tell that you are not an evil man, Jake."

"I am responsible for the deaths of thousands, Isis. By their fruits shall ye judge them. Women, children—an entire race. All dead by my order." Harsh memories erupted into his mind, but Isis flowed over them, forcing them back.

"That cannot be changed ... Deacon. But an evil man would not concern himself with guilt. He would have no conception of it. Putting that aside for a moment, I also share, now, your fears about the Bloodstone. You don't know what to do, but in your memories there is one who could help. A man with great imagination and the powers of a seer."

"Who?" As swiftly as she had merged with him, she was gone, and Shannow felt the pain of withdrawal, a return to the solitary cell of his own being.

"Lucas," she said aloud.

He looked into her beautiful face and sighed. "He went down with the Fall of the world hundreds of years ago."

"You are not thinking," she said. "What are the gateways if not doorways through time? Amaziga took you back to Arizona. Could you not travel the same route? You must get Lucas."

"I have no horse, and even if I did, it's a three-day ride to Domango. I haven't the time."

"Why go to Domango? Did not Amaziga tell you that the stone circles were placed where the earth energy was strongest? There must be other places where they did not place stones yet the energy is still there."

"How would I find one?"

"Ah, Deacon, you lack the very quality the stones need. You do not have imagination."

"Meredith has already pointed that out," he said testily.

"Give me the stone," she ordered him. Fishing it from his pocket, he placed it in her hand. "Come with me," she said, and he followed her upstairs into Mary's old room. She opened the shutter. "Look out and tell me what you see."

"Hills, the slope of the valley, woods. The night sky. What would you have me see?"

Placing the stone against his brow, she said, "I want you to see the land and its power. Where would a circle of stone be placed? Think of it, Deacon. The men who erected the stone circles must have been able to identify the power points. Draw from the Sipstrassi. See!"

His vision swam, and the dark gray of the night landscape began to swirl with color: deep reds and purples, yellows and greens, constantly shifting, flowing, blending. Rivers of color, streams and lakes, never still, always surging and vibrant.

"What is the color of power?" he heard her ask, as if from a great distance.

"Power is everywhere," he told her. "Healing, mending, growing."

"Close your eyes and picture the stone circle at Domango." He did so, seeing again the hillside and Amaziga's Arizona house and the distant San Francisco peaks.

"I can see it," he told her.

"Now gaze upon it with the eyes of Sipstrassi. See the colors."

The desert was blue-green, the mountains pink and gray. The rivers of power were lessened there, sluggish and tired. Shannow gazed upon the old stone circle. The hillside was bathed in a gentle gold, flickering and pulsing. Opening his eyes, he turned to Isis. "It is a golden yellow," he said.

"Can you see such a point from here, Jake?" she asked, pointing out the window.

◇ 13 ◇

When will we have peace? That is the cry upon the lips of the multitude. I hear it. I understand it. The answer is not easy to voice, and it is harder to hear. Peace does not come when the brigands are slain. It is not born with the end of a current war. It does not arrive with the beauty of the spring. Peace is a gift of the grave, and is found only in the silence of the tomb.

From the Deacon's last letter to the Church of Unity

ISIS MOVED OUT into the yard, enjoying the freshness of the predawn air. Several of the wolf creatures were stretched out asleep, but she sensed the presence of others in the ruined barn. She could feel them now, their pain and anguish, and as she crossed the lines of power that stretched back from them to the Bloodstone, her limbs tingled and stung.

Concentrating hard, she narrowed her eyes. Now she could see the lines, tiny and red, like stretched wire, pulsing between the servants and the master, passing through the house, burrowing through the hillsides. Her body aglow with Sipstrassi power, she stared intently at the lines, severing them, watching them wither and fail. An instant later they were gone, snuffed out like candle flames.

Walking steadily forward, she approached the first sleeping beast. Reaching down, she touched its brow, her index finger and thumb taking hold of the Bloodstone shard embedded there. The evil contained in the shard swept back over her, and for the merest moment she felt a surge of hatred. It was an emotion she had never experienced before, and she faltered. The Bloodstone turned black and fell away from the wolf.

"I do not hate," she said aloud. "I will not hate." The feeling passed, and Isis knew she was stronger now. "Come to me!" she called. "Come!"

The beasts rose up, growling. Others poured from the barn. Now she felt the hatred coming at her like a tidal wave. Isis absorbed it all, draining it of energy and purpose.

A creature lunged forward, rearing up before her, but Isis reached out swiftly to touch its huge chest. Instantly she merged. Its Wolver memories were buried deep, but she found them, drawing them into the beast's upper mind. With a cry it fell back from her.

Isis let her power swell, enveloping the mutated animals like a healing mist and sending the power out over the mountains and hills. One by one the beasts dropped to the ground, and she watched as their great size dwindled, the dead stones falling from their brows.

Then the power left her, drifting away as the dawn light crept over the eastern mountains. Tired now, Isis sat down. A little Wolver padded across to her, taking her hand.

The Deacon strode across the yard, holstering his pistols. The Wolvers scattered and ran, heading away into the distant hills.

"I felt him, Deacon," she whispered. "I felt the Bloodstone."

The Deacon helped her rise. "Where is he?"

"He has rebuilt a ruined city a day's ride from Pilgrim's Valley. He has warriors with him, black-garbed men with horned helmets. And the Jerusalem Rider Jacob Moon."

"Evil will always gather evil," said the Deacon.

"The wolf creatures were linked to him, feeding him. Now the supply has stopped," she said.

"Then he'll have to go hungry."

She shook her head. "The horned riders will come, Deacon. The war is only just beginning."

Jon Shannow stood on the brow of the hill, the Sipstrassi Stone in his hand. There was no circle of stones there and no indication that there ever had been one. Yet he knew this was a point of power mystically linked to others throughout time. What he did not know was how to harness that power, how to travel to a given destination.

Was it just imagination, or were there sets of coordinates needed by the users?

Back in Babylon he had learned that there were certain windows in time that would enable travelers to move across the gateways with minimum energy from Sipstrassi. How did one know when such a window was open?

Closing his fist around the stone, he pictured the house in Arizona, the paddock and the red jeep, the sun over the desert. The stone grew warm in his hand. "Take me to the world before the Fall," he said.

Violet light flared around him, then faded.

There was the house. There was no red jeep there now. The paddock was gone, replaced by a tarmac square and two tennis courts. Beyond the house he could see a swimming pool. Shannow stepped out of the circle and strolled down to the building.

The front door was locked. Leaning back, he kicked hard at the wood, which splintered but did not give. Twice more he thundered his boot against the lock, then the door swung inward.

Swiftly he moved across the living room. It was sweltering hot and airless inside. Out of habit he wandered through to the lounge, flicking on the air-conditioning unit. He grinned. So long away, yet as soon as he returned, he thought of the wonderful comforts of this old doomed world.

Moving back to the main room, he plugged in the computer leads, engaged the electricity, and watched the screen flicker to life. Lucas's face appeared.

"Good day, Mr. Shannow," said Lucas.

"I need you, my friend," said the Deacon.

"Is Amaziga with you?"

"No. I have not seen her in twenty years or more." Shannow pulled up a swivel seat and sat before the screen.

"She left here some time ago for Brazil. My dates are

confused. I think there must have been an electrical storm. What is today's date?"

"I don't know. Listen to me, Lucas. The Bloodstone is in my world. I need your help to destroy it."

"There is nothing in your world to destroy it, Mr. Shannow. As long as it lives, it will feed. If you deny it blood, it will go dormant and wait, go into hibernation, if you will. But there is no weapon capable of causing it harm."

"The Sword of God could have destroyed it," said Shannow.

"Ah, yes, but the Sword of God was a nuclear missile, Mr. Shannow. Do you really want to see such a weapon descend on your land? It will wipe out countless thousands and further poison the land for centuries."

"Of course not. But what I am saying is that there are weapons which could destroy him."

"How can I help you? You can have access to all my files, but few of them have any direct bearing on your world save those which Amaziga supplied."

"I want to know everything about Sarento. Everything."

"The question, surely, is *which* Sarento. I know little about the man who became the Bloodstone."

"Then tell me about the Sarento you know, his dreams, his vanities, his ambitions."

"Very well, Mr. Shannow. I will assemble the files. The refrigerator is still working, and you will find some cool drinks there. When you return, we will go over the information."

Shannow strolled through to the kitchen, fetching a carton of Florida orange juice and a glass. Sitting before the machine, he listened as Lucas outlined Sarento's life. He was not a primary survivor of the Fall, though he sometimes pretended to be, but had been born 112 years later. A mathematical genius, he had been in the first team to discover Sipstrassi fragments and use them for the benefit of the people who became known as the Guardians. While he listened, Shannow remembered the struggle on board the restored *Titanic* and the disaster in the cave of the original Bloodstone. Sarento had died there, with Shannow barely escaping with his life. There was little new to be learned. Sarento had been obsessed with the thought of returning the world to the status and lifestyle enjoyed in the twentieth and twenty-first centuries. It was his life's work.

"Has that helped, Mr. Shannow?"

Shannow sighed. "Perhaps. Tell me now of the gateways and the points of power on which they were built."

"You have me at a disadvantage there, Mr. Shannow. The gateways were *used* by the Atlanteans until the time of Pendarric and the First Fall of the World. Whether they were built by them is another matter entirely. Most of the ancient races are lost to us. It could even be that the world has fallen many times, wiping out great civilizations. As to the power sites, they are many. There are three near here, and one is certainly as powerful as that on which the ancients erected the stones. The earth is peppered with them. In Europe most of the sites have churches built upon them. Here in the United States some have been covered with mounds, with others bearing ancient ruins. The people known as the Anasazi erected cities around the energy centers."

"Do you have maps in your files?" asked Shannow.

"Of course. What would you like to see?"

"Show me the deserts of Arizona, New Mexico, Nevada."

"Do you have more specific instructions?"

"I want to see all the energy centers, as you call them."

For more than an hour Shannow pored over the maps as Lucas highlighted sites of power. "More detail on this one," said Shannow. "Bring it up closer." Lucas did so.

"I see what you are getting at, Mr. Shannow. I will access other data that may be relevant to this line of inquiry. While I am doing so, would you mind if I activate the television? It annoys me that my date and time sections are down."

"Of course," said Shannow.

The wall-mounted unit flickered to life, the picture switching to a news text. The date and time were outlined in yellow at the top right-hand side of the screen.

"Mr. Shannow!"

"What is it?"

"You have chosen a strange time to pass through the gateway. We are only twelve minutes from the Fall."

Shannow knew instantly how it had occurred. The last thought in his mind as the violet light had flared around him had been to get to Arizona before the Fall. And he had remembered that awful morning as the plane had lifted off, as indeed it was even now lifting off on that far coast.

"I need you with me, Lucas," he said. "Where is the portable Amaziga used?"

"She took one with her, Mr. Shannow. There is a second in the back bedroom—a small cupboard beneath the television and video units." Shannow moved swiftly through to the room. The portable unit was even smaller than the one Amaziga had carried through to the world of the Bloodstone; Shannow almost missed it, believing it to be a stereo headset.

"Eight minutes, Mr. Shannow," came the calm voice of Lucas as the Jerusalem Man strode back into the main room.

"How do I hook up these leads?" he asked.

Lucas told him, then said, "Take the blue lead and attach it to the point at the rear of the machine immediately above the main power socket." Shannow did so. "Transferring files," said Lucas. "We have five minutes and forty seconds."

"How long will the transfer take?"

"Three minutes."

Shannow moved to the doorway, staring out over the desert. It was still and hot, the sky a searing blue. A huge jet passed overhead, gliding west toward the runways of the Los Angeles airport, runways that would be under billions of tons of roaring ocean long before the plane touched down.

The earth trembled beneath Shannow's feet, and he reached out, taking hold of the door frame.

"Almost there, Mr. Shannow," said Lucas. "I managed to save forty-two seconds. Unhook me and put on the headset."

Shannow unplugged the lead and clipped the portable to his gun belt. There was no on/off switch, and Lucas's voice sounded tinny through the headphones. "I think you had better run, Mr. Shannow," he said, his voice eerily calm.

The Jerusalem Man moved swiftly out of the house, leaping the porch steps and sprinting toward the old stone circle. "One minute twelve seconds," said Lucas.

The ground shuddered, and Shannow stumbled. Righting himself, he ran up the hill and into the circle.

"Get us back," he said.

"What are the coordinates?" Lucas asked.

"Coordinates? What do you mean?"

"A trace. A date and a place. We must know where we are going."

"Beth McAdam's farm . . . but I don't know exactly *when*." The wind began to build, clouds racing across the sky.

"Twenty-eight seconds," said Lucas. "Hold tightly to the stone, Mr. Shannow."

Violet light flared around them as the wind shrieked and rose. "Where are we going?" shouted Shannow.

"Trust me," said Lucas softly.

Clem Steiner eased back from the brow of the hill, keeping his body low as he clambered down to join the others. Zerah and the children had dismounted; Nestor still sat in the saddle.

"What did you see?" asked Zerah.

"Kids, you hold on to the horses," said Clem, smiling at Oz.

"I want to see!" Esther complained in a high voice.

Clem lifted a finger to his lips. "Best stay quiet, girl, for there are bad men close by."

"Sorry," Esther whispered, putting her hand over her mouth.

Nestor dismounted and, together with Clem and Zerah, walked to just below the hilltop before dropping down to his belly and removing his hat. The others crawled alongside. On the plain below, no more than two hundred yards away, Nestor could see a dozen riders in horned helms and black breastplates, holding rifles in their hands. They were riding slowly alongside a walking group of men, women, and children, maybe seventy of them, Nestor guessed.

"What are they doing?" asked Nestor. "Who are they?"

"Hellborn."

"There aren't any Hellborn," snapped the boy. "They was all wiped out."

"Then this is obviously just a dream," responded Clem testily.

"Oh, they're Hellborn, all right," said Zerah. "Zeb and I were with Daniel Cade during the First Hellborn War. And those people with them are being treated as prisoners."

Nestor saw that she was right. The Hellborn—if that was what they were—were riding with their rifles pointed in at the group. "They're moving toward Pilgrim's Valley," said Nestor, thinking of the quiet strength of Captain Leon Evans and his Crusaders. They would know how to deal with the situation.

As if reading the youngster's mind, Clem spoke. "They can already see the buildings in the distance, but it don't seem to worry them none," he whispered.

"What does that mean?"

The old woman cut in: "It means the town is already taken or everyone has gone."

Nestor, whose eyes were sharper than his companions', spotted a rider in the distance galloping out from the settlement. As he neared, Nestor squinted to see better, but he did not know the man.

Clem Steiner swore softly. "Well, I'll be a monkey's uncle," he said. "Damned if that isn't Jacob Moon."

Nestor had heard the name of the fearsome Jerusalem Rider. "We have to help him," he said. "He can't take them alone!" He started to rise, but Clem dragged him down.

"Let's just watch, boy. I don't think Moon has come for a fight."

Nestor swung on him, his face twisted in anger. "Yes, I can believe you don't want to see Jacob Moon," he hissed. "He'd make short work of a thieving brigand named Laton Duke."

The rider closed on the Hellborn and raised his hand in greeting. One of the prisoners, a woman in a flowing blue skirt, ran to Moon, grabbing at his leg. The Jerusalem Rider kicked out to send her sprawling to the dust. A young man shouted and leapt at the rider. The gunshot echoed across the plain, and the man fell back screaming and clutching his shoulder.

"My God," said Nestor, "Moon is with them!"

"I'd say that was a pretty accurate assessment," muttered Zerah. "What I don't understand is why the Hellborn are taking prisoners. They didn't in the old days. Just blood and slaughter. It makes no sense. There can't be that many of them, so why waste time and men guarding prisoners? You understand it, Meneer Steiner?"

"No. But if Moon is involved, there must be a profit in it. The man is a thief and a murderer, and possibly the fastest man with a pistol I ever knew."

"As fast as you?" sneered Nestor.

Steiner appeared to ignore the sarcasm. "I'd say faster. Let's hope it doesn't need to be put to the test."

"Scared, are you?"

"Oh, for God's sake, grow up!" snapped Clem. "You think you're the first *boy* who ever learned that the world isn't made up of knights and damsels? Yes, I was—am—Laton Duke. And no, I'm not proud of it. I was weak where I should have been strong and too damn strong where I should have been weak. But I don't owe you anything, Son, and you have no right to take out your bitterness on me. Now, I've taken it so far because you're a nice lad and learning about the Deacon's lies was a bitter blow for you. But you'd better shape up, Son, because we're in deep water here and I fear we'll be lucky to get out with our lives."

"You heed those words, young man," said Zerah. "I got two children to take care of, and the forces of evil seem mighty strong in these parts right now. I don't believe it would be smart to war among ourselves." Turning to Clem, she smiled. "Where to now, Meneer Brigand?"

"There's a woman I know lives near by . . . if she's still alive. We'll make for her place. You agree with that, Nestor, or do you want to ride your own road?"

Nestor fought down a cutting response and took a deep breath. "I'll ride with you that far," he said.

* * *

Amaziga Archer's mind was calm as the wind screamed above the old Aztec temple, tearing rocks from the ancient walls and hurling them through the air as if they were made of paper. Uprooted trees smashed against the walls, and the noise was deafening as she and Sam cowered in the underground chamber. The storm wind was still increasing, close to six hundred miles an hour, she remembered from her studies of the Fall of the World. As the earth toppled on its axis, the setting sun rose in the west, the winds howling across the earth, to be followed by a tidal wave the likes of which no man or woman had ever seen and lived through.

What strange beings we are, thought Amaziga as she sheltered from the terrible storm. Why are we hiding when the tidal wave will destroy us both? Why not stand outside and let the demon winds carry us up to the heavens? She knew the answer. The instinct for survival, clinging to those precious last seconds of life.

As suddenly as it had come the wind died.

Amaziga stumbled outside, Sam following, and ran up the hill, scrambling over fallen trees, clambering up onto the steps of the pyramid, higher and higher, all the time watching the west for the gigantic wall of death that would soon be bearing down on them. What was it the Prophet Isaiah had predicted? *"And the seas shall tip from their bowls, and not one stone be left upon another."*

Wise old man, she thought as she climbed the last steps to the summit.

"Look!" shouted Sam.

Amaziga swung to the west. The sight was incredible beyond belief, and just for a second she felt privileged to see it. The oncoming wall was black and filled the sky. A thousand feet high. More. Much more, she realized, for here, in this remote jungle, they were already two thousand feet above sea level.

"Oh, God!" whispered Sam. "Dear God!"

They clung to one another as the wall raced toward them. "I love you, Sam. Always have, always will."

Glancing down at her, he smiled. Then he kissed her lightly on the lips.

Violet light flared around them, and a great roaring filled their ears . . .

As the light faded, they found themselves standing on an island no more than sixty yards in diameter, the ocean all around them as far as the eye could see. Jon Shannow was standing some ten feet away, but he was so much older than when last they had said their farewells, his beard long and white, streaked with shades of darker gray. He was wearing the portable computer.

Amaziga grinned at him. "I don't know how you did it, but I'm grateful," she said.

"It wasn't me, lady," he told her, unclipping the machine and removing the headphones, which he passed to her. Amaziga slipped them into place and heard the soft sweet sound of Lucas's voice.

"Electronic cavalry, darling," he said.

"What did you do?"

"I moved us forward six days. The tidal wave has passed, and the sea is receding."

"How did you find me?"

"Ah, Amaziga, I am always linked with you. I need no coordinates. The man Lucas loved you until the moment he died. Beyond, perhaps—I don't know. Therefore, I love you, too. Is that so strange?"

"No," she said, humbled. "Where can we go?"

"Under normal circumstances," he said, "anywhere you desired. But the stone is Mr. Shannow's, and he is fighting the Bloodstone. I need coordinates to bring him home, a date I can home in on."

Amaziga called out to Shannow, who came across and sat beside her. For some time she questioned him about the events leading up to his journey through the gateway, but there was nothing she could use. Sam joined in, asking about the positions of the stars, the cycles of the moon, the seasons. At last Amaziga gave up. "We have to think of something else," she said.

Shannow leaned back, weary and fighting back despair.

"You look more human as an old man," said Amaziga, "less fearsome."

Shannow smiled. "I know. I met . . . myself . . . Not a happy encounter. To see such youth and to know where he was headed yet not to be able to say anything. Strange, as a young man newly wounded with no memory I saw an ancient man who looked close to death. He said I could call him Jake. I recognized nothing of myself in him. And then to meet him again, as Jake, and see a face without lines and wrinkles, a body possessing the strength and suppleness I had long forgotten. He looked like a boy to me."

Amaziga leaned forward. "You met him in the mountains? Before he went to Domango?"

"One day before," said Shannow.

"And how long after the meeting did you travel through the gateway?"

"Eight . . . nine days, I think. Why?"

"Because I met you on the outskirts of Domango. Lucas *knows* that date. If we move forward, say, ten days, we should get you back in the same time line. What do you think, Lucas?"

"Yes, I can do that," Lucas told her. "The question is where. I have no files on the power point Shannow used. We will have to come through elsewhere. You know the area. Where do you suggest?"

"There's a strong power center close to Pilgrim's Valley. I used it myself twice," she said.

"Then that will be our destination," said Lucas. "But I cannot guarantee that we will arrive at the same time or on the same day. Erring on the side of caution, the margin of error could be as much as a week after he left."

Four days had passed. Wallace Nash and Beth had repaired the damaged window shutters as best they could, while Isis and Dr. Meredith had cut what meat remained from the slaughtered farm animals. On the third day the Deacon's mule had trotted back into the yard. Beth had clapped her hands when she had seen it.

"You son of a gun!" she said, smiling and walking forward to rub the mule's nose. "You got away!"

With ropes from the barn they hauled away the corpses of the Wolvers and the slaughtered oxen. Beth dug up vegetables from the small plot at the rear of the barn and stored them in the kitchen of the main building. She also filled several buckets of water from the well and left them inside the house. On the fourth day Dr. Meredith helped Beth carry Jeremiah's body out to the ground behind the ruined barn. Wallace and the doctor dug a deep grave. Isis stood beside Beth as the earth was shoveled onto the blanket-wrapped corpse.

"He was a good man," said Isis, holding on to Beth's hand.

"Even good men die. We all die," said Beth. "Let's hope this is an end to the terror."

"It isn't," said Isis. "Men with horned helms and black armor will be riding here soon. The Bloodstone cannot be stopped, Beth. I felt him and his power, his lust for blood and his terrible determination. And now the Deacon is gone. I think we are all going to die."

Beth hefted her rifle and said nothing.

Meredith stood beside the grave and laid down his shovel. His slender face was bathed in sweat, and his eyes were downcast, his sorrow evident. "I'm sorry, Jeremiah," he said. "You were kind to me, and I killed you."

"Don't dwell on it," said Beth. "You made a mistake. We all make mistakes. You just have to learn to live with them." She turned to the redheaded youngster. "As I recall, Wallace, you have a fine voice. Why don't you sing for us? 'Rock of Ages' ought to be just fine."

"Riders coming," said Wallace. Beth cocked the rifle as she swung.

Clem Steiner rode into the yard and dismounted; Nestor Garrity sat on his horse, hands on the saddle pommel. The boy looked older, thought Beth, his face gaunt, his eyes tired. Behind him came two more horses, one bearing a stick-thin old woman with leathered skin and bright blue eyes and the other carrying two children.

"Didn't find him, Beth," said Clem, "but he's alive."

She nodded absently and walked to where the old woman was dismounting. "Welcome to my home," said Beth, introducing herself.

The old woman gave a weary smile. "Good to be here, child. I'm Zerah Wheeler, and it's been quite a journey. I see you're burying someone. Don't let me interfere with the words of farewell."

"There's food and drink in the house," Beth told her. Together the two women lifted the youngsters from the horse, and Zerah led them inside. "All right, Wallace," said Beth. "Let's hear the hymn!"

His voice was strong and surprisingly deep, and the words of the old hymn rolled out over the hillsides, with Clem, Beth, and Nestor joining in. Isis wept, and remembered the many kindnesses she had received from Jeremiah.

At last the song ended, and Beth walked away from the grave, linking arms with Clem. He told her of their travels and how Nestor had been forced to kill. She listened gravely. "Poor Nestor," she said. "He always was a romantically inclined boy. But he's strong, Clem; he'll get over it. I wish Jon was here. There's more trouble coming."

"I know," he said, and told her of the horned riders herding prisoners toward the town. In turn she explained about the Deacon and the Bloodstone and the spell of changing he had placed over the Wolvers.

"Maybe we should get away from here," said Clem. "Far and fast."

"I don't think so, Clem. First, we've only four horses and ten people, and one of those is badly wounded. You remember Josiah Broome?"

"Sure. Inoffensive man, hated violence."

"He still does. He was shot down, Clem—by Jerusalem Riders."

Clem nodded. "Never did trust that bunch, especially with Jacob Moon in the lead. The man's rotten through to the core.

I saw him with the Hellborn." Clem grinned at her. "So we stay here, then?"

"It's my home, Clem. And you said yourself, it's built like a fortress. No one's been able to drive me off it so far."

Clem swore. "Looks like that's going to be put to the test, Beth, darlin'," he said.

Beth looked up. On the far hillside to the north she saw a line of riders sitting on their horses and staring down at the farmhouse. "I think we had better get inside," she said.

Arm in arm they walked slowly toward the house. The riders were some two hundred yards distant. Beth counted them as she walked; there were around fifty men, all wearing horned helms and carrying rifles.

Inside the house she sent Wallace and Nestor upstairs to watch from the bedroom windows, while Zerah took up a rifle and positioned herself at the downstairs window. Dr. Meredith sat on the floor by the fire beside Isis and the young mother and her baby. Clem glanced at the sandy-haired man. "You need a spare weapon, Meneer?" he asked.

Meredith shook his head. "I can't kill," he said.

Josiah Broome, his thin chest bandaged, a bloodstain showing through it, moved into the main room. "What's happening?" His eyes were feverish, and cold sweat bathed his face. He saw Clem and smiled. "Well, well, if it isn't young Steiner. Good to see you, my boy." Suddenly he sagged against the door frame. "Damn," he whispered. "Weaker than I thought."

Clem took his arm and led him back into the bedroom, laying the wounded man on the bed. "I think you should stay here, Meneer. You are in no condition to fight."

"Who are we fighting, Clem?"

"Bad men, Josiah, but don't you worry. I'm still pretty good with a pistol."

"Too good," said Josiah sadly, his eyes closing.

Clem rejoined the others. The Hellborn had left the hillside and were riding slowly toward the building. Beth stepped outside. Clem grabbed her arm. "What the hell . . . ?"

"Let's hear what they've got to say," said Beth.

"Why?" asked Clem. "You think they've stopped by for Baker's and biscuits?"

Beth ignored him and waited on the porch, her rifle cradled in her arms. Clem took off his jacket and stood beside her, hand resting on the butt of his pistol.

Beth stood quietly watching the riders. They were grim men, hard-eyed and wary, their faces sharp, their eyes stern. The look of fanatics, she thought, ungiving, unbending. They wore black breastplates engraved with swirls of silver and black horned helms buckled under the chin. In their hands were short-barreled rifles, and pistols were strapped to their hips. Yet the most disturbing feature for Beth was that each of them had a Bloodstone in the center of his forehead. Like the wolves, she thought. The Hellborn rode into the yard, fanning out before the house. A lean-faced warrior kneed his horse forward and sat before her. His eyes were the gray of a winter sky, and there was no warmth in the gaze. His helmet was also horned, but the tips had been dipped in gold.

"I am Shorak," he said, "first lieutenant of the Second Corps. This land is now the property of the Lord of Hell." Beth said nothing as Shorak's gaze raked the building, noting the riflemen at the slits in the upper windows. "I am here," he said, returning his stare to Beth, "to escort you to the Lord Sarento so that you may pay homage and learn of his greatness firsthand. You will need no possessions or weapons of any kind, though you may bring food for the journey."

Beth looked up at the man, then at the others, who sat on their horses silently. "Never heard of the Lord Sarento," she told the leader.

He leaned forward, the sun glinting on the golden horns of his helmet. "That is your loss, woman, for he is the living God, the lord of all. Those who serve him well gain eternal life and joy beyond imagining."

"This is my home," Beth told him. "I have fought for it and killed those who would take it from me. I raised children here, and I guess I'll die here. If the Lord Sarento wants me to pay homage, he can come here himself. I'll bake him a cake. Now, if that's all you wanted to tell me, I suggest you ride off. I've work to do."

Shorak seemed unconcerned by her refusal. He sat quietly for a moment, then spoke again. "You do not understand me, woman. I shall make it plain. Gather food and we will escort you to the Lord. Refuse and we will kill you all. And the manner of your passing will be painful. Now, there are others within the house, and I suggest you speak to them. Not all of them will wish to die. You have until noon to make a decision. We will return then."

Wheeling his horse, Shorak led the riders back out to the hillside.

"Polite, wasn't he?" said Clem.

Beth ignored the humor and strode inside. The first person to speak was the young mother, Ruth. "I want to go with them, Frey McAdam," she said. "I don't want any more fear and fighting."

"It would seem the only course," agreed Dr. Meredith. "We can't outfight them."

Wallace and Nestor came downstairs to join in the discussion. Beth poured herself a mug of water and sipped it, saying nothing.

"How much ammunition we got?" Wallace asked.

Beth smiled. "A hundred rounds for the rifles. Twenty for my pistol."

"I've got thirty," Clem said.

"We mustn't fight them," said Ruth. "We mustn't! I've got my baby to think of. What's so hard about paying homage to someone? I mean, it's only words."

"Speaking of which," remarked Zerah Wheeler, "we only have *their* word for it that paying homage is all they want. Once outside and unarmed, they can do as they damn well please with us."

"Why would they want to harm us?" asked Dr. Meredith. "It would make no sense."

"They are Hellborn," put in Isis, "and it was their master who sent the wolves against us."

"I don't care about that!" shouted Ruth. "I just don't want to die!"

"Nobody wants to die," snapped Beth. "Wallace, get back upstairs and watch them. I don't want them sneaking up on us."

"Yes, Frey," he said, and returned to his post.

Nestor spoke. "When we saw them heading toward the town, they were leading a group of prisoners. They didn't kill none of them. Maybe it's just like the man said, just paying homage to their leader."

Beth turned to Clem. "You're not saying much."

Clem shrugged. "I don't think there's much to say. I don't know where these Hellborn came from, but if they're anything like the warriors of the first war, they're murdering savages: they'll rape and torture the women and mutilate the men. And I'm not surrendering my weapons to the likes of them."

"You're crazy!" screamed Ruth. "You'll condemn us all to death!"

"Shut your mouth!" stormed Beth. "I won't have it! This is no time for hysterics. What do you think, Zerah?"

Zerah put her arm around Esther's shoulders. Oz moved in close, and she ruffled his hair. "I got less to lose than the rest of you, being old and worn out. But I've also been trying to keep these children alive, and I'm kind of torn. You look to me, Frey McAdam, like a woman who's been over the mountain a few times. What do you think?"

"I don't like threats," said Beth, "and I don't like men who make them. They want us alive. I don't know why; I don't much care."

"I can tell you why," said Isis softly. "When I went out to the wolf-beasts, I felt the power of the Bloodstone. He is hungry, and he feeds on souls. To go to him would mean death."

"What do you mean, feeds on souls?" sneered Ruth. "That's insane. You're making it up!"

Isis shook her head. "He was linked to the wolves. Every time they killed, part of the life was fed back through the stones in their heads. He is a creature of blood and death. All we are to him is food. The Deacon knew that."

"And where is he?" hissed Ruth. "Gone and left us days ago. Run away! Well, I'm not dying here. No matter what any of you say."

"I think we should vote on it," said Clem. "It's getting close to noon."

Beth called out to Wallace, and he stood at the top of the stairs, rifle in hand. "You called the vote, Clem, so what's your view?" she asked.

"Fight," said Clem.

"Wallace?"

"I ain't going with them," said the redheaded youngster.

"Nestor?"

The young man hesitated. "Fight," he said.

"Isis?"

"I'm not going with them."

"Doctor?"

Meredith shrugged. "I'll go with the majority view," he said.

"Zerah?"

The old woman kissed Esther on the cheek. "Fight," she said.

"I think that about settles it," said Beth.

Ruth stared at them all. "You are all crazy!"

"They're coming back," shouted Wallace.

Beth moved to the dresser and pulled clear three boxes of shells. "Help yourselves," she said. "You youngsters stay down low on the floor."

Esther and Oz scrambled down below the table. Zerah stood and took up her rifle as Beth walked to the door.

"You're not going out there again?" asked Clem.

Beth pulled open the door and stood leaning against the frame, her rifle cocked and ready and held across her body.

The Hellborn rode, fanning out as before.

Ruth ran across the room, brushing past Beth and sprinting out into the yard. "I'll pay homage," she shouted. "Let me go with you!"

Shorak ignored her and looked at Beth. "What is your decision, woman?" he asked.

"We stay here," she said.

"It is all of you or none," said Shorak.

Smoothly he drew his pistol and shot Ruth in the head. The young woman was poleaxed to the ground. Beth swung her rifle and fired, the bullet screaming past Shorak to punch into the chest of the rider beside him and pitch him from the saddle. Clem grabbed Beth, hauling her back inside as bullets smashed into the door frame and screamed through the room. Nestor kicked shut the door, and Clem dropped the bar into place.

Zerah fired three shots through the window, then a bullet took her high in the shoulder, spinning her to the floor. A Hellborn warrior ran to the window. Clem shot him through the face. The door shuddered as men hurled themselves against it.

Beth scrambled to her feet. Several more Hellborn reached the window, firing into the room. Zerah, blood drenching her shirt, rolled against the wall beneath the sill. Beth fired, taking a man in the chest. He pitched forward. Another warrior hurled himself against the window, smashing the frame and rolling into the room. Nestor shot him twice. The Hellborn hit the floor face first, twitched, then was still.

Clem ran across the room, tipping the pine table to its side. Shots ripped into the walls of the house and ricocheted around the room. The door began to splinter. Beth pumped three shots through it and heard a man scream and fall to the porch.

Nestor ran for the stairs, climbing them two at a time. Bullets struck the wall around him, but he made it to the top and moved to help Wallace. Meredith lay on the floor, holding tightly to Isis, trying to shield her with his body. The two children were crouched down behind the upturned table. In the back of the house the baby started to cry, the sound thin and piercing.

"They're at the back of the house!" Wallace bellowed from upstairs.

Beth looked at Clem and pointed to Josiah Broome's room. "The back window!" she shouted.

Clem ducked down and crawled across the floor. As he reached the doorway, he saw the shutters of the window explode inward. Rearing up, he shot the first man through the throat, catapulting him back into his comrades. Broome was unconscious but lying directly in the line of fire. Clem dived across to the bed, dragging the wounded man to the floor. Shots exploded all around him, searing through the down-filled quilt and sending feathers into the air. A shot scorched across Clem's neck, tearing the skin. He fired, his bullet entering under the man's chin and moving up through the brain.

Ducking below the level of the bed, Clem reloaded. A bullet slashed through the mattress to smash into his thigh, glancing from the bone and ripping across the flesh. Clem hurled himself back and fired three quick shots into the bodies massed at the window. The Hellborn ducked from sight. Clem glanced down at his leg to see blood pouring from the wound. He swore softly.

A man leapt at the window. Clem shot him as he was clambering through, and the body fell across the frame, the dead man's pistol clattering to the floor. Rolling to his belly, Clem crawled across to the weapon, snatching it up.

Then all was silence.

Josiah Broome came awake, his mind floating above the fever dream. He was lying on the floor of the bedroom, and young Clem Steiner was sitting some four feet away, two pistols in his hands, blood staining his leg.

"What's happening, Clem?" he whispered.

"Hellborn," answered the shootist.

I'm still dreaming, thought Broome. The Hellborn are all gone, destroyed by the Deacon in the bloodiest massacre ever seen in this new world. A shot clipped wood from the window frame and smashed into a framed embroidery on the far wall. Josiah Broome chuckled. It was the damnedest dream. The embroidery tilted, and the center ripped away. Broome could still read the words: "The works of man shall perish, the love of the Lord abideth always."

He tried to stand. "Get down!" ordered Steiner.

"Just a dream, Clem," said Josiah, getting his knees under him. Steiner launched himself across the floor, his shoulder cannoning into Broome's legs as the older man straightened. Shots smashed into the far wall, and the embroidery fell to the floor, the pine frame splitting.

"No dream. You understand? This is no dream!"

Josiah felt the breath forced from his lungs, and his chest wound flared, pain ripping through him.

"But . . . but they can't be Hellborn!"

"Maybe so," agreed Clem, "but trust me, Josiah, if they're not originals, they are giving a passable fair impression." The younger man groaned as he twisted up into a sitting position, guns cocked. "If you feel strong enough, you might think of getting a tourniquet on this wound of mine. Don't want to bleed to death and miss all the fun."

A shadow crossed the window. Clem's guns roared, and Josiah saw a man smashed from his feet.

"Why are they doing this?" Josiah asked.

"I don't feel up to asking them," Clem told him. "Rip up a sheet and make some bandages."

Josiah glanced down at the wound in Clem's thigh. Blood was flowing steadily, drenching the black broadcloth pants. His own clothes were laid over the back of a chair. Crawling to them, Josiah pulled the belt clear and returned to Clem. Then he broke off a section of the pine frame that had encased the embroidery. Clem wrapped the belt around his thigh above the wound, stretching the leather tight against the skin. He tried to use the pine to twist the belt tighter, but the wood snapped. The bleeding slowed but did not stop.

"You better take one of these pistols, Josiah," said Clem. "I might pass out."

Broome shook his head. "I couldn't kill, not even to save my life. I don't believe in violence."

"I do so like to meet a man of principle at times like these," Clem said wearily. Shots sounded from above, and outside a man screamed.

Clem crawled across to the doorway and glanced into the

main room. Beth was behind the table, rifle in hand. The old woman, Zerah, was below the window, a pistol in her fist. Dr. Meredith was lying by the western wall, the children and Isis close to him. "Everyone all right?" called Clem.

"Bastards broke my shoulder," Zerah told him. "Hurts like hell."

Meredith left the children and crawled across to Zerah. Swiftly he examined her. "The bullet broke your collarbone and ripped up and out through the top of your shoulder. It's bleeding freely, but no vital organs were hit. I'll get some bandages."

"What can you see upstairs?" shouted Beth.

Nestor Garrity's voice floated down to them. "They've taken shelter at the barn and behind the trough. We downed fourteen of them. Some crawled back to safety, but there's nine bodies that ain't moving. And I think Clem hit two more that we can't see from up here."

"You keep watch now," Beth called, "and let us know when they move."

"Yes, Frey."

The baby began to cry, a thin pitiful sound that echoed in the building. Beth turned to Isis. "There's a little milk left in the kitchen, girl. Be careful as you get it."

Isis kept low as she crossed the room and went through the kitchen. The back door was barred, the shutters on the window closed tight. The milk was in a tall jug on the top shelf. Isis stood and lifted it down; then, moving back to the baby, she sat beside the crib. "How do I feed her?" she asked Beth.

Beth swore and moved from the table to a chest of drawers, laying down her rifle and removing a pair of fine leather gloves from the second drawer. They were the only gloves she had ever owned, given to her by her first husband, Sean, just before they were married. Never even worn them, thought Beth. From a sewing box on top of the chest she took a needle and made three small holes through the longest finger of the left-hand glove. Gathering up her rifle, she made her way to the crib. The baby was wailing, and she ordered Isis to lift the infant boy and hold him close. Beth half filled the glove, then waited until milk began to seep through the needle holes. At first the baby had difficulty sucking on the glove and choked. Isis supported the back of his head, and he began to feed.

"They're sneaking around the back!" shouted Nestor. "Can't get a good shot!"

Clem lurched back into the rear bedroom and waited to the right of the window. Shadows moved on the ground outside, and Clem could make out the horns of a Hellborn helmet on the hard-baked earth. There was no way he could tell how many men were outside, and the only way to stop them was to frame himself in the window and open fire. Clem's mouth was dry.

"Do it now," he told himself aloud, "or you'll never have the nerve to do it at all."

Swiftly he spun around, guns blazing through the shattered window. Two men went down, and the third returned fire. Clem was hit hard in the chest, but he coolly put a shell through the Hellborn's head. Then he slumped down and fell against the bed.

Josiah Broome crawled alongside him. "How bad is it?" asked the older man.

"I've had better days," Clem told him as he struggled to reload. The Hellborn pistol took a larger caliber of shell than his own pistol, and it was empty now. Angrily he cast it aside. "Goddamn," he said bitterly. "Those sons of bitches are really starting to get my goat!" His gun loaded, he leaned back, too frightened to check the chest wound. Broome moved out into the main room and called for Dr. Meredith. The sandy-haired young man made his way to Clem, and the shootist felt the man's fingers probing.

Meredith said nothing, and Clem opened his eyes. "You want to tell me the good news?" he asked.

"It isn't good," said Meredith softly.

"There's a surprise." Clem was feeling light-headed and faint, but he clung on. There were not enough defenders, and he was not going to die just yet. He coughed. Blood rose in his throat and sprayed out onto Meredith's pale shirt. Clem sank back. The sun was setting, the sky the color of burning copper.

Clem levered himself to his feet, staggered, and righted himself by gripping the window frame.

"What are you doing?" asked Josiah Broome, reaching out to grab Clem's arm. Meredith took hold of Broome's shoulder, drawing him back.

"He's dying," whispered Meredith. "He has only minutes left."

Clem fell across the ruined window, then lifted his leg over the sill. The air was fresh and cool outside, not filled with the acrid smell of black powder. It was a good evening, the sky bright. Clem dropped to the ground and half fell. Blood filled his throat, and he thought he was suffocating, but he swallowed it down and staggered to the corpses, relieving them of their pistols and tossing the weapons through the window. One of the Hellborn was wearing a bandolier of shells. With difficulty, Clem tugged it loose and passed it to Broome.

"Come back inside!" urged Broome.

"I like . . . it . . . here," whispered Clem, the effort of speaking bringing on a fresh bout of coughing.

Clem staggered to the edge of the building. From there he could see the horse trough and the two men hiding behind it. As he stepped into sight, they saw him and tried to bring their rifles to bear. Clem shot them both. A third man rose from behind the paddock fence, and a bullet punched into Clem's body, half spinning him. He returned the fire but missed.

Falling to his knees, Clem reached into the pocket of his coat, pulling clear his last few shells. Another bullet struck him. The ground was hard against his cheek, and all pain floated away from him. Three Hellborn ran from hiding. Clem heard the pounding of their boots on the earth.

With the last of his strength Clem rolled. There were two shots left in the pistol, and he triggered them both, the first shell slamming into the belly of the leading Hellborn and pitching him from his feet, the second tearing into an unprotected throat.

A rifle boomed, and Clem saw the last Hellborn stagger to a stop, the top of his head blown away. The body crumpled to the ground.

Clem lay on his back and stared up at the sky. It was unbearably bright for a moment, then the darkness closed in from the sides until at last he was staring at a tiny circle of light at the end of a long, dark tunnel.

Then there was nothing.

Nestor and Wallace watched him die. "He was a tough one," said Wallace.

"He was Laton Duke," said Nestor softly.

"Yeah? Well, don't that beat all!" Wallace lifted his rifle to his shoulder and sighted on a man creeping along beneath the paddock fence. He fired, the bullet splintering wood above the man and causing him to dive for cover. "Damn it! Missed him. Laton Duke, you say? He was sure good with that pistol."

"He was good," agreed Nestor sadly. Glancing up at the redheaded youngster, he asked, "You frightened, Wal?"

"Yep."

"You don't look it."

The youngster shrugged. "My folks were never much on showing stuff, you know, emotions and the like. Busted my arm once and cried. My dad set the bone, then whacked me alongside the head for blubbing." He sniffed and chuckled. "I did love that old goat!" Wallace fired again. "Got him, by God!"

Nestor glanced out to see the Hellborn warrior lying still in the gathering dusk.

"You think they'll attack us after dark?"

"Bet on it," said Wallace. "Let's hope there's a good clear sky and plenty of moonlight."

Movement in the distance caught Nestor's eye. "Oh, no!" he whispered. Wallace saw them, too. Scores of Hellborn were riding down the hillside.

Jacob Moon was with them.

As they neared, Wallace tried a shot at the Jerusalem Rider but missed, his shot thumping into the shoulder of a rider to Moon's left. The Hellborn dismounted and ran to the shelter of the barn. Wallace spit through the rifle slit but said nothing.

Nestor backed from the room and called down the news to Beth McAdam.

"We saw them," she called back. "Clem threw in some pistols. Better come down here and help yourself, son."

Nestor moved swiftly downstairs. Isis and Meredith held pistols now, but Josiah Broome sat defiantly on the floor, his hands across his knees.

"Are you some sort of coward?" asked Nestor. "Haven't you even got the guts to fight for your life?"

"That's enough of that!" stormed Beth. "Sometimes it takes more courage to stick by what you believe in. Now get back upstairs and stay with Wallace."

"Yes, Frey," he said meekly.

Beth knelt by Josiah Broome, resting her hand on his shoulder. "How are you feeling?" she asked.

"Sad, Beth," he told her, patting her hand. "We never learn, do we? We never change. Always killing and causing pain."

"Not all of us. Some of us just fight to stay alive. When it starts, stay low."

"I'm ashamed to admit that I wish he was here now," said Josiah.

Beth nodded, remembering Shannow in his prime. There was a force and a power about him that made him appear unbeatable, unstoppable. "So do I, Josiah. So do I." Beth called the children to her and told them to sit with Josiah. Esther snuggled down and buried her face in the old man's shoulder. Broome put his arm around her.

Oz pulled clear his small pistol. "I'm going to fight," said the child.

Beth nodded. "Wait till they're inside," she said.

"They're coming!" Nestor yelled.

Beth ran to the window. Zerah, blood seeping from her shoulder wound, stood to the left of the window with her pistol ready. Beth risked a glance. The Hellborn were coming in a solid wedge of men, racing across the yard.

The few defenders could never stop them.

There was no need to aim, and Beth and Zerah triggered

their pistols into the advancing wedge of attackers. Bullets smashed into the room, ricocheting around the walls.

Upstairs Nestor levered shells into the rifle, sending shot after shot into the charging Hellborn.

They were halfway to the house when Wallace gave a whoop. "Son of a bitch!" he yelled.

More riders were thundering down the hillside, but they were not Hellborn. Many wore the gray shield shirts of the Crusaders.

As they rode, they opened fire, a volley of shots ripping through the ranks of the charging men. The Hellborn slowed, then swung to meet their attackers. Nestor saw several horses go down, but the rest came on, surging into the yard.

"Son of a bitch!" yelled Wallace again.

The Hellborn scattered but were shot down as they ran.

Wallace and Nestor continued to fire until their bullets ran out. Then they raced downstairs.

Beth staggered to a chair and sat down, the pistol suddenly heavy in her tired hand. A face appeared at the window. It was Tobe Harris.

"Good to see you, Tobe," said Beth. "I swear to God you have the handsomest face I ever did see."

Nestor gathered up Beth's pistol and ran out into the yard, where bodies lay everywhere, twisted in death. The Crusaders from Purity had moved on into the fields, chasing down the fleeing Hellborn. Nestor could not believe it. He was going to live! Death had seemed so certain, unavoidable and inevitable. The sun was sinking behind the mountains, and Nestor felt tears well into his eyes. He could smell the gun smoke and through it the fresh, sweet scent of the moisture on the grass.

"Oh, God!" he whispered.

Horsemen came riding back into the yard, led by a tall, square-shouldered man in a black coat. The man lifted his flat-crowned hat from his head and produced a handkerchief from his pocket, wiping his face and beard.

"By the Lord, you fought well here, boy," he said. "I am Padlock Wheeler. The Deacon sent for me."

"I'm Nestor Garrity, sir."

"You look all in, Son," said Wheeler, dismounting and tethering his horse to a rail. Around him other Crusaders moved among the dead. Occasionally a pistol shot would sound as they found wounded Hellborn. Nestor looked away; it was so cold, so merciless. Padlock Wheeler moved alongside him, patting his shoulder. "I need to know what is happening here, Son. The man Tobe told us of the giant Wolvers, but we've now had two run-ins with Hellborn warriors. Where are they from?"

Isis walked from the doorway. Padlock Wheeler bowed, and the blond girl smiled wearily. "They are from beyond the gates of time, Meneer. The Deacon told me that. And their leader is a soul stealer, a taker of life."

Wheeler nodded. "We'll deal with him, young lady. But where is the Deacon?"

"He vanished through one of the gateways. He has gone seeking help."

Nestor stood silently by, his thoughts confused. The Deacon was a liar and a fraud. It was all lies and death and violence. His mouth tasted of bile, and he found himself shivering, his stomach churning with nausea.

One of the Crusaders shouted to Wheeler and pointed to the east. Three riders were coming. Nestor leaned against the porch rail and watched them approach. In the lead was a white-bearded old man; behind him came a black woman, her head bandaged. Beside her rode a black man, blood staining his white shirt.

"The Deacon!" said Padlock Wheeler, his voice exultant. Leaving the porch, Wheeler stepped down to the yard, raising his arm in greeting.

At that moment a body moved beside his feet, springing up with gun in hand. An arm encircled Wheeler's neck, and a pistol barrel was thrust under his chin. No one moved.

The gunman was Jacob Moon. "Stay back, you bastards!" shouted the Jerusalem Rider. All was still except for the slow walking horse the Deacon rode. Nestor's gaze flicked from the rider to Moon and his victim and back again. The Deacon wore a long black coat and a pale shirt. His beard shone silver in the moonlight, and his deep-set eyes were focused on Moon. Slowly he dismounted. The black woman and her companion remained where they were, sitting motionless on their horses.

"Let him go," said the Deacon, his voice deep and steady.

"I want a horse and a chance to ride free from here," said Moon.

"No," said the Deacon simply. "What I will give you is an opportunity to live. Let Padlock go free and you may face me man to man. Should you triumph, not a man here will stop you."

"In a pig's eye!" stormed Moon. "As soon as I let him go, you'll gun me down."

"I am the Deacon, and I do not lie!"

Moon dragged Padlock farther back toward the wall. "You're not the Deacon!" he screamed. "I killed him at his summer cabin."

"You killed an old man who served me well. The man you are holding is Padlock Wheeler, one of my generals in the Unity Wars. He knows me, as do several of these riders. Now, do you have the nerve to face me?"

"Nerve?" snorted Moon. "You think it takes nerve to shoot down an old goat?"

Nestor blinked. The old man could not know who he was threatening. It was madness. "He's Jacob Moon!" he shouted. "Don't do it!"

Darkness had fallen, and the moon was bright in the sky. The Deacon appeared not to hear the youngster's words. "Well?" he said, removing his coat. Nestor saw that he was wearing two guns.

"I'll go free?" asked Moon. "I have your word on that? Your oath?"

"Let every man here understand," said the Deacon. "Should I die, this man rides free."

Moon threw Padlock Wheeler aside and stood for a moment, gun in hand. Then he laughed and moved out into the open. Behind him men opened up a space, moving out of the line of fire.

"I don't know why you want to die, old man, but I'll oblige you. You should have listened to the boy. I am Jacob Moon, the Jerusalem Rider, and I've never been beat." He holstered his pistol.

"And I," said the Deacon, "am Jon Shannow, the Jerusalem Man."

As he spoke, the Deacon smoothly palmed his pistol. There was no sudden jerk, no indication of tension or drama. The words froze Moon momentarily, but his hand flashed for his pistol. He was infinitely faster than the old man, but his reaction time was dulled by the words the Deacon had spoken. A bullet smashed into his belly, and he staggered back a pace. His own gun boomed, but then three shots thundered into him, spinning him from his feet.

The world continued to spin as Moon struggled to his knees. He tried to raise his pistol, but his hand was empty. He blinked sweat from his eyes and stared up at the deadly old man, who was now walking toward him.

"The wages of sin is death, Moon" were the last words he heard.

Padlock Wheeler rushed to the Deacon's side. The old man fell into his arms. Nestor saw the blood on the Deacon's shirt. Two men ran forward, and they half carried the Deacon into the house. Nestor followed them.

The first person he saw was Beth. Her face was unnaturally pale, and she stood with eyes wide, hand over her mouth, as they laid the Deacon on the floor.

"Oh, Christ!" she whispered. "Oh, dear Christ!" Falling to her knees beside him, she stroked a hand through his gray hair. "How can it be you, Jon? You are so old!"

The man smiled weakly, his head resting in Padlock Wheeler's lap. "Long story," he said, his voice distant.

The black woman entered the room and knelt by Shannow. "Use the stone," she commanded.

"Not enough power."

"Of course there is!"

"Not for me . . . and the Bloodstone. Don't worry about me, lady. I'll live long enough to do what must be done. Where is Meredith?"

"I'm here, sir," said the sandy-haired young man.

"Get me into the back room. Check the wound. Strap it. Whatever."

Wheeler and Meredith carried him through the house. Beth rose and turned to face the black woman. "It's been a long time, Amaziga."

"Three hundred years and more," said Amaziga. "This is my husband, Sam."

The black man smiled and offered his left hand; the right was strapped to his chest.

Beth shook hands. "You've been in the wars, too, I see."

Amaziga nodded. "We came through a gateway north of here. We walked for a while, but we were surprised by some Hellborn warriors. There were four of them. Sam took a bullet in the shoulder. I got this graze," she said, lightly touching the bandage on her brow. "Shannow killed them. It's what he's good at."

"He's good at a damn sight more than that," said Beth, reddening, "but then, that's something you've never been capable of understanding."

Turning on her heel, she followed the others into the bedroom. Shannow was in the bed, Meredith examining the wound, while Josiah Broome sat to the left, holding Shannow's hand. Wheeler stood at the foot of the bed. Beth moved alongside the doctor. The wound was low and had ripped through the flesh above the hipbone to emerge in a jagged tear on Shannow's side. Blood was flowing freely, and Shannow's face was gray, his eyes closed.

"I need to stop the flow," said Meredith. "Get me a needle and thread."

Outside Nestor introduced himself to Amaziga Archer and her husband. The woman was astonishingly beautiful, he thought, despite the gray streaks in her hair. "Is he really the Jerusalem Man?" asked Nestor.

"Really," said Amaziga, moving away to the kitchen. Sam smiled at the boy.

"A living legend, Nestor."

"I can't believe he beat Jacob Moon. I just can't believe it! And him so old."

"I expect Moon found it even harder to believe. Now excuse me, Son, but I'm weary and I need to rest. Is there a bed somewhere?"

"Yes, sir. Upstairs. I'll show you."

"No need, Son. I may be wounded, but I believe I still have the strength to find a bed."

As Sam moved away, Nestor saw Wallace sitting by the window with Zerah Wheeler. The redhead was chatting to the children. Esther was giggling, and young Oz was staring at Wallace with undisguised admiration.

Nestor walked from the house.

Outside the Crusaders were clearing away the corpses, dragging them to the field beyond the buildings. Several campfires had been lit in the lee of the barn, and men were sitting quietly, talking in groups.

Isis was sitting by the paddock fence, staring out over the moonlit hills. When Nestor joined her, she looked up and smiled. "It is a wonderful night," she said.

Nestor glanced up at the glittering stars. "Yes," he agreed. "It's good to be alive."

Beth sat beside Shannow's bed, with Padlock Wheeler standing beside her. "By God, Deacon, I never thought to hear you lie," said Wheeler. "But it did the trick; it threw him right enough."

Shannow smiled weakly. "It was no lie, Pad." Slowly and with great effort he told the story of his travels, beginning with the attack on his church, his rescue by the Wanderers, the fight with Aaron Crane and his men, and finally his meeting with Amaziga beyond the town of Domango.

"It really was you, then, in my church!" said Wheeler. "By heaven, Deacon, you never cease to amaze me."

"There's more, Pad," said Shannow. He closed his eyes and

spoke of the Bloodstone and the ruined world from which
it came.

"How do we fight such a beast?" asked Padlock Wheeler.

"I have a plan," said Shannow. "Not much of one, I'll grant
you, but with the grace of God it'll give us a chance."

Zerah Wheeler entered the room, her shoulder bandaged
and her arm bound across her chest. "Leave the wounded man
be," she said, "and say hello to your mother."

Padlock spun, jaw agape. "Jesus wept, Mother! I did not
know you were here. And you're wounded!" Moving to her
side, he threw his arm around her shoulder.

"*Whisht,* you lummox! You'll set it bleeding again," she
scolded, knocking his hand away. "Now come outside and
leave the man to rest. You, too, Beth."

"I'll be with you soon," Beth said quietly as Zerah led her
son from the room. Josiah Broome rose and patted Shannow's
arm. "It is good to see you, my friend," he said, and left the
wounded man alone with Beth. She took his hand and sighed.

"Why did you not tell me who you were?" she asked.

"Why did you not recognize me?" he countered.

She shrugged. "I should have. I should have done so many
things, Jon. And now it's all wasted and gone. I couldn't take
it, you see. You changed from man of action to preacher. It
was such a change. Why did it have to be so drastic, so
radical?"

He smiled wearily. "I can't tell you, Beth, except that I have
never understood compromise. For me it is all or nothing. Yet
despite my efforts, I failed in everything. I didn't find
Jerusalem, and as a preacher I couldn't remain a pacifist." He
sighed. "When the church was burning, I felt a terrible rage. It
engulfed me. And then as the Deacon . . . I thought I could
make a difference. Bring God in to the world, establish disci-
pline. I failed at that, too."

"History alone judges success or failure, Shannow," said
Amaziga, moving into the room.

Beth glanced up, ready to tell the woman to leave, but she
felt Shannow's hand squeeze hers and saw him shake his

head. Amaziga sat down on the other side of the bed. "Lucas tells me you have a plan, but he won't share it with me."

"Let me speak with him." Amaziga passed him the headphones and the portable. Shannow winced as he tried to raise his arm. Amaziga leaned forward and settled the headphones into place, slipping the microphone from its groove and twisting it into position. "Leave me," he said.

Beth rose first. Amaziga seemed reluctant to go, but at last she, too, stood up and followed Beth from the room.

Outside, Padlock and his brother, Seth, were sitting with Zerah, Wallace, and the children. Beth walked out into the moonlight, past Samuel Archer, who was sitting on the porch, watching the stars; Amaziga sat beside him. Beth walked out, breathing the night air. Nestor and Isis came toward her, both smiling as they passed.

Dr. Meredith was standing by the paddock fence, looking out over the hills.

"All alone, Doctor?" she said, moving to stand beside him.

He grinned boyishly. "Lots to think about, Frey McAdam. So much has happened these past few days. I loved that old man; Jeremiah was good to me. It hurts that I caused his death; I would do anything to bring him back."

"There's things we can't change," said Beth softly, "no matter how much we might want to. Life goes on. That's what separates the strong from the weak. The strong move on."

"You think it will ever change?" he asked suddenly.

"What will change?"

"The world. People. Do you think there'll ever come a day when there are no wars, no needless killing?"

"No," she said simply. "I don't."

"Neither do I. But it's something to strive for, isn't it?"

"Amen to that!"

Sarento's hunger was intense, a yawning chasm within him filled with tongues of fire. He strode from the rebuilt palace and out into the wide courtyard. Four Hellborn warriors were sitting together by an archway; they stood as he approached and then bowed. Without thinking he drew their life forces from them, watching them topple to the ground.

His hunger was untouched.

An edge of panic flickered in his soul. For a while, in the late afternoon, he had felt the flow of blood from the men he had sent out to the farm. Since then there had been nothing.

Walking on, he came out onto a ruined avenue. He could hear the sound of men singing, and on the edge of what had once been a lake garden he saw a group of his men sitting around campfires. Beyond them was a score of prisoners.

The hunger tore at him . . .

He approached silently. Men toppled to the ground as he passed. The prisoners, seeing what was happening, began to scream and run. Not one escaped. Sarento's hunger was momentarily appeased. Moving past the dried-out corpses, he walked to the picket line and mounted a tall stallion. There were around thirty horses there, standing quietly, half-asleep. One by one they died.

All save the stallion . . .

Sarento took a deep breath, then reached out with his mind.

Sustenance. I need sustenance, he thought. Already the hunger was returning, and it took all his willpower not to devour the life force of the horse he was riding. Closing his eyes, he allowed his mind to float out over the moonlit land, seeking the soul scent of living flesh.

Finding it, he kicked the horse into a run and headed out toward Pilgrim's Valley.

Shannow, his side strapped, blood seeping through the bandages, sat at the wide, bullet-ripped table, Padlock Wheeler standing alongside. At the table sat Amaziga Archer and her husband; beside Sam were Seth Wheeler and Beth McAdam. Amaziga spoke, telling them all of the Bloodstone and the terrible powers he possessed.

"Then what can we do?" asked Seth. "Sounds like he's invincible."

Sam shook his head. "Not quite. His hunger is his Achilles'

heel: it grows at a geometric rate. Without blood—or life, if you prefer—he will weaken and literally starve."

"So we just keep out of his way? Is that it?" asked Padlock.

"Not quite," admitted Amaziga. "We none of us know how long he could survive. He could move from active life into a suspended state, being reactivated only when another life force approaches. But what we hope for is that in a depleted state his body will be less immune to gunfire. Every shot that strikes him will leach power from him as he struggles to protect himself. It may be that if we can corner him, we can destroy him."

Seth Wheeler glanced at the beautiful black woman. "You don't seem too confident," he said shrewdly.

"I'm not."

"You said you had a plan," said Beth, looking at Shannow. His face was gray with pain and weariness, but he nodded. When he spoke, his voice was barely above a whisper.

"I don't know if I'll have the strength for it and would be happier should Amaziga's ... theory ... prove accurate. Whatever happens, we must stop Sarento from reaching Unity or any major settlement. I have seen the extent of his power." They were hushed as he told them of the amphitheater in the other world with its rank upon rank of dried-out corpses. "His power can reach for more than a hundred yards. I don't know the limits. What I do know is that when we find him, we must hit him with rifle shot and make sure the riflemen stay well back from him."

Nestor ran into the room. "Rider coming," he said. "Weirdest looking man you ever saw."

"Weird? In what way?" Shannow asked.

"Appears to be painted all in red and black lines."

"It's him!" shouted Amaziga, lurching to her feet.

Padlock Wheeler gathered up his rifle and ran from the building, shouting for his Crusaders to gather at the paddock fence. The rider was still two hundred yards distant. Wheeler's mouth was dry. Levering a shell into the breech, he leveled the weapon and fired. The shot missed, and the rider kicked his mount into a gallop.

"Stop the son of a bitch!" yelled Wheeler. Instantly a volley of shots sounded from all around him. The horse went down, spilling the rider to the grass, but he rose and walked steadily toward the farm. Three shots struck him in the chest, slowing him. A shell hammered against his forehead, snapping his head back. Another cannoned against his right knee. Sarento stumbled and fell but rose again.

Sixty rifles came to bear, bullet after bullet hammering into the man, glancing from his skin, flattening against bone, and falling to the grass. Infinitely slowly he pushed forward against the wall of shells, closer and closer to the men lining the paddock fence.

One hundred fifty yards. One hundred forty yards . . .

Even through the terrible and debilitating hunger Sarento began to feel pain. At first the bullets struck him almost without notice, like insects brushing his skin, then like hailstones, then like fingers jabbing at him. Now they made him grunt as they slammed home against increasingly bruised skin. A shot hit him in the eye, and he fell back with a scream as blood welled under the lid. Lifting his hand to protect his eyes, he stumbled forward, the sweet promise of sustenance driving him on.

He was so close now, and the scent was so strong that he began to salivate.

They could not stop him.

"Sarento!" Above the sound of the gunfire he heard a voice calling his name. Turning his head, he saw an old man being supported by a black woman, moving slowly out to his left, away from the line of fire. Surprised, he halted. He knew the woman: Amaziga Archer. But she was dead long since. He blinked, his injured eye making it difficult to focus. "Cease fire!" bellowed the old man, and the thunder of guns faded away. Sarento stood upright and stared hard at him, reaching out with his power to read his thoughts. They were blocked from him.

"Sarento!" he called again.

"Speak," said the Bloodstone. He saw that the old man was wounded; his hunger was so intense that he had to steel himself not to drag the life force from the two as they approached. What helped was that he was intrigued. "What do you want?"

The old man sagged against the woman. Amaziga took the weight, at no time taking her eyes from the Bloodstone. He tasted her hatred and laughed. "I could give you immortality, Amaziga," he said softly. "Why not join me?"

"You are a mass murderer, Sarento," she hissed. "I despise you!"

"Murder? I have murdered no one," he said with genuine surprise. "They're all alive. In here," he added, tapping his chest. "Every one, every soul. I know their thoughts, their dreams, their ambitions. With me they have eternal life. We speak all the time. And they are happy, Amaziga, dwelling with their god. That is paradise."

"You lie!"

"Gods do not lie," he said. "I will show you." He closed his eyes and spoke. The voice was not Sarento's.

"Oh, dear God!" whispered Amaziga.

"Get back from him, Mother," came the voice of her son, Gareth. "Get back from him!"

"Gareth!" she screamed.

"He's the Devil!" shouted the familiar voice. "Don't bel—" Sarento's eyes opened, and his own deep voice sounded. "He has yet to appreciate his good fortune. However, I think my point is made. No one is dead; they merely changed their places of habitation. Now what do you want, for I hunger?"

The old man pushed himself upright. "I am here to offer you . . . your greatest desire," he said, his voice faltering.

"My desire is to feed," said Sarento. "And this conversation prevents me from so doing."

"I can open the gateways to other worlds," the old man said.

"If that is true," responded Sarento, "then all I have to do is draw you into myself and I will have that knowledge."

"Not so," said the other, his voice stronger now. "You used to understand computers, Sarento, but you will not have seen one like this," he went on, tapping the box clipped to his belt. "It is a portable. And it is self-aware. Through this machine I can control the gateways. Should I die, it has instructions to self-destruct. You want to feed? Look around you. How many are here?" Sarento transferred his gaze to the farm buildings. He could see around fifty, perhaps sixty riflemen. "Not enough, are there?" said the old man. "But I can take you where there are millions."

"Why would you do this?"

"To save my friends."

"You would sacrifice a world to me for these few?"

"I will take you wherever you choose."

"And I am to trust you?"

"I am Jon Shannow, and I never lie."

"You can't, Shannow!" screamed Amaziga, lunging at the portable. Shannow backhanded her across the face, spinning her to the ground. The effort caused him to stagger, and his hand moved to his side, where blood oozed through the bandages. Amaziga looked up from the ground. "How could you, Shannow? What kind of man are you?"

Sarento reached out and touched Amaziga's mind. She felt it and recoiled. "So," said Sarento, "you are a truth speaker. And wherever I name you will take me?"

"Yes."

"The twentieth century on earth?"

"Where in the twentieth century?" responded the old man.

"The United States. Los Angeles would be pleasant."

"I cannot promise you an arrival inside a city. The points of power are usually found in less crowded areas."

"No matter, Jon Shannow. You, of course, will travel with me."

"As you wish. We need to make our way to the crest of that hill," said Shannow. Sarento's eyes followed where he pointed, then swung back to the group by the paddock fence. "Kill even one of them and you will never see the twentieth century," warned Shannow.

"How long will this take? I hunger!"

"As soon as we reach the crest."

The man turned and walked slowly toward the hillside. Sarento strode alongside him, lifting him from his feet. He began to run, effortlessly covering the ground. The old man was light, and Sarento felt his life draining away.

"Don't die, old man," he said. Reaching the summit, he lowered Shannow to the ground. "Now your promise!"

Shannow swung the microphone into place. "Do it!" he whispered.

Violet light flared—and then they were gone . . .

Amaziga staggered to her feet. Behind her the riflemen were cheering and hugging one another, but all Amaziga could feel was shame. Turning from the hillside, she walked back to the farmhouse. How could he have done it? How could he?

Beth came out to greet her. "He succeeded, then," she said.

"If you can call it success."

"We're still alive, Amaziga. I call that success."

"Was the cost worth it? Why did I help him? He's doomed a world." When the Bloodstone had appeared, Shannow had called her to him.

"I have to get close to him," he said. *"I need you!"*

"I don't think I can take your weight. Let Sam help!"

"No. It must be you!"

Sam came out to join them now. Laying his hand on Amaziga's shoulder, he leaned down and kissed her brow. "What have I done, Sam?" she asked.

"What you had to do," he assured her. Together, hand in hand, they walked away to the far fields. Beth stayed for some time, staring at the hillside. Zerah Wheeler and the children joined her.

"Never seen the like," said Zerah. "Gone, just like that!"

"Just like that," echoed Beth, holding firm against the yawning emptiness within. She remembered Shannow as she had first seen him more than two decades before, a harsh, lonely man driven to search for a city he knew could not exist. I loved you then, she thought, as I could never love you since.

"Has the bad man gone?" Esther asked suddenly.

"He's gone," Zerah told her.

"Will he come back?"

"I don't think so, child."

"What will happen to us, to Oz and me?"

Zerah chuckled. "You're going to stay with old Zerah. Isn't that a terrible punishment? You're going to have to do chores and wash and clean. I suspect you'll run away from the sheer torment of it all."

"I'd never run away from you, Zerah," Esther promised, her face suddenly serious. "Not ever."

"Me, neither," said Oz. Lifting the little pistol from his coat pocket, he offered it to Zerah. "You'd better keep this for me, Frey," he said. "I don't want to shoot nobody."

Zerah smiled as she took the gun. "Let's go get some breakfast," she said.

Beth stood alone. Her son was dead. Clem was dead. Shannow was gone. What was it all for? she wondered. To the left she saw Padlock Wheeler talking to a group of his men, Nestor Garrity among them. Isis was standing close by, and Beth saw Meredith take her hand and raise it to his lips.

Young love. . .

God, what was it all for?

Tobe Harris moved alongside her. "Sorry to bother you, Frey," he said, "but the baby is getting fractious, and the last of the milk's gone bad. Not to mention that the little fellow is beginning to stink the place out, if you take my meaning."

"You never cleaned up an infant, Tobe?"

"Nope. You want me to learn?"

She met his eyes and caught his infectious grin. "Maybe I should teach you."

"I'd like that, Beth." It was the first time he had used her name, and Beth realized she liked it. Turning toward the house, she saw Amaziga and Sam coming down the hillside. The black woman approached her.

"I was wrong about Shannow," she said, her voice soft. "Before he asked me to help him from the house, he gave this to Sam." From her pocket she took a torn scrap of paper and passed it to Beth. On it was scrawled a single word: "Trinity."

"What does it mean?" asked Beth.

Amaziga told her.

Trinity

THE STORM WAS disappearing over the mountains, jagged spears of lightning lashing the sky over the distant peaks. The rain had passed, but the desert was wet and cool. Shannow fell forward as the violet light faded. Sarento grabbed him, hauling him close.

"If you have tricked me . . ." he began. But then he picked up soul scents so dense and rich that they almost overwhelmed him. Millions of them. Scores of millions. Sarento released Shannow and spun around and around, the heady mind aroma so dizzying that it almost quelled his hunger just to experience it. "Where are we?" he asked the old man.

Shannow sat down by a rock and looked around at the lightning-lit desert. The sky was brightening in the east. "New Mexico," he said.

Sarento walked away from the wounded man, climbing a low hill and staring out over the desert. Glancing to his left, he saw a metal lattice tower like a drilling rig and below it a tent, its open flaps rippling in the wind.

The twentieth century! His dream. Here he could feed for an eternity. He laughed aloud and swung around on Shannow. The old man limped up behind him and was standing staring at the tower.

"We are a long way from the nearest settlement," said Sarento, "but I have all the time in the world to find it. How does it feel, Shannow, to have condemned the entire planet?"

"Today I am become death," said Shannow. Wearily, the old man turned away and walked back down the hillside.

320

Sarento sensed his despair; it only served to heighten the joy he felt. The sky was clearing, the dawn approaching.

He looked again at the metal tower, which was around a hundred feet high. Something had been wedged beneath it, but from there Sarento could not see what it was.

Who cares? he thought. The largest concentration of people was away to the north. I will go there, he decided. Shannow's words came back to him, tugging at his memory.

"Today I am become death."

It was a quote from an old book. He struggled to find the memory. Ah, yes . . . The *Bhagavad Gita.* I am become death, the shatterer of worlds. How apt.

There was something else, but he could not think of it. He sat down to await the dawn and exult in his newfound freedom. Atop the metal lattice tower was a galvanized iron box as large as a shed. As the sun rose, it made the box gleam, and light shone down on the tower itself. Now Sarento could see what was wedged below it.

Mattresses. Scores of them. He smiled and shook his head. Someone had laid mattresses twenty feet deep under the tower. How ridiculous!

The quote continued to haunt him.

"Today I am become death."

Knowledge flew into his mind with every bit as much power as the distant lightning. With the knowledge came a numbing panic, and he knew without doubt where he was—and when.

The Alamogordo bombing range, New Mexico, 180 miles south of Los Alamos. Now that his memory was open, all the facts came flashing to his mind. The mattresses had been placed beneath the atomic bomb as servicemen had hauled it into place with ropes. They had feared dropping it and triggering a premature explosion.

Swinging around, he sought the old man. There was no sign of him.

Sarento started to run. The facts would not stop flowing into his mind.

The plutonium bomb resulted in an explosion equal to

*twenty thousand tons of TNT. The detonation of an atomic
bomb releases enormous amounts of heat, achieving tempera-
tures of several million degrees in the bomb itself. This creates
a large fireball.*

On wings of fear Sarento ran.

*Convection currents created by the explosion suck dust and
other matter up into the fireball, creating a characteristic
mushroom cloud. The detonation also produces a shock wave
that goes outward for several miles, destroying buildings in
the way. Large quantities of neutrons and gamma rays are
emitted; lethal radiation bathes the scene.*

I can't die! I can't die!

He was 127 yards from the tower at 5:30 A.M. on July 16,
1945. One second later the tower was vaporized. For hundreds
of yards around the zero point that Oppenheimer had chris-
tened Trinity, the desert sand was fused to glass. The ball of
incandescent air formed by the explosion rose rapidly to a
height of 35,000 feet.

Several miles away J. Robert Oppenheimer watched the
mushroom cloud form. All around him men began cheering.
"Today I am become death," he said.

THE WORLDS OF DAVID GEMMELL

Author David Gemmell is hailed as Britain's king of heroic fantasy, and through sixteen of his most famous battle-charged adventures, Del Rey brings the action to American shores.

THE DRENAI SAGA: Experience the Drenai cycle that was launched with the international bestseller LEGEND. Meet the heroes of the Drenai people . . .

LEGEND: Druss was a legend even in old age, and he would be called to fight once more, to defend the mighty fortress Dros Delnoch, the last possible stronghold against the Nadir hordes.

THE KING BEYOND THE GATE: Tenaka Khan was an outsider, a half-breed, despised by both the Drenai and the Nadir, but he would be one man against the armies of Chaos.

QUEST FOR LOST HEROES: Among the travelers—the boy Kiall, the legendary heroes Chareos the Blademaster and Beltzer the Axman, and the bowmen Finn and Maggrig—lurked a secret that could free the world of Nadir, once and for all.

WAYLANDER: He was charged with protecting the innocents and journeying into the shadow-haunted lands of the Nadir to find the legendary Armor of Bronze. But Waylander was an assassin, a slayer, the killer of the king.

And don't miss these *new* Drenai adventures, coming soon:
WAYLANDER 2: IN THE REALM OF THE WOLF
DRUSS THE LEGEND
LEGEND OF DEATHWALKER

"Gemmell's great reading; the action never lets up; he's several rungs above the good—right into the fabulous." —Anne McCaffrey

THE STONES OF POWER: Tales of dark magic, sorcery, and conquest stemming from the Sipstrassi Stones of Power . . . a new dark age, a witch queen, a Hellborn army, and a man seeking the child born of a demon. Evil times call for bold heroes, including Uther Pendragon, Culain, and the famed Jon Shannow, the tragic figure known as the Jerusalem Man.

The Stones of Power Cycle
GHOST KING
LAST SWORD OF POWER
WOLF IN SHADOW
THE LAST GUARDIAN
BLOODSTONE

"David Gemmell tells a tale of very real adventure, the stuff of true epic fantasy." —R. A. Salvatore

"Gemmell . . . keeps the mythic currents crackling." —Publishers Weekly

Epic fantasy invades the era of Alexander the Great in tales that unite heroes of history with those of legend . . .

LION OF MACEDON: In every possible future, a dark god was poised to reenter Greece. Only the half-Spartan Parmenion could hope to defeat its evil. And so it had been foretold—Parmenion's destiny was tied to the dark god, and to Philip of Macedon and the as-yet-unborn Alexander the Great.

DARK PRINCE: The Chaos Spirit had been born into Alexander, but the intervention of Parmenion had prevented it from taking the boy's soul completely. But in another Greece where the creatures of legend flourished, a demon king sought the power of the Chaos Spirit. The demon called to the boy who would be king, and only Parmenion could hope to intervene.

"Gemmell works the reader's emotions adroitly. . . . It's a satisfying, often exciting fantasy that will thrill many readers." —*Locus*

KNIGHTS OF DARK RENOWN
The legendary knights of the Gabala had been greater than princes, more than men. But they were gone; they had disappeared through a demon-haunted gateway between worlds. Only one tormented knight had held back—Manannan, whose every instinct had told him to stay. But as murder and black magic beset the land, Manannan realized he would have to face his darkest fears, ride through that dreaded gate, and find his lost companions.

"A sharp distinctive medieval fantasy. Dramatic, colorful, taut." —*Locus*

MORNINGSTAR
Jarek Mace was an outlaw, a bandit, a heartless thief. He needed nothing and no one. But Angostin hordes raged over the borders, evil sorcery ruled, and the Vampyre kings lived once again. The Highland people needed a hero, and Mace inadvertently became that hero, a legend—the great Morningstar returned. But Mace was an outlaw, not a savior. Or was he?

"It seems that every time I read a new David Gemmell novel it is better than the last—and MORNINGSTAR is no exception." —*Starburst*

DEL REY® ONLINE!

The Del Rey Internet Newsletter...

A monthly electronic publication, posted on the Internet, GEnie, CompuServe, BIX, various BBSs, and the Panix gopher (gopher.panix.com). It features hype-free descriptions of books that are new in the stores, a list of our upcoming books, special announcements, a signing/reading/convention-attendance schedule for Del Rey authors, "In Depth" essays in which professionals in the field (authors, artists, designers, salespeople, etc.) talk about their jobs in science fiction, a question-and-answer section, behind-the-scenes looks at sf publishing, and more!

Internet information source!

A lot of Del Rey material is available to the Internet on our Web site and on a gopher server: all back issues and the current issue of the Del Rey Internet Newsletter, sample chapters of upcoming or current books (readable or downloadable for free), submission requirements, mail-order information, and much more. We will be adding more items of all sorts (mostly new DRINs and sample chapters) regularly. The Web site is http://www.randomhouse.com/delrey/ and the address of the gopher is gopher.panix.com

Why? We at Del Rey realize that the networks are the medium of the future. That's where you'll find us promoting our books, socializing with others in the sf field, and—most important—making contact and sharing information with sf readers.

Online editorial presence: Many of the Del Rey editors are online, on the Internet, GEnie, CompuServe, America Online, and Delphi. There is a Del Rey topic on GEnie and a Del Rey folder on America Online.

Our official e-mail address for Del Rey Books is delrey@randomhouse.com (though it sometimes takes us a while to answer).